Is That It Then?

Is That It Then?

Jenny Thomas

The Book Guild Ltd

First published in Great Britain in 2024 by
The Book Guild Ltd
Unit E2 Airfield Business Park,
Harrison Road, Market Harborough,
Leicestershire. LE16 7UL
Tel: 0116 2792299
www.bookguild.co.uk
Email: info@bookguild.co.uk
X: @bookguild

Copyright © 2024 Jenny Thomas

The right of Jenny Thomas to be identified as the author of this
work has been asserted by them in accordance with the
Copyright, Design and Patents Act 1988.

All rights reserved. No part of this publication may be
reproduced, transmitted, or stored in a retrieval system, in any form or by any means,
without permission in writing from the publisher, nor be otherwise circulated in
any form of binding or cover other than that in which it is published and without
a similar condition being imposed on the subsequent purchaser.

This work is entirely fictitious and bears no resemblance to any persons living or dead.

Typeset in 11pt Minion Pro

Printed on FSC accredited paper
Printed and bound in Great Britain by 4edge Limited

ISBN 9781 835740 545

British Library Cataloguing in Publication Data.
A catalogue record for this book is available from the British Library.

"...we long for something profound, sensual and ambivalent as an antidote to the crude, Hollywood-infused cult of modern romance."
André Aciman

24 January 2020

The coronavirus death toll reaches forty-one in China and there are lockdown measures in Hubei province. France has its first three cases.

Gerald sipped his Earl Grey tea and reached for a piece of wholewheat toast. The lip lines around his mouth were deep and strong from all the years of gravitas as a high court judge.

"Chinese experts are saying that the virus has mutated into two strains, one more aggressive than the other, so I don't know how they are going to develop a vaccine."

His grey eyes widened quizzically as he read from his *Times*.

"It could already have spread across the world. They say that eighty per cent of cases are mild, fourteen per cent severe, with lung problems and pneumonia, and five per cent are critical, with respiratory failure, septic shock and multiple organ failure. Can you pass the marmalade?"

Ruth, still in her elegant floral housecoat, pushed her homemade preserve in its cut-glass container across the oak table, the glossy wings of her dark-auburn hair swinging forward with the action.

"Possibly. This week's *Lancet* has a research paper written by Chinese doctors and scientists with its clinical description. Aren't the cities near Wuhan in lockdown? Hopefully it will be contained there."

"Matt Hancock is saying that the risk to us is low!"

"Don't forget the Masons are coming to dinner tonight. Don't be late back from golf."

*

Jo, in her cherry print dressing gown, over a curvaceous, just-showered body, was sitting on what had been her son Jamie's bed. She often came into his old room, that he had filled with his energy and interests – the football heroes still on the walls, the football coverlet and sheets back on the bed of her bright, loud, lovely boy, who went to university, met his partner, Gill, and never came back to live here. *Have I been a weak cipher? Raising, protecting, living through and devoting myself to my child? Being a mother has been the most important aspect in my life. First and foremost, I have been a mother*, she thought. *Teaching, encouraging, comforting. It dominated my job, my marriage – every other part. I lived for Jamie.*

Now I'm no longer needed, who am I? An enigma, a nothing…

29 January 2020

The death toll in China is 132 and 5,974 have the virus. There are cases in Australia, Finland and UAE.

Two Chinese nationals are ill in a hotel in York. There are planes coming in from Wuhan and other Chinese cities every day, and Germany has had its first case, yet our threat level has gone up from low to moderate. It's crazy! Vicky thought as she munched her way through porridge, yoghurt and blueberries. After sixteen years, she still hadn't got used to the strange, empty silence of the house, particularly at breakfast time, when Rob, who had got up an hour before her, would be sitting in his chair, next to the wood-burning stove, commenting on items in the *Evening Standard* from the night before. Now she read it herself, with no one to have discussions with. Rob had had a sudden fatal heart attack; they hadn't known he had a heart problem.

Finishing her breakfast, she went upstairs to clean her teeth, dispassionately glancing at herself in the mirror, flipping it over to the magnifying side to check for hairs on her face. Light hairs were difficult to see, and so, luckily, were the tiny sun-damage wrinkles that greeted her gaze, but which hopefully no one else of her generation with failing eyesight would notice. Age shouldn't be a demographic – but an attitude. She was still the same slim shape she had been all her adult life. A quick comb through her shoulder-length, wavy hair, its wild-honey colour splashed with grey, she pulled on her fleece over her tennis gear, picked up her racket and headed off to her club.

*

Later:

"Did you see *This Morning* yesterday?" Jo couldn't help a little giggle; she looked around the cafe quickly to see if anyone had heard.

Two young women were in earnest conversation, and three men of indeterminate ages were eating early lunch at separate tables while reading their papers.

Vicky sipped her double-shot Americano, hoping to return warmth to her body, and looked puzzled. "Sorry?" The words had landed in her ears but hadn't been taken up by her brain.

"It was a hoot! There was an eighty-year-old woman who had met a good-looking thirty-five-year-old Egyptian guy on Facebook. They got on so well that she flew to Cairo to meet him, and…" She flushed and looked round again, but no one seemed to be listening.

Vicky gave her an encouraging smile. "Yes? Don't think I've ever watched it."

"Well, he looked really hunky in his photograph. They had passionate sex using a whole tube of KY jelly and she could barely walk next day! She said it felt as if she'd been riding a horse. He says he doesn't care how old she is, he's head-over-heels in love with her and they're getting married!"

"Good for them!" Vicky nodded.

"So it made me think. She said she hadn't had sex for over thirty-five years. It's only been fifteen or so for me, I thought that was it, but it made me feel quite horny!" She pulled down the zip of her jacket a little way, sighing at seeing her arthritic knuckles.

Vicky wanted to laugh but bit into her tuna salad sandwich instead. "Are you going to go on Facebook, or fly to Egypt to look for a suitable mate?"

Jo looked down at her croque monsieur and then pushed it away. "Oh God, I don't know. When I was young, having a boyfriend dictated everything – my clothes, jobs – but it's been four years since Al died, and after his long illness I was so drained, I couldn't have considered having an affair, but perhaps now I'm stronger…? I don't want to die without ever feeling desire, without ever having sex again." A vision of a skeletally thin Al came into her head, together with the sour smell of his body, bedpan and pills, in the weeks before his death. She puffed her cheeks out and exhaled.

"When I was young I did it for my boyfriends, didn't get much out of it, didn't know what I needed or wanted, so never asked for it. And apart from sex, I miss the warmth, laughter, hugs and sharing with a partner. I can't stop thinking about it and it's all downhill from here. I'm full of existential doubt about my futile life, too much angst in my head. What's in front of me? Meals for one? Coach trips with scores of other elderly ladies in comfortable clothes and shoes, queueing for the public toilets? Louis Armstrong lies when he sings, 'We've got all the time in the world'. It seems to go faster the older one gets. I know I'm lucky to have my good teaching pension and a second home in Wales, but I'm old, grey, overweight, have dumpy cellulite-riddled legs, drooping flesh, love handles and lead a boring, achingly lonely life. Now I'm older I've got zero body shame. I wear shorts and mini-skirts – even though I've got the huge knees of my grandmother and the bandy legs of my father. No wonder men don't glance at me in the streets anymore – I feel invisible! But I've got the same feelings as when I was young, I still want excitement and affection. Prue Leith says kissing is just as pleasurable now – in her eighties – as it was as a teenager! How am I ever going to find someone for occasional sex? Or even better, another life partner? A kind, sweet, supportive person to spend the rest of my life with? Is that it, then?"

"Hardly grey, you've been that golden-brown colour all the time I've known you. And if you find an older guy, your mortality is mirrored in one another's wrinkles and failing health. My brother has met and gone out with quite a few women. He's done online dating, senior holidays, and there are apparently loads of matchmaking agencies for older people."

Jo blushed. "Jamie said, the other day, 'We want you to be happy, Mum. Look for someone else. I loved Dad, but he's dead and you're alive and need a friend to go out with. You've been a hermit for too long now.' And he's right. I'm like so many of my women friends – staying at home too much, knitting and watching TV. Now we're not fertile, what's the point in our existence? People on their own are vulnerable, lack identity and rarely get invited out. It's easy for men, they can be any size and shape and still seem to find a woman – but for us, you've got to get your man while you're young and hope you both make it to old age. We live longer than men, and I read that three in five women our age live alone. The world is full of older single women! Perhaps not all of them are looking for a partner – they don't want to give up their independence – but some of us want one, and healthy older men tend to pair up with younger women!"

She sighed and her soft brown eyes, with their swirls of grey and green, moistened.

"I've done some research and there's *Telegraph* dating, Silver Singles, Saga, Christian and Our Time dating agencies, ooh lots – but it's having the confidence... My flirting skills are very rusty, I was with Al for forty-five years!"

"Why not leave it to the agency to match you with someone suitable? Though I've heard it's expensive..." Vicky tailed off doubtfully, thinking of her tennis club, choir, U3A classes; she couldn't think of one person who would make her friend's heart beat faster...

She munched her sandwich. "Are you not going to eat yours?"

Jo glanced at it. "Hmm... the older I get, the longer it takes to assemble myself for public scrutiny. I was thinking I'd better lose some weight before I join the meat market. Maybe my body's not up to scratch for a partner to fancy. Do you want it?"

"I'll eat a quarter. Here, you eat the rest, otherwise you'll just be hungry later and eat chocolate or cake. Anyway, you've never been thin, but you're not fat, and lots of men prefer bigger girls. Think about getting fitter and toned – buy yourself a new outfit, try the 5:2. I tried it and it worked. And I read about a research project where overweight people could eat as much as they liked for three months but only between 10am and 6pm. On average they lost three stones! We all eat too much in the evening and then go to bed and don't work it off. Getting fitter will help with better sex."

"Well, you know me and exercise. I'm not like you. I've got good intentions but don't seem to suffer from guilt at being a couch potato. That Mark Twain quote suits me: 'Whenever I feel the desire to exercise, I lie down until it passes.' And I've got no self-control when it comes to food. If I hadn't spent most of my life obsessing about dieting, I'd be twenty stones. Anyway, what about you? When did you last have sex?"

There was a pause while Vicky sipped her coffee. She

swallowed, flushed and looked suddenly rather flustered, furtive…

"Come on, confess!"

"I think I'm emotionally frigid… Yes, it's been years. Sophie's father wasn't aware of my needs, so I used a vibrator when I needed to. Not sure I believe in vaginal orgasms anyway. Rob was wonderful, but as women get older and lose hormones, the desire goes too, doesn't it? It's not as if I didn't get out and about when he died. I joined walking groups, U3A classes, went to lectures and concerts. I even went on Tinder and swiped right a few times. But I think I'd have to retrain my eyes and brain to find men my age attractive."

"Did you go out with anyone?"

She nodded. "Two. There are a lot of self-satisfied, feeble frogs out there, but I find it difficult at this age to be attracted to our demographic, the pool we're paddling around in – men with hairy ears, bald, with paunches, a variety of ailments and too much baggage. We'd have little in common with one another, except for the accretion of years and our historical context. Anyway, I'm not looking to get married again, I've got a lot of single women friends and we do things together. They may not always be there for me, supporting and being interested in everything I did, like Rob was, but it's less complicated, more relaxing than hunting for a special life and sex partner – and now I'm used to how it is. I'm probably emotionally frigid and have repressed any sexual feelings, now my decaying body is creaking, crumbling and withering."

"You're so organised and confident, you probably scare men shitless. You're giving up too easily. I don't like living alone and I miss kissing, touching, stroking, rubbing, the feel of a man inside me – mmm."

"Is it a younger man you want? Didn't the Georgians think older women were wonderful, sexy, exciting lovers? They learnt from them, intellectually and sexually. They'd have been thrilled to get their hands on you!"

"Well, I can't imagine going around with a younger man. I've been invisible since I hit fifty. People would think I was his mother, or gran. I'd be neurotic about the lines around my eyes and mouth, the cellulite, the liver spots, sagging skin… He'd have to be very short-sighted not to notice them. And think of how one would have to keep explaining age-related references and couldn't share the difficulties of getting older. Surely there are some men our age who have kept themselves together physically, are mentally stable, solvent and not gay?"

"Maybe. But going through that rigmarole again of finding out about one another, their foibles, habits, views – I can't be bothered. Anyway, on a different subject, how about you joining the community centre's board of trustees? Two people have resigned."

"You asked me last year, and it's still NO. I'm too lazy. It's enough for me organising my social life in between babysitting. Have you advertised?"

"Yes, and one guy might be good, he's been a CEO of non-profit organisations, just retired."

"What drives you to do so much? You're seventy-seven, aren't you?"

Vicky's brow puckered as she thought about her busy life.

Jo looked at her dear friend, nervously rubbing her fingers, pulling at her cuticles, and heard the defensiveness in her voice and the insistence that what she did was fine for her.

"I've always had a full life, packed it in, and now I'm on my own people think I must have time and ask me to take things on. And I do need a reason to get up in the morning – other than for housework and gardening. I need to be productive, stretch myself, especially because I can't see my daughter or grandchildren…"

She looked at her watch. "I'd better go, I'm playing bridge at the tennis club. Try some dating sites and let's meet here again next week, so you can tell me how you've got on. Or put a personal ad in the *Telegraph*? I know Debs met several men that way, perhaps you should meet her. I think she put something like: 'widow, attractive, healthy, cultured, lively, interested in sport and the outdoors, mid-seventies – seeking a similar man to share travel and fun'. She gave a box number."

"Is that your rather beautiful friend you play tennis with, medium height, vivacious, dark hair, svelte body, in black tight trousers and top?"

"Not dark now, she went grey so has it dyed blonde. She told me the other day that she didn't take HRT until she was sixty-five, and since then – she's seventy-three now – she's gone mad with dozens of dates. Most of her lovers have been in their sixties. She loved Richie, but she doesn't want another partner in a home with Alzheimer's and struggling to walk, as he was."

"Mmm, maybe, I'll try to be brave – nothing ventured." They took their crockery to the trolley, hugged one another and parted.

6 February 2020

The third person in the UK to be diagnosed with coronavirus caught it in Singapore. The government is now telling people arriving from nine Asian countries to check for symptoms and to stay at home and ring the NHS if they have any. The Chinese doctor who issued an early warning about the virus has died.

Vicky had two neighbours, John and Christine, living in the upstairs flat on her right, that she was very fond of. John's wife had left him for her boss when their two sons were at university. He was shortish, stocky, strong and would be retiring from his paramedic job in the summer. Carrying patients had given him two prolapsed discs, and he'd lost all of his hair, from the stress of his work, he said.

Christine, a rather taciturn, tall, slim, attractive, dark-haired nurse practitioner, who retired at Christmas, was his later-life partner. When John retired they hoped to buy a house on the south coast to walk and swim and enjoy the view with glasses of wine...

Vicky came out of her front door and heard footsteps on next door's path. "Hi, John, nice morning, are you on your way to work?"

"Morning, Vic, just off for a walk before my shift – it's such a lovely day. You must be going to play tennis?"

"Certainly am. I've just read that Matt Hancock told the Commons that the UK was one of the first countries to develop a test, and when someone called Steve Walsh returned from Singapore and was identified as the source of an outbreak, all his contacts were followed up. Are Public Health England stepping up the production of tests so we'll have enough if there are more outbreaks?"

"Not sure about that. I've heard they might be letting it take its course, as they would for flu, to get herd immunity, which won't need mass testing. That may of course be the right plan as there is no vaccine available."

"But this is a deadly disease, not flu."

"Absolutely, and I never understand why this country doesn't use the considerable capacity of our private laboratories to mass produce tests. Saving money or what?"

"I wouldn't want your job anyway. You'll be right in the firing line if the virus takes hold here."

"Yup! Hopefully my retirement date will come first. Nice to see you. Can you come over Saturday? I've got a weekend off – I'll cook you one of my Thai curries."

"Ooh, yes please." They grinned at one another and set off in opposite directions.

*

After fifty-nine years of ignoring the annual invitation to her school reunion, Janet wondered if it would be interesting and if she would recognise anyone there. She had kept in touch with her grammar school – sending contributions to various projects, and always her new addresses.

But sixty years since I left? Perhaps that's momentous – that's why I should. Wonder who is still alive?

She decided to wear her green suit which showed off her slimness, her hazel eyes and pale, milky, freckled Irish skin. Her naturally curly hair, the colour of burnt, buttered toast, had been trimmed so it bounced and danced as she walked.

Arriving at the school hall, she didn't recognise anyone and wandered about with a glass of wine, smiling vaguely at the mass of elderly people around her. A woman with thick, pink foundation accumulating in her wrinkles stopped to talk, but they had been in different year groups, so soon parted to look for anyone they had known. After another quarter of an hour or so of wandering about, could that be Barry? Medium height, densely made, strong and fit looking. The flesh of his face had thickened and darkened, and his blond hair was now silvery. Her school boyfriend, she hadn't seen since they left to go to different universities? He looked at her and smiled rather uncertainly; they wouldn't have picked one another out in any other situation, but here? Yes, it really could be…

Time and space dissolved, and she was eighteen again.

"Janet?"

She smiled and felt her cheeks beginning to burn. *This is ridiculous.* She'd barely thought about him all these years and now she was in a state of confusion.

"Barry?"

They couldn't stop talking all afternoon. Didn't look around for anyone else. He was a widower and recovering from a double hip replacement, and she had been a widow for nearly fifteen years. After all this time she could still remember the passion and excitement of their relationship, and how dramatic and painful their parting had been.

"You're the one who ran away," he teased.

"We were starting new lives. I was confused and thought that that was that. You'd meet someone else – someone who'd be better at sex. We were so young! Our love was like a fairy tale."

He laughed. "That's not the way I remember it…"

So quickly they were back in the past, looking into one another's eyes. His a faded blue and hers a lovely violet shone just as brightly as ever, though the skin beneath them was starting to sag and was criss-crossed by fine lines.

After the reunion, he drove her to the coast, produced a bottle of wine, plastic glasses and a rug from his Porsche Boxster. They talked until it was nearly dark. Then, as she had taken the train from London, and he lived only twenty miles from her, he drove her home, stopping for a meal on the way.

"I can't believe you just walked back into my life. Can we meet tomorrow?" he asked, taking her hand and smiling directly into her eyes.

She felt her heart miss a beat and almost hugged herself with excitement. How lucky was she? He had been the sporty, best-looking boy in her year. The rugby captain, whose gentle giant demeanour had been a calming force in their class. Never losing his temper and exuding quiet confidence, he made those around him feel safe. Though broader and stockier now, with more rugged features from taking thousands of tackles on weather-beaten pitches, he looked distinguished, was still attractive, and she knew she had preserved quite well. Her freshness might have faded, like a dimmer switch turned down, but she looked after her body, swimming and doing pilates, and kept her hair a light, golden brown with the help of her hairdresser.

"Why don't you come in?" she asked.

Then, after a drink or two, "I don't think you should drive home, do you want to stay in one of my spare bedrooms?"

He smiled. "Why not?"

They went upstairs together. She gave him a towel and they used their ensuite bathrooms. "Goodnight," he said, appearing at her bedroom door. The lights were low and her curtains were pulled, but neither had been prepared to strip down to being naked in front of the other. She had climbed into bed, so he undid the towel around his waist and slipped under the duvet, reaching a tentative, exploratory hand towards her. After sixty years she felt firm, smooth, young. "A lovely body," he breathed.

She put her arms around him. He stroked her hair, then her breasts. They kissed passionately and she reached between his legs and began to gently milk his penis, already firm and keen.

"You're so beautiful, can I?" His fingers were playing with her clitoris and one entered her. She was moist and yielding. He slipped inside.

19 February 2020

Hundreds of people have begun leaving the Diamond Princess after testing negative for the coronavirus. There are 542 confirmed cases.

Christine looked across the breakfast table at John's expression. He was like a dog who wants his ball to be thrown again – sort of mutely imploring, wordless negotiation, beseeching, big wide eyes and furrowed brow. Never ambiguous, they knew each other so well it was usually welcome, though she was sometimes wearily reluctant. She knew it was good to be desired and she enjoyed sex when it happened, but didn't think about it at other times. Her mind was occupied with other things. He was on a late shift today and had completed his daily meditation, breathwork, strengthening exercises and ice bath, which he believed made him a better human.

"If not now, tonight?"

"Mmm, perhaps," she said.

But he longed for a response that matched his desire; he wanted to be desirable and he needed to know when, so he could mentally prepare himself. "After the news? Promise?"

His face was saying, 'I've tried to be a good husband, trustworthy, doing a worthwhile job, saving for our retirement. We're doing OK, aren't we?'

She relaxed, softened. "Well, if you're home by then." She hated it that he worked such long hours, filling in for absent colleagues. Eat, sleep, work, repeat was his life. "Wish you'd retire now!"

"As soon as the pandemic is over. I'd feel too guilty walking away when our team are dropping like flies."

*

Vicky and Michelle were having supper before seeing the film *Parasite*. They were chatting about the *Diamond Princess* which had been quarantined off Japan for two weeks because someone tested positive for the coronavirus…

"It'll be a breeding ground for COVID. They haven't got masks and the staff sleep in bunks listening to other staff coughing. They share bathrooms and eat in a mess hall, and then go to the guests' rooms! Crazy!"

"And it's generally older people, perhaps with underlying health problems, who go on cruises, isn't it?"

Michelle nodded her red-coloured bob. Her fur gilet, tight pants and high-heeled boots made her stand out in the local bistro. She had always dressed rather outrageously, and being seventy-three hadn't tempered her youthful taste. She always said: "Life is too short not to look the way you like. Be eccentric – wear what makes you happy and comfortable. Remember younger people don't notice older ones anyway."

"Chaika looked forward to our annual cruise around the

Caribbean, but I won't be going without her – not that we'll be allowed to for a while, probably."

They both ordered haddock and chips and Sauvignon blanc. "I thought you were a vegetarian, Michelle?"

"I wasn't when I met Chaika, but I soon got sick of cooking two meals, and she couldn't stand the smell of fish or meat. I thought I'd introduce them to my diet slowly now. *And* cut back on the puddings. Chaika loved them – she had a very sweet tooth – but I struggled to keep my weight down with all that rich, sweet stuff. Now I'm on the downward slope, I must look after my body and mind."

"Yes, there's memory loss, arthritis and absence of bladder control ahead. We've got to keep fit to cope with senescence!"

"My mother looked like an old woman at our age, but we're the Me Generation. We've lived differently. Ageing isn't inevitable anymore, it's a choice and one which I'm not choosing."

"How *are* you going to live your life now?"

There was a pause before Michelle answered. She sighed, and Vicky looked at her closely, wondering what her real feelings were, hoping to catch them on her friend's face.

She shivered as if from the cold wind of the future and sighed again.

"I think most people thought I'd carry on running the house and garden as I've done for nearly forty years, with a little bit of volunteer work on the side. But I haven't done anything without her and for myself since we met. I'm not competent. I didn't drive, pay bills, do the tax forms, plan what to do with savings, book holidays, and I lived within the timetable of her needs. She was the powerhouse, the earner and organiser who took care of everything. I've become helpless. She has left me everything, I'm comfortably off, but I've been on a steep learning curve and I'm so lonely. I haven't worked since I met Chaika, she was so powerful and full of energy and ideas, but I need to discover who *I* am. There's a big space in my day, in my life now.

It's been eleven months and I'm sometimes overwhelmed by aching loneliness. Is that *it* now? I dread my empty weekends. Where do all the older women go? Are they at home watching TV or learning to play bridge? A few weeks after she died, I realised we had two tickets for the theatre, but I had to go alone. Most of our friends were probably actually her friends and they disappeared when she did."

"Oh yes, sorry, I had a meeting. Are you coping with everything? I was a bit similar when Rob died – he'd taken on so much. Then I read somewhere that when you feel down, to look up at a bird, and go above things to look down with better perspective. Fly above life's problems by creating something positive and challenging, and that did help."

"I'll remember that. Though I am starting to get my head above water now. But it's being lonely I must do something about. Needy people are unattractive, we avoid them. Social isolation for old people is a huge health risk and there are so many people around who have outlived the partners they loved. I'm ashamed to admit I'm lonely. What do I do? Wait for the dog to die and then get a one-way ticket to Switzerland? Or do something with my life? Everyone living in my road is part of a young family. They probably think I'm disdainful and aloof – not just shy. I can go a whole week without talking to anyone! I must get on and do something with and for myself."

Their food arrived and Michelle asked for two more glasses of the delicious wine.

*

Vicky walked home, unaware that her shoulders were hunched up to her ears, a habit she had developed since Rob died. A cuticle of moon cast the faintest metallic glow onto the familiar road, where the streetlights were not working, making it look liquid, a mercurial river. She was still absorbed in the five-star, thrilling, tragi-comedy film and also wondering what on earth

Michelle could take up at seventy-three. She had looked after Chaika's every need, fitted into her life and neglected her own for too long. She painted, but had never exhibited, never taken her hobby seriously. As far as she remembered, her paintings were quite sombre – dark trees with roots on the surface, reaching into every corner of the canvas. Nightmarish, not Vicky's taste.

She reached her home, this solid, red brick, Edwardian, four-bedroom, semi-detached house, in a leafy road of very similar ones, where she and Rob had spent thirty-one happy years. Living on her own in such a large house had been very difficult at first. She had had to learn how to coax the temperamental boiler and lose her nervousness of being alone in eight rooms when she only used three. Unlocking the door, grateful for the warm embrace of the central heating, she put off the alarm and put on the kettle for her bedtime herbal tea – which made her sigh for her dear lover and friend. He had always made her bedtime drink, and it was comforting routines like this which knitted two people together. Carrying the tea, she punched the night code into the burglar alarm, put off the light and headed upstairs, thinking of how much Rob, a very practical man, had tirelessly worked to improve this house. It would be very difficult to sell up and leave all the memories.

*

John lay in bed, his head full of the latest news and parts of *Newsnight* that they had watched together. He pulled the duvet close as lack of PPE and coronavirus fears swirled through his head. He heard the click of the bathroom light, then the click of the bedroom light as Christine came into the bedroom and climbed into bed in the dark. She stretched out her arm and gently stroked his body.

Her hand reached his groin and stroked and rubbed. He felt his desire rising and rolled over towards her, his hands on her breasts, his lips on hers. He felt his penis bucking and rearing as his erection grew and they pushed close together. Neither wore anything in bed, they liked to feel skin on skin, hands all over one another's bodies.

"I love you," he whispered, and eased on top of her and inside her.

She wriggled for him to get in deeper. "Love you too," she breathed, and he was thrusting, and she was arching up towards him. Then he felt his penis going soft; he had no control over it. *What's going on? Doesn't it want the big crashing orgasm? It's shrivelling, what's its problem?* "Sorry, love, don't know why that happened."

She kissed him, hugged him. "Doesn't matter, it was lovely, exciting, you're just too tired tonight. Let's do it again tomorrow."

24 February 2020

WHO plays down coronavirus pandemic fears after the seventh person dies in Northern Italy.

"Is the government taking this virus seriously? Their stocks of PPE are low, yet they've sent 650,000 items of PPE to China!" Gerald mopped his brow, then polished his tortoiseshell half-rimmed glasses. "Why aren't we preparing for a possible pandemic? The virus is probably here now! It's taken a foothold in Europe – particularly in Italy. What a load of amateurs!"

Ruth looked up from perusing part of *The Times*, her eyes dark green pools.

"I'll never understand why the World Health Organization hasn't convened an emergency COVID summit. It's not undertaking its role as the global leader, so countries are struggling to respond to the pandemic alone. Do you want any more toast? I read that in those eleven towns under lockdown in Lombardy, there's a 'surreal', 'fearful' atmosphere, everyone is hiding indoors!"

Gerald nodded in agreement. It was perfect to have such a beautiful, intelligent, well-read partner and to have such good sex too, at eighty-one. The thought made him feel quite concupiscent. They hadn't had intercourse for a few days, or was it a week, two weeks? He'd been working on a U3A lecture, and she'd been asleep when he came to bed. *Perhaps later, before dinner. I'll put the radiator on in the bedroom. Funny how once one thinks about it, one can feel desire building up – wonder if she'd be agreeable to after breakfast?*

*

Vicky didn't meet Jo the following week, in fact it was nearly a month before they did.

She was early and had practically finished her hot chocolate by the time a smiling, glamorous-looking Jo breezed up. Vicky parted her hands and lifted her shoulders in a 'What's up?' gesture.

"I'll just get mine, then I'll be with you…"

Jo's hair was glossy brown, bouncy, shoulder-length, not a trace of grey, lips unapologetically red. She looked smart, fresh, younger – what had she been up to?

Carrying her green tea, she sat down, full of smiles…

"Well?"

"Terrible times, it's like a war with an unseen enemy…"

"Yes, the end of life as we knew it. There'll be no theatres, cinemas, lectures, restaurants, groups getting together, and most of my friends are already antisocially self-isolating… But you look full of the joys of spring."

"I did the advert, like you said, and wasn't exactly inundated with responses, perhaps because of the virus scare – but I met up with two, and one is certainly promising. Ted was a doctor, a GP... It's so wonderful to be able to talk to an interesting person, to have proper conversations! I'm thrilled with it after years of poor Al not being able to communicate. We talk on the phone non-stop a couple of times a day, about politics, books, big things, and we've met up six times. We're learning from one another. From him, health issues, the NHS and he's worked with the Red Cross in Africa, and me having always been in schools and with organisations teaching and supporting young people, the advice and research have been my passion. We've got lots to talk about and he's interested in doing volunteer work now – so perhaps I'll get involved in something too... What is amazing is how easy it is being with him. I was scared to date when I was in my twenties. It was nerve-wracking, terrifying. I'd be in a cold sweat, so I thought I wouldn't be able to cope with it now! I was thinking, who'd want to go out with a fat, jowly, sagging seventy-four-year-old, but he's been a revelation."

I haven't done this because my life was bad – absolutely not. I feel grateful every day for my health, how lucky I am, but is this my best life? While Al was here I would have recoiled in horror at the thought of ever being with anyone else... but why am I clinging to the safe and comfortable and sacrificing the elation of progression and learning? What might life be like with a new partner? Is this it? Are adventures all behind me? Have I made all the discoveries of myself and life I was ever going to make? But, of course, this is a difficult time. If Ted doesn't volunteer, he may be recalled to help in this virus crisis, and London may go into lockdown!" Her soft brown eyes were moist, as if with tears.

"You said you had seen two men?"

Jo blushed. "You're my best friend, so I'll tell you, but I felt so ashamed. I met the other one in a pub he knew – around the corner from my house. He wasn't tall, not particularly attractive – a forgettable, vulpine-face. Sort of quite skinny really with a moustache, not much grey hair and a silk muffler round his saggy, wrinkled neck. We got on OK. Had a drink and then another or three. He wanted to walk me home. We were both a bit tiddly, so I'd shed my inhibitions. I felt sorry for him and when he grabbed me and kissed me hard on the mouth and his hand fumbled up my skirt into my knickers, it was quite exciting. We went in and I let him come upstairs. We lay on my bed and I could feel his penis, hard, poking into my groin. It's been so long since I had sex, I just let him pull off my knickers. Who was I to think I was too gorgeous and desirable for him? He pushed in – no orgasm, but definitely pleasure – and when he came, I wondered how soon he could do it again!"

Vicky took her cardigan off; the sun was very warm through the cafe window. Was this too much information? But Jo continued.

"I was ashamed at myself – he wasn't at all my type, I just needed sex. The revulsion and guilt stopped me seeing him a second time. Sex can be elegiac, rhapsodic, but this was disgusting. I regretted it. It seems such a long time ago when I had love and orgasms, I can just remember what they were like… like approaching thunder coming ever closer, until it fills the sky and drowns out your sense – then a shudder and it's all over. Would be nice to have some more of them. Perhaps with Ted? He's definitely someone I could go for, and he doesn't seem prejudiced against heftier women not in their first flush of youth."

"Are you going to try to see as much of him as you can, in case we get lockdown and you can't? Life is just moments – enjoy them."

"He will make a good, interesting companion and friend, and he's attractive, but I don't know if he's interested in anything more."

"Well, stay friends and see what happens – love might be a slow burn. It's been a long time since you had a proper sexual relationship. At best you'll get some good dates and at worst you'll have a friend. Let me know how it goes!"

*

Vicky walked to the tennis club in the cold little wind. The watery sun gave the day a glassy clearness. She was wondering if she would bother again to try to meet a suitable man. How could anyone replace Rob? *He was my other half, loving and supporting me no matter what. I just have to get on with my life and am lucky to be fit enough to be able to teach an exercise class, play tennis and walk for miles. We had such an intense, complete love. Do I want to have sex and intimacy in my life? I don't seem to have a lot of loose lust flying around. What happened to my sex drive? I can't remember when I last used my vibrator, the batteries must be flat as pancakes.* She pondered for a moment. *I seem to have a lot of friends still up for meeting a sex partner, but I'm a typical old person, putting all my energies into tennis, the community centre and gardening, though a garden is so temporary and will go back to nature when I stop looking after it. What does it mean to live one's truest, fullest life? For some people it's not possible without being in a close relationship. Do I feel lonely and unwanted? Well, yes, sometimes. But I've got to accept how life is. Perhaps if I met a man that really attracted and interested me, I'd be up for it?*

Unlikely, though.

The next morning, she was eating her breakfast – her usual porridge, blueberries and yoghurt – and reading the newspaper, when she spotted: *Far more older people now use dating apps, and the Office for National Statistics says that in the past ten years, there has been a bigger rise in marriage rates in the over-sixty-fives than in any other age group.*

She picked up her unopened and usually unread U3A magazine. Flicking through, she noticed a page of personal ads such as: "Attractive lady, early seventies, many interests,

seeks male in London area for friendship. Reply to Box 1383"...
She counted six men advertising, twenty-one women and an introduction agency.

I suppose the U3A magazine is a good place to advertise, as society seems to consider sex between pensioners as repulsive, or 'sweet'.

She sipped her lemon and ginger tea. *All these people looking for love again, what's wrong with me? On my free evenings all I do is watch TV in my dressing gown with my supper.* Suddenly a quote popped into her head: "Life without love is like a tree without blossoms or fruit". *Who wrote that?* She reached for her MacBook – *Khalil Gibran, a Lebanese American, died in 1931. Hmm* – she gazed out of her window at her garden. *Well, it's true that flowering trees attract the most attention, but the others provide the backdrop against which they can shine. I'm happy for all my friends to have lovers and tell me about them, but don't some boring people and trees have to exist?*

Rather appropriately her radio, which she had on in the background, started playing, "If I can't have you, I don't want nobody baby". She sang along loudly as she washed her breakfast things.

9 March 2020

There are more than 110,000 coronavirus cases worldwide. Global markets have tumbled. Italy has had 366 deaths and gone into total lockdown. Germany has had its first death in 1,153 cases. The UK has 319 cases, and Boris says we are still in the containment phase and will not yet be moving to the delay phase.

Vicky telephoned Malcolm, the trustee applicant, who had been chairman of PWC.

"As you know, the community centre needs someone

to oversee the finances. Not a big job for someone with your experience, but it would be wonderful if you were interested in joining us. Shall we meet, say, Wednesday, to discuss it?"

"Yes, sure. I'm free in the morning. How are you fixed then?"

"Perfect. Eleven o'clock at the centre? You've got the address."

*

Vicky's neighbours on the left side of the house were Iranian, though brought up in the UK, and now in their forties. They had moved next door after Rob had died, after completely revamping the house. It had been totally sheathed in scaffolding and plastic for two years, and the noise of excavation and the plaster dust had ensured that Vicky spent very little time at home in the daytime.

Nusheen was beautiful. Unlined, flawless, satiny olive skin, lovely, large, almond-shaped green eyes and slim body, though boredom and petulance were corrupting her freshness. Farzad was also slim, well dressed, with flashing white teeth, salt and pepper hair. Nusheen often visited for tea or invited Vicky there. They had a mutual love of cake, and both made it regularly.

They were chatting over scones, jam and cream in Vicky's garden and got on to the subject of sex.

"Do you know that Farzad said after childbearing that men and women have no interest in sex? It was disgusting to think of old people doing it, even if they could! Persian men! Why did I marry one?" Nusheen said sadly. "I miss sex, don't you?"

"Well, I had put it out of my life and mind when Rob died. Of course, after the menopause, I wasn't as keen – it was the lack of hormones – but he was still up for it."

"You always seem so complete, so competent, empathetic, sympathetic, serene, powerful, as if you don't need anyone or anything. Yet you've got this air of warmth and intimacy which I'm sure makes people tell you everything. Wish I'd known Rob."

Vicky smiled, crinkling her eyes and tilting her head. "I may seem confident and secure in who I am, but when he died, my whole world fell apart. I was lost, bereft, stranded, didn't think I could survive without him. He was a wonderful partner. He supported me in every area of our lives and my life. I didn't know how to put the heating on or how to do internet banking even, and he had taken over paying all the bills. He mended everything, did all the shopping, a lot of the cooking and all the washing up. He rarely grumbled about my choice of theatre, film, or friends for dinner, organised our holidays, and we went for long walks together. He was always there for me, called himself my help desk. I was a quarter of a person without him. I completely went into my shell, hid away in deep depression, curled up with my hot water bottle at night, small, tight and scared. Took a month off and was lonely, lonely, lonely… Then I just had to get on with it. I was just sixty, so buried myself in work and retired at sixty-five."

"I can't imagine how you got over losing him."

"I kept telling myself to think of things that make me happy and things I'm thankful for, at first – but gradually I forced myself to be proactive. To go out more and speak to at least one person a day, especially lonely people so they don't go into a downward spiral, like I had almost done. I took on teaching an exercise class and went to films and plays with friends. I found that talking to people, being busy, lifted my mood, kept me sane."

"Haven't you got a daughter in New Zealand? Did she help you through that period?"

"Well, not really. Rob wasn't Sophie's father, so she hated him coming into our lives. Her father had already emigrated to New Zealand and wasn't bothering to contact her. She took her pain out on us."

"Does she contact you a lot?"

"Sometimes, but of course I don't see my two grandchildren. It's as if the power has shifted in our mother–daughter relationship. We were so close and happy till she was twelve and I met Rob. We struggled through the self-righteous, judgemental, critical and non-communicating phases of her mid-teens. She seemed to want to demolish me and my beliefs with opposite arguments, confident in the knowledge that I loved her unconditionally. She was ashamed when her friends laughed at my opinions that she was parroting – Mummy said this, Mummy said that – so took the opposite view to show her independence. This was the darker side of mothering, the heartbreaking period, when I wondered how to communicate, how I had got it so wrong, and there was no going back. She thought our generation were selfish, in our big houses, some of us with second homes. We'd had full employment, good pensions, whereas our children had insecure jobs, had to pay extortionate prices for rentals or to buy, and then work till they were seventy! And we had been promiscuous and druggy. She was obsessed with how unfair it was!"

"How sad! Now I'm a grandmother times three it's the most exhausting but thrilling thing in my life," laughed Nusheen. "Love it! But with no sex, older men are sour... I just want him to put his arms around me. I hope I've taught my son to be loving, a good partner, not the boss of his wife so she is lonely."

After Nusheen went, Vicky sat and thought about Sophie. Those years before she had met Rob, when there were just the two of them. Her little, skinny body clinging to her: "I'll always love you and look after you, Mum." If only that were true. She would probably never get over her leaving. At times when she couldn't sleep, she would write her thoughts down in an exercise book by her bed – agonising, analysing thoughts, which were never answered, never resolved. *She was everything to me, but she walked away because of Rob, and even though her father and Sven were killed in that road accident, and she's had to bring up Daisy and Ben alone in a foreign country, she rarely communicates...*

That night, as for so very many, she lay in bed staring at the narrow strip of light on the ceiling, rehashing the past. Negative thought sequences replaying, as if on a loop and rewinding, she no longer felt guilty, or blamed herself for meeting and welcoming Rob into their lives, and she had never regretted it, despite losing her daughter. But she didn't sleep well since Rob had died. In the dark, in her big, lonely house, her mind swirled, and sleep was far distant. She knew that there was nothing that she could do to change what had happened, what was, but her agonising anxiety was repeated so often as she thrashed around trying to relax, find a place within herself where there was no cold wind. Empty her brain, and sleep.

11 March 2020

There are 460 cases in the UK, including Health Minister Nadine Dorries, and eight deaths. The US has over 1,000 cases.

Jo met Vicky again at the cafe. Luigi, the Italian owner, had removed half the tables so that people could sit socially distanced away from one another. The coronavirus scare had begun in Italy and some towns were in quarantine.

Vicky could see that something was up. There were telltale signs. Jo's efforts to reduce a beaming grin, her wriggling restlessness, her darting hazel eyes which looked everywhere but at her. "Well?"

"It happened, sex, I mean – and what sex! Only twice, but it was magic! He said it was for him too…"

"I'm so pleased, Jo, so glad you like him so much!"

"Mmm, I do, I really do. But he's talking increasingly about volunteering to go back to help in this crisis, and not in this country but in probably one of the most dangerous places – a refugee camp with Médecins sans Frontières!"

"Oh my God, the people are so packed in, very few toilets, one tap for hundreds and no hot water or soap – they will be death traps."

"Indeed." She brushed away a tear. "We've been exchanging poems, articles and reviews and went to both the cinema and theatre before they closed. Neither of us had been able to go for years because our other halves were a bit deaf. So our social, cultural and intellectual lives have improved with one another. Isn't this just my luck to meet someone I could perhaps be happy with for the rest of my life and he's choosing certain death rather than a new life with me! All the cosy treats I'd planned for us and he's going to put his life at risk in a filthy camp! But changing the subject, I was thinking about your older people's exercise class. You're not going to teach this week, are you?"

"No, though I dithered about it… The question is, which aspects of daily life should we change and which ones can we maintain – to have some semblance of normality in our lives? With all the information out there, it feels as though we are simultaneously being told to brace for the worst, with over-seventies having to stay in for four months, and yet to keep calm, carry on and try to live our lives as normally as possible. Won't staying at home lead to loneliness, anxiety and depression? So I thought we could wash our hands and sanitise them before and after the class, and wear gloves, either plastic or material that you can wash later. I'd worked out a lesson plan with the minimum contact with other people and equipment.

"Then the latest advice came from the government, that over-seventies should avoid social contact, pubs, clubs, theatres, cinemas etc, and within weeks be asked to stay at home for an extended period! So that was that… classes came to a grinding halt."

"What about doing it on Zoom?"

"There are already so many video diaries and exercise videos for people who will be trapped at home if we have to have a lockdown – some dangerous and others pathetic. A third of the class don't have computers, so it wouldn't be fair on them."

Jo put on a sympathetic face. The sun was warm through the glass and she relaxed back in her chair. "Maybe this enforced inactivity they keep saying is going to be a long-haul marathon, not a sprint, will mean that you lose your lovely slim body and fitness and be more like the rest of us. Just joking!"

They giggled, remembering in time to touch elbows instead of hugging and, carefully keeping a social distance from one another, went their own way.

*

Malcolm rang the bell at the community centre. Marilyn, the manager, was self-isolating, Isobelle, the admin person, didn't work Wednesday mornings, and the tai-chi class had been cancelled. Vicky ran down the stairs to open the door and was surprised to find a tall, attractive, silver-haired man with a lovely smile standing outside. She felt a surge in her stomach and hoped she wasn't blushing. They tried to socially distance in the narrow space of hall and stairs, laughed and he followed her upstairs, Vicky filling him in on the usual classes held and how the centre would probably be closed soon, along with other places where groups gathered. They chit-chatted for a while; he had retired to look after his wife, but tragically a few months later, her cancer had killed her. They had had so many plans for their retirement. He joked about how many women had contacted him, offering to bring him food, but after forty-six years of marriage he hadn't felt like eating or socialising.

Vicky, admiring his strong physique, lots of silvery hair, soft, intelligent eyes and warm manner, could see why so many women were interested.

She had been single for nearly seventeen years, but his smile made her feel like a fluttery young girl, with a mind like a bald tyre, spinning, trying to grip on the sand. They talked about his suitability for the post – assuming that he was a fit and proper person, after a DBS check. She gave him the governing document, articles of association and annual accounts, talked about the purpose of the charity, the services it provided and its beneficiaries…

"Unfortunately the trustees meetings will have to be on Zoom, until all this is over. But perhaps you can get up to date? Ring me if you have any questions."

18 March 2020

Testing is supposed to be going to be ramped up and social distancing emphasised, as the peak is coming faster in some places than others. London is ahead of the rest of the country – 224 new cases today. Schools are to close, apart from for vulnerable children and those of key workers. Spain closed its borders two days ago and was already in lockdown, as is France. There was a mass exodus from Paris, thousands of people in masks at all the railway stations trying to get to the provinces rather than stay cooped up in their city apartments. Belgium has locked down. Iran has had 1,135 deaths in total.

On Wednesday mornings, Vicky usually did some office work at the community centre, taught a fitness class for older people from 11–12 and ran a women's advice and support session from 12.30–1.30. All kinds of people came to it, to pour out their stories, and having listened, she would try to direct them to professional organisations for proper help. The mornings were tiring; she did a lot of preparation and practice for the class and worried in case she had not been helpful enough with her advice. However, the centre had been closed for most activities until the pandemic was over, so Vicky was gardening when Maggie, a university friend living in Swansea, rang her.

"Are these the most dramatic restrictions ever imposed in peace time?"

"Absolutely! How are you, Maggie?"

"Oh, good, good! Having a happy relationship helps tremendously. I'm lucky to have put that ad in the local newspaper and met Robert before we got locked down, and if he asks, I'll go and stay with him temporarily till this is all over."

"Do you think we might have caught the virus in January? After that man behind us in the theatre coughed all over us?"

"Could have. We both felt terrible, didn't we? So fatigued and had really bad coughs, throats and headaches for weeks. The antibody test wasn't around then."

"What's he like, this Robert?"

"Married twice, like me, two sons and six grandkids. He was a surveyor. He's eighty-two – but seems much younger. Quite fit really. I don't want to be stuck with someone I might have to wheel about and clear up their poo. He lives in Hereford. We get on well – he's up for most things and the sex is good. Younger people think love is their preserve, it's not at all. It goes on and on and on – whatever your age. And if you're fit and active there's so much to do together. I expect you've realised that my big birthday party can't happen?"

"Oh yes, yes of course, your eightieth in the Grand! I'd booked in to stay the night. After all your planning and organising – what a shame!"

"Indeed, and Robert was going to take me for supper to my favourite restaurant, Slice, the night before. We'll just have to celebrate indoors."

"Can't we have a virtual party on Zoom on your birthday? Perhaps early evening, so you can eat afterwards with Robert?"

"Yes, what a good idea, I'll work on it. Would be great to see you all, even if only on the screen…"

They vowed to contact one another more frequently, blew kisses and rang off.

*

This period is giving everyone the time to reconnect with old friends. So many people I haven't seen for months and years have rung to see how I am. Having the time to catch up has been a boon, Vicky thought. *I wonder how Debs is getting on? We haven't played since January because of her back problems.*

Debs was a few years younger than Vicky. They had been playing tennis with and against one another for forty years. She had dropped out of art school to become a fashion model, then a start-up entrepreneur – a high flyer at the top of her game, influencing the culture of the creative industries, setting up a communications agency in health and science. She had a warm, interested, strong, engaging personality, with a dizzying appetite for life, clear, fresh, flawless complexion, luxuriant curly grey hair with blonde highlights, and a wonderful eye for colour.

Vicky walked in the soft sunshine to her leafy street of halls adjoining three-storey, Victorian houses; the road was packed nose to tail with parked cars. Then she went down the path, into the porch, with its large, glossy-leafed plants either side of the door, wilting thirstily, rang her bell and retreated back through the small paved front garden to her gate. Within a minute, the door opened and her glamorous friend stood there, lips unapologetically red, wearing lilac and yellow patterned trousers and a low-necked yellow cashmere jumper, exposing the cleavage of her full breasts. She was surprisingly, startlingly unaltered by the passage of time and invariably full of verve and vitality.

"How brilliant to see you!"

Even from ten feet away, Vicky caught a familiar whiff of hairspray, cigarette smoke and her expensive musky perfume. "How's your back? Not that we can play, but when we can, will you be able to?"

"Yes, I was thinkin' of ringin' you and startin' back last weekend, then this virus hit."

"So how are you feeling?"

Debs' lovely hazel eyes widened and moistened with the effort of not crying. "OK, can't complain, mustn't grumble. I'm naturally optimistic, but I need social contact like a plant needs water, and I'm so afraid when the huge number of deaths are quoted each day and morgues are full. I've been self-isolatin' for eleven days! I do online pilates lessons every mornin', go out for little walks, and my daughter and a neighbour shop for me. I'm copin' OK, but there might be months more of this. My son came over from Texas in February and wasn't sure whether to hug me when he was goin' back. I said, 'Yes, please do, I've had a good life until now.' You know, life after one's thirties gets decreasingly sad, peterin' out from our golden heyday. Why are we expected to always give the impression that we are physically and mentally younger, so we're not thought to be decrepit crones? I've got a crinkle-free tummy, arms and legs, and I don't have to worry about gettin' pregnant. And right now, I don't want to hide indoors, doin' knittin' or playin' bridge. Life is set up for women who look like little girls. But life goes forward. There's a one-way valve, and us older women in lockdown will be wastin' months trapped indoors, crumplin', crumblin', disintegratin'!"

She bent creakily down to pick up some post and flicked through the pile with her slender hands and their amazing gold nails.

Vicky nodded encouragingly and Debs' tsunami of words flowed on.

"I'm not great at being single, my spirit's hollow, my soul bankrupt. I'm skin hungry! Not touchin' another livin' soul –

havin' no one to dress up for and not even gettin' a smile from a stranger because of masks! I'm so lonely, need company, physical intimacy, intelligent conversations. Life has whizzed by. One minute I'm in my twenties in expensive couture – startin' out on my career and social life. A brief period of sandpit-supervisin' drudgery and tryin' to fit in at coffee mornings as a mother, then suddenly I'm in my seventies and invisible to most people. I no longer exist. All those years, gone… lurchin' from one thing, one man, to another, and now I'm back in the jungle of urban datin', app-based love, where I spend my time scrollin' profiles, goin' on useless dates and havin' it constantly confirmed how many men run away from older women!" Her luminous skin crinkled slightly with her agonised expression. "I want to meet someone whose eyes sparkle – I need a flirtation! Most men of my age are ghastly. Decrepit, boring, dead-eyed, toothless, walrus tendrils of nose hair – yet they still find a younger woman! Where is that man for me, whose eyes are alight, who's fun, liberal, non-judgemental, passionate, unburdened by money worries? Is that it now? Sorry to be buzzin', Vic! Haven't talked to anyone, face to face, for a few days and words are blurtin' out on their own."

"It's fine, we're friends. Like all romantics, I want life to be better, easier, to make more connections, but this isn't the time to be looking for a partner, is it? And you've already tried apps and sites and said it wasn't a good experience."

"Yeah, it's a minefield! Bumble, Tinder, eHarmony, Happn, EliteSingles, Match and Feeld – but that's for the swingers, kinks and polyamorous. You name them. I've been a member of every available datin' app, hopin' I was just one click away from sexual nirvana. Bumble is the best for women – you're in control. Or Toyboy Warehouse, Tastebuds.fm or Drawing Down the Moon – supposed to be for thinkin' people! And if you need a profile on a site, don't be long-winded or make it sound like a job application – more like a warm note, askin' questions so a conversation can start up.

"Trouble is, potential suitors need pre-screenin', to see if there's chemistry. Some looked promisin' through an iPhone lens, but once we met in the flesh, they were either controllin', bitter, bad-mannered or too disastrously pathetic, dull and borin', so my vagina clamped shut. But hookin' up first, even for half an hour over a coffee, is the way to go. Who wants to be stuck with a bore for longer? And have sex early on the first date if you fancy them – so you'll know if you want a repeat. Sex is there to be enjoyed. Who wants to be lyin' there, listenin' to them snorin' or fartin' if they don't give you an orgasm? It used to be that a swipe right was a way to get a shag, but the demographic of guys who have kept themselves together physically, are mentally stable and solvent is tiny. I've met some sleazy, bone-headed show-offs who flash money about, but they can find a woman ten or twenty years younger, which leaves women in my age bracket out of the runnin'. Then there are the guys just wantin' sex. I could really have gone for one or two, but they were married and it's not fair on their wives. And so many are shorter, fatter, unsightlier than their profiles claim, and some just want to be chosen for an ego boost – but have no intention of meetin' you, they just want to play online. Makes you feel used, upset and not good enough… And tell her to be alert for signs that your date can't manage life – doesn't cook or know how to use their credit card and seem to be looking for a carer! Now cougar datin' is good – Toyboy Warehouse. Young men are more cheerful, energetic, less baggage, and they cheer me up, tellin' me I'm radiant and sexy." She paused for breath.

"The current preoccupation of the vast majority of people seems to be pillaging supermarkets and turning their bathrooms into fortresses of toilet roll and sanitiser as they have been advised not to go out…"

Debs grinned and nodded. "Yeah, true. You know, accordin' to 'Datin'.com', the countries most affected by COVID – China, the US, Spain and Italy – have the biggest increase in online datin'! It's boom time for meetin' sites and apps, there's 1,400 in the UK alone!"

"I read that getting on for half of couples meet online now and older people are more likely to pair off. Is it because people are cooped up at home with all social events and meetings cancelled? Isn't it a bit risky, though?"

"Maybe. Datin' sites are tellin' people to make sure they practise social distancin', carry hand sanitisers, wash their hands before touchin' their date's chips, and the search for a partner has been redefined as lookin' for someone to self-isolate with! Because we can't meet, it's been suggested that we're revivin' behaviours on video, from a more romantic, chivalrous age. Wasn't it called courtship?"

"I've got a friend, Jo, who met a seemingly perfect guy with a personal ad. I'd told her that you'd done those. They were really getting on well, but he's a retired doctor who's volunteering to go to a refugee camp to help in these scary times."

"That's so sad. Well, tell her that online datin' is blazin' bollocks! It's a part-time, unpaid job with no trainin' manual. Blind dates and datin' services are a capitalist enterprise. Not focusin' on solvin' the love problem, but how much money they can get out of you. Do you know, some of the 'exclusive' datin' agencies cost £10,000 a year? They guarantee you 'x' dates – but apparently they pay useless men to take you out… and with personal ads one has to be keen because it's an exercise in futility and frustration. You can get a love and datin' coach – more expense, though they'll help you spot scammers and fake profiles… But I keep tryin'… Isn't the definition of insanity doin' the same thing over and over and expectin' different results?" She exhaled irritatedly. "I'll die alone, I'm just too picky. What about you anyway, how are you?"

"As ever, I guess. A few bits of me are dropping off. I've always been active and sociable, as you know, but now I can't swim, play tennis or teach my exercise class, everything's closed. So I'm getting fatter by the minute, as I'm pretty greedy, cook far too much for one and eat it all. I don't have much self-control." She looked thoughtful. "I did, surprisingly, meet a guy I quite liked the other day – but we can't meet up, other than talk from a distance."

"Oh, so pleased to hear you're interested again. You know I was thinkin' about all these random males who come up on datin' sites. It's difficult if they don't have a social media footprint – so prospective partners can get an in-depth look at them, to see if they want to meet them. I mean, I want someone who likes goin' out, I'm just not sure if I want a partner not interested in socialisin' and indeed in social media – they won't have any idea of what goes on in popular culture. We'll have that huge area of my life not in common. I love Facebook and Twitter, and WhatsApp's OK in small doses, and my new crazes are TikTok and Slack. Learnin' the new language and etiquette of these platforms is fun. Could I cope with a partner who found social media an irritatin' distraction? Probably not."

Vicky laughed. "But you wouldn't have met them in the first place! And hasn't texting become our most usual form of communication? The cues we got from body language and eye contact seem now to be derived from written language and semantics and our emojis – delivered from our thumbs! Let's go back to old-fashioned meeting up. Let's set up a friendship group for the single over-seventies on Facebook. Or stone circles in the centre of towns and villages – friendship benches where people can sit if they want to chat to others. There seem to be a lot of lonely people around."

"There's already a 'Facebook friendship' group. Let's specify it has to be singles, with a sense of humour, and see a photo. Mmm... that would be good – circles within circles, stretchin' the tentacles of connection to meet friends of friends. Why not!"

"Mm-hm... I am starting to realise the damaging effects on one's mental and physical health of being alone in the house and life, after years of having a partner. I get more depressed now than when I was with Rob. But I don't seem to want to do anything about it. There are thousands of people in our situation, probably millions. Are we too proud to admit our loneliness? Anyway, haven't you met *anyone* you could really, really like?"

"Yeah-eh, the best is retired lawyer Jonathan. Attractive, daredevil, an adventurer – races fast cars. Endurance, adrenaline and jeopardy are what he lives for. But he's a lone wolf, marches to the beat of his own drum and we haven't in any way got the same tastes. I loved Tamla Motown, he the Grateful Dead. His screen saver is his Dobermann pinscher and I hate dogs. But we had great sex. I enjoyed sex more with him than any time in my life. I don't hold back in sayin' what I want, but it's so rare that men take the time and trouble to help me get satisfaction. Problem is, pinnin' him down! He says he's probably got less than ten years more to be active, travel and see the world. He's more venturesome than me."

"Refreshing to hear about someone who isn't pulling in their horns, giving up on life!"

"Yeah, he's had to self-isolate at the moment. I'm not sure if he'll seek me out, though. He's way hotter than me and thinks I'm a lot more conservative than he is – with a small c – so we'd want to do different things… But then again, is the theory of a soulmate unrealistic? Only another week for him to be hopefully virus free, then perhaps I'll find out if he wants to see me again."

"Well, keep me informed!"

20 March 2020

> The global death toll passes 10,000. Italy and Spain have their biggest daily death toll. Australia and New Zealand have closed their borders. Tehran plans to pardon 10,000 prisoners, including political ones. Forty tube stations, all

> the schools, restaurants, bars, cinemas, nightclubs, leisure centres and all shops except food stores, pharmacies and banks will close when the government passes emergency legislation. Boris says he realises it goes against what he called "the inalienable free-born right of people born in England to go to the pub". Rishi Sunak announces an unprecedented wage-support scheme to try to prevent a tsunami of job losses, revealing that the taxpayer would meet eighty per cent of the wage costs of workers 'furloughed', or temporarily sent home, by firms hit by the crisis.

The usual cafe where Jo and Vicky met was doing takeaway only, through a hatch in the door, and there were seats outside in twos. Everything was spaced two metres apart.

After a hurried greeting, Jo burst out: "He's going to go to the Moria camp on Lesbos, if he can get there. If he can't, he says he'll go to one of the camps near the Turkish border. In Moria there are 21,000 in a space designed for 3,000 refugees and there's only one water tap per 1,000 people! He says that with so much of humanity living under plastic and tarpaulin with little food and hygiene, how can he live comfortably and do nothing while they incubate disease and suffer so terribly. I feel so worthless and lazy by comparison…"

"Sounds an amazing man! I'm sure he'll keep in touch, and perhaps it will all be over very soon."

Jo seemed hyper. She sat on the edge of her seat, eyes bright and flashing. "Life can be so unfair. It takes years to find out what turns you on and ask for it, and then there's no one to do it with. Then someone comes along who is intuitive and could be perfect and…"

There was a catch in her voice; she took a deep breath. "Did you see that the Russian media are claiming that the UK had unleashed the virus on China and Europe to boost its status so it could later announce that it had created a vaccine?"

"Madness. It's known that it came from a fifty-seven-year-old stall holder from a seafood market in Wuhan where they illegally trade wild animals. The virus has a very similar DNA to one found in bats. In London we seem to be in the virus hotspot – 900 more cases yesterday and forty-eight people died."

"Why are all those greedy, selfish hoarders stripping the supermarket shelves as soon as the shops open? It's not happening in other countries, why are Brits more avaricious? I don't understand it…"

"Oh well, if we get it, I suppose it'll help the immunity of the herd, and it can't be that bad for healthy people. Nadine Dorries and that Bond girl – Olga Kurylenko – seemed to get over it pretty quickly. Kurylenko said she felt bad for a week and was mostly in bed sleeping, with high fever and strong headache. The second week the fever was gone, but she was tired with a light cough. By the end of the second week, she felt totally fine. But what's scary is that there seems to be a pre-symptomatic stage of about five days after exposure and in sociable societies that's when it's spread to others. Of course, when the dry cough and fever develop, people can be avoided – but one wouldn't know to keep away from them before."

"What do you actually die of?"

"I think if there's inflammation, and a lack of oxygen from the lungs to the heart, blood vessels and organs, then cells die. It will probably take years to get over the serious damage it does to the organs. There are so many different opinions between scientists and the way each country is dealing with it. From mass quarantine and drastic social distancing in Italy, which probably isn't sustainable, to our 'suggested distancing'."

"It seems to be accelerating faster than governments had predicted. It's going to cost each country so much, with everything closing and people not earning anything and all the rescue packages."

"Yeah. Boris's premiership will be defined by the decisions he takes and the UK recovery. Enjoy your last times with Ted. We've just got to remember that nothing is forever and enjoy the moment, sanctimonious as that sounds."

"You're right, as usual. Hope we can still meet up until the day he goes."

*

Janet had sold her dental practice and retired, but Barry still had his own financial advice company and had taken on an enthusiastic young partner – to whom he enjoyed passing on his knowledge.

Neither had been looking for a companion, but this just seemed so right, and amazingly, after nearly sixty years, they found they still had chemistry for one another. Though they could no longer make love all night, they laughed, were caring and patient, had more foreplay and talked about what gave them pleasure, what they'd like more or less of. They both felt more accepting and accommodating than they had been in their marriages.

"The *Standard* says there are tens of thousands of cases in London and we're going to have tough new restrictions in a few days," Barry called.

Janet came into the lounge from the kitchen. They were at her house for half of the week – the arrangement they had agreed on. Barry was an expert at producing delicious meals out of sparse resources, but each tended to be the cook in their own home. "Oh no, I'm fed up of not being able to go out in the evening already."

"People are ignoring the self-isolation and social distancing recommendations and the total deaths are now 144 here and over 10,000 in the world."

"Did it say how many people have caught it worldwide?"

"Yes, look, here's the figure going across the bottom of the screen."

"Can't see it, haven't got my glasses."

"They think it's now 246,107, up 26,344 in the last twenty-four hours! And Spain has had over 1,000 deaths. They're catching up China, Italy and Iran. People who are caught on the streets in France, now that they've got the lockdown, are being put into police custody for endangering lives. They get a year's jail or a huge fine!"

Janet had gone back into the kitchen and called out:

"I heard earlier that 500 doctors and 4,000 nurses have responded to the call to return. We are being told over and over again that if we stay at home we will save lives. We can shop online and get food and any drugs we need from stores and community chemists. We might think, well, we'll only get a mild version, but anyone can be a carrier! Australia is closing beaches, Snowdon was overrun with people yesterday. National Trust properties, which were leaving gardens open, are now closing – just too many people."

"They've just announced that the armed forces are going to be deployed to help the public services in the UK. They'll transport supplies, run emergency medical centres, help the police and border forces…"

"Can only just hear you, I'm stirring the sauce."

She came into the room holding a saucepan, which she was stirring vigorously. "Do you think soon we won't be able to go out to walk, jog, shop?"

"Well, if huge numbers of people need intensive care and the deaths escalate like Italy's have, the police will have to force compliance."

"Perhaps the next phase will be the closing of all shops apart from chemists and food stores, like other countries."

"It's already happening. I keep getting emails from chains saying I'll have to buy online, and forty tube stations have closed and train services are being cut as there are fewer passengers. What if the virus gets into one of the huge refugee camps, or sweeps Africa?"

"Can't bear to think of it! But I guess it will... Supper in ten minutes?"

23 March 2020

Spain has requisitioned hotels for hospitals and they're turning a Madrid conference centre into a giant military hospital for coronavirus patients, with Europe's second-worst outbreak – having claimed over 2,000 lives and with 33,000 cases. Germany has banned gatherings of more than two people; it has 24,000 cases. UK shops, restaurants etc are closed, business rates scrapped for this period. Facebook and neighbourhood groups are making arrangements to help the elderly and vulnerable. Parks, National Trust gardens and places to walk are closing because people are crowding into outdoor spaces. Local councils are saying, "This isn't a holiday, practise social distancing. Stay at home!"

Jo fell ill. Her muscles ached, she had a dry cough, headaches, nausea... Vicky rushed to see her.

"I've never felt so terrible! I'm icy cold but feverish, can't breathe..."

Vicky rang for an ambulance, and she was carried off to hospital where she was diagnosed with COVID-19.

Vicky then rang her eighty-eight-year-old neighbour, Marion. "Are you OK, Marion? Can I get you anything? I'm going to M&S to get some food."

"This is like living in a terrifying dystopian science fiction film. We have lost so much of what our affluent post-war generation could not conceive of losing. Shopping, going to entertainments and meals with friends and the freedom to go on holiday and to roam. I'm still playing bridge, though, because otherwise I'll go completely insane. Four of us in our eighties have agreed to play in one another's homes and observe strict rules: washing our hands when we arrive, using a new pack of cards, wearing masks and trying not to touch our faces. Do you know that Italy had 799 deaths yesterday? They've run out of masks and ventilators. In Lombardy people aren't allowed to go out to jog or walk."

"Stop watching it! Anxiety and stress can be even more dangerous than this virus. It's all 'possibly', 'maybe', 'there could be'. No one knows, it's all conjecture," said Vicky. "Let's take each day as it comes. Is there anything you need, then?"

"Yes please, the community centre sent me a very helpful lady called Amara who is going to add my orders to her weekly shopping list and deliver it to me, but that's not until the weekend. I'll email you a few things I'd like and pay you by bank transfer, if you give me your details. She showed me how to do it. Nice to see you, stop by any time."

*

The weather was warm, but not too warm, so before going shopping Vicky decided to walk around a nearby golf course. On the way, she saw Nusheen, who had just been to Zaman in Kensington High Street. "I just needed some pomegranate paste for a *khoresh*, a celery stew."

"You didn't get much else?" said Vicky, looking at her small bag.

"No, only spices. I can get other things nearer home."

"Why don't you come for a walk to the golf course with me?"

Nusheen smiled. "I should, I know. I don't do enough exercise."

It was a perfect, sunny, still day and they reached the course through a copse of oaks and larches, to see a symphony of blue and green – the sky above, a shimmering little lake and the perfect grass all around. So calming and restful. There was a seat overlooking the lake, so they sat for a chat.

"How are you?" Vicky asked.

"OK, I guess, though I keep asking myself, why, when I was brought up here, I didn't marry an Englishman."

"You loved Farzad, presumably?"

"He was very attractive and persuasive... and at least we're here. In Iran he could be polygamous. Having multiple women would be the end for me. AND having a temporary marriage, a *sigheh*, so he could try me out. Ugh, then I wouldn't be a virgin and would struggle to find anyone else who would want me. I could never live in Iran, though women seem to have a good time and are socially close. But it feels like the Iranian heterosexual community is a marketplace where women are sellers and men are buyers of sex, and a woman's highest value is in her sexually pristine state. It's so misogynistic. Men think the most important qualities are health, age and femininity – education and career mean nothing and the number of partners diminishes a woman's value. Following a partner, submitting, learning how to please men raises her market value. But I'm not going to be confined to the home. I'm a businesswoman and he's trying to take over my business!"

"I guess he thinks he's protecting you from COVID. Surely it'll be better when all this lockdown is over? Come on, we'd better go back. I'm not sure we're really allowed to be wandering around near the greens."

They stood up, climbed up a slope and emerged from the trees to hear a crack, and a ball bounced onto the nearest green and stopped twelve feet or so from the hole, ten yards away from them. Two men came into view.

"Should you be here?" the younger one called. "It could be dangerous."

"Sorry," Vicky called back, and they headed for the exit.

*

"Listen to this." Ruth switched the sound up. Prime Minister Boris Johnson filled the screen, instructing all

UK citizens to stay at home, to protect the NHS during the coronavirus pandemic:

> "From this evening, people can only leave home for one of the four following reasons: shopping for groceries or essentials; any medical need; one form of exercise per day; travelling to and from work, if it's absolutely necessary and you cannot work from home.
> You will face fines if you fail to comply with the government's new instructions.
> And I am taking the extraordinary step of ordering pubs, clubs and restaurants across the UK to close on Friday."

"Well, that's it then, lockdown comes to the UK!"

"Life is going to change for decades to come. It's an unprecedented crisis!" said Gerald moving slowly, arthritically over to the drinks cabinet. "Shall we have a sherry? Fino or Manzanilla?"

Ruth was staring in horror at the television. "Fino, please. Look at these streets, they're drained of people! In European cities, all life as we know it has vanished. The only things moving are trucks carrying food."

25 March 2020

> Seven doctors at University College Hospital, London, have been infected. They're admitting one patient an hour with coronavirus. The numbers are increasing by twenty-five per cent every day, and London has half the country's total. The Excel centre is being turned into a field hospital for 4,000 people, and the military are delivering personal protective gear to hospitals. London parks will all close if people don't stop crowding into them. Italy hoped that its COVID-19 pandemic had peaked as the daily deaths fell from 793 on

Saturday to 651 yesterday; its total is now 5,470. In India, the 1.3 billion population have been told to stay at home for three weeks. That's one fifth of the world's population!

Janet and Vicky were chatting on the phone. "Two hundred and fifty-two thousand people have volunteered in one day to be an army supporting the NHS with the elderly and vulnerable. Isn't that amazing? I don't suppose they'd want old helpers like us, though."

"No, probably not, though they could if they had testing up to speed. We're still not testing enough people or contacting those who have come into contact with the positive cases, like Germany has been doing. Why haven't we got enough test kits? Why haven't we been producing them since this whole thing started?"

"It's so useless, I blame NHS England… and how on earth does one get food when one is self-isolating? I spent an hour or so on the Tesco website. I've got a club card but can't get a delivery until 18 April!"

"Well, at Sainsbury's – where we've shopped for donkey's years and I have a Nectar card – every time I try to order, there are thousands of people ahead of me. It was 17,610 last time, and I should 'try later', so I can't order, and goodness knows when I'd get the stuff anyway. We're in the 'vulnerable' age group, but we'll have to go out and shop!"

"It's hopeless. Barry can't get a Waitrose or an Ocado delivery either. Did you hear the deputy chief medical officer suggesting that it would be a good time for couples to move in together, to test the strength of their relationship?"

"Is she mad? Moving in with someone is crunch time."

"Indeed, when the rose-tinted glasses come off and you see each other properly. It's stressful enough without the fear that we might get arrested if we try to leave and go home. But I don't want a criminal record for having sex with someone outside my household! So, should I move in with Barry? My house is much bigger and there's the garden too. But he won't move here, he's already said."

Vicky did an intake of breath, remembering their financial disparity. Janet, as a retired dentist, was financially secure, but Barry hadn't been good with his money. She knew he had spent too much on his sporting life and vintage cars and was still working part time as a financial adviser, and that his three daughters and her two sons had been a little worried about their differing finances. Janet had, however, said that they would have to accept who they were now and not beat themselves up about what they were not or hadn't got.

She smiled. "Well, inhabiting the same space isn't easy at any time. We all have our own habits and way of doing things, even to how often we wash our sheets, towels, hair… Wealthy couples often choose to live apart: Helena Bonham Carter and her ex, Tim Burton, for instance. The virus will add an extra level of stress. What a decision!"

"Yes, moving in together is one of the most romantic but stressful things a couple can do – they're trusting that their relationship will survive. But in our current police state, we shouldn't take public transport and may be stopped if we keep driving back and forth to see one another. Should I try it temporarily?"

"What a quandary! You'll just have to go for it. You've got your own personal bank accounts. Pay into a kitty account for bills to minimise resentment. Or have one credit card for joint things that you pay half of. You won't want any financial wrangling. As long as you support one another emotionally, and your children's views and expectations don't get in the way, and your relationship expectations are similar. Yes, go on, try it. Be empathetic and keep talking…"

"Yes, you're right, we want to grow as a couple. We've loved going for little walks – fresh smells, dew on grass and flowers and taking in the beauty of the world. The sex is great. Hopefully our relationship will deepen and remain stable until we drop off the perch."

"Sounds like you're getting on really well."

"There is one area that could be difficult. I love nature, but I'm not a fan of roughing it, and when he's recovered from his hip operations he'll want to be more active. I like ceilings, walls and central heating, and if an insect got into the house, Cliff would get rid of it. I'm not brave or sporty and don't like pushing myself to be different, but I know I must focus on what Barry wants and why. I must try new things and wake up from my old-age lethargy. I must come out of my shell, stop wanting to be comfy all the time – be brave and see what happens…"

Does one have to have another living body near to validate one's existence? Vicky wondered. Having no one to talk to in the evenings made her feel pale and dull, her brain empty. *This is why people have animals and talk to them, I suppose.* She pushed forkfuls of cooling glutinous pasta with tuna, onions and mushrooms around her plate. *And eating so much, so late, will make me double in size…* Finishing the food, she washed up, set the alarm and headed upstairs. There she undressed slowly, throwing each garment onto a chair, as if it were a piece of herself, then into bed and tried to switch off, into sleep.

26 March 2020

> The United Nations Secretary-General, António Guterres, has called for a global ceasefire, saying that "The fury of the virus illustrates the folly of war. It's time to put armed conflict on lockdown and focus together on the true fight of our lives." In Madrid, the services are 'collapsing' as wards are overwhelmed with cases. A total of 3,434 Spaniards have died, including 738 in the last twenty-four hours, now more

than China, though Italy has had 7,503 deaths and the US 1,000. There is tension and occasional violence from this lockdown; a man was stabbed by his flatmate because he was going out with a cough. More than 1,000 people have been arrested and 20,000 fines have been issued.

The next morning, Vicky pulled back her bedroom curtains to see a dull grey sky with no hint of white or blue. It had stopped raining at last and the sounds of thunder gurgling in the distance had receded. There was a dripping calmness and a musky odour came through her slightly open window. The cool breeze swirled the curtains as if they were alive. She went downstairs where the air was still and slipped into the kitchen without disturbing it – feeling that her world had shrunk and she with it. After her porridge, she rang Malcolm. "How are you?"

"I've been self-isolating this week and most of last. My townhouse, with only a small courtyard, feels like a prison. I haven't seen a single person. I've talked to friends and my daughter on the phone, but the offers of food being brought round have dried up. I've managed, eventually, to get an online Waitrose order, but it doesn't come until next week. It's as if there's a war on. I walk or jog from room to room and up and down the stairs, do some shadow boxing and I've got free weights to lift. With all this time, I've been going through my old diaries. We had so many wonderful holidays. But Sylvia died too young and far more quickly than consultants had led us to believe, so we didn't do enough things in her last years." He paused for breath.

"Have you got enough food? Is there anything I can help you with?"

"I've got enough. My biggest worry is how long this will go on for. If it's months of not going out or socialising, there will be a lot of depressed people around, with me head of the queue.

I hadn't realised how lonely I was without her. Lots of people wrote to me after she died. People I could hardly remember, sending their commiserations, saying if I ever fancied a drink, a meal, a weekend stay, just to say. And a few of my male friends have assured me that the world is full of sex-mad widows and divorcees and I'll be knackered!"

"Well, I can assure you that I'm not one of them. We're not supposed to meet up, but why don't I pop round, as my one walk a day, and we can chat about the charity or how you're feeling. Me outside your gate and you come downstairs and stand on your doorstep."

"Sounds good, thanks."

An hour later and she was ringing his bell…

She felt her heart turn over as he opened the door with a big smile. They chit-chatted about the current situation.

"Victoria Park in Hackney closed because people were having picnics and playing games. Why didn't the park staff, rangers, whoever, tell them to stop and chuck them out? Now no one can walk in that lovely big green space. Are you going for many walks?" he asked.

"Yes, every day, though I keep thinking how each infected person infects two or three others. But then it takes a minimum of five days to come out, so there's this feeling of impending doom, waiting for the unseen enemy, and some people are not good at social distancing."

"It's frightening. Yet other problems in the world haven't stopped. The virus will only exacerbate them, particularly in the Middle East where healthcare systems have been destroyed by conflict. Millions of people have had to flee their homes and are in camps, such perfect breeding grounds for the virus."

"My friend Jo has just met a Prince Charming, a retired GP, who is going off to a Greek refugee camp to help Médecins sans Frontières. She's devastated. It might be a very short affair."

"Yes, aren't there something like 20,000 people in areas designed for 3,000? Even the wealthiest countries are struggling to contain the coronavirus. The death toll in France is over 1,300. Their health chief says the pandemic is worsening. What chance have the millions living under plastic and tarpaulins, crammed together with poor nutrition, overflowing latrines and only one or two water taps? He's a hero!"

"How do you remember those statistics? You'll be a brilliant asset to the charity…"

"Can't help it, I've always found that they stick in my head. Like Rishi Sunak's latest. Millions of people across the UK could benefit from his new self-employed income support scheme, with those eligible receiving a cash grant worth eighty per cent of their average monthly trading profit over the last three years. This covers ninety-five per cent of people who receive the majority of their income from self-employment. It's parity then with the coronavirus job retention scheme announced by him last week, where the government committed to pay up to £2,500 each month in wages of employed workers who are furloughed during the outbreak."

"Will cleaners, plumbers, electricians, musicians, hairdressers and other self-employed people be eligible for this?"

"Yes, apparently there's a simple online form, with the cash being paid directly into people's bank accounts."

"Sounds good, hope it works. You've obviously been watching all the virus news. It's horrifyingly compelling, isn't it?"

"You're right, I've been watching it obsessively. Not good for one's mental health!"

"Oh well, I'd better be going."

"Can you come over and chat again in a couple of days. I've enjoyed seeing a human face – it's been quite a tonic!"

Hmm, she thought as she waved and walked away. *Not sure I'm more than someone to talk at. Don't be unfair, Vicky, you hardly know this man.*

*

Carolyn and Vicky had been friends since school. They met up for a meal and chat a couple of times a year when Carolyn came to London for a conference or to see colleagues in other universities. *Wonder how she is*, Vicky thought, *and what happened about Doug.* He had been married to Carolyn's cousin, Sheila, and after she died he kept phoning Carolyn. She had asked Vicky what to do about it last time they spoke. "I'm not a therapist, doesn't he need one of those to get over Sheila?"

I'll give her a ring... "How are you, Cas?"

"OK, so far, but it's only been a week or so, and I've had quite a bit of work to do, trying to finish off the bid for a research funding council project..."

"What happened with Doug ringing you all the time?"

"Well, it's fine now. I didn't want to morph into Sheila, but we have got a lot in common. Both academics, still giving the odd lecture, still researching in our areas. After knowing one another for over fifty years, we feel comfortable with one another. I actually got a date for my knee operation, and he offered to fetch me from hospital and be around for a few days until I got stronger. He said he'd had plenty of practice at being the caregiver, and he's been great! As you know, my daughter is in New York and has only just gone back to work after having had the twins, I couldn't ask her to come over. And my close friends, you live over 200 miles away, and most others have busy lives. Old age is so lonely. We lose friends, one by one, and new friends aren't the same and didn't know us when we were young..."

"So you're getting on well with Doug now?"

"I would say so, yes. When you look after someone, you're together so much that you learn a lot about them. He's a lifetime liberal and I'm a socialist at heart, but we respect one another's points of view. He waters down his washing-up liquid and does most of his shopping in Poundland, but we've tried to adapt to one another's habits and personal idiosyncrasies and have become good friends."

"Do you fancy him?"

"I don't not. We haven't had full-blown sex yet, I've been struggling with pain control and feel like a shrunken, wizened old lady. I've gone grey. The operation seems to have aged me a few decades, and he's not confident. We have cuddled and kissed, but that's all so far. I don't mind. Other things are more important to me than sex, like having a laugh and shared interests. Think it will happen, though, and he's very kind, supportive and wants to look after me, which is nice…"

S'funny how we often talk about sex now we're older, thought Vicky, *we never mentioned it when we were young, never discussed what we did with our boyfriends… We understood the taboos our mothers had insisted upon – no intimacy of any sort. We had to use the pill or diaphragm, which had to be fitted and which one boyfriend told me felt as if he was bouncing on a trampoline. We never discussed it, and perhaps she never got one because she got pregnant and had to have an abortion, paid for by the married father of their embryo.*

They talked about Carolyn's operation and her current mobility, agreed to meet after the lockdown, blew kisses to one another and ended their call. *Yet another friend who has jumped into a relationship*, Vicky thought.

27 March 2020

Prime Minister Boris Johnson and Health Secretary Matt Hancock test positive for the coronavirus.

Vicky had enjoyed sex when she was younger, but she could hardly remember that primeval sexual urge, it hadn't happened for so many years now. *It's the hormones*, she had told herself, when after the menopause she became less and less interested, breathing a sigh of relief if she could get into bed and sleep without an exploratory hand, then arms, lips, body weight entering her sleeping space.

It hadn't been that she was no longer attracted to Rob, but without as much oestrogen, progesterone and testosterone, it was hard to feel desire. So she was very shocked when her heart did a little flip and she had felt tingling in her knickers whenever she had seen Malcolm.

She was sitting in her lovely garden on a warm, sunny day, more overgrown since Rob had died, as he had kept the shrubs and trees under control. He'd loved pruning… She was musing whether she could be attracted to Malcolm. The sun shone down on the golden euonymus, daffodils and kingcups, the white clematis, viburnum, hyacinths and stellata. The many colours of the primula and wallflowers, the blue forget-me-nots and rosemary, or were the flowers mauve? Rob had been colour blind, so she had looked after the flowerbeds and he most of the vegetables and grass. She smiled to herself. *But why would he fancy me? He could easily find a younger woman.*

Her mobile rang, a harsh, crude sound to disturb her reverie. "Oh, hi Ruth, how are you getting on with the virus restrictions?"

"We're trying not to watch the doom and gloom news and coronavirus programmes. Staying in for three months is not going to be an attractive prospect. If we get one of those letters from our GP telling us we're not to go out for shopping, leisure or travel for our own safety, I don't know what we'll do. There were 181 deaths yesterday, and someone's dying every two minutes in Italy! They're struggling, despite the fact that they had twice the number of intensive care beds as us! And this government has gone further than the wartime one in 1945 – amazing they're undertaking a state intervention that goes beyond Jeremy Corbyn's wildest dreams."

"It's only a week or so, but how much weight have I put on?

I keep eating because it is the one thing we can still do. What are you two doing?"

"Well, we thought it was the perfect opportunity to read apocalyptic literature which I'd put off because of lack of time, so I got out Yuval Noah Harari's books. I'd read a quarter of each, but life's too short, I soon got distracted. We play bridge online with friends or Acol and have even got addicted to Zoom quizzes with Gerald's family, and mine too sometimes. And you?"

"I stomp around the streets for a walk once a day, ringing bells of friends and chatting, with me yards away and them on their doorsteps. I need people, not just on the phone or a screen, but physically, seeing them face to face. And I've got the garden. I feel so sorry for people stuck in high-rise flats with none. It's the evenings. There is rarely anything on TV I want to see, and the free plays seem to be ones I've seen or didn't want to anyway. Bridge sometimes, sudoku and I'm making a patchwork quilt and knitting mittens. I seem to have built up an amazing online social life, chatting to friends on Messenger, WhatsApp, Skype and Zoom! But as for enjoying the serenity and absence of routines and deadlines in this strange, slow-motion version of life, no not really. Dressing up to go out would be a change instead of joggers and fleece!"

"How about this man you thought was quite attractive?"

"I went around to chat to Malcolm from a distance yesterday, as he's only got a small courtyard at the back and a bit to park a car on in the front."

"Do you still fancy him?"

"I'm shocked, but maybe I do. I'm not looking for a life partner, but I must admit there's something special about Malcolm. A sexual partner, a companion to have fun with, why not? But sex at our age, and why would he choose me? Do you think that men in their seventies can get it up?"

"Men may suffer from impotence or have more difficulty achieving and sustaining erections as their blood circulation slows and testosterone levels decrease. But if they haven't got cardiovascular disease, diabetes or erectile dysfunction and are reasonably healthy, fit and not stressed, yes, why not? They might need more stimulation and more time between erections. And sildenafil citrate (Viagra), vardenafil (Levitra) and tadalafil (Cialis) have aided some older men. I'm seventy-eight and Gerald's eighty-one, as you know, and believe me it can get better with age! Oh, hang on, there's someone at the door, I'm expecting a Waitrose order…"

Vicky was left holding her phone, remembering that Ruth had been Gerry and his wife Annabelle's doctor. The three had over the years became close friends, and when Annabelle's Alzheimer's had progressed, Gerry often took Ruth as his partner to functions and social events at his golf club or organised by his chambers. When Annabelle died and Gerald proposed, she accepted with pleasure.

She was back. "In fact, we feel like young lovers or newlyweds. I feel like I am able to make love better now I have a whole lifetime of experience. Gerry goes mad about the patronising attitude many people have toward older people who are intimate. Whenever people ask us how long we've been married, we say, 'Two years,' and they say things like, 'Oh, that's so cute.' We're cute?! What does that mean? Why cute? Our love life is very warm. And very satisfying. Our physical changes that occur with age can give us older people a chance to revitalise our lovemaking by focusing more on intimacy and closeness instead of sex alone. Erectile difficulties haven't mattered because of our emotional closeness and sexual compatibility. We're less preoccupied with performance. We can express affection in other ways, such as cuddling, kissing and stroking. We're both very physical, love to touch one another and are best friends. He puts up with my moods, he's very supportive. As you know, his daughter, Catherine, has mental problems. Her life is at risk. We're both committed to helping her."

"Great if you can talk about everything."

"Yes, sexual intimacy among older people is a subject that isn't discussed in the States. People in the UK are far more open. Experts say that not talking about it allows misconceptions to flourish, including the widespread assumption that seniors lose interest in sex and are, or should be, asexual. Gerry says he doesn't feel the *compulsion* to have sex as much as he did when he was younger. There's a great beauty in the freedom from necessity. The actual sex act becomes more a matter of choice and is more interesting and intriguing for each partner, he often says."

"How do you feel about that?"

"Fine with me. I was with the wrong men for nearly twenty-five years at home in America, then on my own for twenty when I was working here, so this is a bonus in my old age."

"You're a remarkable girl, Ruth."

"Mmm, the only thing remarkable about me is that I've never been satisfied with myself. I've always wanted to get better, to evolve, change, become a better person, understand the dynamics of things better, and I've found someone who can help me down that path. Gerry can be pompous and theoretical in his approach to life and I'm more practical and grounded, so we balance one another. He's an old-fashioned man, who hasn't cooked a meal since his student days, but I enjoy the housewife role, having someone to cook for, who appreciates me… I've felt in a zen-like state of peace and happiness since we got together. I adore him, his intelligence, conversational skills, supportive personality, good manners, and he seems to love me deeply too. Most people want to remarry because you need to be of some use. To feel you have no purpose in life is woeful. Women usually take on caring roles. We've been taught to thrive on being pretty and pleasing men, which is often exhausting but can be fulfilling if you're with someone you love. Despite taking on most of the household tasks and always being available to Gerry, I've got time to talk to friends in this isolation period, and he's quite happy in his study doing pro bono work, preparation for U3A lectures and some tutoring. I thought he'd miss golf, but he has hardly mentioned it."

*

"Have you got a retirement date yet?" Vicky asked when she and John bumped into one another, later, outside their houses.

"There are so many NHS staff off with the virus, or self-isolating, I can't think about it currently!" he said and rushed off to work.

Vicky wandered away, aiming for a more distant park to walk around and thinking to herself what a tough job being a paramedic was – having to respond to medical emergencies and rapidly assess a patient and the situation, to provide appropriate care. He had often told her of having to perform lifesaving procedures, such as CPR, administration of medication and inserting a breathing tube to help a patient who was having trouble breathing. *Scary, he's exposed daily to all sorts of viruses...*

Christine was highly qualified; she could assess and examine patients, make a diagnosis and provide advice and treatment including a prescription if required. Vicky had asked her if she was going to volunteer.

"Not yet, I'll wait until the Nightingale hospital opens in Excel and perhaps apply to go there – something different. Anyway, I'm a news junkie, can't help watching it all day. Mind you, working would be a respite from the news, worrying if my sourdough is going to rise and whether I sing 'Happy Birthday' too quickly when I wash."

28 March 2020

The UK has recorded 1,000 deaths, Italy 10,000, Spain 5,700, Iran 2,500, Germany only 455. Brighton was deserted this weekend, after there were hundreds of people on the beach and promenading last weekend, despite being told to stay at home. The police who were posted at the railway station to turn people back and the beach buggy guards patrolling the beach had slim pickings. The Excel centre is nearly ready with its 4,000 beds. They'll need 16,000 staff. Nightingale hospitals are being got ready in Birmingham and Manchester, Glasgow, Cardiff and Belfast. Where did all the beds come from when we can't get hold of masks and protective gear?

Shopping was proving incredibly difficult. Vicky got onto the Sainsbury's vulnerable customer line, at last, and was given a slot and the ability to do an order for her and Marion. When it came, there was no receipt, eight things they said they didn't have and all the veg, meat and fish were best by that date or the next day. *How am I going to eat three packets of French beans, three sprouting broccoli, three different meats and three different fish in two days? It's not as if I can invite someone for a meal. I wonder if Malcolm would want any of it? And without a receipt how do I know how much they charged me?*

And the tragedy of the garden centres being closed. Where was she going to get trays of annuals for her many pots and hanging baskets? *I'd better grow my own...* An hour later, she had found that every plant company she tried had sold out of the seeds she wanted – but a Scottish garden centre was despatching a mixed selection of plug plants through eBay. Then she discovered some cucumber seeds on Amazon. After she had paid, she found to her horror that they weren't coming until June! *June? Where are they coming from? I won't want them by then...*

She rang Ruth to have a moan, but Gerald said she was out walking. "Don't you walk with her?" she asked.

"Walk around the streets? Why would I want to do that? Drive perhaps, but walk? Breathing in all that pollution! Anyway, I'm far too busy."

"There is currently less traffic about, and as you know, physical activity decreases your likelihood of developing heart disease, cancers, Alzheimer's etc. The benefits apparently outdo the harm from air pollution. What are your current preoccupations then, Gerry?"

"I hear the same from Ruth and Amelia. Anyway, I have to prepare my lecture for the U3A politics class, which meets on Zoom every week. Plus, some pro bono work. One rather like the Woody Allen situation. It's a strange world where so-called liberals stop the accused having their say to defend themselves. Allen not only was not convicted but never charged, yet so many think that he's a toxic pariah, a menace to society."

"Well, I agree about that. I suppose we'll never know the truth, but it's a shame his films don't get released. I loved his work."

"Indeed. I'll tell Ruth that you rang."

Suitably dismissed, Vicky wondered whether to go to their local park to see if Ruth was walking there, but then her bell rang. Ruth was standing in the street, her thick, naturally curly auburn hair tied back with a multicoloured scarf, matching her beautiful jacket. "Just saying hello. Are you OK?"

"Strange times. I'm missing chats with you all. In fact, I just rang you, and Gerry said you were out walking."

"Just once round the park every day, trying to keep my distance from all the others doing the same thing."

"Love your jacket!"

"Yes? Josie and Naomi laugh at my devotion to fashion and lovely clothes, especially on days where I'm unlikely to be going out, but I tell them, 'It's who I am.' Your clothes can tell your story, and wearing lovely things cheers me up. I still look at fashion on the internet. Even though we could be in this lockdown situation for months, I don't think I'm just not going to be interested because we're stuck at home for a while."

"You're brilliant, Ruth! I've got two wardrobes and two chests of drawers of clothes, but all I've worn for the past weeks are these old jogging bottoms and shapeless jumper. I can't imagine ever dressing up again or buying more clothes... Somehow, having one's hair done and getting more clothes seems so trivial. Will I ever be interested in doing so again? Wanting the 'must-have' items of each season equals madness to me right now. I'm impressed that you still care."

"And just as shallowly, I find myself obsessed with what we're having for supper, and why I can't get any bread or cake flour... Anyway, enough of my shortcomings, how is your friendship with... er... Malcolm, is it? Going well?"

"We've chatted a few times on the phone, and I rang his bell once, but we're not supposed to go into people's homes, or go for walks with anyone but immediate family, so the answer is, it's stuck, stock still... Gerry was telling me he's doing some Zoom topics for his U3A class?"

"One would think no meetings would mean less preparation, but it hasn't worked out that way. We're sorry for those who lead solitary lives without the classes and the cafe to go to. The trouble is, he has to mute everyone because the group are too big, letting them speak when he chooses, so no one dominates too much. But it tires him out, and between you and me, he's started having erectile difficulties. They haven't mattered because of our emotional closeness and sexual compatibility, but he is now so often tired and distracted that a quick kiss and cuddle is all we manage before he drops off to sleep. I hope that isn't it for my sex life."

"Oh, hope so too. It was wonderful you two were having such fun together. By the way, aren't you missing singing?"

"Both of my choirs are doing online lessons with a Zoom practice together once a week."

"There's so much we can do online now. Did you see the Green Goddess has returned? She's eighty! Doing five minutes of exercise for the older person on BBC, Monday, Wednesday and Friday. And Mr Motivator, who's a bit more energetic, not much though. And the biggest hit, though dangerous for our age group, is Joe Wicks!"

"Yes, it's difficult to choose from so many videos. Are you doing any of them?"

"I've tried quite a few, but not enjoyed them. Either too much chat and too slow, or not what I want to do. I do what I did with my class, it feels right for my body."

"Better go and get the lunch. Nice to chat. Bye."

"Bye."

*

Vicky's road had a community network through a WhatsApp group, and neighbours had become so friendly and helpful to one another. It was amazing what the pandemic had triggered! The street had a mix of elderly people, families, couples and particularly young professionals, in the flats. Nusheen, Vicky and Christine, together with some younger volunteers, tried to make sure that the elderly, particularly those living alone, got food, medicine and support.

Not everyone used a computer, so they had got together and designed a leaflet, which Vicky then ran off at the community centre and they had pushed through every door in their street.

It explained that they were a group of volunteers who wanted to help their community, particularly anyone who may feel isolated or lonely or who were self-isolating. It said:

If you feel that you would benefit from some social interaction, we offer friendly phone calls.

Also pharmacy collections and food shopping. If you use WhatsApp you can send us food lists; if not, contact us at the address or phone number at the bottom of the page.

If you want to volunteer, have a think about how you might bring a bit of cheer or support to someone you know who is having a particularly difficult time. It may be someone who has just lost their job, their business, a loved one, someone who is frightened about what is going on, or someone who would benefit from a kind word or a bit of help. Whatever you do, please do so within government COVID-19 rules.

And if you're out and about, remember, hands, face, space, virus alert on door handles and surfaces, and think optimistic thoughts...

So many people had joined the WhatsApp group that they were now sharing information on good TV programmes and books, recipes, gardening tips or to swap or get an item they needed. People walked dogs for those who were self-isolating, and an egg hunt was planned for Easter.

There were innumerable complaints that doctors' surgeries had stopped seeing any patients and one waited a week or two for a phone appointment.

*

Vicky and Nusheen were talking about countries who were ignoring the virus.

"In Sweden, last week in the bright spring sunshine, families were having barbecues on the beach, all the shops were open, and supermarkets were laden with pasta and toilet rolls. Swedish public health experts argued that it can only be stopped by vaccination, which is probably a year away, or herd immunity. The vulnerable can be isolated while allowing the virus to spread as slowly as possible through the rest of the population, so they build resistance. They have closed colleges, schools and universities and banned gatherings of more than fifty people, and the vulnerable have been asked to stay at home, apart from a daily walk. But people are going to their holiday homes in the country at weekends!"

"Did you see that the president of Belarus, Alexander Lukashenko, has refused to cancel anything. Football league matches are continuing as normal, though some spectators are wearing masks, and he is urging people to drink vodka and go to saunas to ward off COVID!"

"And President Bolsonaro of Brazil says: 'Let's face the virus like a man, not a woman. The media are being hysterical. It's only a little virus, like flu. There are 5,000 cases but only 150 dead, a shutdown would be economically disastrous.'"

"A crazy man!"

"Are you feeling better about staying home from the office, now that most of the people, probably in Europe, are working from home?"

"I guess so, and it's an egoless way to lead the team. It is reducing the 'bosses' to the same pixelated square on the screen, who can be 'muted' any time. It's an incredibly levelling way to work and given us all more understanding of what we do in organisations."

"Did you see that people who work at home and use Zoom a lot are buying books for their colour rather than their contents, to make a tastefully co-ordinated background? Charity shops say that customers leave with armfuls of books intending them to be arranged by the colour of their spines, gold lettering, or back to front, showing weathered pages."

"No, really?"

"And those of us who no longer work are having our egos pricked by having to do our own housework, not that I've had anyone to help me since I've retired. But being important, rich or popular exempts no one from the restrictions of a pandemic."

"It's very moving how many companies and individuals have been making scrubs or hand sanitiser. It's bringing out the best in people."

"Hopefully when all this is over there will be a greater sense of good will, community and 'we're all in this together' neighbourliness. We'll become more generous and thoughtful, less egotistical, instead of everyone being in their own bubble. Or are we being too optimistic?"

30 March 2020

In the UK, over 20,000 retired nurses and doctors have applied to return. There is still a shortage of personal protective equipment for health workers, and the government is asking the public to donate it. The US has doubled its deaths in the last twenty-four hours and 120,000 tests are positive, the most in the world. President Trump says it's because they're testing more people. The UK has had 12,000 deaths. India has imposed lockdown for twenty-one days. There are no buses or trains, so the millions of workers with no money and no food are stranded and are trying to walk to their villages, hundreds of miles away, wearing flipflops and carrying children... They say that hunger will kill them before the virus... In Spain, one in four doctors is sick or self-isolating, and 12,000 care-workers have the disease.

Jo was still in hospital being given oxygen and rehydrated in a high-dependency unit, but, thank goodness, not put on a ventilator. They kept in touch by phone when Jo was well enough to take the calls.

"I heard on the news that Britons who fled to their second homes at lockdown have taken the virus with them," Vicky said. "Apparently areas with high numbers of holiday homes now have above average rates of coronavirus infection."

"Yes, Jamie brought in a letter I'd had from the chief executive of the county saying I'm not allowed to go to my second home, as local hospitals won't cope. And my neighbour who went a couple of weeks ago found banners all over the place saying, 'Londoners, bugger off back to London!' Good job I'm not healthy or I'd be furious not to be able to go."

"It's so sad when it's another wonderful, sunny day and people can't get out in it. The temperature is in the twenties! Over 3,000 people sunbathed and gathered in groups in Brockwell Park in South London, so now the park is going to be closed from tomorrow! It's shocking. Where are people supposed to go for exercise and fresh air?"

"Well, it's not as if we haven't been begged to observe the rules of only going out for exercise for an hour a day, or to shop, care for the vulnerable or go to work."

"I suppose so. That Neil Ferguson, the government adviser, keeps warning that if we don't observe social distancing then the rate of infection will be high 'for weeks and weeks'. You sound OK, a bit croaky, sort of breathy. How are you feeling?"

"Very weak and tired, cos I can't sleep as I'm pumped full of steroids, but I'm lucky, I haven't had it as badly as the people around me. I had a CPAP mask for a couple of days, which passes oxygen into you, and I practised meditation techniques to focus on my breathing with it. Things are getting better, but can't talk anymore, sorry."

*

"I hope to make love as long as I can," Liz said when she and Vicky chatted one evening on the phone and got on to the subject of Vicky's new attraction. "Go for it, Vic! I really believe in the benefits of good sex, at any age. It keeps you active and alive. I'm sure Dave lasted longer when he was supposed to be dead from his cancer. We had excellent sex, and any kind, at any time of day we wanted. Anything that gave us both pleasure was natural and OK. Nothing is wrong in lovemaking if you both enjoy it. Mind you, if you admit you have sexual desires, even when you're young, you're thought of as a slut. Chastity is man's creation. I'm not going to wake up one morning and look younger, but at least life has moved on and widows aren't still seen as witches…"

"It took me five years to get over Dave's death and then I met Paul. Remember I used to fancy him from a distance, waiting at the tube station for my train to work. Most of us were wearing boring dark-coloured suits, but he had trainers and a bomber jacket on, and his silver-streaked hair was in a ponytail. He had an energy about him and looked like an artist, actor or someone in the media. For my last few weeks before I retired, I tried to sit near him, so I could see the books or newspapers he read, or hear the music he was listening to, but he never looked my way. In the end I plucked up courage to speak to him. Older women are braver, don't you think? And anyway, what did I have to lose? Amazingly, I found that we were both in communications consultancy, only he was freelance and I ran McKinnon's.

"I was thrilled when we got into a proper conversation. We had a coffee, and he was quick, clever, attractive, we clicked, and after a few dates he moved in. Julie wasn't happy. I'm financially secure, he's less so, as his wife took half of everything when they divorced. Oh, Vic, remember when we were in college, they were such fun times. We had the pill, it was before AIDS and the world seemed full of attractive, up-for-it men. I was so naughty sometimes, picking someone up for sex and not even asking their name. Out every night drinking too much, parties, pop concerts, festivals, dancing until we dropped…"

"Great times, I agree, we were so lucky, and it was easy to get a job, and you even bought a flat!"

"Yes, our daughters were so jealous of how it was back then."

"So how is it with Paul?"

"He's nearly eighty and on heart medication. He can't always get it up, and I often have help getting me there, but he did last night and we had a new tube of 'Silk' lubricating gel. I'm very dry these days, so have to use it. I couldn't get the bit of cardboard off the nozzle, gave it to Paul to try, and he scratched away. But by the time it was off, he'd gone limp. He was mortified and so disappointed. So we mostly have sex in a different way and are very affectionate to one another. He says it's so nice to wake up next to me. We talk a lot, tell each other everything, and he's very supportive and energetic, with a tremendous appetite for life. Having cancer and shingles knocked the stuffing out of me, but having a loving relationship and a sex life has pulled me through. Sex is supposed to improve physical, emotional and mental health. And it's not like we're dead yet, we're not so bad for our ages. Old people are expected to be serene. It's the mask we're supposed to wear despite the horrors of decay. But I'm still up for things, fighting for things."

"And you look fabulous, Liz, you've never surrendered to time." Vicky was happy to praise her. She was a sexy, young-looking, ashy blonde, though her soft, feathered hair was actually almost white. Her figure was trim, with a fine-boned elegance. She would look fragile, elfin-like, if it weren't for her heavy breasts which she had always shown off by wearing low-necked tops. She was definitely a model of sexy style for the older woman. "And how have you been coping with lockdown?"

"We have had to be very careful, because I do the shopping, but we don't go out at peak walking times and don't meet up with any friends, mainly because of Paul's age and he has high blood pressure and had a small stroke. We were going swimming and to the gym together, now it's mainly walking. He came to church with me sometimes. But I see no reason not to make love in whatever way possible for as long as it's possible. I never thought that sexual feelings could be as strong in older people. I'm crazy about Paul. It makes me panic when I think of him getting the virus, but he's Nigerian and was in the Biafran war, so he must be fairly tough. We eat sensibly, our only problem is being news junkies, which is not good for our mental health!"

"Is Paul missing his social life?"

"He has an urbane, appealing charm, but he's not a socialite. He's actually quite homely and even solitary, so the lockdown suits him fine. I'm hoping this lockdown is over soon, so you and I can meet up. I miss you and your class! Loved the music, it made us want to move. The exercises were just right, and you gave us so much info about the body and health."

They said goodbye and then Vicky got herself a glass of wine and sat in the garden in the dark with just the lights from the house, listening to the sounds of the night and smelling the sweet perfume of the daphne tangutica nearby. The tube trains and traffic rushed past; in the distance, there was the call of an owl and a predatory fox. She thought about how yet another friend had sourced a man and was enjoying a sexual relationship. *I suppose personal relationships take on increased importance as children and careers disappear. We can give more time and energy to our love lives. No matter how wrinkled and sagging a body may be, most people want to be touched and to touch another, to love and be loved. Sex is a physical pleasure we can still enjoy. What has been wrong with me?!*

31 March 2020

Over 42,000 people have died around the world. France had 500 deaths yesterday. There is still a shortage of tests for health workers so they can return to work. One in four is off sick or self-isolating. Germany is testing 50,000 a week. The government has asked university laboratories to help, as they are doing in Germany. On Sunday 29th, Tinder users made 3 billion swipes worldwide. Video dating sites have become very popular in lockdown.

Malcolm telephoned Vicky. "I've got continual bad headaches. I don't want to keep taking paracetamol, it can't be great for my insides."

"Oh no, I'm so sorry! But yes, can't paracetamol damage your liver and kidneys? I've read that aspirin and ibuprofen are better for headaches together with cold compresses and some caffeine."

"I tried the NHS practice I've joined, but they're only doing phone appointments and there wasn't one of those for a week. Took twenty minutes to get through to the reception too."

"Shocking, isn't it? They get huge salaries and pensions and they're refusing to actually see any patients and sending them to A&E. Why should NHS staff in hospitals put their lives on the line while GPs hide?"

"Agreed. I'll go privately if it doesn't get any better. How about popping round for a chat later today? Or can we go for a walk? Walking helps hypertension and cholesterol, and mine tends to be high. I'd love you to take me on all the walks near here."

"OK, let's do that – about three? Let me know if you need any aspirin, I've got loads of those. See you later."

Just after 3pm they were walking around an enormous local cemetery, reading gravestones, looking at the war memorials and chatting. "Is it going to rain?"

He looked up at the wind-blasted sky. The sun, half hidden by greyish clouds, was weak and pale. "Too breezy I should think, and not forecast."

Near the entrance there were mostly Victorian grand mausoleums, ornate gravestones and so many large flat vaults with the writing almost or completely worn away by the weather.

"Did you know that in the nineteenth century, most London churchyards were so overcrowded that thousands of bodies were put under the floorboards of schools and churches? They smelt vile. So, in the 1850s, this rural land was landscaped and also in other areas of London, with flowerbeds, lawns, trees and two chapels, to improve the situation," Vicky said.

Malcolm nodded. "Yes, disposing of bodies was a problem until the Victorians introduced cremation, which is better for the environment and the bodies couldn't be snatched for medical schools."

"I read that if relatives could afford it, they had to put a sort of cage over the grave for a few weeks until the body was no longer fresh. Ugh, horrible! What are you going to choose? I read a Dennis Wheatley book in my early teens. I remember it to this day – *The Ka of Gifford Hillary*. The soul of this man was roaming around trying to get someone to let him out of his grave, as he had woken up. The thought has petrified me ever since. Though waking up being burnt isn't a great fate either…"

He smiled. "You are funny! How often do you think that happens in this day and age? I suggest never. And I really don't have a view. Sylvia was buried and wanted me to join her. Depressing thinking about it. You haven't decided, then?"

They had reached the end of a line of glitzy marble tombs and were walking up a little slope past brightly coloured flat markers.

"No idea, no. Rob was cremated. Who will know where we are, or care, after a few years anyway. Look at all this, so sad!"

They were passing scores of graves which were covered with ivy and had had no attention for many years. Many of the crosses had been upended by tree root movement. Then newer ones with mown grass and pruned trees and graves with plastic flowers, and even a few with living plants.

"Should we be thinking what sort of decoration we'd like? Celtic crosses, snake circles, laurel wreaths, or how about this poem?"

One gravestone had writing not worn off like all the others around it:

> Remember me as you pass by,
> As you are now, so once was I,
> As I am now, so you will be,
> Prepare for death and follow me.

After an area of memorials to young men killed in the First World War, they had completed the circuit and were back at the entrance. The ten-foot-wide gate to the road was blocked by a woman holding the leads of four dogs; she was chatting to a man. They stood waiting for her to move aside.

"Walking in London certainly reveals the true nature of some people," said Vicky. "Just so arrogant! We'd better go back soon and get ready for our Zoom meeting."

"Is it just the manager of the community centre and the secretary?"

"Yes, it's not a trustees' meeting, that's towards the end of April. I'm starting to feel grumpy already. I really don't like Zoom."

"What's the problem with it?"

"Perhaps I'm just too self-conscious. I've never taken a selfie and rather look down at those who do. Zoom is a selfie, as I have to look at myself! What is worse is that I have to pretend that I'm looking at everyone else, rather than being hypnotised by my own wrinkled face, a face I normally never see when it's animated and mobile. I think I'm shocked by what other people see, which isn't the blank bathroom mirror version of myself, but my face making weird movements. I try to focus on other people, but my attention keeps sneaking back to my face, the face of a stranger."

"You've probably just got Zoom fatigue. Your face looks perfectly delightful to me, because it's what I see every time we meet. You need to develop Zoom resilience, because you thrive on meeting people. Though it's true that scientists tell us that we're not neurologically equipped to deal with distortions and delays in video communication, they make us feel isolated, anxious and disconnected. But you can always turn off the camera and wear your pyjamas rather than sit there staring at your own face. Come on, let's get it over with."

*

Vicky walked slowly, reluctantly home. *The internet is wonderful*, she thought. *When my brain feels like Swiss cheese, and I've forgotten a word or name, the web can always remind me. And finding interesting and informative things every week to stimulate and inform my class, just by typing in a few words, is so amazing. No more spending hours at libraries trawling through books, journals and microfiches…*

Bluebells were coming out in the verges, so blue against the white froth of cow parsley. She shivered; it was a cool day. Thin cloud covered the sun. She walked more briskly. "Hello, Vic, not a bad day," called Mary, one of her class devotees.

I miss my class, they were so appreciative, so loyal and keen. They helped me not to feel lonely. But now with this enforced isolating, with all my normal busy social events stopped… There's more time to reflect, lose confidence… I'd filled my life with wall-to-wall activities and friends to banish the lonely emptiness inside me. Some of my single friends, the ones living alone, now talk my head off without pausing for breath. It's not that they're usually garrulous, but they've missed having someone to talk to. And I'm not superhuman, I need to be cared about too. I need people who will give me a cuddle if I need one. She thought of something she had heard Esther Rantzen say: "There are plenty of people to do something with but nobody to do nothing with."

She reached her front door, sighed and turned her key in the lock.

1 April 2020

There have been 563 deaths since yesterday in the UK. The total is now 2,352 in less than four weeks, as the first death was 6 March. Brent has had the most in London, and London the most in the UK. A million people have applied for Universal Credit, which shows the impact of the shutdown. British Airways has laid off 36,000 workers. The government has told local authorities to house the homeless. Wimbledon has been cancelled for the first time since World War II. In New York, a huge tented hospital and morgue are going up in Central Park. The US has had 4,703 deaths. Spain has passed 10,000 and Italy 13,000. Russia has sent the US a planeload of ventilators and other equipment. The global picture shows that South Korea has had the best record of dealing with the pandemic.

Vicky looked out of her bedroom window at her lovely garden, not huge, but big for London, and since lockdown began, it had been her beautiful, quiet world. *It's like the apocalypse*, she thought. *Are we all confronting deep, existential questions about ourselves? How are we living? Are we making the best use of our time? Keeping fit, or fat? All those who panicked and stuffed their fridges, are they now in constant stress snacking, corona comfort eating?*

Through the open crack in the window came the smells of a fine spring morning – growth, but also petrol fumes from the road the other side of the house. It was rarely quiet and there were now so many joggers. People who had never jogged before came wheezing and spluttering past. It was hard to guard one's personal space, and one had to flatten oneself against fences or walk out in the middle of the road to avoid them.

Should we want to go back to 'normal', to the guzzling life of privilege lived by so many of us?

Should it be normal to socialise constantly, travel to entertainments so often, as I and so many others did? Will this pandemic teach us what is important in life?

I suppose my past life was indulgent, full of distractions, organised so I was out most of the time. What will returning to normal be like? Perhaps I won't want to organise tight schedules now I've had to slow down, stay in. But then again, haven't I imposed a different timetable on myself? Housework, cooking, then tennis or swimming, a walk to see a friend, tea, then Channel 4 news and supper. I've still got a schedule.

My normal now is walking on my own, being in my own empty home and bed. She suddenly felt a wave of aching loneliness. *Who cares about me? Not Sophie, and would any of my friends notice much if I disappeared? They're all in relationships or trying to be in one. Since lockdown I've become intrigued with how many of my friends are either searching or have settled for a partner. I wonder what research there is about late-life new relationships?*

She went downstairs, put off the alarm and sat down in front of her computer. Surfing around she clicked on some research by Stacy Tessler Lindau at the University of Chicago: "By the age of 65 nearly half of all couples have stopped having sex and by 75 only 26% remain sexually active."

She thought of some of her couple friends who were effectively separated, yet dependent on one another for the roles they had assumed. Then of a friend who, when she mentioned sex, said, "Ugh, I stopped that after I'd had Julie!" Forty years ago, poor husband.

What's this, the AARP study? "Only 32 percent of women who are 70 or older have partners, compared with 59 percent of men in the same age group," she read. Thirty-two per cent! It seems older men are more likely than older women to be married and have sex partners. Even though older men's erections become less reliable and perhaps don't happen at all, the Massachusetts Male Aging Study found that by age seventy, seventy per cent are affected by erectile dysfunction.

I know that as women age their declining hormones decrease their lubrication and the vaginal canal gets shorter and narrower, and the tissue lining the walls gets drier and more fragile, so sex becomes difficult.

What's this? She became absorbed in various studies showing how oral sex increases older couple's perceptions of relationship quality and increases their happiness and provides the same rush of endorphins. It is, of course, particularly good for those struggling with mobility, painful joints or fragile skin.

"For men, biology or hydraulics is the biggest impediment to sex later in life," says Dr Walter M. Bortz (Stanford Medical School). "Achieving orgasm can take a lot longer as you get older, because nerve sensitivity deteriorates with age.

"For women, it's opportunity and availability. And although not everyone wants or needs an active sex life, many people continue to be sexual all their lives. People that have sex live longer. Married people live longer. People need people. The more intimate the connection, the more powerful the effects."

She sat mulling over this. *I suppose I've thought that was it for me. I've accepted what younger people think, that people of my age should be asexual. That sex is identified with reproduction, youthful attractiveness and power. But why should older people be celibate?*

She went out into the kitchen to make a cup of tea, still deep in thought. *I miss Sophie so much. Will I ever see her and the grandchildren again? How can she be so cruel? At least it's unlikely that they'll get COVID, New Zealand seems to be dealing with it well.*

I believed that if I loved her with all my heart and soul and did everything I could to help her through life, she would love me too. And she always said she did, unprompted. But then Rob came into our lives, the door slammed shut on her love, she left later, and there was nothing I could do.

She thought of her friends Marilyn and Graham, who were blissfully happy after twenty-five years of marriage. He had said: "People ask us how we can still be so in love. Easy – don't have kids! You can be a hundred per cent yourself, a quiet house, long, uninterrupted conversations, and you can do what you want with your lives."

They certainly haven't had to experience all the pain Sophie has inflicted on me!

Her brain hopped onto COVID and how the planet was breathing better, the CO_2 emissions had been halved, but people had lost their livelihoods, couldn't pay bills and some were dying! *Must try not to think about all the lonely deaths...*

The coronavirus is such an unequaliser. If you haven't got a garden or a park nearby, or a car and steady income, and you're trapped in a tiny flat or care home, this lockdown is far worse for you than someone like me with her own house, garden and pension. I mustn't moan about it.

Everyone says that when all this is over, life isn't going to be the same. Taking her tea, she collected a duster, mop and the vacuum cleaner and went back upstairs.

*

Gerald was talking to his married daughter, Amelia, on his mobile phone in the bathroom, where he had been shaving: "We are now risk averse and take security for granted, and death is the unmentionable. Most who die are hidden away in hospitals and homes. COVID is not the Black Death. It mostly kills the elderly with underlying conditions. Yet the government has subjected most of the population to house imprisonment for an indefinite period, resorting to laws to make us comply. This is intolerable for our personal autonomy in a free society. Hundreds of thousands no longer have a job but are on Universal Credit, and at least a fifth of small businesses will be bankrupt, or even a third if lockdown goes on for three months. Future generations are saddled with high levels of private and public debt. Lockdowns are only a way of buying time. Viruses don't go away but are burnt out by herd immunity. We need a sense of proportion."

"I agree, Pops. The city is like a ghost town, and we may as well be at home, there's no new work coming in." Amelia was a solicitor, married to a managing partner in a law firm. They had twin boys aged eight. They chatted for a while longer, provisionally agreed which evening for the next family quiz, and she rang off.

Gerald examined his face in the mirror. Thick, wavy, steel-grey hair that used to be black. He saw the bags under his eyes, his blotched complexion, an ugly mole next to his left eye, and his nose and ears seemed to get bigger and redder. And his body! Sagging buttocks, forlorn scrotum and the beginnings of stomach blubber. It was a long time since he could slip into his size 34 trousers. Obviously not a beauty. Already older than his father ever got to be, he thought how lucky he was to have married a beautiful, incandescently intelligent, capable woman like Ruth…

3 April 2020

> The Nightingale hospital in the Excel centre opened today, and there are at least six others being set up in other cities; 2,000 beds are now ready to be used. There were 932 deaths in Spain today, 684 in the UK, 1,169 in the US. "The disease is still spreading – we can't relax – stay at home to protect lives – this is an INSTRUCTION," says Matt Hancock. Boris still has a fever.

It was mid-morning, and under a sullen sky, Vicky walked around to Debs' house and rang the bell, to chat from the street.

"How are you, Debs? Don't come out, we can chat from here. How are you?"

"Depressed. It's spendin' so much time on my own. I talk to Danni most days, but I have to ring her. I don't know how it is, though, that she's so profoundly ignorant of my needs, values, life, *me*. She lived here till she was twenty-two. We ate meals, did her homework, went on holidays together, and as she got older, I helped her shed her delusionary, uncompromisin' far-left Marxist views. But at times when she was at university, we rarely crossed paths or exchanged a word. She has never bothered to find out what I think, or what I have achieved in life. She thinks I'm deluded, right wing, old, out of touch, shallow – because I appeared in *Playboy*. She never thinks that I sacrificed a brilliant future, getting to the very top, for the sake of bringin' up my family, givin' them a lovin' home. I could have grabbed life and enjoyed it to the full, installin' a nanny to look after them. No gratitude, or acknowledgement. It's depressin'. Wish I'd got some tools when I was young, not just modelled, I might be gettin' some respect now! I wanted to study psychotherapy – it's fascinatin' how brains work and how we get stuck in patterns of thought and behaviour. With no trainin', I've helped so many people to not self-sabotage, self-destruct."

"Yeah, you'd have been brilliant. I saw that the Chinese government has actually threatened to fine people who don't visit their parents often enough. Life has certainly changed. This is how it is now. Danni is probably caught up in her busy life and doesn't realise you are so lonely Apparently a lot of countries won't have enough young people to care for the old, either literally or through paying taxes. I read somewhere that in Japan more nappies are sold for old people than babies. Perhaps we're old and on the cusp of being disposed of as no longer productive or needed. Anyway, let's cheer up. Did you see that Jonathan again? You see, you were enthusiastic about him, so I remembered his name."

"Well, yes, I did, he doesn't care about rules on social distancin', he does what he wants. He rang the bell and just walked in, and the sight of him, a human in my kitchen, made me feel thrillingly fatalistic after two weeks of lockdown. He grabbed me in a bear hug and we snogged – me leanin' against the sink, pale, makeup-free and tousled bed hair. Then he sidled round me and carefully soaped his hands for what seemed like a full minute. The news came on my kitchen TV, and it was so harrowin' that it knocked the stuffin' out of us. Our libidos were suddenly drained, and he was quiet and went off shortly after, not sayin' anythin' about meetin' again."

"What a strange man!"

"Yeah, I guess he's not really for me, too impulsive. But I can't be the only one who would go to extreme measures for a whiff of human connection in this long, lonely time. Last night I watched a film with Idris Elba in avid, greedy absorption and pure uninhibited lust, like a feral cat! And I've read that Ashley Madison, the 'open-minded' Canadian online datin' service for married or livin'-together couples, has added 17,000 members a day during the pandemic – as people find a point for their government-sanctioned daily walk."

"Men!" agreed Vicky. "Hopefully, someday soon, all this will be over and it will just be a bad dream where we ate, slept, walked, repeated."

"The hours drag by, but the weeks have disappeared and what have I achieved? Nothin' but the confirmed knowledge of how I need human contact and the worry about my mental health. I know it's a good time for self-development, to keep fit, eat and sleep well and to think about what has given one most happiness, what motivates one to get out of bed, what legacy one wants to leave behind... But the problem is that we are now too old to fulfil our function of having babies, and though we're free to have as much sex as we like, who with? Men keep on being fertile, they are still part of the evolutionary cycle, but with all the loosenin', thinnin' and wrinklin', women of our age are done, finished. I used to get put up to business class on flights, just by smilin' at the check-in guy, and never had to plan holidays as I'd get invited on yachts. No one notices me now. The next stage is near... being a toothless crone, a burden." She let out a huge sigh. "So sorry to offload on you, Vic, I'm just lonely and frustrated! I need a detox from my addiction to sex." A tear escaped from her hazel eyes, with their swirls of amber and green.

"It can't go on forever... And we've got years ahead of us. There are something like 16,000 people over a hundred in the UK! We'll play tennis again, you'll see your grandchildren..."

"I miss them so much, cuddlin' and rockin' their little bodies, smellin' of soap and milk..."

"They'll ask you what Zoom was and if you made banana bread and sourdough when they learn about the pandemic in history. They're too small now to remember it for themselves. You know, I seem to have quite a few women friends looking for love. Perhaps that idea of a monthly meeting of wine and nibbles would be good, where people can chat, get to know one another, go to the theatre, films, concerts, holidays together, and it wouldn't be just women, like the WI, or interest groups, like U3A, where some people who would really get on would never get to meet, but chatting evenings and joining in with whatever grabs you. We could even get inspirational speakers, have luncheon groups and share news about other things we do which people might want to join, like bridge and choirs. So many people are lonely but are ashamed to admit it." Vicky's eyes were shining dangerously with missionary zeal.

Debs smiled. "Loneliness is an epidemic, sparkin' off so many health problems. In fact, I've read that it has the same impact on people's lifespan as smokin' fifteen cigarettes a day! I eat badly, out of cans or send for takeaways now, on my own. We shouldn't be livin' alone or even in nuclear families. But perhaps with people with similar interests, probity, ethics?"

"Mmm, people may not want to admit they're lonely, it's as if there must be something wrong with them. Shall we do a Zoom meeting to discuss our first social venture, for when we're allowed to meet up again? We could start designing the invitation."

Debs looked more cheerful, so Vicky stopped leaning on her gate, waved and went on her way.

*

Vicky and Ruth met later to walk on the Heath in the cool air, though always at least two metres apart.

"I tried to sign up to be an NHS volunteer – I'm too old to go back as a doctor," said Ruth sadly.

"Life as we knew it has vanished! You were a GP for years and kept updating, it's ridiculous if they can't use you!"

"And what will we look like? No hairdresser, no nail salon, no waxing."

"It's the meetings by Zoom, where they can see my uncut hair and scruffy clothes, that I hate – but I can't bring myself to dress smartly like you do!"

"The invisible enemy has emptied workplaces and city centres, closed schools and sent a fifth of the global population into lockdown, even infecting our leaders. No theatre, cinema or seeing friends for supper. I didn't appreciate that having the Bartletts round was going to be my last dinner party, back in that halcyon age more than a month ago… How can everything change in such a short space of time?"

"Yes, it was only three weeks ago when I was hardly ever in, and now I feel as if going out and interacting with life is not going to happen again for me. Will I even want to? Perhaps I'll carry on being stuck to the couch with my sudokus, crosswords, quilts and knitting."

Ruth pointed a smile at her friend. "I've always thought I'd like to try watching TV all day in my dressing gown, eating ice-cream. It's just confusing that by doing nothing, you're doing what's right and what is your duty."

"I read somewhere that it's like the Old Testament, God purging us with fire, floods and pestilence, for destroying this beautiful planet!"

"Although some people avoid passing close to one in the streets, the majority, arrogantly, seem unaware of me crossing the road or dodging round parked cars to keep two metres between us. And the silence and empty streets in the City and West End are so eerie!"

"It's interesting how different countries are trying different methods to contain it, such as Sweden, doing nothing, and Wuhan, in complete lockdown. The jury is obviously out on which strategy is most successful."

"Yes, Singapore never closed its schools and China is now beginning to unlock the industrial sector. Half the world's population is in some form of lockdown. Germany has ploughed vast technological resources into testing and contact tracing to interrupt the chains of transmission... No one can say what strategy or mixture is right or wrong."

"Italy must have lockdown fatigue. How much longer will they tolerate it, not even being allowed out for exercise? There will be strong pressure from the public to get out of their houses and go back to normal life."

"Ooh it's 4.40. Twenty minutes to Boris time! I suppose it's good that he talks to us. Makes us feel we're all part of the same plan."

"Rod Liddle says his family settle down with snacks and drinks in front of the TV for 'Hancock's Half Hour'. All blunders and apologies. Shall we sit on this bench and look at the swans and coots?" They had reached Highgate pond.

"He's always so funny. Yes, for five minutes. We've got FaceTime with Catherine tonight, and a quiz with Amelia and Josie and their children tomorrow. I haven't had time to get bored yet. By the way, did you know that the lakes are here because of the digging for sand in the Middle Ages?"

"Oh really? From Constable's paintings 200 years ago, you certainly wouldn't recognise the heathland."

"The soil that was brought here to fill the unsightly pits must have hugely changed its character and vegetation."

"At least there are no highwaymen and their bodies hanging from the trees now. Come on, we'd better go."

4 April 2020

In Bangladesh, 4 million workers have lost their jobs as shops have closed and orders cancelled. People will starve and they live so densely that the virus will spread like wildfire. Bangladesh is home to 860,356 Rohingya refugees, needing humanitarian support. Sweden and Singapore, where tight controls were shunned, are now thinking again as deaths soar. Ireland has just spent 200 million euros on PPE from China, and twenty per cent of it isn't fit for purpose. And the British Healthcare Trades Association was keen to supply PPE, but not asked. In the UK, 4,000 prisoners are to be let out, plus a further 500 who are pregnant or old and vulnerable, because if there is a coronavirus outbreak in prisons, the staff would not be able to cope. They will be fitted with GPS tags, but officials are warning that they could well reoffend.

Ruth climbed the two flights of stairs to her study at the top of their Georgian house – chosen because she thought that if she had been sitting for long periods, expending effort climbing up and down would be good for her. She passed their bedroom, with its huge ensuite bathroom. It sounded as if Gerry was shaving. Yes, he must be, it was Saturday, one of his shaving days. The doors to their two spare bedrooms were closed; she opened them to let in some fresher air. They were rarely used.

In the attic room, she looked out of the window at their carriage driveway and the quiet, tree-lined street beyond, then sat at her desk, switched on her computer, logged in, and before teaching a Zoom session with her choir, she opened the latest edition of *The Lancet*, becoming immediately absorbed in articles about psoriatic arthritis and COVID-19.

*

Vicky was watching the nine o'clock news when Malcolm rang.

"How are you today?" he asked.

"OK, I suppose. Did you hear that more than 350,000 people have been fined in France, including the *Sunday Times Europe* editor? She was resting with a friend at opposite ends of a bench having both filled in their attestations, proving they had kept to the rules of not being out for more than an hour and not being more than one kilometre from their homes. But they both had to pay £120. So strict!"

"Possibly we should be stricter here. In Spain they're not allowed out to take walks. I feel sorry for families in high-rise flats with no garden and not even a courtyard, like I have. At least the planet is breathing better because we've halved CO2 emissions, but people are dying lonely deaths in the ICU and others have lost their livelihood."

"If this gets worse, is this how societies collapse? Does it happen so fast?"

"Shall we go for a walk? I could meet you on the Heath."

"OK, I'll park in Hampstead Lane and meet you by the entrance at eleven."

*

They were walking towards Highgate pond and Vicky was talking about her career.

"I've always done jobs that I believe in, and they then take over my life and I'm juggling everything else, like my relationships, my daughter, parents, sport. I'm a focused person and very little diverts me from the path I have in my head. Being a CEO of a big business was isolating, but it's important to be able to work as a team and to know others in similar positions who can act like lifelines, to be able to discuss challenges and how to resolve them. And giving others in the organisation a chance to shine when they might have good ideas is key and accepting that we are not gods with perfect solutions in every area. I enjoyed the interaction, the challenges, as a CEO – didn't you?"

"Yes, loved the buzz of it all, until the last few years when Sylvia became so ill and leaving her every morning was a guilt trip."

"It's certainly not the sort of job to do with only part of your attention. It must have been very hard for you."

"Worrying, certainly. I needed the salary to pay our huge mortgage on our ridiculous estate – we had bought on impulse. Yes, it was worrying. I just put my head down and coped. If I'd started thinking too deeply about my situation I would have gone mad. I kept things going until she was more in hospital than at home. Then I sold up and bought the current house to be near her."

"Men are hard-wired to suppress their emotions, to soldier on, aren't they? Didn't you take time off to cope when she was so ill?"

"Not much, no. I've always found it hard to talk about personal issues or admit that I was fallible and needed help. My work was my security, probably my status in life. I couldn't not succeed at it."

"What did you feel like when you retired, then?"

"Very flat, deflated, depressed, lonely, scared and not knowing what on earth I was going to do with myself. I'd put myself out to pasture without thinking of the next stage in my life. The final P45, game over and then a big blank. I've been lucky that I've been given some status by continuing on the board, and Peter, who took my job, has involved me by asking my opinion on so many issues. And I gradually realised that happiness doesn't come from material things and status, but from friendships, the sun, exercise, good diet, sleep and not measuring oneself against others, but enjoying the moment. I've tried to care less about things that don't matter. Our walks have been lifesavers…"

"Mmm, it's been interesting watching the world almost grind to a halt since February. Will we go back to our busy, rushing, fragmented lives, or will we appreciate a slower pace, enjoy staying in more?"

*

Vicky sat in her car, after the walk, and suddenly her brain emptied. *Where am I? What am I doing?* She looked at the keys in her hand, at the parked car in front and had no idea what she was supposed to do, how she had got here and where 'here' was. She pinched her arms, shook her head, tried to stay calm, breathe slowly and deeply. She had been driving since she was eighteen; it was like breathing, automatic. She put her hands on the steering wheel and it all came flooding back. *This is the brake, accelerator, I'm in Hampstead Lane, I came to walk with Malcolm, to sit by Highgate pond.* These memory lapses were less frightening when Rob was alive, he filled in the missing words and took over, but now! *Am I getting dementia like Mum? Horrors…*

She telephoned Ruth later to discuss her little 'episodes'.

"How long have you been having them?"

"Not sure. Occasionally before Rob died, but they've become more frequent."

"It's not necessarily anything to do with dementia, it can be stress, depression, anxiety, a neurological disorder, like epilepsy. As Samuel Johnson said in the eighteenth century: 'The art of memory is the art of attention.' Perhaps you're just not concentrating. You're not overweight, haven't had a head injury, not diabetic, don't have high blood pressure. Why don't you have a blood test to check your homocysteine levels? It's an amino acid produced when proteins are broken down."

"What foods have that, then?"

"People who eat too much meat have high levels. You have an excellent diet, don't you, apart from cake? It can be treated with Vitamin B9 and folate."

"I eat plenty of dark green leafy vegetables, fruit, nuts, beans, peas, dairy, so I shouldn't have a high level of homo whatsit…"

"True. Are you relaxed enough? You always seem to be rushing about, filling your day with too many activities. And are you drinking enough liquids?"

"I've always been the same, not drinking much. Perhaps it's genetic."

"Well, yes, but try drinking more water and don't worry about it, or that will be counterproductive."

*

Gerald was spluttering with rage. "Do you know that it was Public Health England that thwarted the government's intention to 'test, test, test'?" Ruth looked up quizzically.

"The government wanted to let businesses sort out shortages, like the Mercedes Formula One business did, together with engineers and clinicians at UCL who had devised some sort of breathing aid. Developing something like this would normally take years, but it took days… Yet Public Health England, our state-funded monopoly, refused to allow private diagnostics companies to run tests, though they had already been doing them for private clients and were keen to get involved!"

He breathed out heavily, in irritation. "So, testing has been dangerously slow because they are excessively bureaucratic and hostile to innovation and private sector testing, whereas Germany had an open market from the beginning. It's a heinous crime!"

"Aren't you enjoying your soup?" Ruth asked mildly. "Some more of this delicious bread Vicky gave me? I've been reading that this lockdown could unleash Britain's most creative period since the Second World War. Being asked to do nothing, as we have done for two weeks already, will spur people to start thinking in novel and productive ways."

"Not PHE! Yes of course, everything you make is excellent. I'll have half a piece, please."

Ruth handed him the olive ciabatta and carried on: "Epidemiologists think that for the next eighteen months until a vaccine is developed there'll be a cycle of lockdown and unlocking, with restrictions partially relaxed on an age group or geographical area, until the infection rate starts climbing again."

Gerald smiled wryly and his eyes became hard dark stones behind his thick blue-rimmed reading glasses. "Impossible to think that people would comply with that for eighteen months or more."

8 April 2020

There are 10,000 dead in France, and in Paris there is going to be a 'no exercise outside during the day' rule. In the UK, 786 people died yesterday and Boris is in intensive care for the second night. Excel, which was set up in nine days, has had its first patients arriving…

Vicky walked down the stone steps into her garden, taller, slimmer and fitter than most women of her age. Seeing the wisteria in full flower against the wall almost made her heart stop with delight. It was tumbling over itself in the joy of life. She went down the path, tulips either side like sentinels, and last year's two-coloured snapdragons and purple irises with the cream roses behind, towards the fruit trees. The apple and greengage trees were in blossom, white and deep rose coloured, with rosemary and lavender underneath. The warm, wandering air caressed her bare legs.

She was thinking about her current life. Why she hadn't read more of Claire Tomalin's biography of Charles Dickens, her book group choice, which she had time to finish now, but somehow, going out to walk around the streets for the one walk allowed per day was more appealing; having a conversation with friends on their doorsteps. *Makes me and perhaps them feel less lonely and cut off. It's important to keep in touch with friends, isn't it? To connect with those one cares about. Or am I just too shallow to enjoy my own company?*

Should I stay at home and build up a massive online social life on Messenger, WhatsApp, Skype and Zoom instead?

She sighed. *Will I ever see Sophie and the grandchildren again?*

Two birds flew down and into Rob's bird box carrying moss in their beaks. *Every species seems to want to be in twos, to have a partner. Why don't I?*

This morning I'll drive to Hampstead Lane and walk on the Heath.

Twenty minutes later she was sitting on a bench, watching the swans and coots on a lake, in the sun – a glorious scene, spoilt only by the dozens of dogs and their owners, and the joggers puffing past. To her surprise, in the distance she could see Michelle. Was it her? Walking briskly round the lake towards her, the wind raking through her thin hair, so it flew behind her in undulating waves? Yes, yes, it was. They waved at one another and next minute, a glamorous Michelle, in pink leggings and white cotton jerkin, plonked down at the other end of the seat.

"I'm so unfit. I've let myself go!" She took a glug from the bottle she was carrying.

"Americano with an extra shot for an adrenaline rush. When did I last play tennis with you? Must be fifteen or so years ago!"

"You had tennis elbow and never restarted."

"Chaika wanted to go on long walks. I guess they took over my time."

"How are your plans for you?"

"I've spoken quite a few times with my sister. She's busy with her own life, but we'll meet up when all this is over. I was so lonely that I was thinking of paying for 'Rent a Friend', but then I saw an ad for a yoga retreat in Koh Samui in Thailand. I went for two weeks."

"Well, how wonderful. I didn't know you were interested in yoga. Have you done it before? And what's 'Rent a Friend'?"

"I guess most artists live in a perpetual state of anxiety and unconfidence. Thinking, 'Is this pointless? Should I be doing something more useful like volunteering to work in a hospital?' I decided to go to the yoga retreat to sort out my head. And yes, I'd always done some yoga poses every morning before Chaika got up. I breathe deeply, count the breaths as I go through the movements and afterwards sit cross-legged connecting myself with the morning light. It keeps me calm, helps me to cope with deep stress, low self-esteem and anxiety. I was doing a yoga class when I met Chaika, but she was scornful of it so I didn't go back to my group or pursue it further. And 'Rent a Friend' is a US company which offers platonic friends to hang out with, take to a party or even give you a hug. In the States many people work in the gig economy, working long, antisocial hours and having no meaningful interaction with anyone. They are starved of company and affection."

"A typical American idea, sounds good, but how was the yoga?"

"Wonderful. Thatch-roofed cabins, a paradisiacal beach, raw food, lentils and tofu, inspirational stretching and breathwork. From eight in the morning, the nurturing, nourishing, enlightening, healing programme was packed. Expensive wellness for the privileged, but my tension faded away and positive energy and inner harmony came back. So now I know I'll experiment with different styles, until I find myself. I've always been sceptical about the value of things like these. Wary of psychobabble, touchy-feely stuff. But being in a group was invaluable in terms of realising that my life and circumstances are so much better than most. We all seemed to have had relationships which hadn't been good for our personal development but we stayed for the security. I feel ready to move on, look forward, not back."

"Wow, Michelle, I'm so pleased you're sorted. You seem so calm and philosophical, full of positive energy, and… and you're such a talented artist…"

Michelle suddenly grinned. "AND I've been using something that has changed my life."

Vicky's brow furrowed. "Tell me more."

"Doesn't sex define all our psychologies? Isn't it the core of all of us? I was in a depressive, bulimic, suicidal state when I met Chaika. I'd never had an orgasm – no man had ever made me come and I couldn't even get to it myself. I'd had to have therapy to detox from an addiction to self-harming. Chaika changed everything for me, she unlocked me sexually. Before her I'd lie there pretending to enjoy it… Thank goodness I've managed to find the perfect new vibrator. I can pretend it's her." She smiled and her grey eyes twinkled. "Sex toy sales have gone through the roof in this pandemic. Even Poundland introduced one last year. Shall I get you one?"

"Um, I had one years ago. It was so noisy, though."

"I'll order it when I get home!" And she was gone.

10 April 2020

There have been 980 deaths in the UK today; that's over 9,000 in total. France has had over 10,000 and the US over 20,000. Three and a half million have claimed Universal Credit in the UK.

Diana's sister Amy had set her up at a dinner party. She wasn't looking for anyone. She had been divorced from Robin for thirty-five years, but found Alex, a tall, distinguished-looking thespian in his late eighties, silver hair curling over his collar, who was sitting next to her, very easy to talk to. They realised that they had met at Amy's daughter's wedding four or five years before, when his wife had been alive, but they could barely remember it.

Towards the end of the meal when they were talking about their past lives, he said: "I admire you, Diana, you're a strong, beautiful woman. I'd like to get to know you better."

Diana felt herself blush; something was happening to her! It was as if she were in a long tunnel with loud, echoing noises. The world was receding into the distance… *Surely he isn't fancying me? It's been years since someone has noticed me, fancied me. I'm old, faded, worn out, but he's made me feel like a gauche teenager – lost for words!*

He gave her a lift home and by then she was thinking it might be nice to have someone to go out for a meal, to concerts, cinema or theatre with, occasionally.

So they started to meet, and it became four or five nights a week. He wasn't looking for anyone to take the place of his wife, but both were enjoying their relationship and had plenty of sexual energy. Diana saw things in a scientific way – she was a pharmacist – and Alex more subjectively and emotionally – he was an actor, then a theatre director. When the lockdown came, they were not together and so, obeying the rules, had to stay apart.

*

Vicky walked further than usual one morning and came to Diana's street of small, semi-detached houses with small gardens behind, and only a very small paved area in front. She passed a house where men were taking down scaffolding, expecting not be noticed, when suddenly there was a whistle, a lone whistle.

She looked up to grin at whoever was being flattering but met only indifferent glances or no eyes at all. Perhaps it had been sarcastic or directed at someone other than herself. Wearing her baggy old track trousers and shapeless jumper, being old enough to be a grandmother to these guys, it certainly couldn't have been genuine appreciation.

She thought back to when she did attract wolf whistles – half a lifetime ago, before it was non-PC and thought to be stressful, sexual harassment. She had always quite enjoyed it as a harmless act of admiration, but as a feminist, could see that it was only OK if one was confident. She remembered how she had smiled to herself when, as soon as she was obviously pregnant, and then when she was pushing a pram, the whistles had totally stopped...

She rang Diana's bell.

"How lovely to see you! Shame it couldn't be on the tennis court." Diana's hair was now more grey than brown, and she was wearing similar clothes to those which had become Vicky's uniform, though in brighter colours. She seemed to have put on a little weight, though she had always been tall and strong looking.

"How are you getting on?"

"I'm so missing tennis and the gym. I walk the dog and do a few fitness classes on the internet, but it's not the same as going out to do them. But I think I've got used to diminishment, I've sort of accepted it, which I suppose is better than being miserable and resentful." Her voice wavered and her eyes looked tearful behind her glasses. "I talk to Alex every day, sometimes two or three times. I'm lucky to have Adam near who drops off my shopping, but I can't see him or my grandchildren properly. It would be terrible if I got it and passed it on to them. I'm in the vulnerable group because of my asthma and stents. It doesn't matter about me, I don't matter anymore. But although I wasn't looking for anyone,

I never thought I'd find this much happiness at this time of my life."

"How is he getting on?"

"Oh, he's OK. He's got a gardener and a live-in housekeeper, so he's well looked after. He reads, listen to audiobooks, watches streamed plays and Netflix, and he's trying to set up a radio station for boomers to hear music from their era – '50s, '60s and '70s – and he's got a lot of the old DJs interested in having slots. He says he misses seeing me, of course."

"Weren't you discussing selling your house and moving into his larger one?"

"Yes, just about to exchange and ditto with a flat in Deal. We were going to spend weekends walking at the coast. As it happens, we wouldn't have been able to go there anyway, second-homers are being told to stay where they are. 'Super-spreaders' are unwelcome. Local hospitals won't be able to cope with their retired elderly population – who make up the heart of many of the coastal towns – all getting ill. Let alone extra people!"

"It's great that you're getting on so well and so quickly."

"We don't actually sleep together, so we'll always need two bedrooms. I'm restless, wriggle all over the bed, and neither of us would get any sleep. And his snoring, dear God, his snoring! After nights of me sighing, kicking, shouting, and experiments with nasal strips, high pillows and so many other devices, we decided that two bedrooms was better than sleepless purgatory. But we love to cuddle, touching is so important, so we get together when we wake up well rested in the mornings. I suppose people might think it's funny that old people want to do things like that. And he has shown me how my life has been stressed because I fill every moment of the day. I'm going to refuse inspection and consultancy jobs – retire. The lockdown has given me time to sort out my perspectives and the junk in my house. I've got things ready to go to charity shops when they open again. I loved my work, but I'm retiring properly, otherwise I know I'll get overwhelmed by taking on too much. I need time to spend with Alex. It's been wonderful to have someone to spend evenings and weekends with. I know the U3A was great for me – all those National Trust holidays I did with them, repairing footpaths, surveying butterflies and plants – but Alex is interested in nature and enjoys walking, and of course we both love opera, theatre and films. It's nice to have someone special to do things with. And he's so enthusiastic about everything and such a good listener. With Robin we had too many prickly silences."

"What does Adam think?"

"He's happy for me, I've been alone for a long time. He was apprehensive at first, he thinks I can be impetuous, but after he'd met him he was OK with it, and we've made a prenuptial agreement, even though we're not married. We wanted to make sure that our assets we had before we got together would go to our children and grandchildren. He's got three daughters who are starting to accept our relationship, and luckily our grandchildren get on so well. My vision of how I would be when I retired is having lots of projects. As you know, I've kept updating, doing courses, and I sometimes work for CQC. I never wanted to be that negative stereotype of an old person in a rocking chair. But I had never thought I'd be sharing my life with a partner!"

"It's great, Di, so pleased for you!" Though mean little subtitles about her friend's self-absorption flickered through her brain.

"Will we ever be able to play tennis again?"

"Not looking good, is it. Perhaps younger people will be released earlier, but our age group, could be a year or so. We'll be too old to move and see the ball when we're allowed back!"

They chit-chatted for another five minutes, then Vicky carried on with her walk, thinking, *I'm very fond of Diana, she's very lovable, always laughing and cheerful, but she has been on her own too long, she is desperate to talk. She tends to bombard people, talk at them and not let them in. Like a tape recorder, you press 'play' and out pour words. Did she ask me a question? Hmm.*

Having brought up her son alone, she's had to organise her and his life like a military operation. She's always been busy and became even more so when he left home. There have been no men in her life until Alex. She persuaded herself that she didn't need one and had a lot of interesting and strong women friends. It was quite a shock when she met Alex and they got on so well… Perhaps she is different with him, or he doesn't mind and is deeply engaged by her intelligence and wit and is fascinated by her sometimes tedious, endless conversation and apparent belief that everything she says is interesting. Ooh, why am I being so spiteful!

*

Nusheen rang the bell and went back to lean on the gate post. Vicky opened the door, with a big smile. "Hi."

"Am I disturbing you?"

"No, not at all, I was pricking out some kale seedlings. Are you OK?"

"I miss our teatime chats. I've done twenty minutes on the stationary bike and a YouTube pilates lesson, some housework, made a cake and now I'm missing the office. I love, chaos, noise, constant interruptions and dramas, it's stimulating. I definitely can't find that inner calm people talk about. I could never meditate – too restless, easily distracted. I've got a grasshopper mind and I'm bored on my own…"

"Where are Farzad and Kalil?"

"They went in to the office. I don't see why I couldn't have gone, it was my brainchild. I get the ideas and the business."

"They're protecting you. You're at risk – you had bronchitis before Christmas."

"Mmm, but I'm a city girl. I'm happiest bustling and rushing on pavements or in traffic. Don't like the great outdoors, it ruins my heels. I'm BORED at home!"

Her lovely face was free of bags, sags, lines, and definitely no Donald Duck lips and skin stretched like parchment. She always looked glamorous and perfect, and her strong personality shone through her heavy foundation, black pencilled eyebrows, long, curly, jet-black hair and curvaceous body.

"Can't you Zoom or FaceTime some colleagues or customers?"

"We all go online at 9am, drink coffee together and discuss the day ahead. We need camaraderie to keep everyone facing in the same direction. Regular communication is vital. Young people are used to connecting digitally, but they also need human contact and Zoom is so shallow compared to actually being with people! We need to make sure we're looking out for one another and being flexible and supportive in case anyone has problems with parents, children or being on their own all day. They need to feel part of a team and share information about their projects. I think this is my strength, being empathetic and motivating. But, going in? They've told me not to get involved, to just look after the home… I criticised some of the younger people's ideas and now they're saying I'm too old! I should let youth take over! It's pejorative and ageist to think that an older person's lack of enthusiasm for an idea stems from being stuck in the past. It's just as likely to be because they have tried it before or thought it through and it won't or didn't work. The passing of time doesn't necessarily erode one's faculties, it can sharpen them. Probably a life well lived, greater insight and experience make you wiser. There can be late-onset zest to think of new projects to put energy and vigour into the company."

"You're absolutely right. Many people have a third wind and often a fourth, look at Trump and Biden! Hopefully not everyone's personalities, intellect and energy erode every year until they become an amorphous, ancient blob, waiting to die."

"The only thing is... I'll admit something to you, you'll understand. New clients were always a problem. I'd dress in a perfectly tailored business suit, scrape my hair into a severe top-knot, discreet, no-nonsense jewellery, positive approach – yet they'd look past me for the person they were expecting to meet. As if I was fit only to get the coffee or answer the phone! I'd stride up, firm, confident handshake, tell them my name, then wait for the adjustment between reality and expectation. And when they'd recovered, so many of the men then tried to date me, make me into one of their decorative appendages. My professionalism was sorely tested. Not to mention the business associates who complimented me on how articulate and impressive my pitch was, in surprised voices!"

Her eyes were dark and her lips set tight. Her words were like pistol shots. "So degrading and frustrating! And do you know, Farzad has been talking about getting a better work-life balance. He actually wants to move to the country and have outbuildings and countryside all around us! He keeps showing me estates in Ayrshire, Montgomeryshire, Languedoc. We can run the business from there, he says."

Vicky could imagine her friend, a vision of high-maintenance, immaculate glossiness, similar to a Kardashian, would be frustrated by the slow pace of life in the country.

"What will he and you do there? You're not big gardeners or walkers. Do you like animals?"

"He seems to see himself as a country gentleman. He says I can do pottery and paint. Pottery! Painting! I don't even like the countryside, I like pavements and shops!"

"I'm sure you could run your business from anywhere, you're so talented. Perhaps he's winding you up. If you're going to be moving, let's talk about when and how we're going to get our social project off the ground, then. Perhaps an introductory cocktail party? You could start designing publicity."

Her lovely eyes lit up and she nodded, black curls bobbing. "Good thinking, are you sure I can't come in?"

11 April 2020, Easter Saturday

> There were 917 deaths yesterday in the UK, and in Spain, only 510! The lowest number for three weeks. The UK has Europe's highest number of deaths and seems to be on a similar trajectory to the one Italy was on, and we might exceed their total in the end! Sweden has admitted not being properly prepared as deaths rise. The decisiveness of Norway and New Zealand has meant they have had relatively few deaths. The US has had 2,000 deaths.

Gerald finished preparing his lecture on the dot of 12.30 and went downstairs for lunch. He passed Ruth going up and down the first two steps of the staircase.

"We need to exercise much, much more, and stretching and toning don't strengthen the brain like aerobic exercise does. Why don't you join me? Come on." She held his arm and half pulled him into her rhythm, of up, up, down, down.

He reluctantly let himself fit into her pace. "This is hard. What other ageing problems is my body encountering?" He wondered if she would mention sexual dysfunction; it had been weeks since he had felt desire, although Ruth was no less attractive and had tried to arouse him.

She smiled. "Well, you asked me. Up, up, down, down. Our cell renewal slows down. Cells can only divide a limited number of times, programmed by one's genes, so everything changes. The skin gets thinner, drier, gets age spots and skin tags, and the body no longer functions smoothly without pain. Bones are less dense and the discs between vertebrae shrink, so the bones rub together and we lose height. There are changes in the cranial vertebrae, so heads tip forward, called 'senile kyphosis', compressing the throat, so swallowing is more difficult and one chokes more easily. Vascular function in the brain decreases and fewer neurons are produced, so we decline cognitively." She changed her leading leg and ensured he did too, then carried on.

"Ligaments and tendons are less elastic, so are tight and stiff. The more we work on our muscle mass, strength, flexibility, balance and aerobic capacity, the lower the rate of degeneration. By age seventy-five, our percentage of body fat doubles. Exercise won't halt ageing but will preserve our cognitive and physical functions and many of the factors like our telomeres, the caps on the end of the strands of DNA, that keep us feeling and looking youthful. It's the most potent longevity drug!"

"Sounds as if death will be a happy release. Can I have lunch now?"

*

Vicky and Malcolm were wandering around the Heath, along with hundreds of others.

"This huge area has so much history, has attracted so many famous people through the centuries. Like Karl Marx and his family? C.S. Lewis? Constable? Dick Turpin – and wasn't he born in the Spaniards pub?"

"You're probably right," he said, and as a jogger passed them very closely: "Hope it's not a good place to pick up the virus. There are so many people huffing and puffing all over us."

"Apparently minority communities, BAME, are being disproportionately affected," she said.

"Why on earth is that?"

"More in a household? More likely to have diabetes, high blood pressure? And from what I've seen in shopping streets, just not so careful about social distancing."

"Boris has come out of intensive care, saying the staff saved his life… and 1,000 people were fined by the police force. They're supposed to engage, explain, encourage, and only if the person refuses to change what they are doing and observe social distancing do they enforce. It's a new world for the public and police – we're all adapting to a new way of life."

They reached Highgate pond and, spotting an empty bench, quickly claimed it, sitting at either end.

"I'm amazed that three weeks has gone so quickly," said Vicky. "Have I read *Middlemarch* or learnt Italian? I read that Shakespeare wrote *King Lear* while England was fighting the bubonic plague and Isaac Newton discovered gravity while self-distancing! We all probably have good intentions, yet *North and South*, my book group choice, is unopened by my bed while I catch up on old colour supplements and magazines. If Newton and Shakespeare had had as many social media and TV distractions as we do, would they have discovered or created anything?"

"Yes, true. None of my intentions for this quarantine period have got off the ground yet, and by 6.30 it's time for a shower, cooking and eating supper with a glass of wine and whatever programme one can find which is remotely interesting on TV."

"Mmm, I've rediscovered what terrible programmes there are. Too many cooking, buying houses, animals, reality stuff, so I watch endless analyses of the news about the coronavirus. It's odd how comforting the news is. Despite its terrible tales of death and destruction. Is it because the misery is inflicted on others, so we are relieved to be safe from harm? Anyway, I'm certainly not going to finish this isolation more cultured, fluent in a language, an intellectual titan – perhaps just fatter and more stupid?"

He looked at her fondly. "I don't think that you've put any weight on, look at this little fat gut here!" He patted his stomach area. "Yes, reading, I thought I'd devour novels. I started to reread Albert Camus's *The Plague*, but haven't got far."

"That's appropriate. People going about their lives, taking things for granted – the human condition of not really thinking about others suffering. Then the plague strikes, the town is quarantined, people are powerless against fate and they learn moral responsibility for one another. An existentialist classic!"

"I should join a book club, because one tends to only read authors who confirm one's opinions and world view. It's like surrounding yourself with people who believe the same as you do, so your views are never challenged. You started one, didn't you?"

"Yes, and we could do with a man or two – we are a dozen women. I often wonder if books give one secondhand thoughts, sort of stifle one's creativity. Maybe having to read a book a month stops me trying to write one myself? So many people don't read books at all, just newspapers. Does it matter? Are we moving away from reading? Oh no, was that a spot of rain?"

They jumped up, he produced an umbrella from his rucksack, which he insisted she have, as his jacket was old, and they hurried to their homes.

13 April 2020, Easter Monday

> There have been 717 deaths in UK hospitals today, which doesn't include deaths in care homes and hospices, as people there haven't been tested, so it's not proven that they had the virus. This will be the fourth week of UK lockdown and people generally agree with it. Spain and Italy are easing their lockdown restrictions; France has extended its restrictions until 11 May, India until 3 May.

It will soon be warm enough to plant out my seedlings, thought Vicky. *The sap is rising. There is a sensory explosion in gardens and amongst wildlife. Is all this fecundity stirring my sap? The tomato, runner bean, broccoli and kale plants have grown enormously in* this hot weather. *All the experts say not to put them out until late June, though I usually do so in late April. Perhaps mid-April this year.*

She met Ruth at Paddington Old Cemetery – twenty-four acres of rural land in Willesden Lane, which had been laid out with a horseshoe path with two chapels at the entrance. They chatted from two metres apart, remarking on how the style of graves had changed since 1855 and looking for the advertised apiary, which apparently produces 'tombstone honey'.

"How are you, Ruth?"

She sighed. "Rather fed up without the theatre, films, concerts, my two community choirs, U3A and lectures at the Royal Society. And never getting dressed up for anything. But really, OK, I suppose. I can't seem to do a lot, apart from playing Boggle with Catherine, or Trivial Pursuit and quizzes with Amelia, Josie and other family on Zoom or FaceTime. And Gerry and I play bridge online with some friends. My whole day revolves around what to cook, what to keep for other meals, when I'm not staring bleakly at the news. It's so stressful and I'm only cooking for the two of us. What does it matter? I'm still struggling to get flour and yeast. There are too many people sharing their recipes, filming themselves on their phones. I'm drowning in social media's hundreds of discussions of how best to make sourdough, in their locked-down kitchens. I used to love cooking, it gave me purpose, order, unleashed creativity, but now…"

"Isn't cooking for loved ones the way one shows affection? About giving them something good so you're taking care of them?"

"Hmm, well, Gerry's quite happy, he tutors on Zoom and reads newspapers online. But humans are social animals and the diminution of my enjoyment caused by this lockdown – being deprived of the intimacy of my friends and family, the things I value most – make the days empty and meaningless, threateningly amorphous and tinged with anxiety. The fracturing of social bonds is as painful as physical pain to me. The epidemiologist Neil Ferguson says we might have to socially distance for years, to preserve life! That's not the same as *living* life. The thought makes me quite depressed…"

"Clearly the over-seventies with underlying health conditions need to take extra care, but hopefully there have been enough letters in the press, petitions and support from the famous and powerful, for the government not to set age restrictions which breach our equality laws. I couldn't have got this far without visiting someone every day, and it amazes me how many long-forgotten people have telephoned. Let's meet more often… I love your hair, it suits you at that length."

"I was going to say that to you too. We've probably been stuck in ruts keeping our hair at the same length for years. I had long hair until I was thirty-something, then it seemed unsophisticated and a bit muttonish." She ran her fingers through her auburn, splashed with grey, thick locks. They both smiled. They had arrived back at the entrance. "We must have missed the apiary."

"Oh well, next time." They waved goodbye.

*

Alex was seeing his daughters, and Diana had pretended that she was busy with Adam, Ruby and their children, Ellie and Mark – but actually, they were seeing Ruby's mother in Birmingham. So Diana was at home, in fact, studying her long face, naked and blotched in the bathroom mirror, her once-glossy black hair now looking rather greasy and flecked with grey. She was thinking that she needed to keep up with her appearance – it had been so long since it mattered. *But I mustn't obsess about which outfits, my hair and perfume – must stop reading advice in magazines and the internet. Better to be understanding, thoughtful and not keep worrying that he will go off me.* She wondered if Alex knew her at all. He was obviously entertained by her opinions, but did he actually take them on board? Change his views, because of her good points? *He loves to talk with men and is amused by women, but are we a lesser species? Is it because he's old fashioned and sees women more as homemakers? Perhaps I'm being unfair, he gives me more attention than I've ever had before. More reason to make an effort.*

When she had been with Robin, perhaps she had stopped thinking about how she looked, but she hadn't known she was in a competition, thought she was loved for herself. She remembered the shock, the sharp spear of rejection, the thought that this was how it felt, how other people had felt whom she had pitied when they were ditched, and now it was her.

After all the pain of his leaving, she remembered finding an old sweater of his and burying her face in the blue wool, breathing in his masculine smell, the scent of him trapped in the fibres. He had said they had had good sex and she had never thought or asked for her own pleasure. She enjoyed his orgasm and the way he was limp, satiated and tender to her after his explosion – though Alex, now, was far more attentive to her needs. Dozing with her face in the sour fabric, she had felt cold, unloved, alone. They had been mismatched, at least from his point of view. He was so charming and popular, flirted with waitresses, any woman who came into his orbit – but somehow never around when she needed him, always busy somewhere else or on his phone. And the bickering and simmering, flicking onto one another's sore points – perhaps purgatory had lain ahead. He said he would have come back, but his wretched secretary was expecting his baby.

Stop thinking about Robin. He had been my life, I lived inside his love and care, but now it's Alex. She wandered into the garden; the sun was clinging to the last vestiges of the day, lingering, before burying itself behind the houses opposite. A plane flew overhead. She thought of all the squandered years where she never went anywhere, was carrying too much unconfident baggage, and was tied by her job and looking after Adam. Shivering, she turned back. *I should give this a go. I've been too long on my own.*

16 April 2020

The 2019 Global Health Security Index has ranked 195 countries in order of capability and readiness to prevent, detect and respond to a pandemic. First is America and second is the UK. Yet bodies are piling up in these two countries and not in India or African countries. COVID-19 is affecting industrialised rich countries more than low- and middle-income countries. COVID attacks the lungs, so shortness of breath is a key symptom. A UK study of 17,000 patients showed that only twenty per cent of those requiring mechanical ventilation were discharged, fifty-three per cent died and twenty-seven per cent were still in hospital. And although healthy lungs produce an oxygen saturation reading of ninety-two per cent – there is 'happy hypoxia' where patients are normal at fifty-four per cent not on the ventilator. It also gives heart, liver and kidney problems, neurological complications and lethal blood clotting. Is the obesity rate one of the factors which kill people? The proportion in intensive care is twice the proportion in the general population. When they lie down, the extra weight of the stomach pushes the diaphragm up, reducing lung capacity, and they are more likely to have high blood pressure and type 2 diabetes. Or are the UK's problems due to slow lockdown, lack of mass testing and tracing, tourists arriving without checks and population density in cities?

After three weeks in hospital, Jo was starting to walk, had better levels of oxygen in her blood and was released to go home, because Jamie said he would move in to look after her while he was working from home. Vicky had been phoning her for updates and had checked first that a visit was welcome. She opened the gate of the large front garden of Jo's semi-detached Edwardian home, and went down the patterned, tiled path to the porch, peering in the windows of the two reception rooms either side. There was no sign of life, so she went into the porch and rang the bell of the door with its beautiful stained-glass window. Then she retreated back towards the gate. A very pale Jo came to the door with a fold-up chair, which she sat on.

"How are you feeling now?"

"Today is possibly the first day I feel human and able to read a newspaper. Washing, speaking, everything takes it out of me, so we won't be having our usual long chats for quite a while. The NHS staff were outstanding, and I'll be out there next Thursday joining the neighbours in cheering for them. In fact, I panicked a bit at leaving all that wealth of knowledge and caring. I didn't have to go on a ventilator or have a tracheotomy, thank goodness, but for a couple of days I was locked in my body, couldn't respond to anyone or anything. I could hear, but not show I could. That was the first time I've had to face up to my own mortality – it was frightening."

"You've just got to take it slowly and not get impatient, I suppose."

"Coming home from hospital, clutching a bag of drugs, was terrifying, but having lovely casserole dishes left on the doorstep from local friends – thanks so much for yours – and thoughtful cards from those further away has been cheering."

"Did you keep hearing from Ted?"

"No, nothing, and I couldn't contact him to tell him. Perhaps he has had it too? I texted him a couple of days ago, but no answer."

"He's probably incredibly busy."

"Suppose so. This experience has taught me a lot about myself, and I've realised how precious life is. When I learnt to breathe normally again, the air going into my lungs felt so wonderful. My ancient face looks like an elderly alien, so browless, saggy and wrinkled – the ageing process has really speeded up! I know I can't look young, but it's going to take a month or so for my strength to come back, and to feel less anxious. I'm hoping the weather will be good enough for me to gradually get out and about again. Being confined to the house is a lonely, infantilising, prison cell existence. My garden is very neglected. I look forward to being able to do some weeding. I need to get my fitness back. As you can see, I can barely walk. I'll have to start with staggering around the house. Shame we're not allowed to walk together."

"Yes, you can understand it, though, so many people are ignoring social distancing. They seem to think that they're impregnable, superhuman and they can't catch it! What about Captain Tom Moore finishing his hundred laps of his home before his hundredth birthday! Soldiers from his old regiment were there to witness his last steps. He had thought he'd raise £100. It was his family who said to go for £1,000, and didn't he get £16 million and still rising?"

"Amazing. He's one of those quiet, modest, brave, determined war heroes – so inspiring. I've just read that 15,000 people have died in the UK."

"Yes, so there'll be at least three more weeks of this, despite Spain, Italy, Denmark, Austria, Switzerland, Germany, New Zealand, Iran and others relaxing their lockdowns in some way. Our curve isn't flattening, though – there are over 800 deaths most days, which doesn't include people dying at home or in care homes."

"Sorry, but I'm starting to feel really weak."

"Oh, so sorry, Jo, how inconsiderate of me…"

"No, no, I was desperate for a chat, please come again, any day – tomorrow? It's just I have to lie down now."

They blew each other kisses and Jo shut the door.

Vicky then walked over to Malcolm's house and rang the bell.

"Hello, how nice to see you. Have you been for your walk yet?"

"No, not yet, do you want to come – two metres away from me? I was going to the Heath today. There'll probably be too many dogs and joggers, but I love sitting looking at a lake."

"I'll just get a coat."

An hour or so later, they were sitting apart on a bench, by Highgate pond, watching the ducks, swans and coots...

"I enjoyed living in the countryside, except for the journey to work. I often stayed overnight with my sister. Walking, one saw so few people. The air felt cleaner, the skies clearer, birdsong louder and so many flowers. I haven't seen a primrose, cowslip or daffodil this year. They're in abundance in the countryside. Could you live in the country?" he asked.

"I was brought up in a very small village. But no, I wouldn't want to go back to that sort of life. I love the energy, the different cultures, foods, theatres, galleries, my tennis club and friends I've had for so many years. But of course, groups of people and crowds spread viruses, and being squashed up against strangers might not be a good idea for a while."

"So glad I retired when I did. I wouldn't like the problem facing every CEO now of how to survive the looming recession and who and what they can cut. So many companies and high street stores won't survive, and CEOs won't be able to cream off vast salaries and bonuses as the government will want a say if they bail them out. I see Air France is not to be allowed to provide short-haul domestic flights – the French government wants people to take a train."

"Cleaner air, but another hit on the air industry."

"Exactly. Is that one swan or more?"

Vicky laughed. "Really, can't you see it's one? Its partner is over there. Have you got another headache?"

"Mmm, yes, sorry, but I think the aspirin are wearing off again. I'd better get back, so sorry."

*

Vicky was chatting to Marion, standing in the street, telling her how she was keeping sane by doing a lot of walking and exercise at home.

"Well," Marion said, "my week looks a little different to yours. I haven't left the confines of my house and garden for two weeks. I'm shrivelling and rotting with a patina of bluish mould, like an old plum. My exercise is mainly gardening. Yesterday I mowed the lawn and pulled out some of the periwinkles down the path. Picked up the dead camellia flowers – the rain made them go brown and squishy. The front garden has never been so tidy! We've been so lucky to have had such good weather during the lockdown. I've spent hours in the sun, planting seeds, pricking out seedlings, with the noisy birds for company. Perhaps I'm getting used to the new normal all too easily. Maybe I'm a bit lazy and antisocial. The 'Stay at Home Choir' has been challenging but fun. As long as the weather holds, I'll keep pottering in the garden. The key for me is to achieve something each day, but not set my goals too high."

Vicky smiled. She had been envisaging Marion practising her singing in her garden flat, which overflowed with pictures, ornaments and books. Weighty dark furniture, with antimacassars along the backs of the chairs, and high, bushy plants in front of the bay window, where she pulled back the heavy, dark curtains to let in some light. Such a contrast to her own bright, light decor.

"Gardening keeps us both going. It's eternally forward looking, with planning, ambition, expectation. What we do now is in the interests of seasons to come, but I can't wait for the end of lockdown, whenever that may be, so we can meet up with friends. Won't it be wonderful when we are all able to sit around a table and have tea together again?"

"Whenever that is…"

Vicky changed feet and leant on the wall. "You're not going to rush out when I've gone and disinfect this bit of wall, are you?" And not waiting for Marion's response, she carried on. "Did you see about a mother who is a full-time carer for her schizophrenic son posted a message on Twitter about her loneliness, as not one person had said happy birthday to her? Eighty thousand people then sent messages from around the world. All these people who are at home and on digital messaging. Friends I'm not usually in contact with are emailing, phoning, texting and my usual friends are wanting us to Zoom. Everyone wants to chat and everyone has time, and the most staid of neighbours can be seen out on the streets, banging saucepans for the NHS. I guess it's *carpe diem*."

"Not me, I'm too busy in my garden. But I do wonder if we will ever be able to go back to how it was before. The economic realities of resuscitating bankrupt businesses will mean that our world will look very different."

"Wonder if we're thinking more about how to live and what to value?"

*

"What *will* happen when we are released from lockdown? We just won't be used to going out and being free from this strange slow-motion existence," Vicky mused as she and Ruth did a walk around Richmond and Ham.

"Mm-hm, will we be able to just slip into our previous lives, or will we go mad trying to pack in everything we've missed? Perhaps there will be drunken orgies in the streets. Or perhaps we'll have a better idea of what matters and what is important. I know I'm spending more time reading and making a rug and less cooking dinner party food. It's strange,

I used to set my easel up in the garden and paint for hours. Gerry used to do the same, but we seem not to have time now."

"Love Old Palace Yard, these houses are to die for." A plane passed overhead. "Except it's on the flight path. They must have been pleased to have had a reprieve from the constant noise in the past few months."

"I've always had this feeling that I mustn't waste a minute, keep pushing forward, but yes, the days slip by so quickly and I'm left wondering what I've achieved."

"I think we're allowed to do things we enjoy, and perhaps chatting to lonely people is what you've been achieving lately? Let's go this way, so we can avoid all those shouting, exercising youngsters." They had reached Richmond Park.

"I do wonder if COVID has caused a new relationship between older and younger people, that we now see them as a dangerous risk? Though perhaps that's unavoidable when they don't wear masks and seem unaware of social distancing. It's always us who do the avoiding, dodging into the road behind cars. Wonder if any older people have been run over while performing avoidance tactics?"

18 April 2020

Another three weeks of lockdown! There have been 631 deaths today and a total of 13,729, not including those who have died at home or in care homes, as most of those were not tested for the virus.

Vicky walked over to Debs' house to ask about her son, Mark, as she had read that 22 million people in the US had lost their jobs and applied for unemployment benefit, which was the worst economic slump since the 1930s. The sky was heaped with glowering, mutinous clouds promising rain, though it hadn't been forecast.

Debs came to the door wearing scarlet leggings with a hole in the knee and a long yellow shirt.

"Yes, you're right, Mark lost his job! The only good thing is that he might come back now."

"Has he suggested that?"

"Not yet, no…"

"Are you OK?"

"Feel a bit old today. I know the internal changes associated with agein' have been happenin' inside me, unobtrusively, but I'm conscious of them today. I'm a bit creaky and stiff."

"About time too, you've never looked your age. Don't worry, feeling hasn't translated into looking. What are you doing with yourself?"

"It feels as if the digital revolution was set up for this lockdown. We can order food, clothes, any item to our homes rather than goin' shoppin', and I'm surfin' and buyin' too much. There's email so we don't have to write letters, and I can watch any film in high quality, and I can do all these things in bed, and I do. Skype and Zoom have been waitin' for us to have to use them, and with people one didn't know well, we can now see their house and children, which makes them more human. Oh yes, I can be very busy, but I so miss actual human contact. I've got skin hunger, touch deprivation. I'm even missin' being squashed up to people on the tube!"

"Are you still a sex terrorist, trying to meet men in the lockdown?"

"No. Even though I so miss adventure, excitement, the frisson of flirtations – but I'm tryin' not to angst about what I might have. I'm tryin' to enjoy celibacy, like some seriously impressive people have done before me."

"Who are you thinking of?"

"Apparently, Mother Teresa, Isaac Newton and the Dalai Lama were all virgins!"

Vicky laughed. "You are funny. Anyway, glad you're keeping

busy. I'm sure Zoom is effective one to one, but when I've tried it, with the book group or the community centre meetings, I didn't feel at all connected. The slight time lag and the fact that sometimes the internet loses one person and their face is left in a gurn as if the wind has changed. Or someone disappears and everyone talks as if they're not there, though they are. It's so self-conscious. Can anyone stop staring at themselves and wondering if everyone else is counting their wrinkles or whatever? It's a weird distraction to be looking at oneself and the strange faces one makes that one isn't used to seeing. Not to mention the embarrassment if the background of one's room is in a mess… And there are awkward silences, then everyone speaks at once and some then don't get to say what they wanted to… Zoom doesn't answer what I want. I don't want to talk at a group of friends, but to have meaningful, real conversations with them and hear their voices, not see their face watching their own face in the camera of their computer. I'm weary and wary of Zoom, it should be kept for special occasions. It's like junk food and a phone call or FaceTime are more like a real meal. It's good to talk, but on Zoom?"

Debs was grinning from ear to ear. "You're the funny one. The general opinion is that one in four personal Zoom calls with friends will be fun, but perhaps only to make fun of those in the last three? OK, Zoom doesn't bring out the best in most people's personalities, it can be a circle of snipin'. If you want a catch-up use the phone. Though then you can't blame a bad internet connection for an event you'd rather not attend. It certainly professionalises friendships to an alarmin' degree. Social media does provide a lifeline, I'd be suicidal without it. But it's no substitute for bein' with people."

"Well, are we both going to broadcast to friends and everyone we can think of that when all this is over, we are hoping to be more sociable and community orientated and meet up once or twice a month, starting with drinks and snacks evenings and then organising theatre, film, concert visits, even holidays? It would be something to look forward to in this period of losing our liberty, access to places, goods and services, sex for some, and our security, as we can't feel safe from the virus. We must all be longing for something, whether it's fish and chips at the seaside, a visit to a pub or a foreign hotel with a beach for a holiday. So wouldn't it help to get people through this lockdown? Why don't we ask if they would come and what day and time of day is best for them?"

"If it'll help me get dressed up to the nines and goin' on lots of dates with up-for-it men," said Debs, "I'll be all for it. See how shallow and single-minded I am!"

*

Janet and Barry were walking from Finsbury Park station along a disused railway track – which was now a green corridor to Highgate. It was three and a half miles. Not much for Barry, who jogged most mornings with his phone and watch to measure everything from his blood pressure and heart rate to his speed and time. Trotting around the same route and jumping up and down if he had to wait to cross a road. He did it even when there was snow and ice, as he didn't want to feel lazy and old. Three miles was quite enough for Janet. The trees made it feel as if they were in the country, though after the first mile, they started passing quite a few people going the other way, and then faster walkers overtook and passed them. "This is a bit busy."

"Anywhere in London is going to be," Barry answered.

She was feeling guilty and guarded, wondering what he was thinking after last night. He had reached out to cuddle her and her body had contracted away from him. Even though her mind wanted him, she felt as if she was hiding inside her body and being touched was a violation. She couldn't explain, she didn't understand it herself and no words would come, so she rolled over, away from him. He hadn't said anything about it and was warm and solicitous today.

The sun came out as they entered Queen's Wood, one of the ancient woodlands that had once covered Middlesex. It was quite a balmy day. After a while, they sat on a fallen tree to have a drink of water and to share a sandwich. Barry opened the packaging with meticulous care. Janet idly wondered how he had acquired such magnetic qualities, so that no stray bits of bread, chicken or avocado fell from the packet or his hands. Similarly, liquids he handled never spilled, as if they recognised that he was a more powerful force. She wouldn't have blamed him if he had shown irritation at her sloppiness, but he never did…

19 April 2020

> The death toll in Europe, excluding Russia, has passed 100,000. China and South Korea report the lowest numbers of new cases. Americans in a number of states have taken to the streets to protest against lockdown. Tomorrow the furlough scheme starts. Companies can apply to the government for eighty per cent of employees' wages, so they can get up to £2,500 a month and keep their jobs.

Gerald banged on the breakfast table with his fist. "This is diabolical incompetence!"

Ruth got up and walked round behind him. Putting her hands on his shoulders to massage and gently calm him, she read over his shoulder.

"38 DAYS WHEN BRITAIN SLEEPWALKED TO DISASTER."

She squinted down at the double-page spread in the *Sunday Times*. "But you've thought the government was doing well, consulting with all the experts, making decisions based on their evidence."

His neck was red with anger and the newspaper shook as he read: "On 24 January, Hancock told reporters after a Cobra meeting that the COVID risk to the public was low, though *The Lancet* had published an article saying that the lethal potential was as high as the 1918 flu pandemic which killed 50 million. Johnson didn't even attend that meeting or subsequent ones for another five weeks! By then it was too late, and no preparations had been made. Two pages of evidence of complete incompetence, where even plans that had been made were not put into action! It's true, Johnson is a part-time prime minister, not capable of leading a country. Why was I hoping that he had stepped up this time?"

He threw the paper onto a nearby chair.

"I hope that history attributes the 15,000 deaths, or whatever number we get to, down to his lack of leadership…"

"These insight reporters like to be sensational. They're probably very left wing and they find a few dissenting voices and make a big drama. And as you said, whose science? The government says it 'follows scientific advice'. But scientists rarely agree. They criticise one another's modelling and methodology and are too often proved wrong!" She moved her hands up to gently rub the back of his neck.

"When the politicians wanted to prepare, they said, 'Not yet', and when blamed for the delay, they said, 'But if we'd spent a fortune preparing and then we didn't have a pandemic in the UK, we would have been blamed for that too!'"

He pushed his glasses up the ridge of his nose and twisted around to look at her. "You read it, it's very damning and rings true, though I take all your points. Anyway, I'm starting to think that if we hold politicians responsible for everything that goes wrong, they will be so terrified that we and history will judge them incompetent that they will lock us down for their own protection. They were panicked into making a decision which has shut down our economy, based on an unlikely worst-case scenario modelled by Neil Ferguson, who has since been discredited. Infuriating. Perhaps I'll come for a walk with you today, I'm getting quite sedentary since the golf club closed."

*

Ruth and Vicky were chatting on their phones.

"Did you see that President Bolsonaro says that COVID is just 'the sniffles'?!"

"Yet they've had nearly 2,500 deaths!"

"And how about Captain Tom Moore being top of the charts? Amazing!"

"I loved his regiment being there at the end. He's part of a huge, loyal family – one of their own. One of the few good things one can say about being in an army…"

"Our friends in America said they'd like to ditch Trump and have Captain Tom Moore instead."

"I was amazed at how all the US channels showed the Queen's address."

"Yes, they really love the Queen. Do you know a left-wing activist said something like, Americans were more moved and hopeful watching an unelected monarch – the solid, durable bedrock of another country – than anything Trump has said in this crisis! Much too much bitterness and polarisation in the US – the Queen's words have nothing to do with party politics."

"Are you swimming in Hampstead ladies' pond at the moment?"

"I wish! One of the great joys of my life still closed."

"I'll come with you sometime. There are too many swimmers in the sports centre pool, and I dream of gliding through the water, body at full length, arms pulling, legs and feet flapping rhythmically. I'm not a great swimmer and like the sea best, but moving meditatively through water, that sense of peace, the physical and mental balance from swimming, is what I yearn for," sighed Vicky.

*

Vicky and Malcolm were walking on the Heath, wild garlic, primroses and flowering blackthorn lining their path. They were talking about the place of women in society and how Vicky had been refused a mortgage without a man's signature on her application form, and the jobs she had applied for where a woman wasn't even interviewed.

"However, I feel lucky living now, not having to marry out of the need for economic survival and social acceptance. So many authors have shown us what happened to women who didn't have the sense to get married. Leo Tolstoy, Gustave Flaubert, Edith Wharton and Henry James's independent, foolhardy heroines die, and Jane Austen and George Eliot's often pragmatically accept men they don't love."

"As a white man I feel guilty that I am part of the historical oppression of women. Yes, at least you don't have to marry for social correctness, security or money now."

"No, but I was brought up to be nice to men, though I soon rebelled when told not to beat them at tennis. Winning meant more to me than acting the sweet supportive loser. And I couldn't stand bullies. I'd challenge them to a fight, though don't remember many of them taking place."

He smiled. "I can imagine they were probably all petrified of you. Wish I'd known you then, not to fight you of course. Hopefully life is moving on for women."

"Mmm, my generation may have been the first to mostly have careers. I remember my mother saying when I agonised about which university and which subject: 'It doesn't matter which, you'll be married soon.' She had to give up her job in a bank when she got married, and though she was very bright, there was no question of her or her sisters going to university... I have always worked and fought all my career to succeed in a man's world. When I gave birth, there were only nine weeks off, either five or four before and the balance after, and only full pay for two, was it, or four weeks? Can't remember, but it was very different from today."

"There was no question of Sylvia going back. She was a top PA at the BBC, but it was just before the Employment Protection Act of 1975. You had Sophie in 1978, didn't you? By the way, will you think about doing a walking holiday in Italy, when all this is over?"

"Mmm, sounds good. Rob and I did one most summers with Headwater or Ramblers. We loved the colours and smells of the wildflowers in the country, the red roofs of the buildings, the light and warmth, and at the coast, the soft lapping of the little ripples on the hot sand and rocks."

"We'll talk about it again when travel is allowed."

*

Michelle had driven Vicky to Isleworth in her Mazda MX-5 to do a beautiful walk, following the river to Richmond. They had chit-chatted during the journey, but after Michelle had parked, Vicky asked:

"How are you feeling now, Michelle? What are you doing in this lockdown?"

"I have the radio on all day, but I'm overwhelmed by aching loneliness. I know what I should do, get a rescue dog, to get more exercise and for company now Diva has died. Plus learn new skills, volunteer, force myself to be proactive. I just dread the empty weekends, and I won't be going on any more holidays without someone to share them with."

Vicky sighed. "It takes time. It's been sixteen years for me, and getting used to being alone didn't happen overnight. Home is dark and empty when I come back in the evening. And I'm still afraid of the randomness of fate and chance and pain and how, all at once, everything can be taken from you. I wake up in the morning and unless I motivate myself, the day stretches ahead, lonely and pointless."

Getting out of the car she squinted her eyes up at the vast, never-ending blue sky.

"But if you like dogs, why not? You and the dog, after all, may be rescuing each other."

Michelle joined her and they set off, talking. "When I walk down the street, younger people's eyes slide past me. I am of no interest, too old, someone's grandmother. When people say, 'You don't look your age,' I wonder what I will look like when I do look my age? Should I not go out anymore then, hide away? I cut myself off from my past, stepped into Chaika's life, acted as her support. Am I too old to make my own life? Find my own friendship group? Now I'm on my own, I'm conscious that I could entirely retreat from life! I hated parties – all that small talk while eyes peered over one's shoulder for someone more important. I just used to get drunk. And the dinner parties! At least if we gave them I could hide in the kitchen between courses. I'm not on WhatsApp, haven't got my own group of friends, no one in fact. I don't know why you bother seeing me!"

They stopped for a moment to admire the view of Syon House, the last surviving ducal house and estate in Greater London.

Vicky, keeping socially distanced, said: "I can't put my arms around you, just imagine a big hug! I'm in a similar situation. It's difficult being on one's own and having to constantly make the effort to contact friends, when you didn't have to bother if you didn't feel like it, as you had a partner to do things with. When this is over, why not join an art class and art appreciation at U3A? And a few of us are going to set up a sort of friendly group, where we meet occasionally for drinks and chats, sometimes book theatre etc together and possibly organise trips or even holidays if we get on with one another. But meanwhile, you could contact neighbours or people you'd like to be friends with, check they're OK and perhaps meet for walks or have them round to your lovely garden for a socially distanced chat or tea or drink. You have so much to offer, so much to give."

In front of them was a beautiful scene. The hedges were covered in hawthorn blossom, guelder roses tumbled from the trees and kingfishers flashed back and forth over the water meadows.

Michelle sighed. "You know, I haven't minded the parameters of my life shrinking with lockdown. I've enjoyed silent roads, skies devoid of vapour trails, seeing more wildlife. The quiet has been good for me." She smiled. "You're such a good friend. Sounds what I need to do. I will try."

*

Vicky woke up during the night; the moonlight was poking through the curtains, peeping incuriously through the crack where they didn't meet. She had been thinking about Malcolm's suggestion to do a walking holiday when life went back to normal. How would it be? Two single rooms and a sexless friendship? They hadn't touched because of COVID. Would they? Did she want to? *We flirt a bit and I enjoy his company, but more?*

22 April 2020

There are 2,592,000 cases of coronavirus around the world. Eighty-four tons of PPE has at last arrived from Turkey and is being checked. Matt Hancock says the UK has reached its peak. Spain is easing its lockdown from tomorrow.

"Spanish children have not been out for forty days, they'll go wild!" said Ruth.

"What about the uppity Americans protesting against lockdown, carrying banners saying, 'Land of the Free'?"

Vicky and Ruth were walking two metres apart around

their local cemetery, admiring the crumbling mausoleums and cherubim and straining to see the inscriptions on the very old headstones. It was sunny, so from the trees came so much birdsong from blackbirds and chaffinches, and there were bluebells pushing through the long grass.

"They need to work." Said Ruth. "We're lucky with our pensions and living in the UK. They are saying that if you're paranoid about the virus, stay in, but everyone shouldn't be prevented from living their lives. Unfortunately, one of the most militant has died of COVID!"

"They've had over 40,000 deaths, haven't they?"

"Well, there have been 20,000 here and that's not counting people dying in care homes or their own home, and compare the size of the two populations!"

"It will be interesting to see how other countries come out of lockdown. This is an enormous expanse, isn't it? I don't understand the big gaps, and there's acres of room here, yet Joanna said when she enquired about a grave for her uncle and then possibly for herself, she was told it was full."

"Strange. Makes you think about your own mortality and that unfortunately nature's rules apply even to us, we're just biological organisms. It's interesting how some people have been prepared to sacrifice so much in the past months, to protect their lives, while others haven't."

"So many friends have found gardening has carried them through the first four weeks of lockdown and made not going out bearable. With this sunny and hot weather, we've been returning to nature, which many of us had lost touch with."

"I'm not one of them, I've always had a gardener. But you're right, human nature and green nature are intertwined. There are so many projects in prisons, for war veterans, those with depression and mental breakdowns, and research has shown that access to trees and grass reduce violent crime, domestic aggression and that students perform better if they first walked in an arboretum rather than urban streets. Wonder why I love and appreciate gardens but have never been interested in actually getting my hands dirty?"

*

Vicky rang Maggie wondering if she was at home or staying with Robert.

"I'm here at home. The lockdown happened so quickly it was too late to negotiate living together."

"Just heard that the UK is the fifth country in the world to get more than 20,000 deaths!"

"Who are the other four? It must be the US, they're way over 50,000, and I guess Spain, Italy and France, and they've had much stricter lockdown measures."

"Lucky Australians, allowed onto the beaches, and children are going back to school in New Zealand. Although Tory grandees and famous baby boomers are threatening a grey revolt, it's not happening here yet. I'm amazed that Sweden seems to be quite happy with the way they've handled this pandemic. They said that harsh measures can't be sustained, so didn't have a lockdown till way after the rest of us."

"But then they had a higher incidence of deaths, far more than Norway and Finland."

"We're down to 360 deaths yesterday and there are only fifty-one patients in the Nightingale. Boris is back in charge asking us to keep to lockdown rules, and it looks as if at last we are going to be doing aggressive contact tracing, testing, quarantine like Germany did at the outset."

"Yes, I pray us over-seventies aren't the last to be released from lockdown. It shouldn't be for the healthy over-seventies, just the vulnerable ones. The Nightingale wasn't really needed, was it? There were only nineteen patients last week and it's designed for getting on for 3,000! I suppose it's easy to criticise in hindsight."

"I woke up feeling a bit down this morning. It's four weeks since Robert and I were together. We email and talk on the phone, but it is not quite the same as actually being together! It's probably the rain that is depressing me. I'm stuck here and feeling I have had quite enough of this isolation. It's thirty-two days today since I saw him!"

"It's such a complete change of lifestyle, perhaps we'll get like hermits and not want to go back to normal. But perhaps being stuck in lockdown together would have been a passion killer? Do you Zoom one another?"

"No, he's a bit of a technophobe. I am definitely fed up… Pictures of the M4 show it's very empty, but there are so many webcams, I probably wouldn't get very far. Wales is like a police state now. I do lots of little jobs all day, time passes. I have a weekly Sainsbury's delivery. Today is just a 'fed up' day, for whatever reason. It will pass, hopefully. Think I need a cuddle, to be touched, I'm horny… Do you remember in college when we used to lie in our beds in the dark, comparing notes about our dates. I've not talked about such intimate things with anyone since!"

"Yes, and giggling over sex books like Mary McCarthy's *The Group*. I read somewhere that the sale of sex toys has gone through the roof, so there are a lot of horny people missing sex."

"Glad to have a chat, let's ring one another more often."

"Yes, we must. Wish you were nearer, but it's good to stay connected to people one cares about. Helps, particularly when one lives alone."

*

Gerald sat in his office in his comfortable chair, reviewing his life. Both Amelia and Charles were lawyers, they had been no trouble, and he was proud of them. Catherine had wanted to be a doctor, until her mental problems became too much for her to cope. But the fact that they had done well would be due to

Annabelle. She had concentrated on the children and expected little from him, except to pay for everything. Their relationship was like a business arrangement: they shared few interests other than the children and she obviously received little pleasure from their sexual congress, so that tailed off when they were in their forties. He was faithful, though, and he assumed she had been too. She had become deaf as the years passed and had to read lips and the scripts of films and plays before seeing them. How lucky was he to be spending his last years with Ruth, an infinitely more stimulating companion in every way. He heaved himself out of the chair and went downstairs to the kitchen for the salad Ruth had left for his lunch. Perhaps he should be exercising daily with her, getting fitter; she was younger and much sprightlier than him. He was just being lazy.

His phone rang. It was Amelia. She often FaceTimed him at lunchtime. "Why are you frowning so dreadfully, Pops?" she asked.

"Didn't know I was." He walked over to the cupboard with the mirror inside the door; his cross-looking face looked back at him. His eyes seemed to have retreated behind his jutting cheekbones. "That's gravitas. Not sure I can change it now."

"You're not worried about anything?"

"Only my idleness, lack of exercise. Ruth is always out walking or swimming, while I sit at my computer."

"You used to draw and paint, are you doing that now? Outside, *en plein air*? You could walk to a viewpoint and sit and paint it."

"Yes, yes." He didn't want to be nagged. He'd had enough of that with her mother. "Maybe I will…"

*

Nusheen and Vicky were having tea in Nusheen's garden.

"I feel we should have got to know more of our neighbours before. Has Marion got family? Was she married?"

"Don't know, she has a daughter and two grandsons. She mentioned once that she'd had a life-long affair with a married man, who always said he was going to leave his alcoholic wife. But of course he never did – sounded sad!"

"Very. I'm missing the WI. The interesting lectures and friendship. I know since lockdown that people have been more generous and helpful to others – like our WhatsApp group – but I looked forward to the WI meetings. My mother and aunts were always part of community groups in Iran. Wonder when we'll be able to meet again."

"Could be months. This cake is delicious, what's in it? Think I can taste cardamom, orange, ground almonds?"

"Yes, and rose water. It's called 'Persian Love Cake'. I made two and cut one into four to give to people who are isolating and don't cook."

"That's good of you. I feel guilty not making PPE. I just hate sewing, and my machine is old and doesn't work properly."

"I've put together some shields. No sewing."

Vicky lay back in the garden chair, legs stretched out in the sun. "It's so peaceful, with the fountain and water circulating. Gardens certainly help with anxiety and depression, both in doing it and in observing nature."

"Farzad is so proud of his engineering. He's always saying it's paradise on earth for us to relax and contemplate. But it's much more formal than yours – I love all the flowers and shrubs you've packed in."

27 April 2020

There are now over 3 million global coronavirus cases. Trump is mocked for his sunlight and disinfectant-injected-into-the-body speeches. Emergency hotlines say they had thousands of calls asking how to do it and which disinfectant? He now says that he was being sarcastic to bait the journalists.

Gerald was reading his newspaper and as usual was getting aerated about contentious articles. "Why did the CQC, the organisation which should be protecting the elderly, not stop the discharge of untested people into care homes? There's a letter here from a man who runs a group of care homes in the North. He emailed them to stop the Department of Health sending 15,000 patients back into the community, including to care homes, yet nothing happened, and other residents caught the virus from those released too early and died. He says the sector is berated for not being caring, safe and responsive, but it was the CQC who failed the elderly. Apparently there have been 12,700 more deaths than usual in care homes!"

"Finish your egg, dear, it's getting cold. Yes, we seem to have protected the NHS at the expense of the elderly…"

Gerald ground his teeth together as he picked up his unfinished 26 April *Sunday Times*. "Us oldies are blamed for the huge economic cost to the country for keeping us safe, but the billions of pounds paid to British workers and companies will be borrowed, and who will buy this debt from the Treasury? British savers and pension funds with abysmally low rates of interest and our dividend payments cancelled. We'll get next to nothing for our investments, and the benefits will go to future generations!"

Ruth buttered her toast and reached for the marmalade. "Well, we're always slated for getting on the housing ladder so easily and being comfortably off with our savings, perhaps we need a bit of hardship? Fiscal sacrifice? Is it our turn? But changing the subject, I worry about newspapers coming into the house. I know the printing process will kill it, but then we don't know who has touched them subsequently. I spray the outside of your *Telegraph* and *Sunday Times*, but we probably need to leave them a few hours, in case."

"Am I to have NO pleasures? The *Evening Standard* has cut right back with the loss of advertising and people like you refusing to have it in the house, so now it's mostly read online.

There's no evidence either way at the moment, different experts say different things."

"I read that COVID was found on a cruise ship seventeen days after the passengers had left. We can't be too careful…"

Sighing, he heaved his way half out of his chair, fell back, so that the chair creaked in protest, pushed up again, and made his way upstairs for his morning ritual with the *Telegraph*. Ruth constantly surprised him with her knowledge and insight into areas which he had not considered.

*

"When this is all over, will this pandemic have exposed how ridiculous the cult of celebrity is? Seeing our spoilt idols, safe in their luxury compounds, telling us to stay home, which for many people is a couple of rooms with no outside space." Vicky had rung Jo's bell, had stayed in the street, and they were chatting.

"The good thing about all this is when communities have come together to help elderly neighbours or clap the heroic NHS. You're looking so much better, Jo, and you've lost weight."

Jo was dressed in a flowery housecoat covered with a beautiful pink silk shawl. There were vases of lilies on the hall table behind her – she could be a Renoir painting.

"Yes, more than half a stone. I needed to. Just got to keep it off now. I did a beginners' pilates class earlier, am trying not to eat much before lunch and Jamie has bought me a stationary bike. Will do some walks and ten minutes on the bike. I don't want to have grey hair *and* sagging flesh. Can I follow you now? I'll keep two metres away. Where are you going?"

"Just as far as the Heath, a quick look at a lake and back." Vicky could see that Jo was pale and there were dark circles under her brown eyes, but if they walked slowly… "OK, you're on."

Jo got dressed and they set off, talking about Ted. "Is that it now? Are you going to see if there's anyone else you might like, or wait for his return?"

"Hmm, well, he's emailed a few times this week, saying that there are constant emergencies. He's so frustrated not to be able to give the aid needed, because of a lack of communication, co-ordination and drugs. I mean, it's an overcrowded, filthy, dangerous place, not enough food, water, hygiene. There's rotting rubbish everywhere and stabbings, rape and thefts. COVID must be rife as well as other diseases. I can't see him surviving. Oh, I don't know. 'Find me a find, catch me a catch'," she sang quietly. "This trying to find a match is tricky. We're all set in our ways by this age and their ways may not be yours. Most people I know have settled down with someone in their socio-economic bracket, a clone of themselves. Life is less stressful if you are both comfortably off and you don't have to worry about dependents or career paths. No, I'm not going to give up. If I can find one suitable guy, there might be more out there, and I can't bank on Ted coming back. And I'm lonely, very lonely, but I've got to stay positive. So, when this is over, I'm going to put an ad in the *Telegraph* and *Times*, an ad like Jane Juska, saying, 'Before I'm seventy-two in October' – OK, I know I'm older – 'I'd like to have lots of sex with a man I like,' and then invite all the reasonable applicants to meet me for the weekend in my Welsh cottage. If they're not domesticated, not sociable, not interesting to talk to, not reasonably fit, I'll find out in one fell swoop rather than having to see each one a few times. Don't you think it's a spectacularly efficient way to find a suitable partner? Just like that programme on the TV. What's it called?"

"I think you told me on the phone on Wednesday. *Five Guys a Week*? Which men would you put on your fantasy guest list?"

"That's a hard one. I'd have to think about it. David Attenborough's a bit old, I might have to be wheeling him about and clearing up his poo before too long. Barack Obama?"

*

Christine sat at her lounge window, looking out into the street, mopping her mascara-stained face with a sodden tissue. Why, why, why? What had she ever done to deserve this pain? John was such a good, kind human being. Not like Josh, her first husband, who had had an affair, even though they had had a good marriage – solid, predictable, comfortable. Josh said it wasn't her fault. In fact, when the gloss had gone from his fling he had tried to come back, saying life was habit and routine and he preferred it with her. She had been dignified, had never scratched his car or cut up all his suits, even though he betrayed her. But by the time he'd seen the light, she had a relationship with John and wasn't going to be powerless and humiliated again.

Why? What had she done in life to deserve losing John? She saw his photo on the bureau; they were both laughing, he had always been such fun. If only she could have had children, his child, someone to remember him with…

*

"Why don't you come in?" Malcolm asked when Vicky called for him. They were going for one of their usual walks. "You haven't seen my house. We can socially distance if you shut the door behind you and follow me up?"

"OK." She closed the door carefully and went up the stairs of the tall, brick, terraced house, past the huge kitchen on the second floor, to the big lounge with high ceilings and glass doors onto a terrace on the third. All very tasteful, modern and pristine. The sun shone in, so the room was bright and light, a place of possibilities.

The sills of the large windows were cluttered with photographs. "Who is everyone here?" Vicky asked.

"This is Sylvia and our daughter, Bec," he said, lifting a large gilt-framed photograph of two blonde, attractive women. "It's strange, they both called themselves feminists, but they both chose relationships with men that looked very like Sylvia's mother's marriage – dependent and sheltered. Living their lives within their husbands' strength and competence."

Vicky took it from him and studied it. "They look lovely. Kind and fun." Bec was standing very upright, a space between her and her mother, staring directly at the camera. There was an independence about her, as if she knew where she was going and what she wanted. "Where is Bec living now?"

"In Winchester, with her son, Will, and husband, Simon. All our married life our purpose was directed at Bec's education and life, and then you have to stand by and not interfere when things go wrong, as they seem to have at the moment with her and Simon.

"This is my sister, Alison. Everyone says we're two peas in a pod. This is Sylvia's brother, Philip, and the other two photos are mine and Sylvia's parents. No longer around of course. Can I make you a coffee?"

"That would be nice, thanks. Small, no milk or sugar."

She went on looking at photographs, trying to imagine what the people were like and wishing that she had known Sylvia. The wedding photograph was of two fresh, upright young people. He was handsome, she, tall, fair, long hair, smooth, pale skin, their faces showing their love for one another. Their eagerness to be together in their new life.

The coffee came; it was delicious, strong and rich.

"It seemed very strange moving from our country home – well, I suppose it was an estate – to a Georgian terrace, but Sylvia could no longer drive or cope with her old life. First, she had a cyst on her spine which had to be removed, then she started having strokes, poor girl. Would you like a tour of the rest of the place?"

"Would that be too nosy?"

"I think it helps to understand people by seeing them in their environment."

He led her upstairs to the ensuite master bedroom, another

bedroom and bathroom and the third bedroom, which he had made into his study. "This has become my office."

Vicky looked at the neat shelves of labelled files and boxes, the neat desk. "You're so tidy and organised!"

"People who are not creative tend to be organised. Anyway, now you've seen my home, it's supposed to rain later, shall we head off?"

30 April 2020

The government is recruiting 18,000 human contact tracers. It's paying £8.72 an hour and some people will be trained and others act as call handlers. So many people have lost their jobs, this might tide them over for a while.

Vicky and Malcolm were walking in a nearby park. She was tutting every time they saw a discarded mask. "They can be washed. I don't know why people discard them so cavalierly."

"It would be a huge task to wash the amount of PPE used in hospitals. There just aren't the facilities or personnel to cope with doing that. The gloves, visors, masks and aprons have to be thrown away after seeing each patient. So, billions of items are needed of these single-use plastics, produced by the petrochemical industry – who are apparently working twelve-hour shifts in some of the American plants to produce the raw materials to be worn on the front line of the pandemic."

"But where will all those plastic items end up? Don't they take 500 years to rot in landfill? What are we doing to the planet?"

"Infectious PPE is usually incinerated."

"So what are all those rubbish piles of single-use plastic items we see in less developed countries and clogging up rivers, lakes and floating on the sea?"

"Yes, agreed, Western countries should incinerate more of their waste. Paper and cotton products generate far more emissions in the production process, and paper comes from trees which capture carbon dioxide gas."

"The whole thing is so wasteful and depressing. I shouldn't watch the news so much, I know. It's emotionally draining and repetitive. A few statistics, then sobbing relative and/or frontline worker telling us to stay home. It's so relentlessly emotional, but where is the intelligent inquiry into such questions as to how the deaths of our frontline staff compare with elsewhere? And examinations of the different schools of thought between scientists, and instead of patting us on our backs for staying indoors, tell us how we can do something useful, even if it's just making our face masks. And we would like to know how the government is weighing up the various considerations for ending lockdown and compare them with what other countries are doing."

Malcolm smiled at her fondly. "Do I sense another letter to the press? It's the first pandemic our government has experienced. They're blundering around and possibly not everyone is as interested. *The Guardian* has good comparative reports, perhaps you should read it online?"

*

"The trouble was that they didn't get PPE gear early enough, only masks and gloves, and how could they know if the people they were trying to treat for non-virus conditions were clean or incubating it? They were cannon fodder," said Christine, a tremor in her voice. Vicky had just heard that John had been a victim of the coronavirus, and she had gone to their flat to say how deeply sorry she was. They stood two metres apart at the door.

"John had a dry cough, which he ignored. Then a temperature in the hundreds and a deep pain in his chest, aching limbs, headache and stomach cramps. I said: 'You have to stay home, John. I know there are now so few of you, but even wearing your mask you could be so contagious!' But he worried that there would be no one left to run the service. In the end, he was in so much pain and had practically lost control of his bladder, that he had to stay at home. He admitted that he'd never felt so wiped out." She sobbed…

"You don't have to tell me everything now," Vicky said softly.

"After three days at home he wasn't getting better. His lungs were full of fluid, so he could barely breathe, he was retching up blood into the bathroom sink and had uncontrollable diarrhoea. Sam, his best paramedic friend, took him into hospital and in case I tested positive, I had to self-isolate and couldn't visit."

"Oh, Christine!"

"If only he had given in and gone into ICU days before! He was given antibiotics, put on the ventilator and then the ECMO machine, but after two days they phoned to say he had gone downhill. He died a few hours later from multiple organ failure and septic shock. I didn't even see him to say goodbye. He had the top team of experienced staff working night and day on him – everyone knew John. Thousands of people have died, I know, and he was a smoker when he was younger, but he was so strong, fit and knowledgeable. If only he'd given in and gone into the ICU before… I hope he knew how many people tried to see him and sent messages of love and support as he lay there alone! He couldn't breathe to hold a conversation and was too unwell for the staff to let anyone visit!" She choked, pushed her hair off her face and behind her ears and started to weep. "It was so quick, and I didn't even get to say goodbye and tell him how much I loved him!"

Vicky felt tears running down her own face and took out a tissue to try to surreptitiously mop them up. "I'm so, so sorry, Christine. John was one of the best, so kind and dedicated and never bitter about how hard he had to work. It's such a wrong-place-at-the-wrong-time disease. He was confronting, cohabiting with the virus every shift. I'm here for you, as I'm sure all your many friends are, though you're in quarantine now, aren't you? What about the funeral?"

"We were talking about getting married and now it's his funeral!" She was sobbing loudly.

"Well, though churches are closed and only immediate family can be at his grave, we can make a video, stream the burial to others who loved him and have a memorial service with a wake when all this is over?"

"He deserved so much better! I get really angry when I see pictures of queues outside supermarkets not social distancing, people having fun in parks, and I can't even have a funeral! And how am I supposed to register his death if I'm not to leave the house?"

1 May 2020 – Test, Track and Trace

> The media have at last discovered that forty-five per cent of the PPE from 2009, when retested, wasn't safe or suitable, e.g. there were 15 million goggles, but visors are now used. Too many people are staying away from the NHS with serious health conditions like cancer and strokes. We are being told that there are beds and staff, and to go to hospitals. Hong Kong has a densely packed population of 7.5 million. It has had over 1,000 cases of COVID-19, but only four deaths, and none are healthcare workers or any of the 80,000 people in care homes.

It was the seventh week, and Vicky was pulling out self-seeded forget-me-nots, which had finished flowering, and planting cosmos and antirrhinum plants, which she had grown. It was late morning. The trees shimmered in the heat, and the air vibrated with the sounds of lawn mowers and children playing in their paddling pool nearby. She was thinking that isolation wasn't necessarily quiet. *Living on my own should be peaceful, but my phone makes pings and beeps as people contact me to exchange texts, have a chat, Zoom, FaceTime, do a quiz, play bridge, and because we're all permanently available, there's no escape and to refuse is rude. It's a minefield. If you don't answer, the person will know you're ignoring them, as all the useful excuses like being too busy to answer no longer work, and anyway, the person the other end might be lonely, sad or feeling ill. I almost wish mobile phones had never been invented. No one has anything to say because we're not going anywhere and it's too embarrassing to say goodbye.*

That morning, she received and sent on a 38 Degrees petition to prevent over-seventies being locked down for longer than the rest of the population.

She was doing a circuit of the nearest park, when she caught up with Ruth, who said: "I've signed and sent that petition on to fifteen people. It's illiberal and immoral if they lump baby boomers and upwards in with those in care homes! You know that various MPs and media personalities are rebelling, as surely most of us are no more 'vulnerable' than other ages. We will be careful, but draconian restrictions on us because of our age are unfair if the rest of the population are able to resume their lives. Boris has said to be patient, as we have reached the peak, so they should be able to make a plan next week for some sort of return to normality for workers and schools. Just hope the petition stops him 'shielding' our age group! And by the way, how are you getting on, spending so much time on your own? Are you eating properly, not drinking too much?"

"I love fruit and veg and eat tons of them. Cake and cheese are my downfalls and the bread that I make. As you know, I have to cut the cake and bread up and give it away or freeze it in daily portions. I love eating but can't be bothered to go to much trouble for one."

"We'll have to get you to hook up with that Malcolm, or someone, when all this is over."

"I expect you're getting cold, I am. Oh, and it's raining again. Gotta go, lots of love!"

Vicky half ran home in driving rain and hail, praying that her beans and tomato plants wouldn't have been beaten down by the force of the hailstones...

*

Liz came out of Sainsbury's and saw her daughter on the other side of the road, finishing using a cash machine.

"Julie," she called, and waved. Julie was carrying two large Waitrose bags. She put one down to wave back. Then picked it up and crossed to her mother.

"Do you want a lift, or did you come by car?" Liz asked.

"No, tube. Martin is out at a business meeting, then dinner, with the car."

"Well, Paul is visiting his sister, how about having early supper with me? Just a vegetarian lasagne, but you always liked that."

Julie paused; they hadn't been getting on well for some months. Perhaps an evening with her mother was better than one alone. "Alright, as long as you don't nag me about anything."

Liz swallowed but decided not to say anything. She knew better than to go back to their argument about why they kept James in a top boarding school, when he hated it and Martin wasn't earning enough to cover the fees, plus their own living costs. Perhaps later over a glass of wine?

It was a bright, sunny, late afternoon and her small garden was bathed in golden light. They sat drinking tea and chit-chatting politely. "The garden is looking good, so much coming up, much better than when I lived here."

"Well, I was working all hours then and trying to be a good mother and wife. I've got the time now," Liz reminded her. "A glass of wine while the lasagne warms up?"

After eating in the small conservatory and a few glasses of wine, Julie brought up the difficulty between them.

"You know we only wanted you to move because this house is too big for you. Is this Paul actually living here? Hasn't he got his own place? Is he living off you?"

A whisper of guilt passed through Liz's head, but like a solitary cloud in an otherwise blue sky, it cast no shadow. She spoke determinedly. "Yes, but his sister has come to live there, so yes, he's living with me, and we're very happy together."

"Living here rent free, stopping you selling and helping us out? You'll have to pay such a lot of tax on it."

"You mean you will if I die seven years before selling."

"But you know we need the money. Don't you want your grandson to be in a top school? I hardly see Martin, he's working all hours to pay the fees. And I can't get a full-time job and not be home in the holidays for James."

Julie was an accountant and did clients' tax returns at home.

Liz was deeply disturbed at her daughter's unhappiness. Her insides felt as if they had been speared and twisted around with a fork. She tried to breathe deeply and evenly. "Wouldn't you be happier to have him living at home? There are plenty of excellent day schools near here. It would be cheaper, and you'd see so much more of him. He'll have grown up and be off to university before you know it. Paul and I pay into a common bank account, monthly – for joint bills and holidays – but otherwise are independent of one another. End-of-life situations will come soon enough. We're healthy now, but we'll have to see what happens. And I've lived in this house since you were born. It's full of memories. Your father and I painted, papered, tiled, repaired, upholstered and French polished all the old furniture we found, together, and made it into the home you know. I love it and don't want to move. Unless I get dementia of course and have to pay for a care home."

"Martin and I think you're going a bit batty now. What on

earth do you think you're doing living with some old guy, after a happy life with my father? It's disgusting!"

"Hello, girls, any wine left?' Paul joined them. "The keys were in the door."

Julie nodded to herself – definitely going batty.

5 May 2020

The death rate has gone back up again and Neil Ferguson, the epidemiologist whose projection changed the government strategy to full lockdown, resigns. The media lynch mobs led by The Mail on Sunday and The Telegraph blamed him for people being under 'house arrest' and caught him breaking lockdown rules with his married lover.

Liz went in to the spare bedroom that Paul used as a study. "Is there anything you want? I'm going shopping." She could see he wasn't really listening, still absorbed in the poem he was writing. He looked past her vaguely, as if she wasn't there.

"I don't know, apples? Spinach? Tender-stem broccoli?" But he wasn't interested really.

"Do you want to come?"

He still didn't focus on her. "No, no, I don't think so, I'm trying to finish this poem."

She walked behind him and gently massaged his shoulders. Julie's words kept coming back to her: "living with some old guy". He was fitter and seemed younger than most of the people she knew in their sixties. She hadn't been as happy as she was now since Julie had been a baby.

As for him, he had been enjoying his retirement, with a nearby park to stroll in, a daily routine and for the first time in his life, precious time to write. But though he had friends and family, he had been missing a loving partner, a special person to be close to. He reached up and caressed her hands.

Before she left the room, his thoughts were back with his writing and his fingers chased one another over the keys, accurately; he rarely had to correct. His typing was as immaculate as the rooms he inhabited. As the dishes he cooked, as the sexual pleasure he gave.

*

Vicky was standing leaning on the wheelie bin outside Malcolm's house. He had brought out a cushion and was sitting on his front step...

"Sorry to be sitting down while you stand. Shame you can't sit on the wall – too many shrubs."

"It's fine, and this purple lilac smells wonderful. As long as you don't mind me leaning on the bin? My neighbour told me not to, as she'd have to disinfect it after I'd gone!"

"Rather neurotic?"

Mm-hm, but she is eighty-five with asthma. Hasn't been out since before the lockdown but doesn't seem at all fed up or depressed. Not like me, I'm so missing my normal life, but glad to have met you. Are you OK?"

"I don't know. I'm suffering a lot of headaches and migraines at the moment and pills don't help. My muscles are stiff and I can't watch TV – it's blurry."

"That doesn't sound good. You really must call 111 or, even better, go to the emergency department of the Royal Free or St Mary's. I know it's scary with all the COVID around, but the newsreaders keep saying not to neglect one's symptoms and to go to a hospital. Please do! Will you go today, or tomorrow, and ring me to let me know what they say?"

"OK, I will, but I'll have to go and lie down now. I feel very strange, another migraine. So sorry, don't know what's the matter with me." He got up falteringly, waved and disappeared indoors, leaving a very worried Vicky to wander home.

*

Michelle and Vicky were walking around the local park.

"I've had the chance to slow down, look inward at myself and think about what art is to me and what it can do for me," Michelle said. "Art sustained me when my world fell apart, but why have I always painted nightmarish scenes? I thought I was happy with Chaika, but that's not what my subjects showed. Was it because I was a slave to fruit and vegetables? Now at last, I'm seeing their beauty, painting them instead of cooking them. And I entered a competition for people over seventy. There are various categories. You used to write poems and short stories, why don't you enter? It's called King Lear Prizes, have a look. How are you anyway?"

"OK, I went to a party last night."

"What?"

"Oh, a virtual party. I think I've got Zoom fatigue, it went on for far too long. We had to have our drinks and snacks so others could see them. We sat there in our sequins and black tie, appearing as a tiny thumb-sized box among sixty others, being yelled at – 'Will everybody else please press MUTE!' It was my dear friend Maggie's eightieth. She had had a weekend party in Swansea planned, but of course it was cancelled. I didn't know many people, and those I did know, I couldn't talk to them. It was all structured socialising. Maggie led the topics and responses, so people popped up on the screen and stared with strangely blind eyes, tried to think of something to say, then disappeared. Some people couldn't really cope with it and kept saying, 'Something's gone wrong.' Is that the most appropriate metaphor for humanity and COVID?"

"How funny, you could well be right. Parties... before I met Chaika they seemed to be almost every night, staggering around pissed, in feet-destroying stilettos. In grotty flats, full of empty bottles and overflowing ashtrays, competing to be the most exciting person. I was full of furious energy, ready to take anyone on, or gripped by utter self-doubt, desolation and worries about where I was going. In fact, I lost sight of who I was. Chaika calmed me down, gave me love and security, but what has happened to my life? Tortoise-like neck, tits and arse hanging down, cellulite legs, can't remember names, dates and pin numbers, and everyone looking straight through me. Think that's why I'm sticking with my eccentric clothes, and anyway, life is too short not to look the way you want… I guess without being loved I should aim to be respected, or even admired for what I can achieve, don't you think?"

"Just don't be heartbroken if you don't win all the competitions and acclaim, they are just the icing on the cake, aren't they? Being active and happy day to day is the best aim, and getting out meeting people, having a purpose, doing more things is the key."

"That's what you've done, isn't it? You're amazing how well you've coped on your own. I feel a cow that I didn't see your pain and try to help you through it. Chaika blotted everyone else out of my life. So sorry."

10 May 2020

> **Boris speaks to the nation, praising citizens for staying at home and following the rules, and is hoping to tentatively reduce the lockdown in England. Scotland, Wales and Ireland are carrying on with it. The new rules are to only travel if necessary, go to work from Wednesday, if it's safe there to socially distance, and if one can't work at home. Some primary school years can return from 1 June. 'Stay alert and aware' are the new rules. Singles tennis, along with golf and angling, have been cited as sports that can be played safely, while keeping two metres apart from anyone else. Doubles are only allowed if all four are from the same household.**

Gerald and Ruth were sitting at the breakfast table, watching the BBC news.

"Well, he's trying to give people hope. Going around with a 'catlike tread'. No more 'Stay at Home', the new mantra is be 'Alert and Aware'. Sounds a bit of a joke!" He popped his last piece of toast into his mouth.

Ruth nodded, pushed her chair back and walked around the table to plant a kiss on his head. "So many people going to markets and shops haven't been socially distancing anyway – it's a lifestyle change. And there were thousands of people and dogs, walking, cycling, jogging, chatting in groups at the weekend in the parks. What lockdown? And why Years 1 and 6 from 1 June? Keeping little children apart from one another will be impossible! Poor teachers, in old schools with narrow corridors and small playgrounds, and people congregating at the start and finish of school as they bring their children. Why not the older ones?" She slid her arms down his body and rubbed.

He smiled wryly and reached up to squeeze Ruth's left shoulder. "I expect the government want to get people back to work and they can't leave small children at home."

She was on a roll. "And meeting up with no more than one friend or relative, outside! One would have to see couples separately. Ridiculous! But at last, wearing masks on public transport is mandatory and we can play tennis and golf." She sighed. "But I guess we're lucky to be retired, being able to walk and have good pensions!"

Finishing his mouthful, he twisted around and pulled her down onto his lap.

"I think that until they've got the 'Test, Trace and Isolate' going, all this is too soon. If only we'd tested and traced like Germany and South Korea did right from the start! I've started to think however that 'Protect the NHS' was a ridiculous rationale, depriving the UK population of its liberty, destroying millions of businesses and jobs and giving us all a crippling debt to repay. The economic price of this virus will be stratospheric, as will its social costs. The government did an amazing job increasing intensive care capacity, but were all the beds occupied? We didn't need the Nightingale hospitals. It was pushed into a decision which mocks our humanity and terrified us into submission by making us think that COVID was dangerous for everyone, not just those who are seriously vulnerable. For most of the population the symptoms are mild, and it will probably be with us for a very long time anyway."

Ruth nodded. "I think you're right. They're trying to protect their backs and we can't be in lockdown forever, and meanwhile it's all very confusing. You can go for a walk in the park but not sunbathe, you can drive to the Lake District but not go to your second home there, meet someone in your front garden, but not your back – it's become absurd and just putting off when we're going to have to face the risk. Anyway, how about coming for a walk with me today, Gerry? You'll be too unfit and stiff when you can start golf next week."

He was rubbing her legs and back and wondering if his heart was pounding with salaciousness or indigestion. "The club and England Golf are advising over-seventies to stay home as much as possible, and most of the staff have been furloughed, so not sure I'll be starting yet."

"Is that an excuse not to get fit?"

Gerald shook his head. "You know I rarely come for walks."

Ruth shrugged, brushed her soft lips across his temple and stood up to start clearing the breakfast things. "You said you quite enjoyed it when you came that once, and were going to keep it up."

His passion ebbed away. "Maybe tomorrow."

*

"How are you, Debs?" Vicky had rung her bell and was standing in the street.

"I should come and visit you sometime, Vic. You're so sweet to pop round to cheer me up…"

"Aren't you cheerful, then? What's happened? How are you doing?"

Debs welled up and burst into tears. "Badly," she sobbed. "I'm desperately missin' my daughter, grandchildren, friends. Walkin' on one's own, being in one's own empty home and bed feels achin' lonely. I find myself talkin' to plants and inanimate kitchen objects, and I'm scared to go back to normal. I'm so petrified of this virus and any others, I don't want to come out into the world, to travel on buses and tubes. It negates all this sacrificin', of hidin' away. I want to stay in here, I know it's best, but I'm also so lonely and anxious, my emotions are all over the place. It's the evenin's which are worst. Six o'clock comes and I'm alone and really lonely. I may seem to have it all, with OK health and enough money, but I need human contact. I'm havin' to confront who I am as a person, and I don't like it."

"I don't know who you're thinking you are, but loads of people love you, and I wouldn't come around so often if we weren't good friends. Cheer up, this is just a blip! Apparently, the mental health charities have been getting fifty per cent more calls than ever before. So many people are lonely, often their families live far away, and they are not allowed to visit one another. They're working at home, everything they did has stopped. No classes, lectures, going out with friends, it's hard for everyone. The hug deficit is leaving people anxious, depressed and so lonely, perhaps psychologically damaged. I've always envied the way you're always up for more experiences – you inhale the world as if it were perfume!"

Debs mopped up her tears and blew her nose with a lace-trimmed hankie before stuffing it back into the waistband of her red leggings. "Sorry, I'm bein' self-centred. I speak to Danni most days and we do FaceTime with the grandchildren and Mark. I get Waitrose deliveries now. I'm relatively lucky."

"Don't worry, it's a natural response, particularly because you've had such an exciting life. You travelled the world when you modelled, didn't you?"

At the thought, Debs seemed to grow a few inches and her face lightened up.

"Oh, yes, that was such fun! Our hotel room would be laden with gifts. We'd get private guided tours in every city. Restaurants fell over themselves to have us, even though we couldn't eat much. I loved the glamorous life, even the dead-eyed billionaire designers and the stupid celebs and coked-up party boys who licked you all over – but then I met Louis and gave it all up for him."

"Apparently, I keep reading, we should be using this time to be brave enough to explore our inner selves, so we know ourselves better and our capacity for solitude. Most humans operate best with routine, but it's the opportunity to bring change and renewal into our lives. You're still doing exercise every day – pilates and a walk – aren't you? Exercise relaxes, it's a great antidepressant."

"Most of my energies lately have been directed at Matt – we matched on Feeld, the go-to app for the sexually adventurous. You have to tick off your desires from a list, includin' bondage and foreplay. We've been sendin' detailed descriptions of what we were goin' to do to one another when we were allowed to get nearer than two metres. He sent me a picture of him lyin' on a beach, which inflamed me even more. We sent one another voice notes to mutually masturbate to and messaged one another for two weeks. But when I tried to organise a date, as the virus infections seem to be fallin', he didn't ever reply! Do men prefer you when you're not real? Do they want you to be pen pals, so they can imagine the perfect version of you? Is the hypothesis better than the real thing? What's happened to me? Maybe he was right not to meet me. That speculation and dreamin' are way better than the real thing could ever be."

"You've been too long on your own and lost sight of who you are and what you want. When we can get out again, everything will calm down and we'll go back to being ourselves."

"Whatever that is. As a younger woman, I was so full of furious energy – I would take anyone on. But then I was often the opposite, utterly desolate and full of self-doubt. I spent so much time competin' and tryin' to be an exciting person that I lost sight of who I really was. And marriage is a con trick. I was a flattered, indulged, spoilt model and had to learn self-sacrifice and eternal good nature with unnoticed efforts when I became a prisoner and slave to family. So perhaps bein' old is when you become the person you always should have been, and because you've got a wealth of experience you know who and what you like. Dunno, I'm still a confused mess! But how are you copin', Vic? And how did you cope when Rob died? You're like a guardian angel goin' around, keepin' in touch, cheerin' us up."

"I thought I'd die with the pain. Life seemed empty and I wasn't interested in living it anymore. It's taken a lot to move on… I think that having a big empty notebook by my bed undoubtedly helped me. I downloaded all my problems and misery into it when I woke up in the night, so I was empty of them and could get to sleep. And in the day, if my depression was dragging me down, I wrote in another book, all my achievements, small victories and what I'd enjoyed that day, so I'd not feel so worthless. Eventually I got on an even keel and here you see me, missing Rob terribly, but surviving."

"Wish I could hug you! You bring sanity and sunshine into my life, thanks so much!"

"Shall we play tennis in a few days? We can firm up then, about how to advertise our social group and the party we're going to have."

*

Diana rang Vicky that evening. "How about a game of tennis this week as soon as the club lets us?"

"Oh, OK, I don't seem to have any other pressing engagements. Will you book a court?"

17 May 2020

There has been the lowest number of deaths for a long time – 170 – though there is often a lag at the weekend. Tomorrow, Mental Health Awareness Week starts…

Vicky and Diana met to play tennis. There was huge demand for the courts, so they'd waited five days to get one. The gates of each court were tied back so no one had to touch them. They had to finish ten minutes early so that they could leave the grounds before the next people arrived. The clubhouse was locked, and they each had to have two balls which they served with and only touched the other person's balls with a racquet. It felt strange playing after more than a two-month break.

"Have you seen Alex?" Vicky asked as they knocked in the service boxes, to warm up.

"Yes, we've met on the Heath nearly every day. I was quite tearful the first time. I had to keep reminding him to keep the social distancing and it was upsetting not to give him a big hug. But seeing him is a boost, I get really excited."

"You're still keen, then?"

"Definitely!"

They moved back to rally from the baseline.

*

Vicky and Malcolm were walking their usual route on the Heath. It was Sunday, so joggers and walkers were out in force. Groups of people and twos and threes wandered along, takeaway coffee in one hand and dog leads in the other. Untethered dogs ran around everywhere, sniffing one another, ignoring the shouts from their owners.

"Most of London seems to have bought a dog," Malcolm observed. "The Heath and the parks are overrun with them."

"I read that prices have soared and it's quite hard to get one now. And the Kennel Club has had something like 150 per cent more enquiries than usual. Shame these people don't realise that we're not all in love with their dogs." She pushed away a huge Labrador which was sniffing at her legs.

"Don't you like dogs?"

"We had them when I was a child, and I can see that if one is on one's own, a loyal, loving friend and companion, which doesn't answer back and gets you out of the house for a walk, is attractive. Especially when so many people are working from home. I feel sorry for the dogs who will be locked indoors all day when their owners go back to work."

"They're certainly dominating the parks and open spaces at the moment. Let's count the ones in sight."

They got to twenty-seven and decided to talk about something else.

*

Liz and Paul had gone to his flat for an early supper with his sister, Aretta. After her husband had died she had moved there, out of her home, so that her son, Sani, and his family had more room. The lounge had changed in style. The grey furniture was the same, but their arrangement subtly altered and was, to him, in less attractive positions. His decor of uniform white and greyness now had bold black and white patterned rugs, bright green curtains and chair covers, and a carved shrine panel on one wall. Paul had not been an accumulator of extra things, apart from books. He had been surprised at how much 'stuff' Liz had, and no matter how full her cupboards and shelves had become, she seemed unable to throw anything away.

Aretta had cooked what had been Paul's favourite Nigerian dish, of egusi soup and pounded yam. She served them while Paul opened the wine they had brought.

They talked about family and the past, plus the time he was having therapy. All of which was fascinating to Liz.

"What did you understand differently about life and yourself after the therapy?" she asked.

"It straightened me out. After the three-month course, I was trying to learn something every day and not shy away from new experiences. Later-life learning I think is important to keep our brains developing and changing, throughout our lives. We should probably work for longer. And it made me realise that I should invest in my wellbeing, by keeping fit, eating healthily, sleeping well and keeping in touch with people I care about. It helped me to understand myself and what I needed in life."

"What was that?"

"I think most people, both sexes, want the same thing: love, companionship and security." He reached out and took her hand. "I think we've found those in each other?"

She smiled and nodded.

After the fermented corn pudding and fruit, Paul jumped up saying he was going to clear up, make some coffee and then look through his books. He was feeling a little guilty, as he hadn't been that friendly and grateful to Aretta when she had made such an effort with the dinner. The trouble was, she had cooked what had been his favourite dishes when he had been ten.

"Come on, Liz, let's have a chat and eat some of the chocolates you've brought," Aretta said, steering her towards the couch. "Don't you love these?" she asked, pulling off the cellophane and digging in to the chocolate mints.

'No,' Liz wanted to say, 'I keep away from chocolate so I stay slim.' But she muttered, smiled and took one from the proffered box.

"I've never lived on my own before. I got married young and moved from home to live with Femi, but even in the lockdown, I've been so happy here and haven't needed Sani and the grandchildren. I love this flat, and I think Paul is happy at yours. He's got so much more room and a garden."

Liz hoped that this was the case. She gazed around the lounge. It was a nice flat, but only one bedroom. She would find living without a garden unbearable – and they certainly couldn't tell Aretta to move out. But had she lost her daughter by not selling up?

*

Ruth and Gerry were drinking a pre-prandial glass of Chardonnay in their garden, lit by the full moon. It was rather a bland, neat garden, cared for by their once-a-week gardener, but this evening it seemed enchanted, as all the white flowers seemed to be reaching towards them after the warm day.

"Are you not starting golf now that you're allowed to?" Ruth asked.

"Maybe next week. Derek and Neville want to play on Tuesday."

"You don't sound very keen."

"I know I'm lucky to be able to walk around the course on a sunny morning with my friends, but it's being old and slow and stiff which makes me hesitate. Some part of me is always creaking or aching, nothing is smooth and pain free. I used to be full of energy and drive and wonder why the older golfers shuffled and dragged their feet round the greens. Now that's me."

Ruth put her glass down, looked lovingly at his shapely head and strong jaw and got up to give him a hug. "You know we've got to adjust to all our age changes – ligaments and tendons getting tight and stiff, muscle hardening – but you don't have kyphosis, are not deaf and still have a wonderful brain and perfect teeth!"

He smiled, hugged her back and they went in to dinner.

18 May 2020

There were 160 deaths in the UK today, making a total of 34,696. Northern Ireland restrictions eased: six people can meet outside, garden centres can open and churches for private prayer. Everyone should wear masks and have a temperature check when entering shopping areas and hotels. Tourists may be welcome in July. Italy opened restaurants and hairdressers, and church services resumed. Trump says he has taken an antimalarial drug every day for a week, though his medical regulators say that it is neither safe nor effective. Refugee camps are struggling; for instance, Moria, which was built for 3,000, now has over 20,000. People are living in terrible conditions, very crammed in and quarantined by police, with no food or clean clothes. The EU has given thousands of euros and has taken in many refugees, but still they come.

Vicky and Ruth met at the tube station and took a train to Baker Street. There were trains every two minutes and theirs was totally empty. No one on the platform, no one on the train. At an eerily empty Baker Street, they put on their masks, rode up the escalators to the street and walked down the Marylebone Road towards Regent's Park. No one was wearing masks, even the tube staff hadn't – though there had been signs and announcements on the PA system, saying that they had to be worn. The few people in the park weren't bothering to socially distance as they walked or jogged past one another.

"I'm shocked," said Ruth. "It's not like China and South Korea, or in fact any country we've seen on the news. People just don't care about this virus."

"Did you see Southend beach yesterday? I know it was twenty-seven degrees, but it was packed! Why are people so cavalier?"

"Perhaps the media have been too heavy-handed, constantly telling us that it's mainly BAME or older, overweight people with underlying health problems that are affected. All the people we've passed today, who have made no effort to be two metres away from us, have been young and white. Perhaps they think they're inviolate."

The sun shone, it was warm, and for the first time since lockdown had started they felt free of the virus dread. "Hello clouds, hello sky!" said Vicky.

Ruth looked at her quizzically.

Vicky grinned. "When I was young I was the school librarian and there was a magazine in the library called *The Young Elizabethan*, which you would never have seen in America. It had a Nigel Molesworth column. He went to St Custard's, where there was another pupil called Fotherington-Tomas, who was a 'gurl', a sissy, and skipped around saying 'Hello clouds, hello sky!' Lovely days make me feel like he must have."

Ruth smiled and turned her face up to the sun.

The park was beautiful. They walked next to the water, watching coots, swans, geese and ducks at play.

"This is an amazing park. Think how many people have enjoyed walking here."

"Yes, Sylvia Plath wrote about the rose garden, and there are scenes in *Mrs Dalloway*, and some of Dickens' writings are set here and it's something like 470 acres."

"You're becoming an egg-head, how do you know all that?"

"We've been doing virtual pub quizzes with Naomi, Catherine, Amelia and all the children, so I try to look things up I'm interested in and memorise them so I'm not a complete duffer."

"You'll be a trivia geek after this lockdown is over. I'll make sure you're in my team when we have the next community centre quiz."

They sat in the blistering sun, near the Triton and Dryads

Fountain, which wasn't on. Then wandered around the rose garden, choosing which ones they would like to have.

"Will you come for socially distanced tea in our garden now?" Ruth asked. "Gerry says he doesn't want to eat as much cake and I know I should stop making it, but I can't do dinner parties in lockdown, so my creative, artistic urge is frustrated. Especially as I seem to have gone off painting and am just cooking plain meals for Gerry and me. You make patchwork quilts which will be treasured for years, Michelle's art will hang in galleries and on people's walls, but mine leaves no trace behind after it's eaten, just momentary appreciation, if I'm lucky. Plus, possibly a note of thanks later, before it completely fades from memory."

Vicky laughed. "How sad. Are you feeling unappreciated? We all know what a wonderful, imaginative, original cook you are! Of course, I'd love to come to tea…"

*

Vicky and Debs had finished their game and were sitting in the sun, either end of a bench, swigging at their water bottles. Vicky had said she had put on weight with no tennis and too much eating.

"I haven't noticed. Have you always been so slim? And how come you don't seem to mind not having a man?"

"Slim? I used to be. Then when I retired, one day in the shower, I looked, really looked, at my naked body in the mirror. I seemed to have become shorter and wider. What had happened to me? Well, I know the long bones shrink and the vertebral discs lose liquid – so get closer together – but I'd never been this squatter shape! So, I tried to improve my body by doing more exercise. I volunteered to teach the class, worked out more in the gym, played more tennis and went on walks, but I've got fatter in lockdown again. And men? I haven't felt interested since Rob. I wondered if there was something wrong with me, so I did try the dating apps, but I didn't want to have sex with someone I didn't love, or even like much. To have sex, I want the full package, someone to rock my boat, to romance me, turn me on – a kind, sweet, supportive man like Rob was. There don't seem to be many of those around."

"No, you're right. On the surface, I had everythin'. A successful career, a beautiful little house, good looks for my age and self-confidence. But now, having stepped back from the agency, I've got more time to get extremely lonely. I like masterful men. I enjoy surrenderin' to a passionate man, feelin' desire transferred from them. Love, good sex, makes one glow."

"But how do you look so young? I know I've ruined my skin in the sun and not using creams, but you haven't got wrinkles!"

"Well, I learnt a beauty routine from Joan Collins, who was my neighbour a very long time ago, and I've stuck to it. I put ice-cold pads on my eyes for five minutes when I wake up, then I cleanse, apply oil with hyaluronic acid and retinol on my face and let it sink in for ten minutes, then a base, a light foundation containin' sunscreen, then makeup for day or evenin' from there."

"Sounds far too complicated and don't suppose it would rescue my ancient face, I've let the ageing process go too far."

"Silly girl, you're beautiful and strikin' and you don't seem or look old, you must have been doin' somethin' right! However, when are you going to take off the track bottoms or the shorts and dress up again? I read somewhere that one adopts the characteristics of one's clothes."

"Perhaps that's why I've become so bad at tennis. I'm drab and boring, and my life and tennis are too. I should put on a dress and makeup next time I'm in a Zoom meeting. If I can be bothered."

23 May 2020

There's a £62.1 billion deficit this month, greater than that which had been forecast for the whole year! Anyone coming into this country, whether a tourist or someone returning from holiday, has to self-isolate for fourteen days unless they are fruit and vegetable pickers, freight drivers or those taking up jobs. If they are found not to be doing this, there is a £1,000 fine… So many education authorities are saying that their schools will not be opening on 1 June, even though the research shows that children are less capable of spreading the virus and have a low risk of getting it. However, until Test, Track and Trace is in place, many people do not feel safe. Brazil and Peru have been hit hard. President Bolsonaro has been called "Trump of the Tropics" with his pronouncement that "It's just a little flu" as 27,000 are dead.

Vicky hadn't seen much of her neighbour Christine for the last few weeks. She wondered if she had gone back to work, so rang her bell.

A tired-looking Christine came to the door in her dressing gown, her hair hanging lank and greasy. They exchanged greetings. "How are you and what have you been up to?" Vicky asked.

"Nothing," Christine said in a flat, exhausted-sounding voice.

"Have you been going out shopping or for walks?"

"No, I'm stuck in a rut, lost confidence, depressed and scared of going out. I can't sleep. I listen to the *World Service* and *Farming News* all night, like so many other solitary people. Our tribe of the forgotten, the forsaken, whose lives are pointless. Then I sleep in the afternoons. My hair's a mess, I can't be bothered to pluck my chin hair, or wear anything other than comfortable night clothes." A tear rolled down her cheek.

"This isn't like you, Christine, you're so ballsy, though you have every reason to grieve. You're entitled to go feral for a while. Lots of people are in the same state, scared to go on public transport or in shops, agoraphobic and just wanting to be comfortable in their own cocoon. I've seen it called FOGO, fear of going out. You're not old, you'll work out how you want to live soon, and you know you can get sleeping pills if you want them. Come over to my garden, walk down the side and we can sit two metres apart and chat. Don't know if you're eating cake?"

She gave a slight smile. "You and your cake! OK, it's time I went out, perhaps tomorrow, thanks."

"See you at four tomorrow, then!"

*

Later, Vicky was in her bedroom when she heard car doors slamming. Through the open crack in the window came the smells of a fine, spring night, growth, plus petrol fumes from the road which was never quiet.

Looking out, she saw three beautifully dressed people going into Nusheen's house, the women carrying covered dishes. *Is it the end of Ramadan?* she wondered. Checking on her computer, she found that it was indeed the end, when the festivities of Eid al-Fitr were held. She had barely seen Nusheen for the past month; not being able to eat or drink from dawn to sunset had meant their cake-eating had taken a break. Another car arrived, and two children got out and ran down the short pathway. A bent old lady was levered out of the car by Kalil, and then a white-haired old man with two sticks was helped into the house with great care and attention.

It was lovely to see a family gathering, even if it were currently illegal. How she missed hers, with all the older generations dead and the younger in New Zealand.

*

Liz had come for tea and a chat in the garden. She sat under the big umbrella on the lawn; her pale, translucent, freckled skin was age-spotted and starting to get crepey and slack on her bones, and sun made it red and painful. She was like a nineteenth-century English beauty, when any semblance of a tan meant that one did outside work, like a labourer in the fields. She was explaining how she had been agonising about what to do after Julie had called her selfish for not selling her house so she could pay James's school fees.

Vicky swallowed. "Hmm." If she said that Julie and Martin were being unreasonable, would that be destructive to the mother–daughter relationship? She knew how painful that would be. "Where would you live if you sold your house, the house you love?"

"I suppose I could go and live at Paul's, with him, if his sister left. But if we split up, I wouldn't have enough to buy anything remotely comparable by the time I'd paid for James's schooling."

Vicky was treading carefully. "How likely is it that you would split?"

"On my side, not at all. It's been heaven to be loved, not to be lonely, to have excitement, intimacy, companionship, and he's so laid back and easy to live with, thoughtful, helpful, cheerful. He's a glass half full, always. There are so few people one clicks with and he's a wonderful lover. He understands instinctively what gives me the most pleasure." She got up, popped on her sun hat and wandered around the lawn restlessly. "I thought that that was it, but I've had the best sex, ever, with him."

"Wow, that's some reference!"

"I know that if Paul left, the house would seem too big for me. It's old and I would start not being able to cope. I was a bit scared coming back to it when it was dark. Paul has put outside lights up, which come on when I'm on the path, and the house seems warmer and more welcoming since he moved in."

"You and Paul have to decide on your own future, but

it's too soon to start pushing him into making decisions now. You love Julie and will leave her everything, no doubt, but she shouldn't be demanding a share now. Presumably you don't have lots of cash saved which you could give her? You could do an equity release, but she wouldn't thank you in years to come when she inherits very little. Julie seems to be a little jealous of your new relationship. Perhaps she'll calm down when she sees how happy it's making you."

"Yes, if I hadn't met Paul, I would probably have sold up and bought some small flat somewhere to help them out, as she probably realises. But I don't want to force Paul into having to decide whether to invite me to live with him, just yet. We should see how it's going in a year or so. Sad for James, but he doesn't enjoy his boarding school. They should cut their cloth, not expect me to change my life. Wonder if they've asked Martin's parents? Mustn't hate him. I guess it's that he wants the best for James, to keep him safe and give him a background to be successful in life."

27 May 2020

Children in South Korea have gone back to school, with frequent temperature testing, hand washing and wearing masks, but they fear that they have another spike in infections, so will lock down again. Every news broadcast and political discussion is going over and over, since Friday evening on the 22nd, whether Dominic Cummings broke the rules, even though he said he was doing the best for his four-year-old son, by driving 260 miles to his parents' farm estate in County Durham because he feared that he and his wife had COVID and wouldn't be able to take care of the child. Over forty Tory MPs think he should resign or be sacked. Deaths in the UK have gone up again to 412 and the total is now 37,460. Test, Track and Trace has gone live in the UK

with thousands of people employed to contact those who have been in contact with anyone who has tested positive. The massive state intervention, where twenty-five per cent of the UK workforce is furloughed and eighty per cent of their salary paid by the government, is costing billions, so from September employers will contribute ten per cent and in October twenty per cent, after which it will finish. Some lockdown rules have been relaxed: one can meet in a friend's garden, observing a social distance and taking one's own food, drink, plates, cutlery and glasses.

Vicky woke up feeling flat and a little depressed. *Mustn't get down. I'm lucky in many ways*, she told herself, *but with Rob dead and Sophie and the grandchildren lost to me, I'm entitled to some sad periods. Old age can be so lonely, losing one by one the people one shared memories with, until there is no one left who knew one when young. I MUST be positive, think that maxim, 'Don't cry because it's over, be glad it happened!'* She got up and pottered about, surrounded by her own silence. Made some scones, which she then forgot about, so they burnt in the oven. She picked at bits of food, didn't feel like attacking the cleaning and hung about disconsolately, unable to go in the garden or out for a walk, in case a novel she had ordered came, which was too big to be pushed through the letter box. *This isn't helping, sometimes the post doesn't come till mid-afternoon!* She wandered over to the fridge for perhaps the tenth time, opened it to take out the cheese, but then closed it. *I must stop this. Too much time on the couch watching TV and eating!*

Jo telephoned. "Have you heard, I still can't go to my Welsh cottage! One can meet up with another family, but not travel far from home or stay the night! How dare they say I still can't cross the border!"

"What happens if you do?"

"They have threatened that one'll be arrested, fined and sent back home! There are signs and police everywhere to see that people 'stay local'."

"They should refund your extortionate rates."

"No chance. I had a letter from the county chief executive telling me I could NOT go to my second home, and when I wrote back asking for a rebate, he said the tax was on the property not whether you visit it! With all this lovely weather we're stifling in London. If only we could swim in the sea!"

They agreed to meet later. Jo wanted to walk over to sit in Vicky's garden. "I'll come at four for tea. Hopefully I won't catch it twice."

This is ridiculous, feeling so down, she thought. *I'll go out, to hell with the book.*

There was a 'ping' from her phone; it was Malcolm: "A walk today? I could meet you at the entrance to the park at eleven?" She texted back, "OK", and her mood lightened.

*

They were walking around the small park and chatting about their careers, a comfortable warmth between them.

Vicky said thoughtfully, "I've always had plenty of ideas for new, innovative ways of working. I created new ways of thinking about subjects, new courses, new events and have set up so many things that people have flocked to and have become so popular in this country and beyond. But no one knows where they originated now they're in common currency. I've found it hard sometimes, that the new people who take them up have no idea that they are only doing whatever it is because of me. It was difficult walking away from the industry. It was like leaving one's babies. No one knows or cares who I was, let alone that what they are doing and accepting as *de rigueur* were all my ideas. That so much of what they do now was created, invented, established by me. And no kudos, thanks or recognition to me for any of it. One goes from being at the centre of things, the instigator, creator, innovator, with all the satisfaction that comes from its success, to being outside it with no further involvement or use. It sounds as if I want to be feted, put on a pedestal, but no, not that, or is it that? It was just difficult to retire and be an old nobody, as if I'd never had an idea, never achieved anything."

He had listened carefully, smiled. "Yes, perhaps we should work, be involved for longer, not retire so early. This part of our lives is like a preparation, a stripping away of who one was, a winding down to extinction, yet one still feels able to be part of the world, to take an active role."

"Look at the two presidential candidates in the US. They don't think they should be preparing for death and they're our age. You're right, I shouldn't have retired so early."

"You have breathed life into your community centre and were teaching a successful class. I haven't worked out how to live my life yet, you're way ahead of me."

"Sorry to bare my soul like this. I hardly knew I thought like that until I put it into words. Guess it's the thing of not being useful to society anymore. In some societies when that day comes, one is supposed to creep away from the village to die quietly somewhere."

"Not just yet, Vicky, you can give an old guy like me a lot of pleasure if you agree to come on a walking holiday in Italy with me, when this lockdown is over. I haven't had a proper holiday for ten years and I'm just ready for one."

"You're hardly old, you're younger than me!"

"Is it yes, then?"

"With pleasure!"

On her way home, Vicky marvelled at all the different smells. First, a garden with overwhelming jasmine, then a privet hedge, followed by lime trees and now honeysuckle. Without the exhaust smells, each perfume was very distinct and strong. *Sadly, the volume of traffic is coming back, so this delight will disappear*, she thought.

10 June 2020

> There were 245 deaths in the UK today and 730,000 people have lost their jobs. From Saturday, one person and a child can visit another household, so people living alone can see relatives or friends in England. Our economy shrank by 20.4% in April; we're heading for a recession. The return to schools has stopped; the government has given up fighting the unions and some schools. Brazil has more than 500,000 cases; the gravediggers can't keep up. President Bolsonaro still does not wear a mask and shakes hands with supporters. The take-up of exercise has vastly improved: most people have been walking and 1.3 million Brits have bought a bike. Online yoga and pilates have been very popular.

Ruth and Vicky were taking a walk in Kenwood Park, which had just reopened.

"There's an entirely digital London Fashion Week starting today. It's three days of live streamed interviews with designers and videos. So much of fashion is now seen and bought online."

"Are you still interested? Not going anywhere but for walks has certainly dealt buying clothes a serious body blow for me, perhaps forever. Though it might have been the lovely weather. When I can go around in shorts and T-shirt all day, why would I think of buying or looking at clothes?"

"Did you read that Britain's electricity grid hasn't burnt coal for sixty days? Apparently the longest period since the Industrial Revolution, 200 years ago. So electricity is being made almost free by renewables: turbine, solar and hydropower!"

"Life is certainly changing, and we've got cleaner air and clearer skies..."

*

Michelle came over to Vicky's for tea and stayed on for a glass of wine and some falafels. "I've been having really vivid dreams – one is that Chaika comes back. I get so upset when I wake up alone! Didn't Freud say that dreams are disguised wishes?"

"I read an article about how many people are having vivid dreams, out of frustration, reflecting their helplessness at being locked down. It's because we're going through a new set of experiences and have more time for sleeping. Are they giving you ideas for your art?"

"Well, yes, I think that's right. I've been experimenting with more Daliesque, colourful, vivid paintings, but what I haven't told you is that I'm teaching a Zoom drawing class now. Structuring it and looking at their homework takes quite a bit of time."

"How did you get that off the ground?"

"It's been running since last September – a beginners' class, through adult education. A friend of Chaika's asked me if I'd take it over when the teacher was ill with coronavirus. And I'm enjoying doing it and they seem enthusiastic. So many people are shielding and want things to do, I may put on some workshops, inspired by Frida Kahlo or Gwen John, or do both. Will have to cut the numbers down, though. Haven't had time to sort out getting another dog, and anyway that would be very tying if I wanted to go off on holiday." She took a falafel and, munching it quickly, said hurriedly: "You know you told me to go to the doctor to get something to help me with getting over Chaika's death?"

"Yes, did you?"

"Mmm, he said I was depressed. Not unsurprisingly. It's a chemical imbalance. He wrote me a prescription."

"And?"

"I decided not to take them. Of course, I'm unhappy and discombobulated. What kind of relationship did we have if I wasn't? But dulling my feelings isn't going to help me make a new life. I want to have a clear head and be fit and healthy, and now I don't have to cook and be at Chaika's beck and call – not that I wasn't happy doing both – I've got the time to discover what I want, who I am." She took a gulp of her Sauvignon blanc and straightened her shoulders. "I need somewhere to exhibit and sell from, and some friends to socialise with and perhaps go on holidays with. That'll be a start for me."

"Well, U3A runs tons of classes, you could teach or be a student when they start up again. We haven't started that friendship group for over-sixties yet, but hopefully soon."

"Oh yes, you're going to invite anyone on their own to come for a drink and snacks once a month and perhaps plan holidays together, go on walks, to films, plays, concerts, whatever?"

"Yes, we must get on with starting it. Lockdown has made it difficult. Meeting others gives one a community for those who have left work and don't have families. Don't be hard on yourself, you need a bit of self-compassion and to appreciate what you've got and your talents. I was reading an article this morning about inner happiness – that it doesn't come from material things, but from sunlight, exercise, diet, rest, self-confidence and friends. You've got all but the last one and hopefully that'll soon be remedied."

They lay back in their chairs and sipped their wine. It was a warm evening and the air was still. There were almost soundless 'pops' from the evening primrose flowers opening in the border next to them, and the white lilies, everlasting sweet peas, phlox and roses stood still and glowing in the twilight.

*

Vicky and Diana had to finish their singles duel because the next players were waiting to come on the court. They sprayed their hands and wandered off, swigging at their water bottles.

"Remember when we sat in the clubhouse and had a drink

after our game, then a shower and sauna? It's only four months ago, but seems much longer…"

"You know, I thought I'd read so much, being stuck at home every evening, but I haven't. Do you think that generally people are shifting away from reading towards the internet and TV?"

"Probably. Accessing information from them is amazing, but doesn't reading teach us empathy? We get inside the world, the consciousness of the writer. We don't get inside their head on screen. Look how boring *Normal People* was – just pornography."

"Mmm. It was disappointing. The scene-setting and dialogue was too plain and unrevealing – we weren't inside the writer's head. Though do we invariably read just the writers who amplify our world view and what we believe? Do most of us live in our own bubble, surrounding ourselves with people, programmes, literature confirming that what we think is right?"

"Maybe, yes, probably. Are you still thinking about moving?"

"Perhaps, though is it all a bit quick? It seemed like a great idea to start a new, exciting life. I don't seem to have tried enough ways of living. But having to make the decision is rushing towards me and it's not like me to jump into something like this, so I've got a bit panicky. I hardly know Alex and he's always had staff to look after him. Am I ready to take him on? I'd like a bit more time to work out how it would be. Do you think he's right for me?"

"I don't know how to answer that. It seems that you are the one who has to change. There's a delicate power balance between men and women that drives relationships. As long as it isn't subjugation by one and dominance by the other. But you're too ballsy for that. It takes time to know people and that's not what you've had. I know time is running out for us oldies, but you should be sure."

A tear rolled down Diana's cheek, and a sob broke in her throat. "I've been on my own too long and haven't had any other offers, or interest in me. The idea of having someone to share life's ups and downs... I'd just had great results with my evening class and I wanted someone to be proud of me, and he's so flattering and impressive! Perhaps I've been too impulsive. I thought I'd get to know him better after." She shrugged and shook her head to try to shake away the self-pity. "My son was thrilled, and he interrogated me, in his lawyerish way. We all want to be loved. Perhaps it would be better if we didn't live together, because he likes modern things and I like traditional. I'm sporty and he doesn't do exercise, but is far more cultured than me, and he's on the board of two theatres. I could stay over, then come and play tennis with you, carry on with my life..."

"The advantage of being older is that one doesn't have the illusion that there is a perfect person out there. Go for it, Diana, but cautiously."

15 June 2020

There were 'Black Lives Matter' demonstrations in the US and cities across the UK yet again this weekend after the killing of George Floyd in Minneapolis on 25 May. A hundred far-right protesters were arrested and twenty-six police officers were injured. There are twenty-seven new infections in Beijing, having had none for fifty days. It's been traced to a market, which has been shut and the surrounding area locked down. Imperial College London is trialling its vaccine. And Oxford University has shown that dexamethasone, an off-the-shelf, cheap steroid, reduces deaths from COVID-19. Over 80,000 people have been told to self-isolate by the NHS test and trace system, but a third of people found to be carrying the virus wouldn't or didn't pass on their contacts. It is now mandatory to wear masks on public transport, but at least one third, mainly young people, are refusing to do so...

Vicky hadn't seen her neighbour come out of her home since lockdown began. She rang her bell and retreated to the street, under the impossible sweetness of a lime tree in flower.

A cheerful-looking Marion came to the door. "Oh hello," she said and turned to pick up some post on the hall floor, her hand like bird bones, loose in their pouch of withered skin. Vicky could see her pink scalp peeping through her white hair, which was thinning at the back.

"Have you been out for a walk yet?"

"On no. I contacted my GP last week to see if I am shielding more than I need to, since I didn't get one of those letters. She said that only the most severely compromised got them, but I was very definitely on the next level, and should stay self-isolating for at least the next two months, not to go any nearer than two metres from anyone and not into shops. Also carry on washing my shopping. She says it's a very nasty bug, and quite unpredictable in who is going to get it, or how ill they are going to be."

"That sounds a bit extreme. If you wear a face mask and avoid getting close to people, you should be OK. I went to Oxford Street this morning, and the tube was empty. Everyone is supposed to wear masks on public transport now, but people still are not travelling. Surely you can walk around one of the parks wearing a mask?"

"I think I'm scared to start. The days slip by, I read, garden, sing, practise my violin and watch some TV. People over seventy have been told to stay indoors and I'm over eighty!"

"Yes, but do you feel old? We need to develop policies, advise people by acknowledging the diversity in health and fitness. I read that in the flu pandemic of 1918–19, about one in seventeen Brits was over sixty-five – now it's one in five, and a 104-year-old lady recovered from COVID. You and I have had better diets, do exercise and have a sense of purpose in life. You're probably not as vulnerable as your age suggests. Are you practising for going into a care home or something?"

Marion laughed. "Hadn't thought of that."

"Come out! Though I don't want to act as the devil and tempt you into catching COVID!"

"Hmm, I'm quite happy with my own company. My daughter and grandsons ring every few days, as do friends. I'll wait for the R number to come down."

*

"Farzad watches so much news. I'm sure it's not good for his health. There's this cold anger in him. He's coiled, waiting to leap up in fury at whatever he sees as an outrage. And he's refusing to wear a mask, or muzzle, he calls it – not that he ever goes on public transport. But if it's made compulsory in shops like it is in Germany, Spain, Italy and Greece, he'll refuse. He says how can they possibly work, when there are hundreds of thousands of cases of COVID in India, Pakistan, Iran and Turkey where women wear full face coverings?" Nusheen and Vicky were sitting in the latter's garden, eating apple cake and drinking tea.

"Well, that's a fair point. There are plenty of others outraged by what they're saying is the 'surveillance state'."

"But if most scientists and epidemiologists all over the world think we should wear it to benefit one another, I'm not going to listen to the few who say they are useless or that our freedoms are being taken away. It's embarrassing. He's flouting the rules."

"Unfortunately, the government and the World Health Organization did say that there was no evidence that they were beneficial, but now they've changed their minds. Did you see that Twitter meme: 'If I can pretend your mask works, then you can pretend I'm wearing one?' At first, it seemed people put their egos aside in favour of caring about others, but now arrogance and selfishness are back. And look at our examples: Boris in March shook hands with all the patients in a COVID ward with no gloves, mask or sanitiser and was the first world leader to catch it. The government has been hopeless at handling this crisis – slow and contradictory. Farzad is a libertarian, didn't he vote for Brexit?"

"Yes, but he's calling me a coward, is trying to influence Kalil, and I don't see why I'm wearing one to protect others when they're not trying to protect me!"

"Another piece of cake? More tea?"

"Regretfully, I'd better not, thanks."

*

"Sad about Vera Lynn dying a couple of days ago," Malcolm said as he and Vicky walked down the canal path from King's Cross to St John's Wood.

"Yes, loved her Second World War songs, 'We'll Meet Again' and 'The White Cliffs of Dover'. My mum used to sing them to the forces too."

"Really? In other countries?"

"Only to Belgium with her church singing troupe. I didn't inherit her voice, though I enjoy singing, which we can't do now. Do you sing?"

"As a boy chorister, yes, and for a while I sang in the church choir with Sylvia. I was a tenor, were you an alto?"

"Yes, the same as Mum. Oh look, what a lovely, peaceful scene." A proud mother duck was leading her eight ducklings purposefully across the canal. "Wonder where they go at night, there are so many foxes in London."

"I'm sure not many make it to adulthood, though the mother tries to protect them for up to two months and then they're on their own. The male duck moults early, round about now, and then they can't fly, so they're not much help. We had ducks on our estate."

24 June 2020

In England, holidays, libraries, restaurants, pubs, hairdressers, cinemas, museums, galleries and church

services – though no singing – can be back from 4 July and one metre replaces two, but with caution and masks on transport. Where possible outside space must be used, and diners and drinkers must give their names and contact details on arrival for Test, Track and Trace if someone falls ill later. Groups of friends from two households can meet indoors. The vaccine developed by Oxford University is being trialled in Britain, South Africa and Brazil.

"I miss music, culture and socialising so much," Ruth sighed as they ate their breakfast in the conservatory.

Gerald looked up from his newspaper. "I keep reading that researchers think that the country will emerge from lockdown with a new set of rules for living, working and getting on with others much better than before. Boredom forces us to think differently and come up with creative, novel solutions. We'll just have to see."

"Or of course they become anxious, depressed, angry and drink too much. What do they mean anyway? Because of the change in the way we're living? Home schooling and virtual working? Will work practices change? Will companies be looking at their offices and the enormous bills for their heating, maintenance and upkeep and wondering what is the point of the office? Meetings are much shorter when conducted remotely and various studies have shown that productivity rises hugely when workers work from home. Does it mean adapting to a drop in income, no more secure employment?"

He looked over his glasses and smiled. "Or how we communicate technologically with friends and order the shopping. Amazon has suddenly become a vital public service and hired 200,000 more workers. And apart from cost savings to companies, all these buildings could be the answer to the housing crisis and all those wasted commuter hours be used more productively. Plus, upskilling or reskilling may be necessary in multistage life. Living longer gives us more time for more transitions."

"Mmm, I think that social distancing and remote working have removed the boundaries of our life, the boundaries between home and work. Scheduling too many meetings, those long commutes and spending too little time with our families may be a thing of the past."

"I read that there has been more domestic violence. And the social isolation won't suit everyone, particularly those who live on their own."

She smiled back; he really was a perfect companion – supportive, interesting, so lovable. She offered him the toast. "Maybe bosses will be more empathetic, particularly as they will have seen their employees' home life and bookshelves."

*

The next day, Vicky and Malcolm went to Bournemouth for a swim on the hottest day of the year so far.

Malcolm got first-class train tickets, and they had the first-class carriages to themselves. However, scores of people got off the train with them, and there were streams of groups of young people heading towards the coast. The electronic notice boards they passed, giving the numbers of spaces in two of the three car parks, said 'Full'. They walked along, trying to keep out of the way of the crowds in front and behind, but there was no social distancing, no evidence that anyone cared about COVID-19.

"This might have been a bad mistake!" Malcolm was sweating in the thirty-four-degree heat. After the airconditioned carriage, it was rather a shock.

"Well, as long as we get a swim, it will have been worth it. And I haven't been here since I was a teenager. I did waitressing in my summer holiday. There are seven miles of sandy beaches – surely there'll be lots of room?"

As they arrived at the coast, to their horror, the beaches as far as they could see were packed. Gangs of people were appearing from all directions, to add to the throng. They walked to the right for a kilometre or so until they spotted a space and camped down on it.

Stripping off to their bathers, underneath their clothes, they rushed to the sea. Warm ripples fawned at their feet like attention-seeking cats. After a long swim and a short time drying off in the sun, they decided to go home. Vicky had volunteered to make a sauce for pasta with last year's tomatoes from the deep freeze, together with tinned tuna and mushrooms.

*

"I'll get you a couple of bottles tomorrow," Malcolm said as he opened a bottle of Merlot in her kitchen.

"Don't bother. Rob belonged to the Wine Society and I kept on with it after he died, as they deliver."

Twenty minutes later and they were eating, and most of the bottle had been drunk. They were chatting about all sorts of things, including sleep patterns.

"I sleep better now. When I was working, I'd wake in those early, dragging hours and worry about being a poor father and husband and about the meaning of life. Forever on a hamster wheel, having to keep going, to keep up."

"Life is set up for successful white men, you're not continually knocked back and trodden on like women are!"

"Far more men than women commit suicide. The pressure to succeed is horrendous. To get top grades, get the best women, have a lovely house and children, and to keep climbing the ladder. It's expected. When you talk about Rob, I've felt so envious of his life."

"Why?"

"He exercised and kept himself fit, looked after your lovely house and garden with his talented DIY, in addition to working.

I was never able to stand back, take time out, I always felt pressure to keep my nose to the grindstone. Sylvia didn't work and organised our home and social life. I suppose I was trapped! Sorry, I sound ungrateful, and many people would envy what we had – expensive foreign holidays, a lovely daughter in a top school, wonderful home and garden, friends."

"Sounds amazing. Don't you miss that life?"

"Not really. When Sylvia was ill our life telescoped down. As I've said, we sold the estate because we were spending so much time at London hospitals. Our social life disappeared, as did many of our friends. I could have kept working and paid for her care, but I felt I wouldn't see enough of her and be able to keep on top of my job. So, I retired. Lockdown has been more of the same quiet life for me. You have added another dimension to my rather boring existence. Are we going to go and see a film, now that we can?"

"We'll be able to go to the cinema on Saturday the 4th, but will we? I've waited so long for this time to come, and am so sick of slumping on the sofa every evening, searching for something to watch on TV... but what if it's not managed properly? Too often I've caught things from people coughing on me from behind!"

"Apparently, the ones which have opened on the continent are all arrows winding you round the building, plexiglass and sanitiser. Masks are optional and one third of seats are closed, so there are gaps around each bubble."

"If only it was like that here! When *Little Women* opened in Denmark last month, it made as much as they would have expected before the virus lockdown, so people are certainly going. I read all the reviews, so know what I'd like to see. Shall I look at what films are being shown and what the safety arrangements are? I have to warn you, I don't like sci-fi or action or adventure films, poor Rob never got to see any of those. Will you mind subtitles?"

Malcolm smiled. "Whatever you choose will be fine with me."

*

Later:

Vicky's thoughts darted here and there as she washed up after he had gone. She was attracted to Malcolm and they got on so well, but did she want to fall in love and need someone as much as she had adored and needed Rob? Suppose they had drunk too much, would something have happened? Or did he just see her as a friend? *I can't help fancying him, but starting a sexual relationship is often embarrassing. I can't ask for him to do the things which turn me on – zero sensation in my nipples, and my clitoris is half an inch lower, please. Not the first time anyway, and men usually could get gratification, while women pretend.*

She went slowly upstairs and opened her bedroom window. The warm night air rolled in, dusty and polluted. She sighed and got ready for bed.

*

Barry lay next to Janet wondering why his penis refused to stiffen, no matter how much Janet stroked, rubbed and even sucked. It stubbornly stayed floppy, though it had gone bigger. Should he lay off the alcohol? Was he no longer attracted to Janet? This had happened before with other women; he'd had to walk away as it was too embarrassing, but he'd never thought it could happen with his childhood love, so recently rediscovered. Why had he no control over his penis? Perhaps he'd ask the doc after this virus was over. Prostate might have got worse…

1 July 2020

A hundred days since lockdown. Pubs and restaurants can open on 4 July. Apparently, last month mental health

absences for NHS staff and care workers were three times higher than for COVID-related sickness.

Malcolm and Vicky had taken the Met line out to Little Chalfont to do a seven-mile circular walk in the beautiful valley of the River Chess. Through the charming village of brick and timber cottages, then a wood, they crossed stiles and over fields, chatting all the way.

"Wimbledon would be on now. All those years of getting the tube to Southfields and walking with mounting excitement to the ground. When I went thirty-plus years ago, I would drive there, park in a side street and walk about the outside courts, bumping into friends, watching bits of matches. It's not like that now, there are so many people, one is rather stuck in one's seat."

"I did go years ago but found it rather boring. Hushed silence apart from the thwack of tennis balls and grunts or screams, then the enthusiastic clapping at every point, no matter how pedestrian. I seem to remember watching good old Tim Henman dragging a match into five sets."

"Yes, five sets is an awful long time to watch something. That's one of the reasons I rarely bother to go now, and because one is at the mercy of the weather. Either baking or rained off and then unable to get into the tube station for the horrendous queues. It can be quite a marathon. I prefer to pick and choose matches on TV."

They stopped by the river, under a chestnut tree, and ate cheese and lettuce rolls which Vicky had brought. Kingfishers and dragonflies swooped over the water, and they were sure that they had seen a water vole.

Then down a quiet valley through beds of watercress – unfortunately, currently none for sale, due to pollution from a water purification plant up stream. Past the brick-built tomb of William Liberty, more fields, stiles, a church and to the model estate village built by the Duke of Bedford in the 1850s. His wonderful Tudor manor house of Chenies, with its tall intricately twisted chimneys, crow-stepped gables and stunning gardens, was sadly closed, so no stop for tea. "I felt a ghost there when we went around the house a few years ago." Vicky shivered. "There was an unmistakable presence in one of the bedrooms, and the guide told us as we exited that Henry VIII's ghost walks the corridors looking for his wife Catherine Howard."

"Do you believe in ghosts, then?"

"I can feel presences, and have seen grey protoplasmic, see-through versions of people who have died. So I have to think they exist."

They went on through a woodland and down a stony track called the Ridgeway, and in front of them, the sun had dropped and was peering through a thicket, so the two trees in front of them were flares of gold in the summer stillness.

They got back quite late, and after some soup at Vicky's house, she said, "Why don't you stay here? I'll make up a bed for you."

*

Waking up from a deep dream-filled sleep, with the sun peering through a crack in the heavy curtains, she was unsure where she was. She gazed at the ceiling while her mind gently woke from a strange dream set in her childhood. She felt for the side of the bed. When she was a child it had been single; this was a double. *I'm at home.* She moved her arms so she could begin to push herself up; her back was stiff, she must have slept awkwardly. She fumbled for her phone by the bed, lit up its screen. Time to get up.

In the bathroom, cleaning her teeth, she stared at her reflection – lines around her mouth, bags under her eyes. Hopefully her lithe body and smile disguised the old-age signs. From the shower room came sounds of Malcolm, the rush of water as the toilet flushed, his happy whistling.

She went back into the bedroom and dressed for a community centre course-booklet meeting. Dark blue dress, red cardigan and sandals, a comb through her shoulder-length, wavy hair and down to her big oak-panelled kitchen. Malcolm was sitting at the far end of the long table with a mug of tea and piece of toast with her homemade strawberry jam. He looked up and smiled. "I hope you don't mind, I helped myself. Did you sleep OK?"

She nodded. "Did you?"

He wanted to raise the subject of sex but thought he should wait until after the meeting. He didn't want her to think she wasn't attractive to him, but he didn't want to start a romance with his illness hanging over him. Vicky was making her porridge; he preferred her wholewheat bread, toasted. It felt healthy with all the different seeds she added. She was standing by the hob, stirring, her mind on the subjects they were to cover when she chaired the meeting in an hour's time. He watched her and felt her awareness of his eyes, as if his arms were around her body.

The morning sun made her hair shine like gold. He wanted to stroke it, stroke her all over, make love to her... She was deciding between Activia or plain yoghurt with jam on her porridge. And blueberries of course, always blueberries.

*

Marion had stayed in her flat and garden for four months. After encouragement by Vicky and all the very hot weather, she decided to go out for a walk at 5am. But it was difficult to step out of the flat; she hesitated on the doorstep, unable to cross that boundary. Then with a deep breath she plunged forwards and down the path. Being on the pavement felt so vivid, as if she were an alien looking at a new world. Down the street, around the corner, two more streets, into the little park. The flowerbeds hurt her eyes they were so colourful. She exulted in every shape, colour, and the sunlight through the trees felt so new. She drank, sucked it all in to review it later. Her eyes, her very being, tingled with the newness, the brightness of it all. People were arriving with their dogs, there was more traffic, she must go home, but what a walk! She would do it again later in the week.

*

"Why don't you go to my house in Wales for a few days? We're allowed to from the 11th. The weather isn't as good as it was, but you can do walks and it'll be a change of scene," said Jo. "I'm going to do the ad soon and invite the best to the cottage at the beginning of September. Surely life will be back to normal by then?"

"Why not?" Malcolm said when she rang him. "Sounds a great idea. It's not Italy, but we can't go there yet…"

*

Liz hadn't seen Julie since she had been asked to sell the house. She had rung a few times, but the conversations had been stiffly polite and short. She missed their mother–daughter gossips and mourned sadly, guilt padding behind her like a well-loved, reproachful dog refused a walk.

6 July 2020

> In Wales, the 'stay local' restriction is lifted, people are allowed to go to their second home and two households can meet. In England, hairdressers, and bars and restaurants can open, the latter two outside if possible. England (the Scots and Welsh have been told to wait) has lifted the travel ban from 4 July, after an agreement for 'travel corridors' with fifty-nine countries and two weeks of quarantine on returning to this country lifted from

10 July. This also applies to travellers from the fifty-nine countries. The Chancellor is giving £1.57 billion to try to save cultural and heritage organisations. **Victoria state in Australia, including Melbourne, is locked down for six weeks.**

Malcolm rang and, sounding distinctly upset, asked if he could come for a chat, as she had a side entrance and they could sit in the garden in the sun, an appropriate distance apart.

Vicky felt a sudden frisson of fear. "Are you OK?" This sounded ominous. "Would you eat cake and have a cup of tea, or is that one step too far? Some of my friends are happy to come to tea, others will visit but not eat or drink, unless they bring their own."

"I'm very happy to, love cake and haven't had much for some time."

"See you around four, then?"

Vicky had an orange, ground almonds, dried apricots, eggs and walnuts, so she stewed the apricots in the orange juice and made a cake.

He rang the bell at four and then walked down the side passage, which she had unlocked for him. Walking past a window, he stopped. He could see Vicky pounding away on the treadmill. Churn, swish, churn, swish; she had headphones on, so she probably hadn't heard the bell. The muscles in her toned arms and legs were shining with the sweat, her hair was tied back and she seemed to be muttering: "Come on, come on." Should he disturb her? He tapped on the window and then again, louder. She came out of her trance, spotted him, stopped the machine, took off the headphones, smiled and indicated she would meet him in the garden. She emerged in a sweat top with a towel round her neck, carrying two cushions. "Sorry, I'm sweaty and disgusting. Why don't you sit on this chair in the shade?" She dropped a cushion onto it. "I'll sit over here."

He admired her lithe fluidity and ease in her own body. It was another beautiful day; the sun had raked over the soft pastel sky, so it was scarred with rosy welts.

"This is a wonderful garden, you must spend so much time on it."

"Rob was a very hard-working and keen gardener. I miss him terribly. He kept it under control. I just grew things from seed, weeded and did most of the planting. It's going a bit wild now without him."

"I didn't know you were a gym bunny."

"We didn't use the little gym that often, only if our more interesting ways of exercising were not available. I'd prefer to play tennis or swim, or dance about with my dumbbells and bands. Dance is the quickest way to boost my mood. The stretching, circling of all the joints, helps uncoil all one's knots and it releases all the good hormones, like serotonin and endorphins. Do you use a gym?"

"Yes, we both belonged to an expensive, but very well-equipped one. Sylvia preferred the pool and sauna, though. Can't see gyms and leisure centres opening for a while, and I'm in no rush to visit them, or pubs and restaurants, are you?"

"I'd love to go to a restaurant, but sitting in a perspex cubicle isn't attractive. It's connection that makes us human, but proper connection, not a Zoom call or shouting at a friend from a distance. Oh, for normal life to return. You're on edge, what's the matter?"

"Look, Vicky. I've got something I must tell you, related to my headaches."

She stiffened; her mouth suddenly felt as if it were full of sand – this sounded serious. He seemed to be pulling himself together to speak, and she realised how frighteningly powerful his attraction was for her, like electricity restored after a powercut. She faked a bright, warm smile. "Yes?"

He swallowed and out it came in a rush: "I've got

glioblastoma multiforme, probably grade 4. It's a malignant brain tumour and surgery is possible, but its position and the difficulty of removing all the tendrils from it means it's a death sentence. I've got a maximum of a year."

"Wha… what?" It was as if a rocket had hit her. She tried to stay calm, though her heart was thumping. "Are they sure?"

"I've seen the CT and the MRI scans for myself. There is no doubt that they're right."

"Oh, Malcolm, how earth shattering, I'm *so*, so sorry!" She gave him a painted-on smile to disguise her agony.

"It's very strange, I seem to be experiencing the world with such heightened intensity, living each moment as if it is the last. I look through my window at the most frothy, glorious blossom and budding trees in next door's garden, and when I go outside, the birdsong makes me want to weep. The only time for me now is the present and that has become so vivid it has made this lockdown period wondrous. Yet even though I know I'm going to die, I still behave as I have always done, paying bills, doing jobs, keeping up with friends on the phone, seeing you, as though I'll live forever."

"This period has exposed our human fragility. It's such a shock to find we're not immortal, that terrible things can happen to us and to our friends. What are you supposed to do next? Is there nothing that can be done, no treatment to stave it off, reduce it, stun it?"

"The country is reeling from high infection rates and death tolls, none of us are invulnerable, though I secretly thought I was immortal. I have to say, though, that nothing concentrates the mind better than time running out."

"I know you've got family and closer friends, but how can I help?"

"By giving me tea and being around when I need a chat. I want to live my life as fully as possible, get on with living in the face of my impermanence. And I still want to go to Wales."

They had a delicious tea and chit-chatted as if he had never broken the terrible news to her.

*

Vicky's first thought after a restless night was to ring Ruth, she was so knowledgeable.

Glioblastoma multiforme. It was too early, they wouldn't be up yet. Ruth would say, "Keep calm, perhaps he could have a second opinion, why don't you look on the internet and find out more about the condition?"

Eight thirty. Maybe I can ring her now?

Ruth answered. "Haven't spoken to you for a couple of days, how are you?"

"I've got some terrible news. I know you don't know him, but Malcolm has got glioblastoma multiforme, probably grade 4. It's a malignant brain tumour. He might have surgery, but apparently it's difficult to remove all the tendrils from them. Of course, he has to have chemoradiation after the surgery. His prognosis isn't great."

"Oh, Vicky, I'm *so* sorry. Just when you two were getting friendly."

"He seems normal at the moment, but it says here that there will be progressive gait difficulties, psychomotor slowness, cognitive impairment, headaches and nausea. Well, he's got the last two."

"Let's find out all the top people in this field, contact them wherever they are. There'll be somewhere in the world where there's been a breakthrough of some sort. I'll come over later. We'll sit in the garden and get on it today!" Ruth said enthusiastically.

"Yes, thanks, Ruth, that's what we'll do, research every possible option. There must be something which could be tried other than palliative care and wait to die!"

*

They sat, socially distanced, near the house WiFi for their computers. Ruth, as an American, checking out the US, and Vicky the rest of the world. "China uses T cells and Addenbrooke's Hospital in Cambridge seems to be a leader in the research field, and Dr Gilbert is a great figure in the area for a second opinion."

"I keep coming across a US-approved drug to ward off malaria, which is often used. But how about this? A US company called Ziopharm has two options: 'Sleeping Beauty' which targets multiple antigens, or IL-12, which 're-establishes the immune system to get the body's own defences to destroy the tumours'. They say that radiation, chemotherapy and surgery don't cut it against glioblastoma, it's such an aggressive type of brain cancer that often recurs with a vengeance. Ziopharm is working on a 'remote-controlled' gene therapy to buy these patients more time, and early data show it extended patients' lives by more than a year. And at Duke University cancer centre they injected a woman with her own blood cells and a vaccine to rev up the white blood cells. She's had four injections over a hundred times already, but she's lived ten years since diagnoses and even if people have the tumour removed and chemo and radiation therapy, they don't usually live more than fifteen to sixteen months."

"Why is it so lethal?"

"It seems to be resistant because the cells within the tumour are of different types, some of which keep on growing, and also the tumour has thread-like elements so it's difficult to tell where its edges are, even though the patients having surgery drink a drink which makes the cells glow bright pink under UV light."

"Let's contact Dr Gilbert, see if he can recommend someone in the UK, and go from there."

"Good plan. Didn't you say you'd made a cake?"

11 July 2020

The global total of infections is 41,332,899 and 1,132,879 people have died. In the last twenty-four hours in the UK, there have been 820 positive results and forty-eight people have died.

In the morning, Vicky opened her curtains to see the sea lying asleep in the sun. Around the bay, the hills of different shades of blue and violet were asleep too, and below her window, the flower-starred, grassy slope stretched quietly down to the gate. Then came the sea, blurring into the horizon.

They had arrived late the night before, after an exhausting drive with too many roadworks and diversions, so had eaten the sandwiches she had brought, with camomile tea, made up a bed in each of the bedrooms and got into them. There was no sound from across the landing, so she used the bathroom quietly, dressed and went down the steep, narrow flight of stairs. The front door was open, and Malcolm was sitting in the front garden with a cup of tea. He looked up, smiling.

"I could sit here, listening to the sea and gulls, watching the boats and clouds forever," he said.

"Mmm, lovely for a change, but it's the middle of nowhere. This little row is all second homes and apart from the pub, which is also the shop and cafe, there isn't exactly a social life."

He smiled. "Peaceful and beautiful, though."

He had a strong face, a kind and gentle face, one she had come to look forward to seeing…

After toast and tea, with which Malcolm took strong painkillers for his headaches, they put on their walking boots for a walk. Several sailing dinghies were now swooping about in the morning sun. Their coloured and white sails scattered gaily, forming random patterns amongst the sparkling waves. "Who would not be happy in such stunning surroundings," she said.

Up a gentle slope they toiled and through a kissing gate into a field. "Hey," said Vicky, "don't you know what this is called?" She explained and they gave one another an embarrassed peck. She could smell what she thought was 4711 aftershave and wondered if he could smell anything on her.

Down through two fields, long grasses and cow parsley rippled in the breeze, the sounds of a stream rushing down to the sea, birds singing in the trees and sunlight filtering through the branches onto the path in front of them as they passed through a copse of trees. A tractor in the next field turned the rather stony-looking earth, birds streaming behind.

Then puffing up a steep hill, over the top and down to follow a brook which reflected the sun, like a shining path. Across the big stepping stones with wild watercress growing strongly on either side. She held onto him as they crossed.

"I used to greedily pick and eat the watercress," she said.

"Why don't you now?"

"A man once warned me that I would get liver flukes, which rather put me off. Do you know wildflowers?" she asked.

"Not many. Sylvia wasn't a walker and we had a gardener. Do you?"

"Yes, a friend and I used to press them when we were in school, and Rob and I tended to remember different ones, so between us we weren't too bad, but got better by the autumn every year and had forgotten lots of them by the following spring."

"What's this, then?"

"Rosebay willow herb, and the purple-headed flower next to it is knapweed. You know this dandelion and this buttercup?"

"Just about, yes, and this?"

"Ragwort, and that's an ox-eye daisy. But this? There are so many ox-tongues, hawkbits, hawkweed, cat's ear, nipplewort that look vaguely similar, I can't remember which is which. I think this is a squill, they grow on cliff tops."

Down a long green lane, sun streaming through the overhanging trees, making bright patches. The only sounds their feet, crunching and crackling over fallen twigs and leaves, occasional bird calls and the brook below, which long ago had been a millstream.

They reached a bench looking out over the sea. In the distance were climbers scaling a scary-looking vertical rock face, and seagulls swooped and dived over an area of churning sea below. Sitting peacefully in the sun they absorbed the view. The breeze on their backs whipped her hair across her face.

"Are you wondering why I haven't made a move, as I'm obviously very fond of you?" he asked.

"No and yes, I suppose, but isn't it fine just to be close friends?"

"I don't think I've ever felt closer to anyone in my life!" He looked at her with intensity and reached for her hand. She put her hand in his and he held it gently, then tighter as if he were afraid she would withdraw it. "This may sound conceited, but if you fell in love with me and then I die, you'd have had two tragedies. Might it be better for you if we have a less intense, close relationship? And by the way, don't think I don't fancy you and am just using you as a companion. I can't think of anyone I'd like to make love to more than you. I've been forcing myself to hold back." He squeezed her hand.

She flushed. "However you want to play it is fine with me." Though really, she often felt she would love him to give her a hug... and more. Though would it be fair to Rob's memory, to have sex with someone else?

*

They had tea when they got back, read for a while, then cooked their evening meal together and ate outside looking at the calm sea.

Next day, they had another walk, around the tranquil woodland gardens of a nearby medieval castle. After some delicious soup, they went to the nineteenth-century walled garden with its exotic and rare trees and plants, herbs and beautiful fountains. On the way back, they passed the beginning of a jungle boardwalk through lush, huge planting. "Let's have a go, there are Japanese bananas and all kinds of tropical trees and shrubs to see!" She jumped onto the raised foot-wide boardwalk, completely forgetting that Malcolm struggled with his balance.

He fell off immediately into the soft undergrowth. She looked back, to see his agonised expression. "Oh no, I'm so sorry, Malcolm, how stupid of me." She rushed to his side as he shamefacedly struggled to his feet.

"Come on, let's go."

Back at the cottage, it was so warm they swam, and later, when the sun was low, burning gold through the trees, they walked to the pub for fish and chips, their shadows long and distorted behind them. Malcolm had a child's portion as he was never hungry. As they got back to the cottage, a summer storm rolled in – loud claps of thunder and resonant echoing booms, followed by rushing, fast rain. They sat on the sofa in front of the TV to watch the news.

She could feel his heat and was acutely conscious of his every breath and movement. He was thinking that in the golden light of the lamp, she looked so beautiful. The news was finishing. "Shall I make some camomile tea?" she asked.

"That would be nice, thanks," he smiled.

She tried to get up, but the sofa was low and she got half up and unbalanced. He put out his arms to catch her and she tumbled onto his lap, his arms around her, his breath on her cheek, then his lips on her skin. His hands reached under her shirt and onto her braless nipples. She twisted round to search for his lips and the swelling in his shorts.

I want this, she thought. *It's been so long and I want this now.* She had unzipped his fly, was rubbing his erect penis. He was sucking her nipples, kissing her, then his hands were pulling down her shorts and pants, fingers inside her. They rolled down onto the carpet, entwined together, the shock of their mutual desire firing their passion. Their unknown bodies linked together; he eased gently inside her. They moved together as if they had been born for this, and suddenly she could feel a gradual, then increasing stimulation inside her… and they orgasmed together.

They lay entwined on the carpet. *Did that happen? We both orgasmed together? That's never happened to me before*, thought Vicky.

Was it wrong? Did I start something he didn't want? Her body was throbbingly still alive, still feeling him inside her, her skin burning from his touch. *Was it my fault, or was it the force of gravity, then did the intensity of our desire for one another take over?* She looked up at his face and he was smiling, his eyes warm and shining. "Perfect," he said, "perfect!"

14 July 2020

Antibody treatment is to be available to protect older people from the coronavirus for six months. All the workforce of a farm in Herefordshire have been quarantined after seventy-three pickers and packers tested positive. Similarly, in Germany, 1,500 workers in a meat-packing factory are quarantined. The UK has the highest number of deaths of health and social care workers; only Russia has more. The UK has the third-highest number of deaths in the world, and the highest per 1 million of population, but is thirty-fourth in the total number of new cases, with only 650.

Back from Wales, Malcolm had stayed the night at Vicky's, but this time in her bedroom. When she woke, her clock said 8.10.

He was lying with his back against hers, warm and somehow part of her. She wanted the moment to go on and on, so didn't move to spoil it. But somehow, he sensed that she was now thinking real thoughts, not dream ones, and rolled over to press his face against hers, his lips on her cheek. His arm came over to encircle her. "Are you awake?" he whispered.

"Mmm."

He moved slightly back and let his eyes run over her body. Over her prominent hip bones, over her caesarean scar, over the fine, blonde hairs on her thighs.

"I wish…" He stopped there, though hoped she knew that he'd like to wake up every morning next to her, but today he was going to Queen Square for his operation, with the neurosurgeon suggested by Dr Gilbert. The comfortable warmth disappeared at the thought. They disentangled and climbed out of bed to face the day.

Malcolm's sister, Alison, was coming to the operation with him to support him, then was going to stay until he was on his feet again.

*

Vicky and Diana had finished their game and were having a drink and chat, sitting outside.

"Don't know what I'd do without tennis and chats during and after," said Diana.

"Yes, one of our basic needs is social interaction – there's Zoom, FaceTime, phone calls and others to connect one to people. But for me, I can't beat having friends coming over for tea or supper in the garden. It means the day is broken up."

"I read that people are not having their hair coloured during this period and are not bothering with 'sets' as they are rarely going out. So hairdressers, after the initial rush for cuts, now have so few customers. People are apparently putting on weight, wearing old clothes more…"

"You're describing me!"

"...but taking up hobbies, learning things and doing stuff to keep calm, like yoga and pilates. Lockdown has done strange things to us all. People have turned to gardening, cycling, cooking, but an awful lot of people have watched an awful lot of bad TV."

"Isn't it called hate-watching?"

"At least people aren't going to be hugging us and feeling spare tyres. That has to be a good thing!" Diana sighed.

Vicky laughed. "When we meet one another, will we say a cheery 'Good day' or 'Hello' from a safe distance as we used to when we were young? Rather than the hugs and *'moi-moi'* kisses we imported from the continent? I found that so alien when people started doing it to me when I was in my thirties. Now *not* doing it and touching elbows feels strange."

"Mmm, touch reduces stress hormones. But perhaps we'll go back to the greetings, like, 'Good to see you', or 'How are you?' Much safer too."

*

The operation had removed as much as possible of the tumour and a shunt was fitted to drain the build-up of cerebrospinal fluid, which otherwise would cause the pressure in the head to rise.

Vicky sat in the white, bright waiting room, feeling invisible as people came and went. She fought against a rush of tears as she saw a flash of bird wings passing the window – Malcolm's soul? She knew she wouldn't be allowed to see him – his daughter and sister would be enough after the operation. They didn't know her, and she had only seen their photographs.

A nurse, realising the situation, came to tell her that Malcolm was awake, though very drowsy and unable to communicate. He would be in hospital until his wound healed and there was no longer a risk of infection.

"Why don't you ring up tomorrow, and come and see him when he's able to speak to you?"

*

Debs had gone to a social tennis evening at the tennis club. In two of the rounds, she was paired with a newcomer called Tom, who was trying out the club. He was obviously twenty or thirty years younger, but he looked hot. They joked and laughed and had good chemistry. After their second game, the coach had called that it was the last round, so he asked if she'd like a drink. Three gin and tonics later and lots of knee contact under the table, she said she was going home. He jumped up too and said he'd take her, as they had found that he lived in the same direction. Leaving the club, he put his arm proprietarily around her back to shepherd her along and she felt the tug of lust. He tucked her into his Mercedes and when they arrived, escorted her up the path, and by then, there was no question that he would come in. He pulled her to him as soon as they had got through the door, and she could feel the hard lump in his trousers. She knew how to orchestrate matters to keep him horny, so they had an enjoyable few hours in bed, and then he left.

In the morning she had a hangover and stumbled into the bathroom to look forlornly at her face. Creased and crumpled, with blotches of makeup in the grooves and mascara under her eyes – she felt and looked ninety. She had enjoyed the evening, though she was pretty sure she wouldn't see him again. But what fun it had been.

18 July 2020

In Victoria, Australia, there is a $140 fine for not wearing a mask. Brazil has over 2 million cases. Positive cases have soared in Manchester. The death statistics are being reviewed.

Vicky could hear Ruth playing the piano as she walked up their path. She was so talented musically. Vicky had been brought up in a silent house, with no musical instrument or radio playing, but she could appreciate both Ruth's and Gerald's knowledge and abilities. She peered in through the half-drawn blinds of the lounge window, the sun pouring in behind her, and tapped on the glass.

They waved to one another, and Ruth came to the door to take the book Vicky had enjoyed.

"It's about time and place and how they have an effect on our thoughts and deeds," she said. "I found it amazing that a book written a hundred years ago gave me so much pleasure and delight! It was so charming and witty, sweet and heart-warming that it cast a spell on me. I could smell the wisteria and freesias, see the apple and plum blossom. *The Guardian* called it a 'sun-washed fairy tale'."

"*The Enchanted April*." Ruth smiled and took the book.

*

Vicky and Debs were having a drink at the side of the courts after their game.

"There are so many things now that make me feel ancient. No one ever told me that after the menopause I'd develop a furry face," Debs sighed.

"Yes, chin hairs are so embarrassing. Rob used to point them out on me. We should do it for one another. I don't look at my face enough in a bright light to keep up with them."

"Yours probably don't show, they're fair, but mine are dark and I can look as if I've got a beard!"

"I pluck mine if I notice them. What do you do? Threading is apparently good, as it pulls them out by the root, but I'm too much of a baby to have someone do that."

"Laser is best for dark hairs, and I tried electrolysis, but they came back. Are we goin' to get on with this idea of sort of meetin's or Zooms for older singles?"

"Yes, why not. We've agreed on what to say in the email and the date to meet – 22 August. Of course, some people may be away, but let's get started before we get locked down again. But where?"

"Your garden? It's big and lovely. Would you mind? There may not be many people the first time. We don't have to get too close. In fact, shall we say we'll all wear masks? I'll get the snacks, if you get the drink? We can put the costs down and when we get organised as a group, charge joinin' fees and refund outlays like this."

*

On the way home, Vicky saw a figure in a black hoodie and cape around her full figure. She was scuttling along determinedly, though carefully; her feet were obviously giving her trouble. Catching up with her, she called, "Hi, Marion!"

Marion turned and smiled. Her face was a mask of fine lines, her jaw less defined than it had been, her blue eyes sunken but still with the glint of intelligence. "I've taken your advice, I'm walking every day. It makes me feel fitter, but also hungrier. How are you?"

"Oh, overweight, stiff and fed up of never going out in the evenings."

"Mmm, you know you're getting old when everything dries up, leaks, wrinkles and a simple walk is such an effort!"

"At least you haven't reached the point where instead of lying about your age, you brag about it."

"That's to come. I read a pertinent saying, though, which goes something like this: 'Grant me the senility to forget the people I don't like, the good fortune to see more of those I like, and the eyesight to tell the difference!'"

"You are funny. Are you missing your community class?"

"Absolutely not. I didn't mind the exercise, though I preferred your class. But it made me depressed and anxious about my lack of accomplishments. We were asked to write our life story! We were told it would improve cognition, lessen depression, stress and anxiety and boost self-esteem. It was doing the opposite for me! No doubt they found me very ungrateful and curmudgeonly. COVID was a blessed release for both of us."

*

Gerald was driving his Mercedes to the golf club, when a lorry in front of him suddenly slowed to turn left, and he had to slam on his brakes. The Fiesta behind him managed to stop, but the BMW, which had come quickly up behind them, piled into the back of it. Gerald had watched this in horror in his rear-view mirror, so pulled in and heaved himself out. A young woman had got out of the Fiesta and was crying in shock. "So sorry, my dear. I don't think he indicated. Are you alright?"

A young man, shirt sleeves rolled up, holding his phone had got out of the damaged BMW. "You stupid old sod!" he spat out contemptuously. "You shouldn't be driving!"

"Don't speak like that, it wasn't his fault," the young woman said through her tears. "You were driving too fast up behind us."

"It's a new car!" he shouted. "You'd better be insured," he spat at her.

"Why don't you go?" she said to Gerald. "I'll give him my details."

Gerald felt in his inside right pocket. "Here's my card. If we both say he was travelling too fast?"

She smiled and took it. *What a kind young lady*, he thought. *She's had the back of her car stoved in through no fault of hers and she's being so kind.* "Please contact me," he said. "I'd be so pleased to invite you to dinner with my wife, after all this is over. So sorry to have caused you this bother."

She pushed him into his car and he drove on, with the BMW driver's insults still ringing in his ears.

It doesn't seem too long ago since I was young and driving like Stirling Moss, but the way he spoke to me, it's as if by entering my eighth decade I've exited the human race!

*

Liz came back from tea and a chat at Vicky's, to find, to her surprise, Julie sitting on the doorstep of her tall, narrow, Georgian house. Her hair was greasy, and the usually milky, translucent skin of her face rather red and puffy. "Why didn't you go in, darling?"

"I saw Paul through the lounge window, and not you. I didn't like to go in – he might be hating me for trying to get you to sell the house."

"I haven't discussed it with him, he doesn't know – you would have been quite safe. Well, come in now. It's lovely to see you. How is James? He came home a few days ago, didn't he?"

"Yes, that's what I wanted to talk to you about."

Liz opened the door and they went in, walking through to the kitchen; a delicious smell of lemon chicken was wafting from the oven. Paul was an excellent cook. There was no sign of him. He was probably in the shed at the bottom of the garden.

"Let's have a cup of tea, and you can tell me about whatever it is."

Julie walked up and down restlessly, stopping at the six pots of geraniums on the windowsill and absentmindedly pulling off the dead leaves and flowers, which she had done with her mother when she was a schoolgirl.

Liz put the tea leaves in the pot, poured on the boiling water and reached above for some mugs and the biscuit barrel. "Shall we sit in the conservatory?"

They moved through to the sun-filled room. The garden and conservatory faced south, and it could get very hot when it was sunny. Julie plonked down, looked up at the new sail blinds above her, that Paul had put up, and plunged into: "James has begged us to take him away from that school. Half his friends from junior school went to UCS and he did pass the entrance exam, but Martin wanted him to go to his old boarding school. But he hates it. He'd like to be living at home."

"You'd like that, wouldn't you?" Liz smiled.

"I would, but Martin is furious. He says I mollycoddle him and he'll get used to it and love it after a while."

"He's disappointed that James isn't settling in. I expect he thinks he hasn't given it enough time?"

"Why are you taking his side, Mum? He tried to get you to move so we could afford to keep James there."

"Perhaps you need to be calmer about this. Do you think that James realises you miss him and feels guilty about being away at school?"

Julie looked shocked. "Oh," and after some thought, "maybe, I hadn't thought of that. Maybe I do mollycoddle him. Maybe I don't want him growing away from me."

They both sat in silent thought.

"Perhaps all this is my fault. I'm trying to keep James tied to my apron strings and I upset you. I should never have said that you should sell your home. It's your link to all your memories and I can see that Paul is a handyman, so unlike Dad. And if you get on well… I seem to be messing up all your lives!"

Liz got up and gave her a hug. "Why not see how James gets on next term? Don't tell him that he can leave if he hates it, or he won't give it a chance. I'll cash those shares that your father and I bought when things were being privatised. They're not doing very well at the moment, but they should pay for one more year, and after that you and Martin may be making more money. This pandemic has not been kind to many people."

Tears had been pouring down Julie's face. She rubbed at them with a damp paper handkerchief. "You're wonderful, Mum. If I can be half as good a mother as you…!"

26 July 2020

Face coverings are now compulsory in shops, takeaways, banks and public transport in England. Police can fine people who refuse £100. *It was compulsory in Scotland on 10 July, but not in Wales or* **Northern Ireland. All travellers must quarantine for two weeks when they return from mainland Spain, the Balearics and Canaries. There has been a spike in infections, so the government is saying that Spain is an unacceptably high risk for travellers. People are cancelling their holidays and Tui has scrapped all its bookings.**

"Look at this! TFL needs another taxpayer bailout! Shocking!" said Gerald.

"It certainly is." This was one of Ruth's hobby horses. "I've emailed TFL twice and written to the *Standard* about it. They're running empty trains every two minutes, both ways, since the beginning of the lockdown, and the buses are the same. If they had cut their services they would have saved so much money. Everyone says when they catch a tube there are virtually no other travellers. And all the gates are open, so no one has to pay. It's crazy… so incompetent!"

*

Vicky and Debs were sitting on the tennis club balcony, looking down on the grass courts where they had just played their first game of lawn tennis in 2020.

"They're in good condition at the moment – a few funny bounces, but they usually open on 1 May, so are worn out by July."

"Yes, not bad – considerin' they were reseeded in the autumn."

"I read in *The Times* today that protesters went into a Morrisons in South London with a megaphone and bellowed at the customers to resist their new world order and its conditioning and remove their 'face nappies' or 'muzzles'!"

Debs sighed. "Hope they don't get COVID then, or pass it on! There are so many people, mostly young, refusin' to wear masks on public transport. Hope they refuse a COVID vaccine so there are more for the 'sheeple'."

"They are also against lockdown and say, 'This country is like North Korea'!"

"Well, they're hardly being shot dead or sent to a labour camp for demanding their right to cough on everyone!"

"Rod Liddle made me laugh in *The Sunday Times*. Always so bolshie, he points out that there are just as many 'experts' and 'studies' showing that masks are useless as those saying that they are essential, but in this case, as it's been decided that on balance it's prudent, he's going to be a dupe and coward and have his mask ready for going on public transport, into shops and when he's having sex. Though the last is not to do with the virus, but because his wife prefers him to!"

Debs giggled. "He's brilliant!"

"How is your dating going?"

"Mmm, as you know, I feel pretty negative about the datin' apps and services, would obviously prefer to meet a partner more naturally. You get excited, meet a guy, it doesn't work, because who wants to have their cake and eat it when they can have the whole bakery and can look for the next person on whom to pin their hopes? I read about a Facebook group called 'Are we dating the same guy?' which is in various cities in the States and is startin' in London. Single women share a screenshot of a guy they've matched with, and then others share any info they've got on him, so there's a database – like his datin' CV. So, while he may say he's looking for a long-term relationship, the comments say otherwise. Great idea!

"I used to assume that the people you met would treat you like a human bein' with feelin's, not an instantly replaced avatar in the endless game they play on their phones. How much better to meet a friend of a friend, or someone you worked with or played tennis with – so you can't get rid of them with one click. It would be too shameful, and you can't tell lies like you can online. Snatched copulations in hotel bedrooms, masturbatin', watchin' porn or hookin' up online isn't intimacy. I don't want to go on like this. Apps don't work, they're a money-makin' capitalist enterprise. Bumble, Match, Silver Singles, Singles Over 70 and all the rest with all their gimmicks, what the hell is the point? It's a free-for-all. I want to meet someone the old-fashioned way, spend time with them doin' things like watchin' TV and goin' to sleep and wakin' up with them. I'd rather die alone than carry on like this, there's more dignity in that. If only there were some likely matches here at the club!"

"There's David, on that court over there, but I'm pretty sure he's gay, and the guy he's playing with seems to be free – but is weird."

"Yeah, and a total turn-off! I want an emotional connection, to fall in love, not casual sex with multiple partners I don't even see again. Life can be so unfair. If a woman has sexual desires she's thought of as a slut. Chastity is a male creation… Could I cut my hair short, join a book group and U3A class and continue indefinitely the long evenings of unnecessary existence that I have been livin' through lockdown? No, I'll go mad. Somethin' MUST change!"

*

Vicky's day was now in the rhythm of visiting Malcolm in hospital in the morning, so his daughter Bec, or sister Alison, had the rest of the day to choose from. She did some cleaning, then watered all the pots, the vegetables, and sometimes the borders and trees, though she knew it was better to water in the evening. Her daily walk was now mostly to the hospital.

Only once did she bump into another visitor – Alison. When she introduced herself, Alison broke into a big smile. "Malc said you've been his lifeline since Sylvia died. So glad to meet you at last. Give me your phone number."

They chatted for a while about Malcolm. Apparently, he was having physical therapy and had started radiation therapy, which makes the brain swell, so his headaches were back. But if everything went well, he would be out in two days, so they had employed carers, and either Bec or Alison would see him every day and take him back to the hospital for his radio and chemotherapy.

"I'm ten years younger than Malc, you know!" Alison suddenly said.

Vicky looked puzzled, not sure why it mattered.

"I've had six months of chemo, like Kylie Minogue… It horrifyingly aged me twenty years. I'm an ancient alien. A browless, hairless, sunken-cheeked, razor-jawed, bony, wizened, spectacularly weird being with a sad, mangled torso. I'm ashamed, embarrassed of how I look now!"

Vicky gulped. "But you're alive."

"Just thought I'd tell you. I haven't always looked like this…"

*

Vicky spent hours every afternoon thinking of interesting things to tell him the next day, and often making delicious things to tempt him with.

Her phone rang. "Hi, Carolyn, how are you?"

"Oh, good, good. Doug and I have booked a cottage in Norfolk, the first week of August, and wondered if you'd like to join us?"

"Tempting, but…" and Vicky explained about Malcolm. Then asked if their relationship had really blossomed.

"Yes, it has. I wasn't looking for a partner, but our friends kept asking both of us to things, putting us together, and we got used to it and found we both liked it. I told him from the start that I didn't want to get married, and he said he didn't want to either, it would complicate things with our families. We don't live together, but see each other most nights, taking it in turns to cook dinner. Then we have a cuddle and the one who is 'away' goes home to bed. It suits us – though some people might think it's a bit weird."

"How lovely, Carolyn. I'm so pleased for you."

"I must admit, I'm surprised how well we get on. We play bridge online, at a club and with friends. Garden together, watch films, go away for weekends when it's allowed. I know some people wouldn't want to start up a new relationship at nearly eighty, but we're alive and fit enough to enjoy our lives together. We don't argue or get irritated with one another, and our children seem pleased, so why wouldn't we want to give this a chance? Anyway, so very sorry about Malcolm and that we won't be seeing you this time."

"Have a great week and stay safe. Hope to see you before too long…"

*

Nusheen tossed a lock of hair back with a flicking motion of her head. "I love parties, the more people the better. In my country it is more sociable. Families and friends get together all the time."

Vicky imagined her dancing around a room, a beautiful girl, light and colourful.

"But Farzad always thinks I am flirting if we meet other men. He is very, very jealous. He wants me to stay in the home."

Vicky wasn't sure what to say. She couldn't criticise this sexist, old-fashioned behaviour Nusheen had to live with. "Well, he loves you too much."

"But I don't want to live like some sort of aristocrat from another era, not working, not even doing housework, while all around me people are working punishingly hard. I want to work hard, get involved, but I'm a peacemaker, I hate arguments, discord. I'll always keep quiet to appease, but I'm going to admit something to you, as my good friend... I've been brave and resorted to phone sex."

"Phone sex?"

"Apparently, it's a lockdown trend. I don't want people to see me in case I get found out, and with no cameras you can masturbate, be yourself. As long as they use the right words to describe every sensation, and I can imagine everything they're saying – I get self-pleasure. Embarrassing to admit, but I've been quite desperate – very frustrated. We haven't made love for months. He comes to bed late, then pretends he's immediately asleep."

Vicky was poleaxed. What could she say?

"Can I eat the other half of the pistachio eclair?"

10 August 2020

There was the biggest increase in the number of people testing positive for coronavirus since 25 June yesterday – over 1,000. However, the number of people in hospital has fallen ninety-four per cent since the peak of the pandemic.

Localised restrictions have been imposed on Preston, following Leicester, Greater Manchester, East Lancashire and West Yorkshire, and almost half of the new cases are in people under thirty. Tent sales have soared 750 per cent as most people take staycations rather than self-quarantine after holidays in countries abroad.

Vicky was driving herself and Janet to the south coast for the day. It was sunny and warm, so they both wore shorts and T-shirts and looked healthily tanned.

Out of London and the sprawling suburbs, where a dry, hot wind was pestering the city and dust was everywhere – until either side of the road were fields of sheep and their lambs, grazing contentedly. Two chased one another, gambolling in the lush grass for the joy of living. "They must be ready for slaughter. Isn't 'lamb' less than four months old? Lamb is my favourite meat, but how can I eat those cute little animals? Should I give up meat?" Vicky asked. Janet seemed very quiet. "Are you OK?"

"Yes, fine thanks, it's a lovely day, why shouldn't I be?"

"You said you've walked away from Barry? Did you mean for good?"

"Well, the last straw was the unexpected criticism from our children, of us moving in together. They didn't want to see us as sexual beings, just friends. Fiona even caught us in bed. She just walked in one morning early. It upset her. Forced her to acknowledge her father wasn't too old to have sex. It was knowledge she didn't want, and we couldn't take it back. She went running to her sister and my sons, and they made such a fuss, made it so awkward. It compounded all the doubts we'd been having. Young people refuse to think that older people's sexual organs are there for anything other than show – rather like a false pocket. They imagine that we stopped using them after progeny.

"I don't want to keep going with him out of inertia or guilt. I thought at first we could be good together, but I think I was remembering how we were at school, and in the last sixty years we've of course changed and grown in different directions. He's not interested in gardening, or the theatre particularly, and I know I'm very controlling. His flat is incredibly tidy, OCD-ish, and I'm messier. I went to his flat because, though it is smaller and in a very built-up area, the bedroom is half the flat, with plenty of cupboard space for my things. But I got angrier and angrier with him, and what made it worse was because I was on his territory, I was holding back from saying anything. I even wrote angry emails but didn't press the 'Send' button. All that repressed anger bubbled inside me and after all those weeks of cohabiting, enough is enough and do I ever want to do it again? No."

"Apparently divorce rates spiked in the wake of the pandemic, too much working from home. Don't you have feelings for him?"

"Yes and no. Perhaps by the time we've reached this age, we're fixed, like waxworks. I don't feel we've got much more to say to one another; and we've got such different ways of doing things domestically, and such different interests. We couldn't even watch the same TV programmes. I like to sleep late, but he bursts out of bed so energetically, so full of life, so early, it exhausts me. And I might have been a '60s rock chic and loved the fun, fashion and free love of that hedonistic time, but now I seem to have lost my sexual appetite. Perhaps it's because I had to do without sex for too long and I got used to a bath, cosy pyjamas and a hot water bottle and going off to sleep. At first, we were like rabbits at it, but then it palled, and if I cuddled up to him, he thought that was the come-on, which I didn't want, and it turned out he couldn't perform after a while. So, what started as a natural, passionate thing we both enjoyed became the elephant in the room. I've lost my libido and he's lost his erections."

"Poor guy, he must have been really confused."

"It's too difficult having to compromise in how you do things – what you eat, your lifestyle – and hibernating in the lockdown in his little flat brought our differences into clear perspective. Although we both understood that sex wasn't going to be the same as when we were young. It would take more time and experimentation. So many couples have stopped having sex by our ages and we were just starting. We tried to change our behaviour to fit in with one another. We agreed we wanted to achieve a loving, tranquil relationship. We worked out our finances, our household jobs, so we were fair and considerate to one another – but our age, stiffness and medical issues have made us more short-tempered and intolerant than we would like to be. We've realised that despite huge efforts, we're both too old and selfish to adapt, adjust and accommodate one another."

They stopped at some traffic lights and Vicky turned to look at Janet's expression.

"You're upset about it, though?"

"Well, yes, we're both lonely but want someone just like ourselves. We're too set in our ways to compromise. What is love anyway? Infatuation? It's not friendship – and without sex, it's a desperate longing for something so as not to be lonely. Two people agree to do a deal with one another, to be responsible for the happiness of the other, to bare their body and soul. We should call it quits now – before we get nasty and blaming and mean."

"Do you think you could go back to 'living apart together'? Isn't that what it's called? Plenty of famous couples have done it – Margaret Drabble and Michael Holroyd, and Simone de Beauvoir and Jean-Paul Sartre. You could see one another sometimes, whenever you want, but be independent, then perhaps the irritations will pass? Did you address the low-grade niggles early on and try to recognise what sets you off, before you react – so you could talk calmly about it? You both like walking – you'd get on best on holiday! Weren't you happier when you could escape if either of you got tetchy and you could see your families and carry on with your normal lives as well as seeing one another? You've just been stuck in his tiny flat, with no garden, no outside stimulation and got on each other's nerves. No love is perfect. It can be chaotic and messy, with irritations, pain, as well as joy. It's not about finding the perfect fit but someone you can rub along with, learn how to compromise with. Someone who will support you through life's ups and downs."

"What and be like furniture to one another, without the sex? It started off so well. Neither of us had made love to anyone for years, and age brings infirmities, debilities, so we were both afraid of failure – but we were fine. But now he's got prostate problems and yet he's blamed me for his impotence. I'm not exciting him enough. I can't get on top – my knees are too painful! Men can't bear to think they're not sexually potent! No, it's hopeless, we irritate one another. He's very tidy and organised and I've got too much stuff. He hasn't got a garden and isn't interested, and he says I'm controlling! You know, I even came to hate the way he chews – hardly at all and loudly – and the way he swallows as well... it's like a gulp, like a heron gulping down its prey. And end-of-life situations will be upon us soon... Oh, I don't know, we'll see if absence makes the heart grow fonder."

Vicky couldn't help a snort of laughter. "But you know that men are taught to equate success with happiness and they find it hard to talk about personal issues. He will be feeling a failure because he has been taught to aim to be a superhero – to be tough, show no weakness and have sexual prowess. Apparently, a huge number of older adults give up on sex because of medical and emotional challenges, which get worse if one is stressed or anxious about it, and then they get out of the habit. At the community centre we've had to have a man's shed for retired or soon-to-be-retired men, so they don't drop dead as soon as they leave work. There's such a high rate of depression and feelings of anxiety among older men. They're not like most women, they don't engage socially very easily or adapt to leaving full-time work."

"A man shed, what on earth is that?"

"There's no WI for men, but there are hundreds of men's sheds where they meet up and make stuff. Perhaps the shed, first, then other things like bird boxes and wooden bowls. Men can connect and create. So many guys have done little more than work, parent and sleep, they're lost when they retire. A lot of women push their husbands into joining. I know Barry isn't fully retired and you've been the thing that has kept him happy and stimulated, and suddenly his sexual prowess is challenged so he naturally looks outside himself for the reason. Fallibility is not something most men are conditioned to show."

"Yes, I see that. We're all pushed, educated into roles, and for guys of his age, they've got one foot in the patriarchy and traditional manliness of the past, and another in the greater equality of now. I know it intellectually, but in the situation – I just get infuriated. Should I try to be more understanding? Focus on tenderness and contact? But now I've told him what I think of him! Words are dangerous things. Once they're out, they have consequences, they induce reactions, make definite what had only been shadowy before and able to be ignored and forgotten."

"You need to talk."

*

Jo was still keen to advertise for sex partners, then to invite suitable respondents for the weekend to her second-home cottage. Like a programme she saw on TV, *Five Guys a Week*.

She was sitting in Vicky's garden eating carrot cake. For so many months now, it had literally been illegal for two single people, not living together, to have any physical contact. It had been life on hold, an enforced period of celibacy. Isolating alone caused so much anguish, with no one to hold and life's big questions consuming one's thoughts...

"I don't want to have to meet a lot of frogs to find a prince, and I'm ready to move on. I had a good marriage and am ready to try again, rather than be a burden on James. I don't feel old, and I think I've got a lot to give. I could have died with COVID, and I've got anosmia, and still get very tired and breathless, but I'm walking OK and on the mend now."

"What's anosmia?" Vicky interjected.

"It changes the way you smell things. I can't smell some strong smells like curries, but I smell other things which aren't there. I haven't got brain fog or chest and joint pains anymore, but I'm hoping I get my ability to smell back soon. I sniff essential oils. I'm working towards a blindfold test. But here I am, alive with everything I need in life – but love. I don't have much time left, so I want romance. I want to be swept off my feet... by a good kisser and hugger... who is accessible and whom I like."

"Sounds reasonable. Are you putting an ad in a newspaper again? But making it more risqué, like Jane Juska's this time?"

"Mmm, yes, but don't want people feeling sorry for me and thinking I'm a horny old bird looking for a dirty old man. I want to have some dignity! Remind me what sort of thing she said?"

"She was brave, something similar to: 'Before I'm...' whatever age she was, but in your case seventy-five, '...I'd like to have a lot of sex with a man I like', and she said something about Trollope. I suppose so she wouldn't get someone uncultured?"

"Wonder if I'd have got on with Jane Juska? Though not if liking Trollope was a precondition. I've always felt that he was conservative, plodding, unexceptional, his characters lacked life blood, were unreal. Perhaps I could mention the theatre? Do you think I'm mad? I know my hair is dyed, my face is lined, my teeth aren't as white as they were, but they're all my own and my body is looking better than it has for years – now I've been ill and lost weight."

"You do say some rubbish things. I've always told you that you look like Catherine Deneuve! What does James say? Or haven't you run this past him?"

"Yes, yes, I did, and he said, 'Go for it, Mum. I said to you before, it's your turn to have fun.' I don't want to feel desperate or ashamed about this, but perhaps Jane has made it acceptable, to most people I care about anyway. What the hell, the virus is receding. I'll check out the cost of ads and try a tabloid and a broadsheet. What an adventure!"

*

Vicky was walking to the tennis club under a sullen, grey sky, when she saw Michelle cycling towards her. A rather different Michelle. She was wearing dark-coloured cycling shorts and T-shirt, and her hair was tied back and under a cap.

They saw one another and stopped to speak, Vicky becoming aware that a slim, dark-haired woman had stopped behind her friend. "Hi, Vicky, off to play tennis? This is Stella, my new best friend."

Stella smiled in greeting. "Hi, I've heard a lot of good things about you."

"She's making sure I'm properly fit, getting me to do weights and pilates, and I'm teaching her tennis." Michelle turned and grinned at Stella.

"Well, you're looking much healthier – some colour and as if you're eating properly. I read that something like 1.3 million Britons bought a bike since the beginning of the pandemic, for exercise and because they don't want to go on public transport. I don't remember you cycling before."

"No, you're right, we bought them to get around. I mean, wearing masks is mandatory, but some people are not wearing them to be bolshie, particularly young women."

"Yes, TFL is saying, 'Perhaps they don't know.' How could they not, with the notices everywhere on the stations and the PA system blaring out the 'You must wear masks' message? Unfortunately, they probably won't be the ones who develop the symptoms."

"Why don't you come over for tea or early supper when you've got a minute? How about tomorrow?"

"That would be nice, but not free till Saturday for tea."

"Saturday it is, then." And they cycled off.

*

"Do you fancy coming here for a socially distanced barbecue? Paul is keen on barbecuing and we can sit three metres away from one another, on the terrace, in our thermals if it's a cold evening. You could bring that guy you're seeing." Liz had telephoned Vicky.

"Yes, would love to! Sitting in every evening, eating, is making me fat and boring. It will be great to go out. Malcolm is just not well at all, so it'll just be me."

"We'll cross our fingers for a speedy recovery for him, then. Hopefully we'll meet him when he recovers. Yes, all this staying in is becoming the norm, though we drove out to a North London cricket club last night with folding chairs and a picnic, for a bit of comedy entertainment and to support the dying live arts."

"It's strange the government hasn't done more to help theatre and live entertainment. I so miss going to the theatre every week. If my next move is to a care home, I'll be well prepared and morph seamlessly into the lifestyle!"

"Next Saturday then, at 6.30? So sorry about Malcolm."

15 August 2020

Thousands of British holidaymakers have made a last-minute dash to get home before a fourteen-day quarantine requirement came into force for people arriving from France. The isolation measure also applies to the Netherlands, Monaco, Malta, Turks and Caicos, and Aruba, amid concerns about a rising number of COVID cases. Eurotunnel trains have sold out and ferries increased capacity. Air fares are up to six times more than normal. Countries who were targeted for quarantine restriction are those whose infections rates exceeded twenty cases per 100,000 people over seven days. In the UK, the 'Rule of Six' became law yesterday.

Vicky walked to Michelle's semi-detached Edwardian brick villa, in a wide avenue near Hampstead Heath. It was a cloudy day, but the bright flowers in the front garden made it seem almost sunny. Stella, a tall, slim, attractive woman with dark hair in a top knot, answered the door with a big smile. "Hi, Vicky, we can't touch, but do follow me in. We'll sit in the conservatory unless the sun comes out. Michelle is just finishing a Zoom tutorial."

The huge conservatory was warm, and the garden looked still glorious. "My garden is starting to look a bit autumnal. The colours here are stunning," Vicky said, sinking into a comfy chair.

They chit-chatted for a while, and Stella said that she had met Michelle at the Zoom drawing class and there was an instant attraction. "I was married for over twenty-five years. Our sons are forty-three and forty-one. We divorced twenty years ago, though we're still friends. It's been such a revelation how many interests and opinions Michelle and I share. We started spending time together and found that we felt a strong attraction for one another, far more than I have ever experienced before. I was wondering what she was doing every second of the day. My strength of feeling took visceral to another level – when we were together, time stopped. It felt glorious, warm, bubbly, exciting, natural, normal."

"How wonderful," Vicky said.

"Yes, I feel more equal, though I had never been attracted to a woman before – it was foreign to me. I loved my husband deeply, but not my role as a wife. I often felt that I was the support and people identified me through him – though we were both engineers. I wasn't looking for anyone. I had a full and rich life with a circle of friends, babysat for my son – Dominic's two children – and went on painting holidays with my ex-husband. Our culture is afraid of sex. It's like a monster in society and liberation hasn't changed how puritanical most people are. As long as we aren't hurting anyone, there should be no taboos. I read that the Romans would have sex in front of their children. It's now too often in a locked room with the light off! To my surprise I found – and find – Michelle irresistible! Even her ability to get lost in areas she knows doesn't irritate me in the least!"

"Oh, tell me more."

"Last weekend we went to Norfolk and stayed near where she was brought up, so she could show me the wonderful countryside. It was cold and grey when we arrived – but we decided to go for a walk before dinner. We didn't have a map and I didn't realise that Michelle doesn't have a sense of direction. 'We've got Google Maps and I know the paths round here,' she said. Anyway, we meandered about, enjoying the scenery, the emptiness and the clear, fresh air. The light was fading, so I thought we should go back, but she was clueless about where we were and which direction we had to go in. We got out our phones, but there was no reception, blank screens, no Google Maps. So we couldn't phone for help, and even if we could, how could we tell a cab driver or anyone else where we were? We had no idea ourselves and we realised we were in trouble. We wandered about a bit longer – it was almost dark when a cyclist came along. We could have kissed him as he directed us and came some way with us to make sure we didn't get lost again. Eventually stumbling into the hotel, we felt as if we'd walked the Camino de Santiago, not just gone around in a few circles!" She laughed gaily and Vicky joined her.

Then the door opened and in came Michelle.

"Hi, Vicky, so sorry to keep you waiting, the tutorial took longer than I thought."

"Oh, it's fine. Stella has been filling me in on how you met and your exploits last weekend."

Stella went off to get the tea, while Michelle explained that they had recently decided to live together and rent out Stella's flat. "We share the cooking and gardening, and even though this house was Chaika's, we're putting a lot of effort and energy into making our home and garden reflect both our tastes."

"So pleased that you're happy and have found a soulmate – lucky girl!"

"I loved Chaika, but Stella and I touch one another far more. It's like electric shocks sometimes and we have such fun together, say we love one another often, and I feel safe and loved. We share the same studio, so we can see one another as we work. I feel so lucky, because when it comes down to it, aren't friends what we need most in life? If they're a lover too, great, but we need someone who has plenty of time for our relationship, a true... companion."

*

Malcolm was gaunt, with yellow skin and eyes, and was trying not to be depressed with his slow recovery. "My left side is weak, I'm dizzy and my co-ordination so poor. I continually feel sick, and I can't see properly to read. I know removing the tumour entirely is impossible, but I was reading that tumour cells double every ten days! What chance is there for me to get back to normality?" His words came out slowly, as if he were drunk.

"Well, you're hardly missing anything, we can't meet in groups, have to wear a mask and the weather isn't as good as earlier in the year. Be patient," said Vicky. "You know that the pressure of the brain tissue and fluid has altered in your head, so you're bound to have headaches and feel sick. You're doing all the right things – eating healthily, not drinking, trying to exercise when you can – but they said it would take six to twelve months for you to get back to feeling normal."

"I feel so helpless! Being looked after, unable to do much. When you stop working you have to learn to live a new life; to find new challenges, not to rot, as one suddenly has no power. But one still needs to be taken seriously; to be able to achieve things, be given respect. I've set myself goals of self-improvement, without work pressures. Having worked all my life, this is supposed to be the time of the harvest! But I feel as if I've gone into my second childhood, I'm so helpless. It's humiliating. I have always dreaded being a burden, being helped to walk, wearing nappies, and this is before the inevitable deterioration of old age. I've jumped a stage."

He found speech difficult, so this came out in fits and starts, some of which she could barely hear. His silver hair was greasy and lank, his nose red and sore, and cheeks alabaster white and clammy looking.

"Be patient, it will get better." She stood behind him and massaged his tense shoulders, until Alison came to take over his care.

*

Paul had been in love quite a few times in his life and now there was Liz. Why did he love her? Well, she was very attractive, bright and vivacious, in fact beautiful, when her smile lit up her high-cheekboned, almost perfectly symmetrical face. She took pleasure in the little tasks that order the day, like washing, watering, cleaning, gardening, and her face showed contented happiness when they sat down for a meal together. She made him feel like a roaring engine, an essential part of her life; he wanted to be useful to her. They listened to one another, had strong, intellectual discussions, cared, tried to please. And he was lonely. Men are encouraged to be self-reliant. He was an urbane, fun, party type, and at the peak of his career he could be out drinking champagne every night. He had 500 friends on Facebook and over 800 followers on Instagram. But if he didn't call these 'show ponies', it was so rare that they called him.

Liz had come out to the shed, where he was making a bird box.

"All these months at home have turned you into a brilliant man about the house!"

"I didn't have a toolbox before, and I hadn't realised how satisfying building, mending and fixing things could be," Paul said with a smile.

"You're brilliant at it. And grilling, you've become a pro!"

"A grill snob, you mean! I loved my propane barbecue. Now, unless other grillers have got black fingernails, smell of wood smoke and can discuss the merits of different types of charcoal, they're amateurs to me. And you're the salad queen. Everyone is always impressed with those."

"What's great about the Rule of Six is that we don't have to invite any boring partners of our friends," said Liz happily.

"Who are you referring to?"

"Come on, who's got the charm of a damp grey towel and rarely says anything interesting?"

"That's cruel. Mike is a great companion, so supportive to Annie."

"That's as may be, but he's had a charisma bypass and we all dread being trapped in a corner with him telling us about his latest cycling trip. Vic can come, but Malcolm's still too ill, so I've invited just Annie, plus Gaby and Stephen, as we're not allowed to be more than six! I'm sure that in this strange period, even those of us who are normally courteous and well-mannered will pare down the things we do and cross out the things which don't fill us with joy, because each outing carries an inherent risk of illness, so we will be weighing up how much happiness each one brings us. Seeing a depressing friend who moans and never asks you about yourself, they'll be out, and no more eating not very nice food at dinner parties. We will have the phrase, 'What a pity, rules are rules.' We'll be able to engage more closely with the activities and people who interest us. We can pare our social circle back to those who are important to us!"

Paul smiled. "Mmm, maybe," he said in a humouring tone, and wandered off towards the house with his tape measure.

*

Ruth and Vicky were walking on the Heath. "I was reading about a report from the Royal College of Psychiatrists which found that the number of people drinking too much has doubled in lockdown. That's certainly the case with us. How about you?" Ruth asked.

"I've tried really hard to not drink half the week. I know it's not a destresser. I could never understand how Rob slept, as he always had to have a glass of wine last thing."

"Yes, it increases our heart rate, stops us sleeping and is a depressant. If someone feels pressured and stressed, using alcohol as an escape is no good – it just suppresses your emotions, so you think they're gone. Your body needs sleep, water and good food, not alcohol. Anyway, how is Malcolm?"

"He's having radiation therapy and oral chemo, which means nausea, exhaustion, headaches, aching joints, stomach ache and hair loss. I feel so sorry for him. I called for him yesterday to take a gentle stroll in the park and he had on a woolly hat, cos he's bald now, a jumper and thick jacket, though it was a warm day."

"Removing tumours can cause huge damage. He will have focal neurological deficits. Has he got epilepsy and spatial dyslexia? That's if he tries to move one way, his body goes the other."

"No, thank goodness. Shall we go to Kenwood cafe for tea and one of those round, flapjacky cakes covered with nuts?"

"Need you ask?"

25 August 2020

Various other countries have now gone over the UK government's threshold of twenty coronavirus cases per 100,000 people and may be considered for quarantine

measures. Switzerland, the Czech Republic and Greece may be the next. Tory backbenchers are attacking the 'chaos' of the government's quarantine policy and calling for airport testing, which thirty other countries are doing. Heathrow has set up the UK's first COVID-19 testing facility to test passengers on their arrival, but it is not being used. The Prime Minister has done a U-turn and masks are to be worn in secondary schools in lockdown areas, and other schools can choose whether pupils wear them.

Debs and Vicky were relaxing with a drink on the balcony of the tennis club after their game of singles.

"That was quite successful for a first event, in a possible pause in a pandemic."

"Yes, we kept socially distanced and eyed one another up. Everyone seemed keen to do it again, even if we have to use Zoom next time, and expand it to others. I was glad to meet Jo, we hear such a lot about one another from you. She told me she had invited six men for a weekend. She's *so* brave! Wish I had the guts – but of course she has got a seaside cottage to tempt them."

"Christine was talking to Tony from the tennis club most of the time – they seemed to get on well."

"Yes, ten people isn't many, but it'll grow. Shall we call the group, 'The Silver Foxes'? I know it's usually a name for older men, but vixens doesn't sound as compellin'."

"Sounds good, why not. Did you see that Adria tour was cancelled after half a dozen players tested positive. They were playing basketball, then dancing about in a nightclub, hugging after their games and… Djokovic is so stupid."

"Mmm – I know there haven't been many cases in Belgrade, but the whole world is being careful and he organises a tour and shakes hands with umpires, gives ball-boys their towels and sells tickets to 4,000 spectators!"

Vicky swivelled her legs out from under the table and stretched them in the sun. "Did you see them after the matches? Surrounded by fans, taking selfies and signing autographs. Do you want another drink?"

"No thanks, it's time for some lunch. I've put on weight over this lockdown *and* got COVID face!" She craned forward towards Vicky. "Look at it! Grey, lined, two chins, I look like some exhumed ancestor! I could pass for eighty!"

Vicky smiled. "You don't look any different to me. Apparently, half the women in the UK say they have aged with all the stress, anxiety, too much alcohol and food generally. I've piled on the pounds. Eating is one of the few things we're still allowed to do."

"Well, I notice it at Zoom meetings. I look ancient. All the blue light from extra time on the laptop makes the skin dull, wrinkly and aged. Crow's feet at the corner of my eyes, little vertical lines at the corners of my mouth. God, can six months age one so quickly? When we get back to dressin' up, will I look like resplendent mutton in this age-phobic society? We both try to be outside exercisin' most days. I need to stop worryin' about the future, sleep longer, eat more healthily. Shall we try to not drink for a week?"

"A bit more age positivity, please! But you're right, we all know what to do, it's doing it that's the problem. I don't drink if I'm with Malcolm anyway."

"How often do you see him, and how is he?"

"Most days. I don't go when his sister or daughter are there. He's having difficulty walking now, and concentrating, and remembering things. He has occupational therapy and physio, but he's had a few fits – sort of epileptic fits. He's not well at all."

"Terrible. I'm so sorry, Vic."

*

Gerry had been into the city for a socially distanced drink with an old friend. He wandered into the kitchen where Ruth was making a casserole. "The city centres are ghostly, empty. If people won't come back to work, as Boris has asked them to, why not employ some bright young people in India at a fraction of the wages?"

She turned, smiling. He really was clubbable, suave, charming; he made her heart beat faster. "People don't want to do the long, expensive commute, eat overpriced sandwiches, wear sweaty suits. The reality of white-collar life seems a waste of human life. At home they feel like captains of their fate and masters of their souls."

She had a smudge of flour on her nose; he rubbed it off and felt her body heat. She smelt of roses and really was very sexually attractive – soft, slender and supple, interesting, and always cheerful. "Shall we go to the south coast to a hotel at the weekend? We need a change, something special after these months of hibernation – don't we?"

"That would be nice, while the weather is still warm."

*

Vicky and Jo met at their usual cafe.

"Well, I didn't get sixty-three replies, not even twenty-three. Got twelve in the end. But remembering Jane Juska coming to regret some of those she put into the 'No' pile, I didn't use distance from London as a criterion, only arrogance and really old men – there were four of them. I'm replying to eight, sending my photo and a bit about me – like, I was an English teacher, one son, husband died, and asking for a recent photo of them and asking a few questions. Such as: where did they grow up, what did they work at, children, their music, reading tastes. And asking them if they would be prepared to have a lateral flow COVID test just before they come to Wales for the weekend – as I will. I'll invite them to my cottage. If I borrow Susan's house next door, that will be three bedrooms, so I can ask six. Should I ask them for their sexual history, you know, if any of them have had venereal diseases?"

"I think not, Jo, that sounds rather rude, but otherwise, go for it!"

"Learning to live around a highly transmissible virus has made me worry that everyone could have asymptomatic COVID. I can't switch off my hyperawareness of proximity and hygiene. You know, it's a paradox. What am I looking for? Someone different from me who is exciting and challenging, or someone comfortably like me? Isn't it true that humans tend to pair-bond and form relationships within their social class and level of attractiveness? It's the human condition to want to share one's existence with somebody, isn't it? But if their post-lockdown outlook is not to wear a mask or have a vaccine, that would be the end for me. Do you want to come and see who I choose?"

"I don't think I should be sticking my oar in, we go for different types. And I'm taller than you, so would be worrying that they could be midgets. I read that men add an inch or so and women subtract fifteen pounds. You can tell me about them after, though."

*

From the replies, Jo chose her six and wrote them invitation letters. Ray got cold feet, he'd changed his mind. Pity, he sounded good. She asked the first reserve, Sammy.

Simon, the college professor, said he was a luddite and to make sure she rang or wrote the directions to him as he rarely did email. He was seventy-three and was divorced ten years ago. He had a deep, warm voice which would be easy to fall in love with. They started chatting every day. "I might be falling in love with you," he said.

*

"Vic, I know I'll end up back in hospital," Malcolm said. "The thought of it is making me weaker."

The dark creases under his eyes seemed to be spreading and becoming blacker in his anguish.

"Why? Surely things will improve if you're in there, seeing the top consultants daily?"

"In hospital I'm a patient, a medical case, my body is taken from me, and things are done to me over which I have no control. I'm a case, described by a technical vocabulary. The subject of impersonal attention, and I've lost my selfhood. I lie, waiting, not hungry, not thirsty, not thinking, not me…"

"Hopefully you'll be back to being you very soon."

But he had gone back deep inside himself, with no more energy for the outside world.

30 August 2020

> There are 25 million COVID-19 cases in 188 countries. In Germany, 40,000 people have demonstrated against the government's COVID protection measures. In the UK, Leicester, Luton, Northampton, Manchester, Preston and Glasgow are hotspots. Most are linked to big indoor gatherings. The 'Eat Out to Help Out' deal ends today, and schools start back tomorrow.

"How are you, Marion?" She and Vicky were passing in the street.

"OK. I'm trying to stop watching the news and all the programmes about the virus so obsessively to protect my mental health. So I thought I'd go for a walk when the lunchtime news was on. My garden is looking good, but I've still got projects to complete in it. Not when those children are screeching, screaming, howling, yelling and kicking balls over, though. It's hell when they are let loose."

A young family had bought the garden flat next door to Marion, their noise was ruining her life in her garden.

"Have you started to play bridge again?"

"Not meeting with my friends, just Joyce and I play online – badly usually. We were last this morning. She's starting to dement, I think. It doesn't matter that she weaves in false memories from the TV into her stories about herself, embroidering and embellishing, but she's losing the thread when we play and playing with yesterday's cards – not the ones in her hand."

"I'm sure it's good for her to keep trying to play, though. Did you read about the crime rate in Japan by women over sixty-five quadrupling?"

"No, why is that?"

"It's because they want to be sent to prison where they are fed and they have people to talk to! Isolation for the elderly is such an issue."

"Luckily I like my own company."

*

Barry didn't understand how it had happened, but a strange coldness had arisen between himself and Janet. The unspoken understanding they had was gone, to be replaced by unfriendly indifference. He felt that what he said to her didn't penetrate; her essence was off somewhere else. He watched her on her phone. How beautiful she was, how perfect, how radiant. Without her, life was meaningless. She had finished her call.

"I don't want to lose you, Jan."

"Don't you?"

"I know I've been stupid, refusing to live at your place, accusing you of not exciting me sexually, not compromising my way of life as much as I should have. We have spent so much time together, circumstantially, it might have been too much. But we've learnt how to fall in love again and got to know one another even more deeply." He felt her relaxing, softening. "Can we try again?"

"Are you sure you want to?" Her voice was gentle. "I've been selfish, set in my ways, and I was so thrilled to get this chance at the end of our lives, to be with someone I loved and could love again."

"Neither of us has tried hard enough. I've expected too much of you and though I wanted this adventure, I also missed my single, selfish life." His fear of her leaving him was beginning to recede. In long-term relationships there's a balance of power; it becomes easy to hurt and also how to please one another. But if you matter to one another, massive compromises have to be made. "So can we try again, at your house this time?" he said.

She smiled. "Sex is powerful, important and fun, but it is only sex. If we find we can only rarely manage it, well, so what, there's the rest of our lives together."

He put his arms out, and she went inside them and they hugged.

"Let's try to be patient with one another. We've both been on our own too long. We'll try to be more loving, patient and honest. I'm going to stay with my sister tomorrow. Let's talk about it again when I get back?"

"We'll make it work," he agreed.

*

Gerry and Ruth were staying at the Grand in Eastbourne. They had walked the esplanade, she had had a swim in the sea and then they had both had a massage and swum in the hotel's heated outdoor pool. After a delicious dinner and perhaps too many glasses of wine, they were lying on the bed watching the ten o'clock news.

"Sorry I'm getting so old and forgetful," he said. "If I get too doddery, just put me in a home!"

"Silly man," she said. "Just try not to get distracted. Wasn't it Samuel Johnson who said, 'the art of memory is the art of attention'? You've often got too many things to think about."

He couldn't remember when they had last had sex, they often went to bed at different times. Was it two or three months, more? She was a younger woman and had always seemed to enjoy it. Was he being thoughtless? It had been spontaneous lust for so long, perhaps they should make appointments now, so it actually happened.

She was naked underneath her dressing gown; he could feel her quickened, excited breathing as he moved towards her and she pressed herself against him, her lips on the little silky bristles on his jaw. He could smell a perfume on her hair. *Touch me all over*, she thought, and he mind-read, running his hands up her legs, round her shoulders, past her breasts and to her clitoris. She fumbled for the remote control and stabbed the TV to silence, then slid her hands over his bottom, cupped his scrotal sac and rubbed behind it. Gently milking his penis, it sprang into life... "Put it in me," she demanded, "it's hard enough." So, he did, wetting it with his saliva and easing it in. After a few minutes of gentle in and out motion he felt himself shrinking.

"Touch me, rub me, please," she asked.

He found the most sensitive part of her clitoris and could feel her body vibrating. "Harder, harder, please! Yes, yes, yes!" Then her orgasm hit her, she shuddered, and her body bucked with its power. She lay there, limp, sweating and trembling, and he stroked her gently, until she drifted off to sleep. *I've been selfish*, he thought. *Must give her more pleasure.*

*

Nusheen had come to chat to Vicky in her garden. It had rained and the sun refracted through the drops of water on the leaves so they glistened. "I haven't seen you since you had the party here."

"No, what did you think?"

"It was pleasant, but I couldn't get rid of that Alistair. It was irritating how intensely he kept looking at me, as if I was going to do an exotic dance or something. He wouldn't leave me alone."

"Well, you are rather stunning, Nusheen, you can't blame him."

"The point is, I told him I was married. But even so, he asked me to have dinner with him! He's a bit chubby and pale for me, and reeks of coffee, cigarette breath and expensive aftershave – so even if I were free… Farzad would have killed me if he'd seen me chatting to him. I'd better not come again. He was eating more than his fair share of the vegetable crisps, greasy fingers dipping into the bowl, so others hung back. And he called me an Asian woman a few times. I said to him, 'Don't stereotype me, why should that describe me? Everyone who is reduced to a category feels like this. Women, disabled people, black people, they all want to be seen as themselves, not their label.' He did apologise." Her large, well-spaced, heavy-lidded eyes were wide and her lips drooped with her hurt.

"Nusheen, you've been wanting some more social life. Yes, Alistair has a big belly. He's had it so long, it's who he is. He wouldn't be Alistair without it. Hopefully there will be more people next time and you can smile and walk away from him and chat to them."

"Yes, I suppose so, at least he isn't casually racist. So often at parties someone has said to me something like, did you have an arranged marriage? Do you know any suicide bombers? Or did you have FGM? Or they speak slowly to me as if I don't understand English! I was brought up here – it's always so upsetting!"

*

Malcolm was sitting in the kitchen watching Vicky. "I don't seem to be getting better, in fact I'm getting worse, and I feel everyone must be getting impatient with having to devote parts of their lives to being with me."

"Bec and Alison wouldn't want to be anywhere else, and neither would I. Don't worry, don't feel stressed or you certainly won't improve." She was making vegetable soup with kale and broccoli from her garden, together with the remnants of the organic veg box Alison ordered.

"I've never asked you, but are you comfortably off?"

"Well, most of my 'wealth' is the house, which has really increased in value. But yes, I've got enough to last me. As you know, women CEOs are never offered the same financial packages as men, but I wanted to do the job, so I didn't haggle. I was living with Rob, so didn't have all the bills to pay myself. I never asked him to share the expense of bringing up Sophie, though. She wasn't his daughter and she resented him."

"How did he get on with her?"

"He didn't try to be her father, he understood her devotion to her real one, who by the way rarely bothered with her. But Rob was there for her if she needed lifts, or any kind of help."

"Sounds the perfect partner."

"Yes, he was rather. I was lucky to meet him."

*

Jo's excitement and tension mounted as the date got nearer. How had she dared do this? A few days before, her terror increased. What had she been thinking of? She hadn't been able to sleep, constantly felt she might faint, and the closer the day got, she was so panicky she almost cancelled it.

5–6 September 2020

Melbourne remains in hard lockdown despite a fall in cases. The US has more than 50,000 new cases, though New York State infection rate is below one for the twenty-ninth day.

India has 86,432 new cases. South Korea has the lowest daily total for three weeks. Despite the UK government exhorting workers and putting pleading ads everywhere to try to get people to go back to the office, people are still working from home, and a third of the Pret a Manger sandwich workforce have lost their jobs.

Jo sat on the wall outside the 'fourth cottage from the end' that she had described to the men. "You'll have to park in the station car park if you come by car. There's one train a day which arrives at 5.16. You have to wear a mask on trains but not in shops in Wales. I suggest you all aim to arrive at 5.30. Walk down through the village towards the sea and turn right when you get to the end. The little road is called Winklesea Lane."

It was 5.20 and she felt a vague anguish, like a shadow or mist, pressing over her soul. Sitting on the wall in front of her cottage, in the sun, in her shorts and T-shirt, swinging her newly slim, brown legs, she wasn't registering the bank in front of her on the other side of the lane. It was covered with big daisies, in a tangle with herb robert, red bladder campion and convolvulus. Or, beyond that, a faraway ship, melting hazily into the blue of the horizon.

The first one to arrive was the apparently self-assured Clive. She had been rather shocked by his arrogant reply. He had written:

"I consider myself a rare animal. I'm strong, from regular weightlifting, perfect teeth, tattoos on my chest. Was a chief constable in the CID and divorced. I'm confident that girls will perceive me as high SMV (sexual market value)."

But she had decided to see if his confidence was just bravado.

He came striding down the sun-whitened lane, marching as if he had been in the army, barrel-chested, bald, very strong looking and tall. She thought it must have taken a lot of effort to find a shirt as awful as the one he was wearing – turquoise with red and orange swirls.

"Hello there," he shouted as he spotted her.

They touched elbows; she stood on tiptoe so her five foot three inches reached.

She was nervous, her mouth full of chalk. "Thanks for coming, did you have a good trip?"

"Yes, drove too fast probably, but had rather a late start."

"It's a lovely spot for a few days, isn't it? Would you like to freshen up, either in this cottage or this one, and choose your bed? I'm afraid you'll all be sharing rooms."

Three other men were approaching. Would she recognise who was who from their photographs?

Mmm, I think the bearded one in the front is Simon, the college professor. Thin, receding hair and a tweed jacket, walks like a speed walker, his feet low to the ground. He's not so gorgeous as his voice. Then that could be Adrian, the ex-civil servant, gliding like a slinking panther, with a pale face, pale hair, gold-rimmed spectacles. The sun making him look buttered. Or is it Garry, the computer guy? That must be Chris, the insurance man, curly, thick grey hair, elegantly dressed, a lined face of indeterminate age.

They reached her and introduced themselves. She was right, it was Adrian. But before she could show them around, Sammy, the rather Mephistophelian-looking restaurateur, was hurrying towards them, walking on his toes, bouncing along.

She made tea or coffee for them all, and they sat in her garden with the cake she had brought with her, and chatted about their journeys, the view, and when they would wear masks. Then they went for a stroll on the cliff path, to a little bay where she and Chris, minus the cashmere jacket and linen chinos, swam. The others had 'forgotten' to bring their bathers.

Simon had recently retired. He loved long walks and went off with Adrian to walk further. His voice was still the one which gave her goose bumps.

She had asked them to bring the wine and she provided a cold spread for Friday evening. Ciabatta, cheeses, chicken legs, quiche and a couple of salads. Sammy had brought an aubergine dish to add to the spread. The second night she had booked the pub/diner which had just opened up again, where they could eat outside.

Chris had brought two bottles of champagne. So, when they had all gathered back in her small garden, they opened them and discussed relationships. "I'm a romantic, an idealist and a dreamer," said Chris. "But I've realised late in my life that relationships have to be worked at. They're not a walk in the park. I've been divorced twice and Sonia, my lover, died a few months ago. I should have married her. I was selfish not to have realised till the end – it was what she'd wanted."

Sammy's wife had died three years ago. He was passing his restaurant to his son and daughter and hoping that they could bring it back to life after lockdown. Adrian's wife had also died, twenty years ago, and Simon and Clive were divorced. Simon admitted to having affairs with students when younger, and Clive said his wife thought he cared more about fitness than her. They were all surprisingly honest about their failings and were all younger than her, apart from Adrian, who looked a very fit over-eighty, though he didn't disclose his age. Sadly, Garry hadn't turned up and Jo found a text from him, saying he was chickening out of the 'beauty contest', but he would be happy to take her to the BFI to see a film of her choice sometime.

She felt pleasantly tipsy as she went inside to lay out the supper dishes. Standing at the sink, washing the salad, she felt someone's hands cupping her buttocks, gently rubbing and squeezing. She stood still, enjoying it for a few seconds, then turned and handed a masked Chris the washed salad to put on the table. Did she fancy him? *Mmm, he got me going there, and he's very smooth, articulate and confident, could give me a good time.*

It was dark outside, so they congregated indoors, with their masks on. When she bought the cottage, Jo had all the downstairs knocked into one big room with the kitchen at one end. She had bought a big table, worn to whiteness with the years of being scrubbed, which the six of them fitted around easily with social distancing. Sammy warmed up his parmigiana in the microwave and Adrian poured wine for everyone. Then they sat down to eat and chat.

Clive narcissistically talked and talked, and talked some more, about himself and his love for musical comedy such as *Hairspray*, *Kiss Me Kate* and *Cats*. Adrian loved live theatre, particularly classics, and Chris, opera and films. They all bemoaned the fact that live shows wouldn't be back for a long time, if ever. Sammy had of course worked every evening and hadn't had time for anything else, and Simon seemed to have lectured in universities far from cultural centres, but they both discussed their love of travel. Simon was writing a novel and obviously thought he was destined for greatness. This weekend meant he was now behind schedule. *Half the world are writing the great novel*, she thought scathingly. *Only a few get published. Perhaps he has friends in the industry, or his college would publish it for him.*

At first, she had been very nervous, having got all these men here. What were they thinking of her? She got up and opened the door to the garden a little further, letting the cool night air flow over her. But as the evening progressed, she became more confident and talked Proust and Eliot with Simon, fringe theatre productions with Adrian, and French cinema with Chris.

In no time it was eleven o'clock and time to start thinking about sleep. As Clive had arrived first, he had bagged the bedroom in her cottage and they had left the other bed in that room for Garry, in case he came late. So Chris and Simon reluctantly headed off to next door, while Sammy and Adrian washed and dried the dishes before following them. Jo put all the uneaten food in the fridge, then went up to bed.

In the bathroom while cleaning her teeth, Jo stared in the mirror, noting the lines around her mouth and eyes and her wrinkled saggy neck. *I'm certainly no longer beautiful, but in a poor light, with the fuck-me smile that Al always said I had, hopefully I'll do.*

She was undressing, when her door opened and a completely nude, masked Clive came in. Without a word he backed her up to the bed, pulled down her last items of clothing and drew her towards him. She touched his erect penis; it was warm and smooth and bucked at her touch. He lifted her onto the bed and his hand played over her clitoris. She came in seconds. Then he pushed into her and very quickly came. *What about my G-spot?* she wondered. It was too quick; she lay there hoping for a rerun.

But he seemed rather abashed at his actions, apologised and retreated to his room. *Shame*, she thought, *that was rather nice, it had potential.*

The next morning the sun was shining, and it felt hot at eight. She got up, made herself a cup of tea and laid the table with muesli, yoghurt, eggs, wholewheat bread and the strawberry jam Vicky had made earlier in the year. Strawberries had been cheap, because there had been no Wimbledon. The sun was pouring in, and the fridge was doing its usual thing, of shaking itself like a wet dog and then clicking off. She wandered into the garden to drink her tea.

The sea lay asleep, hardly stirring, and behind the cottage the blue-grey mountains were asleep too. Lovely scents came up from her herb bed as she watered it, and a gentle breeze lifted her hair and swayed the penstemon, phlox and verbena in the flowerbed by the gate.

She was at the sink, washing her mug when she felt hands on her buttocks again; they slid up to her breasts and cradled them. "Look what you've done to me," Chris said, turning her around and directing her right hand to his erect penis, pushing through his trousers. She was feeling quite aroused, when there was a voice from behind. "Is this a help oneself breakfast?" And Adrian was there, reaching for the kettle.

He smiled at them shyly, and up close she admired his lovely lips, startling blue eyes and unlined skin as Chris slunk away. *Well, this is turning out to be fun*, she thought.

When they had all had some breakfast, they talked about what to do for the day. Sammy and Clive thought they'd like to look at the nearby small town. Chris thought he'd laze around, read and swim, while Simon and Adrian said they'd take a walk in the opposite direction to yesterday. "Are you thinking of swimming today?" she asked them.

"I might," said Adrian.

"I'm no swimmer," said Simon.

"Well, I'm no walker, but I'll come for a while with you and then swim," she decided. So off they went.

After a couple of miles, they arrived at a lovely cove, which Jo couldn't resist. "Think I've walked far enough, time for a swim and read," she said. Simon carried on, but Adrian stripped to his briefs and plunged into the water. It was delicious, calm, clear, velvety. He swam out with a stylish, powerful crawl and lay looking up at the cloudless sky and boats on the horizon. Jo rarely went out of her depth, so breast-stroked back and forth looking at the endless heather, the sky reflecting its colours, the rock strata patterns on the cliffs and the seagulls' nests on the ledges…

Then she lay on her towel on the warm sand.

He hadn't brought a towel, so they sat on hers. He really had a nice body, slim and supple. He moved well, in a compact, graceful motion. "How many men have fallen in love with you?" he asked. "And how many have you manipulated and intrigued?"

She smiled at the thought. "What made you answer my ad?"

"I've had a long-standing relationship with a past colleague, but she went to Australia to visit her sister and is staying for six months. So when I saw what you wrote, I thought, I've always been so predictable and safe. Why don't I do something out of character, something to take me out of my comfort zone? So here I am. Not debonair man of the world, though, more like a panicky teenage virgin on a first date."

His beautiful lips parted in a smile, and she wanted so much to kiss them. She leant towards him, took his face in her hands and kissed his sensuous mouth. He was immobile and stiff. *Does he find me too fat, old, plain?* Then suddenly the tension in his body relaxed and he put his arms around her and pushed her down, the few strands of his dark hair that he still had falling forward over his brow.

She was aroused and wanted more than anything for him to take her, though this made her feel embarrassed and needy, like a sex-mad beggar. *It's been so long since I've been near men like this.* Then he was on top of her, half kneeling, straddling her, so she wasn't bearing his weight.

"Hasn't this weekend made you feel vulnerable?"

She was arching towards his penis, both their bodies wet and slithery. She wanted him entering her, inside her, filling her.

"Well, yes, but I'm hoping for so much pleasure."

A ghost of a smile passed his lips, revealing his perfect white teeth. His mouth was very distracting. And then he moved her bikini down, and slid inside and plunged, plunged. His penis was long and warm, and she felt it on her cervix, bumping. Their hip bones ground together, but after many minutes, she still hadn't had an orgasm, so he slid out, asked her to spread her legs and rubbed and licked until she became frantic and crashed, and then he subsided onto her.

"But you didn't have an orgasm?"

"I wanted you to enjoy it."

I think I could love this man, she thought.

Minutes later and he was stripping off his briefs, stepping into his shorts and pulling on his socks and shoes. "I said I'd catch Simon up, perhaps I'll meet him on the way back."

And he was gone, scrambling up the heather and gorse-covered bank to the path…

Jo lay a few more minutes, exulting in the passion, her clitoris still tingling. What an amazing weekend.

*

The second night at the gastropub went quickly. She wore her 'throw-on' dress, the sort that sold out several times over last summer – a tiered, broderie, white midi, loose and comfortable, yet still looked pretty. Everyone chatted, enjoyed the food and got a little inebriated. Simon left early, having taken an indigestion pill. "I suffer badly with food intolerances and digestive problems," he said. "Sorry to be a wimp, but I think bed is the place for me." Jo felt a little sad that she hadn't got to know him. He was tallish, pleasant-looking, cultured, a good storyteller, interested in nature and gardening, had named all the wildflowers on their walk to the pub. He had potential. *Seems a bit up himself, though*, she thought, *don't know why he came. Perhaps he just doesn't fancy me.*

Sammy seemed to be nursing grief for his wife and closed restaurant; he didn't really join in the chat, just too preoccupied and distracted. He wasn't very fit, tended to shuffle rather than walk, had very hairy ears and admitted that his daughter had pushed him to come on this weekend. Adrian couldn't have got much sleep, as he said that Sammy emitted a symphony of grunts, snorts and whistles most of the night.

Chris seemed a bit of a joker; he had a quip for every topic but was highly knowledgeable and amusing. Clive was very confident, but his descriptions of things felt rather ponderous, particularly his description of one's SMV, which apparently goes up if you're seen with a good-looking partner. This makes you more attractive to potential partners. And how you can gauge your SMV is by seeing how many attractive women/men look at you when walking by. She was staggered by his lack of humility. Adrian was fairly quiet, but observant, seemed sensitive and kind and was certainly a good lover.

They walked back to the cottages, loudly singing old Beatles songs, led by Clive, who sang in a choir. "Valerian tea?" she asked Clive. "It helps you sleep."

"Don't get much of a problem sleeping," he said. "But yes, why not, I'll try it."

They carried their tea up to their bedrooms, and she had no sooner come out of the bathroom, stripped and was standing sipping her tea, when he opened the door and without asking, backed her up to the bed again. "Hang on, let me put this mug down," she said and wondered if she should resist, but his warm, smooth, hard penis was poking between her legs and he had his hand on her clitoris. *Why not*, she thought and lay down with a thump on the bed behind and came in seconds with his insistently rubbing fingers. He pushed inside her, a few thrusts and he climaxed. "You need some lubricant. You're so dry I can't last long."

Oh, so his short performance is my fault? she thought.

She lay in bed. *Well, three orgasms in two days isn't bad, though not vaginal. I didn't really have one with Al either, I thought it was him. Perhaps I don't have a G-spot. If I did it's been dormant for too long, so forget it, Jo.*

The next morning, Sunday, a soft mist had rolled in from the sea, settling all over the garden, like sticky, grubby wool and blanking out the view. It seemed to augur the ending and they all left quite promptly after breakfast. There was a train at ten which Adrian and Simon were catching; the others were driving. "Keep in touch," she said to the group as they collected at the cottage door. "I've enjoyed meeting you all." And off they all went.

Well, I enjoyed the weekend and the sex, she thought. *Do I want to see any of them again? Hmm, I thought Simon had potential, but he wasn't interested, he's in his own world. Sammy wasn't up for anything, Clive was too full of himself and would go for a younger model. Chris was rather disturbing, touching me, and Adrian was the best, but has a partner.*

Twenty minutes later, there was a knock on the door and Chris opened it. "I think we have some unfinished business."

He dropped his man bag, strode towards her and cupping her buttocks, pulled her towards himself. She could smell the aftershave on his smooth skin, feel his erect penis.

His fingers were expertly removing her G-string and rubbing her clitoris. She squirmed with pleasure. Then he pushed her down onto her furry rug, straddled her and pushed himself in. They humped for a few minutes, rolling over so their loose skin flopped over one another, until he came inside her. He collapsed next to her while his insistent fingers brought her to orgasm.

Lying there, she thought how very nice this could be.

He was relaxed and his eyes were closed. "Do you want a tea or coffee?" she asked.

"Would prefer to finish off the wine," he answered.

She got herself up and fetched two glasses, the Rioja left from the first night and some bread, cheese and bits of quiche. It was cloudy and cooler outside, so they ate, propped up against the couch on the thick, furry rug.

Not long after, he rolled on top of her and aroused them both by rubbing himself up and down. She took his penis in her mouth; it was a nice size and shape and smooth and warm. He was getting towards orgasm but pulled out of her mouth and pushed inside her. It felt such a good fit, so right, such pleasure, then he filled her and straight away put his tongue inside her until she felt she would burst with ecstasy.

He lifted himself off her and she couldn't help seeing that the skin on his face was falling towards her, off the bones. *We are both deteriorating, dying, but until we do, I want to keep doing this...*

After a five-minute rest, he got up, dressed and made himself a coffee. "I've got a long drive, better go. Thanks for the weekend."

It seemed rather an abrupt ending to the delicious sex. "Are we going to meet up again?" she asked, her voice coming out breathily as she was still feeling euphoric with afterglow.

He was slipping his feet into crossover-strap Prada sandals. "Only if you get some lubricant, like 'Silk'. You're too dry and I can't get in you easily, so come too soon." He smiled, but it didn't reach his eyes, saluted and said, "Thanks for the weekend," and was gone.

9 September 2020

> Moria camp on Lesbos has been completely destroyed by fires, fanned by high winds. There are now 13,000 people homeless and sitting on the streets near the scorched remains, forbidden to leave by the police. From the 14th, people in England cannot meet people from other households, either in or outside, in groups larger than six, and people in Wales must wear masks in shops. The rates of infection are increasing; it has doubled in Birmingham, and that city, like Caerphilly, will have to have stricter lockdown measures enforced. A Department of Health report says that there are 1,100 new coronavirus cases every day in care homes currently, mainly among the workforce.

Jo and Vicky met up for a walk on the Heath.

"So how was it? Tell," asked Vicky enthusiastically.

"Well, definitely interesting and because my ad said I wanted to have sex, I certainly did, with three of them!"

"Wow, really? How did you manage that in two small cottages with six men?"

"Only five turned up and three guys used their opportunities." She described the scenarios. "But though it was all very exciting, none of them lasted long inside me and two were quite rude about how dry I was, saying that was the reason for their quick performances. And no one asked to see me again, though I suppose they might contact me."

"Why do you think they came, then? Adventure? A last fling? To test their sexual prowess?"

"All of that, I should think. Being old and alone isn't an attractive prospect and death is coming closer. They probably thought I wanted it badly and that's why they'd been invited. They were all fittish and healthy. Don't people who have sex live longer? Perhaps they've found their virility waning, so wanted to try it out with a different partner, a keen one, and that's why they blamed me for not going on longer. Though they were all skilful at giving me clitoral orgasms. Getting partners gets harder as we get older; we're seen as 'horny old broads' or 'dirty old men'. It must have made a change to have a fully compliant, no-strings-attached partner."

"Tell me about them. Who did you like best?"

"I thought at first sight, Simon, the college history professor, who loves travel. He had a deep, melodic voice and was fit, but he was rather into himself and his novel writing. He seemed to be sorry he came, though that could have been when he saw me. Sammy is a restaurateur, there was something Mephistophelian about him. Dark hair in his ears, broken blood vessels in his nostrils; he'd been sent by his daughters because after fifty years of marriage to their mother, he was lonely when she died. Men struggle to manage loneliness as they are less likely to have friends to talk to. But he was never up for anything really. Clive, ex-CID, thought too much of himself, was tough – a bit bitter and argumentative – and Chris was also up himself – a libidinous opportunist really. He's a partner in an insurance company – long divorced, loves opera and art movies. Don't know when he did any work, as he said he was a member of the Groucho, Savile and the Chelsea Arts clubs!

"So, Adrian, I suppose. An ex-civil servant who goes to classic theatre. He was the oldest, but had good skin, lovely lips and nice body. He has a partner, though – who has gone to Australia for six months. I may try to see him while she's still away, if he doesn't feel too guilty. He respects and esteems her, but she may well be more like a sister. He seems to have had a life of routine and self-denial and refused adventure and insecurity. Perhaps I could spice up the rest of his life? And of course, I haven't met Garry yet. He's still working as a project manager in computers for a bank. He loves old films and belongs to the British Film Institute."

"Mmm, so it was all worth it, then? You certainly look glowing and healthy!"

"I'll have to do something about being dry before I meet anyone else, don't you think?"

"Perhaps you should have said, 'Well, you weren't very stimulating – to arouse me!' Ruth and I talked about it once. As you know, it's because of the hormonal changes women get. In midlife the ovaries stop making oestrogen, the vaginal lining becomes thinner and less elastic. Fortunately, there are plenty of lubricants on the market. Or go to the doctor and get a prescription for oestrogen-releasing pessaries. I tried them once, years ago, and the doctor mistakenly gave me 25-milligram pessaries, which had a huge effect on my heart. I couldn't sleep and was hyper. Then I saw on the internet that 5–10 milligrams was the correct dose, so stopped using them immediately, but they still affected me. I had little sort of fainty bouts, as if blood wasn't getting to my head, so I had to flap my arms, then I was OK… Some research I saw from Indiana University showed that women who use vibrators have better sexual function and satisfaction because every orgasm one has increases the blood flow to the genitals, keeping the vaginal tissues hydrated and healthy. You could try that… But go for lubrication, it's easiest…"

*

Barry secured his bike inside Janet's garden fence, took off his bicycle clips and helmet, her spare keys from his pocket and went to the back door. He rang the bell to warn her, before putting the key in the lock, then opened the door, feeling nervous and unsettled. "Janet," he called, "Jan." No answer. Could she be having a nap or be in the shower? He wandered upstairs, treading quietly in case he woke her, and gently pushed her bedroom door open. The bed was made and the bathroom door was open; she was out somewhere. It was after two o'clock. She finished at the community library at twelve, and they had agreed to meet. Where was she? He was hungry after his morning's bike ride, ravenous in fact, so he headed for the kitchen, where he found dirty breakfast things on the table and some plates and saucepans by the sink from last night's meal. Collecting up the dirty crockery, he stacked it neatly by the sink, ran the hot water and squeezed the washing-up liquid into the bowl. He never ate or prepared meals until the kitchen was clean, immaculate even. After washing up, wiping all the surfaces and putting the hand towel in the washing machine to join the next wash, he took a couple of slices of bread from the bin, a chunk of cheese to put between them, and a plate. He was not a crumb-dropper.

Into the lounge, he switched on the TV news channel, feeling restless and impatient, wanting to get their discussion about their future relationship over with. The news finished and he started to worry. Where could she be? Should he go and look for her? Irresolute, he stood in the middle of the lounge floor and then began pacing up and down the room. What did he want from this discussion anyway? His daughters liked Janet and he got on well with her sons. After a series of unsatisfactory short relationships, finding Janet and it feeling so right was more than he had ever imagined could happen. But learning to live with her after being on his own was a challenge. He flicked off the TV and walked to the kitchen door and looked out. It had started to rain again. Where was she?

The rain was getting harder. Should he take an umbrella and walk to the library in case she was still there? A car came into view and stopped in front of the house. Janet got out. "Thanks, Vic, so kind!" And she was walking up the path towards him. "Where have you been, love?" he asked quietly. "We arranged to have a chat."

"I needed to talk to Vicky, so I went there after the library."

He felt upset, bewildered and even irrationally angry in his anguish. Was she pretending that everything was alright, rather than admitting that things were very far from that and she wanted out. He helped her off with her damp anorak, hung it up and sat in his usual place at the kitchen table. She sat opposite, her elbows on the table, her chin resting on her upturned hands. She looked into his face, the face she knew so well. Grey eyes, smooth skin, mobile mouth and blond hair now grey. He was speaking. "Are we going to continue to get to know one another? I hope so. I've learnt from you every day, but know that having been married to one person for so many years, adjusting to a new person was never going to be easy."

She looked at him, took a deep breath and replied: "Now that we've tried living together, if we carry on with our relationship, should we go back to being together but living apart? We can spend time with our families, do our independent activities and our interests like my concerts and volunteering and your sports and work. We don't have to live together totally."

He reached for her hand. A tear rolled down her cheek. He didn't want to spoil the feeling of togetherness by getting up for a tissue. "Well," he said, "let's give it a try. As long as we're honest with one another. Plenty of other couples live apart/together. It doesn't mean we don't love one another or wouldn't look after the other in illness or injury. And learning to listen properly will be the best thing that can be learnt from our first bash at being together. Listen before responding. We're not getting any younger. If we're going to be happy it had better be now. And let's be honest about our sleeping arrangements, the cuddling and making love has been the best ever, but we both really like to sleep in separate beds, if we're honest, don't we?"

She sniffed and took out a handkerchief. "I'm sorry I thrash about so much and keep you awake, but I've always done that and don't know how to stop it, and we get up at different times in the morning."

"So, though it seems a bit sad," he continued patiently, "I'll keep on going into the spare room, after a cuddle, when I stay here, and you take the study bed at mine. It doesn't mean we don't love one another." He gave her hand a squeeze. "Shall I make us a cup of tea?"

Later, Barry was lying in bed, watching Janet over the book he was reading as she undressed. Her brows and muff were still dark, but her hair that she had had cut short before lockdown 3 was threaded with grey. There was a little slack around her tummy; she still had a girlish figure, but an ageing girl. He was reading about Viagra.

"Viagra helps with erections but doesn't enhance desire – men might have to have their testosterone levels checked – might need testosterone patches to renew the sexual spark. Bodily changes affect sexual life – need extra time and touching to be aroused and time to reach orgasm, which might not be as intense."

He had seen so many adverts for erectile dysfunction medication on TV, it must be quite common. *Shall I send for some, or can one get it from one's doctor? How embarrassing. I'll make an appointment. No, I can't, they're not seeing patients, so it'll just be a phone chat. If I get it online, it might be dangerous, too strong or counterfeit and affect my heart. Perhaps I'm too old. I won't chance it, I'll ring the doctor.*

21 September 2020

The UK government is about to introduce fines of up to £10,000 for people who breach self-isolation rules. There

> are 90,000 hospitality sector workers still on furlough;
> many will lose their jobs next month if it's not extended.
> Daily infections rose to 4,368 and there were eleven deaths.
> Newport, Bridgend, Merthyr Tydfil and Blaenau Gwent
> go into lockdown tomorrow, joining various cities and
> areas in the North West, Yorkshire and the Humber, North
> East and Midlands. Bolton has the highest rate in the UK.
> Spain and France have very high numbers of infections,
> and various areas and cities are in lockdown. Germany and
> Belgium's cases have also risen. The Chief Medical Officer,
> Chris Whitty, and the Chief Scientific Adviser, Sir Patrick
> Vallance, spoke to the nation about the seriousness of the
> current situation. Like Spain and France, the infections
> started amongst younger people, but have spread to older age
> groups. The lowest infection numbers are amongst children
> and seventy- to seventy-nine-year-olds. The pandemic is
> doubling every seven days; if we don't change what we are
> doing, this will continue and there will be 50,000 infections
> by mid-October. They see no evidence that it is a milder
> version than in April. They warn that if you increase your
> own risk, you increase the risk to everyone around you. There
> are over fifty labs doing the testing, and many private ones
> are being brought in to help.

Gerry and Ruth were, as usual, reading newspapers at the breakfast table, and as often happened, Gerry was irate about something and getting quite red in the face.

"What are you reading about?" Ruth asked dutifully, hoping to decrease his blood pressure.

"Sir Paul Nurse, you know him – runs the Crick Institute? Says he's tried to be part of a testing plan for London. The city should be leading the response to COVID, not be a victim of it. Think of all the scientists, tech start-ups, project managers, teaching hospitals, all the skills and resources that are not being used! Our official data shows new infections are low, or is this because testing is such a disgrace?"

"Are you saying London should go it alone?"

"Absolutely! Scotland's population is 5 million, GDP about £170 billion. London's population is 9 million and our GDP is £550 billion. It's paying the bills for the rest of the country. Yet Scotland has its own crafted policy, though London has not."

"I see what you mean. Workers being told to stay home again, pubs and restaurants shutting by ten, empty tubes, trains and the city centre, our wonderful theatres, galleries and museums wounded perhaps forever! Yes, we should have our distinct policies to help our economy to survive and recover."

"Does this government have any clear aims? Johnson is a flailing, inward-looking waffler. London should step away from the national chaos, set up quick, easily available tests, made in the UK, and open up London to businesses. Shutting everything down again is not the answer for this great city."

"Boris can change the rules and impose fines as much as he likes, but if they aren't being enforced, he may as well not bother. People are STILL not wearing masks on the tube, and TFL says that its staff have been told to 'avoid confrontation', which is presumably why they hide out of sight, leave the gates open, so people don't have to pay and if they do appear, are not wearing masks. I was waiting at the station yesterday and when a tube drew in and ten people got out, guess how many didn't have masks on?"

"Two?"

"No, seven! And they weren't all together or young, there was only one couple. It's shocking! Why aren't they being fined by TFL staff? Priti Patel says she'd snitch on her neighbours if they broke the current rules. Matt Hancock agrees, but Boris doesn't. Families, couples have been reduced to their nuclear states. We're locked down in our homes. To snitch on neighbours when they are maybe the only people we see is not a good idea. Preferable is the old-fashioned community spirit, sharing and supporting one another!"

*

Barry had been prescribed medication and Janet had ordered a sexy nightie. They were lying entwined on the couch, listening to music after supper. Janet was reading poetry and Barry was watching the turquoise sky through the window and massaging her back. He could just see two parakeets in the huge copper beech at the end of the garden, but the light was draining away as the music soared.

Smetana depicted the river flowing more slowly and fading to a trickle. Janet yawned and closed her book. "Bed?" she asked, and they rolled off the couch and went upstairs.

She quickly did her teeth, stripped, pulled on her nightie and turned the bedside lamps down low. He undressed in the second bathroom, came in and got into bed under the sheet and light coverlet. She moved towards him and he ran his hands all over her body under the nightie. She put a hand on his penis and stroked gently; he felt a strong tingling. She rubbed it up and down and it rose, strong and commanding. "Thanks be," he said, feeling a rush of love and tenderness towards her. "I do love you."

"That's lust talking," she said. "Take it slowly."

Janet's house was detached. She always felt embarrassed at Barry's flat, because she couldn't help moaning and even screaming as she let go and neared orgasm. But in her home, she didn't have to worry. Her back arched, her head pressed back into the pillow, she shuddered and got louder and louder as their bodies, slippery with sweat, moved in rhythm together. Then they climaxed. "Wow," she said. "That was heaven!"

They lay, exhausted, replete, then reached out their hands to one another, a squeeze, and they rolled over to sleep. He would move beds later, perhaps.

"No meeting friends at a gallery for a look and snack, or a swim at Hampstead ponds or a trawl around dress shops. No seeing family, cooking for friends. We are all worried about what is safe. Can't go to second home in Wales, life is drab," Jo said to Vicky as they wandered around Golders Hill Park.

Vicky smiled. "It's depressing. No kissing, hugging or hand shaking with anyone other than a partner or bubble. We seem to have eliminated so much in this COVID new world, including spontaneity. So much of our lives now has to be meticulously planned, from supermarket delivery and library picking-up-book slots to when it is safest to go for a walk. We – well, I do anyway – sit on my sofa, eating too much and getting obsessed with house plants, gardens and nesting activities. Making plans on the hoof is no longer allowed. Will this be a permanent change and we'll no longer find being flexible appealing? And will I be too slow and useless to play tennis if we get stopped for months again!"

*

Hannah, who ran a cafe/gallery in an outbuilding of a mansion in a nearby park, and was doing Michelle's art course on Zoom, asked her and Stella to hang some of their paintings to sell. She said, "We'll put green dot stickers on them when sold but keep them there for a month. If prints are to be made, please indicate how many you are prepared to sell."

"How did you get into running an arty cafe?" Michelle asked her.

"My husband, Adrian, was an artist. He was quite famous, an academician. I met him at art school and when he died, I realised I had been living through him. I hadn't pursued a career, I haven't any talent for anything. I never even did my own housework or learned to cook and had a nanny for Fredo.

I didn't know how to fill my days, so a friend persuaded me to start up this cafe, with her, and I found I loved it and stuck at it when she dropped out. So, shall we advertise your paintings are coming? And will Stella want to hang a few?"

25 September 2020

> There has been the largest number of cases since April – 6,874 people tested positive and thirty-four deaths. Retail spending is down by seventy-one per cent. The most infected group is the seventeen- to twenty-four-year-olds. Infections have multiplied in universities, despite all the signs and help to sanitise and social distance. Glasgow has 172 cases, Edinburgh 120, Liverpool eighty-seven, and many others have outbreaks and so many people are having to quarantine. More areas in Wales are being locked down – Cardiff, Swansea and Llanelli. There is to be a £200 fine for not wearing a mask.

Vicky rang Maggie to see how she was, now Wales was in lockdown.

"Oh fine, fine, thanks."

"And Robert?"

"Don't know. I haven't seen him for a while.'

"Oh, what's happened?"

"Well, I might be an intolerant old bag… our relationship was light-hearted fun at first, but gradually I found we had opposing political views. He hid them because he knew I was a Labour Party member. But gradually I realised how polarised we were, and if he had just been honest it would have saved huge amounts of time, hope and emotion! Do you know, I found a 'Vote Leave' poster on the inside of his wardrobe door?"

"That's so sad. Why can't you keep off political subjects and agree to disagree? You haven't changed. Remember you had that 'Never kissed a Tory' T-shirt?"

"Mmm, it's the privilege that gets me, the lack of caring about inequality and the disadvantaged. He went to Harrow and Oxford! Maybe he's sometimes guilt-ridden, but he won't be able to help falling back on old patterns inherited from his past. He belongs in a class of the flawed and indulgent, and often wears red trousers like a male Sloane!"

"Aren't they a metaphor for being red-blooded? If he could put up with your views, can't you put up with who he is?"

"Just goes against the grain! All those weeks of lockdown when I couldn't see him, then we did, and what did I find? He'd been hiding his right-wing views, so that was that."

"Aren't you missing him? What are you doing with yourself?"

"I'm coping with isolation quite well. I'm good at pottering and I like my own company." She laughed. "You introduced me to Zoom. Remember when we had my birthday party, and friends from all over the world were dancing and coming into focus to say things? I've kept in touch with them all since, with Zoom... And taking on a relationship at our ages was a big step, you know. In the future, one of us will get ill and be a burden on the other, and death is never far away. I'm not going to experience that everlasting, mythic love we used to dream about. That's probably it now. I've had plenty of adventures, and I'll get more of a thrill sitting down to eat a duck wrap from Pret than I will fancying someone. Thinking of them getting incapacitated and having to change their nappy when I haven't known them long is a passion killer. Being eighty is the moment of truth, you know. I'm no longer elderly, I'm old. My knees are gone, eyes are dim. I'll be carrying a stick, taking pills and talking about health all the time, very soon."

"Not you, Maggie. You're eternally young."

"Hmm, I haven't told you, but my cancer came back. I've had two chemo cycles. Got no hair, no lashes or brows, and huge clumps of the stuff fell out, so I wear a wig or a hat. Couldn't bear to let him see me bald, or big from the steroids, so at first lockdown was convenient!"

"Oh no, Maggie, no. I'm so sorry. How devastating. How can I help?"

"By keeping in touch regularly. I've got to go, sorry, I'll be late… appointment with my consultant."

*

It was a balmy, still day, just right for tennis, and Diana was playing particularly well. She had been included in her young neighbours' fours, which had sharpened her up considerably, and she and Vicky hadn't played for a while.

"Well done, you're so much quicker today. You were much better than me!"

"That's down to having to be, playing with Helen and her friends. Let's have a socially distanced drink on the terrace."

"OK, and you can give me any news."

Settled with their soft drinks, Diana blurted out, "I took the plunge."

"Have you moved in together?"

"Felt it was now or never, so put my flat on the market and moved in with Alex. I had to get rid of all his wife's clothes and personal effects. Luckily his daughters helped me with them. I'm having the house decorated in my taste and we're currently going to buy a house on the south coast somewhere, which our children can use too. We've been pulled into all our children's lives, and we seem to all get on, and Alex is so flattering and loving to me, saying how beautiful I look and how proud he is of me."

"I'm so pleased it's working out well."

"Yes, when I was young, I was looking for the perfect person. When one gets older you realise that everyone has bad habits, can be irritating and not look their best in the mornings. I'm more patient and tolerant now and grateful to have found someone like him. I worked all my life, brought up Adam, looked after my mother – now it's my time. When you get to our stage of life and you don't have to argue about money or kids, there's no point in arguing about anything else and we are trying to enjoy every day. He's got a house on Bute, an island off Scotland, which was his wife's family home. We're going to go there very soon."

*

Malcolm couldn't walk or move his legs, had blinding headaches, seizures, confusion and twitching muscles, plus difficulty breathing and swallowing. He was back in hospital.

Vicky stood for a while looking at him, feasting on his handsome, pain-ridden face, his silver hair, listening to his laboured breath from those parted lips she had so enjoyed kissing. She sat in the chair next to him, leaning over, so his warm breath touched her skin. He stirred but didn't wake.

*

"Delicious, my dear!" Ruth had tried a new recipe; Gerry leaned back in his chair. "These scientists don't seem to understand probability. They're entrenched in their positions with a complete absence of doubt, so there are a range of competing certainties. SAGE, for instance, the advisory body, contradicts the government at every turn, and other scientists are trying to build followers for their viewpoints, rather than presenting the evidence. Your hair is looking lovely this evening, by the way."

"Thanks. It's so long and thick. I've had it in a ponytail all day, which gives it a lift when I take out the band. Yes, their confidence in their own point of view rather than concrete fact is staggering. I know we hope for certainty, but epidemiological abstractions are being treated as fact, even though the 'evidence' they input was what might happen. It's not a binary choice, lockdown v herd immunity. Lockdown just defers the problem."

"Brexit and COVID have both been reduced to false polarities, illusory certainty. They produce Sweden's policies, or South Korea's, as examples to back up their prejudices, rather than other examples of countries that have reacted similarly but that have had different results. Did they model the consequences of not treating other illnesses or the financial harm? No, none of what they have done has been modelled, it's a learning process, they have lost sight of uncertainty. And these slogans!"

Ruth smiled. "'Hands, Face, Space'?"

Gerry grimaced. "And 'Take Back Control'! Ugh!" he said gloomily. "Is there a pudding?"

*

Today had been the day of the second meeting of the Silver Foxes.

Nigel had offered his garden, and he and Tony had organised the drinks and snacks.

Vicky was too upset and depressed about Malcolm, so didn't go.

She wandered around her garden as the shadows lengthened, like ghosts dragging their cloaks across the beds and grass. The scents, the delicate texture, from the nicotiana, bergamot and evening primrose, filled the air. The day was draining out of the sky and the thin slice of moon was like waxy alabaster. She was lonely, unbearably sad and lonely.

"I'm so sorry, Vic," said Ruth when she phoned her later.

Some lovely classical music was playing in the background. Vicky could imagine Ruth lying on the couch in a pile of cushions, Gerry sitting in his wing-back Edwardian chair, feet up on his footstool. Both with their decaf, or maybe a glass of port.

"Apparently in patients over seventy, the treatment he has had is not always tolerated. Think they'll struggle to alleviate or improve his symptoms, but I pray they can."

28 September 2020

> In Germany, infections rose to 1,192 a day. Angela Merkel says they will rise to 20,000 unless there is action, but the economy must be kept running and schools and nurseries stay open. The UK had 4,044 new cases, particularly in North East England, so further restrictions have been imposed. The US had 36,919 new infections yesterday and India 82,120. Italy's cumulative number of COVID cases over the past two weeks is currently just over thirty-seven per 100,000 people, among the lowest rates in Europe. The UK is at over a hundred, France exceeds 230 and Spain has around 330.

Vicky's close friend Lucia was spending the summer at her family home, north of Milan. Her son and daughter were with her. "I'm worried to come back," she told Vicky in a phone call. "Mask-wearing has been scrupulous here since the start of the outbreak. Compulsory inside and in busy outdoor areas in the regions that have seen an increase in infections, such as Rome. Those breaking the rules on mask-wearing face fines of up to €3,000. Because people are strictly complying, restaurants have remained open and are largely free of the early closures some other European countries are imposing."

"That sounds brilliant. You're right. Generally, people won't wear them here. What about university?"

"Yes, we will have to come back in a few days. It's worrying, I feel much safer here than in England!"

*

Vicky was sitting by Malcolm's bedside, watching his waxen, still-breathing face, learning it by heart. *We all have to die*, she thought, *but why now, when we were just getting close? I had flung open all the doors to the rooms of my life for him. All this terrible suffering he's going through. Is he in pain? Dreaming?* She imagined those bright, kind eyes opening, the way his gentle, heart-stopping looks lit up the room when he smiled. He had been shaved and his silvery hair combed. He lay on his back, groaning occasionally. A ray of sun came suddenly through the window, lighting the corner of his soft lips and an eyebrow so he looked quizzical. 'Why be sad?' was he saying? 'Remember the passionate tenderness of our lovemaking, nothing is forever.' She had wondered a hundred times since that night if it had been disloyal to Rob or whether he would have understood: *Would he have lent me to him, have liked him if they'd met. Surely Rob would have known that I could never have loved anyone but him? All those thousands of times we lay entangled in one another, wanting never to be anywhere else. Feeling as if we could merge, move out of our body space and be one. Was I searching for you, and Malcolm for Sylvia, as we hungrily embraced?*

*

Ruth and Vicky were eating cake in Vicky's garden on a lovely late September afternoon.

"Poor, poor Malcolm. It's just not fair. What was it? An intracerebral haemorrhage?"

"Yes, and only fifty per cent of people recover from them and probably not those who had already lost part of their brain function and are having seizures. I think he's probably had it."

"So very sorry, Vic, what can I say? We're all on the downward slope. He's just got there before his time."

Vicky sighed and gazed around her lovely garden. At the white everlasting sweet pea, the white and yellow dahlias and yellow cosmos and sunflowers. The acer leaves were turning red or yellow, and they were all against a background of different shades of green.

"Yes, everything dies. And is this the new normal, being locked down, released, locked down? London is on the verge, isn't it?"

"Sounds like it," said Ruth gloomily. "But not doing so might be a lethal gamble which might lead to a more severe lockdown later on. Either option is hugely harmful. This apple cake is delicious."

"Can you eat some more?" Vicky offered her the tin and knife.

"Better not, thanks, I've put on weight. The national debt is horrendous, restaurants and theatres are bankrupt, our cultural life is zilch, the testing system is a mess and I'm fatter than I've ever been!"

"You don't look any different. And yes, until testing and tracing works, across all the country, limits on what we can do seem unavoidable. New York, Paris and Madrid are having similar crises. Did you see that in the Netherlands, before they went into lockdown, single people were advised to find a '*seksbuddy*'? Very thoughtless of our government not to do the same. Us single people have found it hard…"

"How about coming swimming to the women's pond one morning?"

"I've never fancied swimming in muddy, pooey water, with moorhens, ducks and fish. And it's no doubt freezing!"

"The chalkboard tells us the temperature. Yesterday it was fourteen degrees, and yes, it's muddy and cold, and I have to get in in one movement, not bit by bit, or I'd be there all day. So, in, up to my shoulders, in the very cold, dark, silky water. Every bit of me hurt, stabbing needles, especially my extremities, and my breath balled in my throat. 'What am I doing here?' I asked myself. 'Would I notice if my foot was chopped off?' I forced myself to splash off and two ducks moved quickly, disapprovingly, under the weeping willows. There was a heron on a branch, kingfishers were darting past, my toes brushed reeds. It was raining a bit, and the trees sagged with moisture. Droplets splashed into my face and the wind circled above, rippling the water. My mind drifted, lost in the wildness of the place.

"I don't like getting my hair wet, swim with my head high, like a periscope, even though I wear a hat. I tell myself that it's good for my white blood cell count and an adrenaline/endorphin release, and then suddenly it was OK, my body was one with the water… swimming was like cutting through cream."

"But I like the local sports centre pool. It's not too cold, I get a hot shower and if I choose my time, the lanes aren't too full."

"But in a pool, you just go up and down, here you can go around, and look at things and your brain empties with the cold. You're back in the womb, floating, meditating, in a dream state. When everything in life changes, or is difficult, here is a sanctuary, profound solace."

"Mmm, well, surprisingly, you're tempting me."

"All sorts of strong, powerful women swim there and write about it too. You're keen on Deborah Moggach's writing? Well, she says it's like slipping into bliss. It's wild, free and anarchic."

"OK, OK, I'll try it. When?"

"Tomorrow? You can wear neoprene socks and gloves. A lot of swimmers do."

*

"It went well, then?" Vicky and Debs were chatting about the last Silver Foxes meeting. Fourteen people had come, and Debs had been impressed with one man called Steve.

They had finished their tennis game and were sitting outside, swigging at their water bottles.

"We all talked about what we would like from the group – theatre visits, film and music evenin's where people bring their favourite CDs and we eat fish and chips together. Everyone said they would keep in touch with Zoom parties if we go back into lockdown."

"Did Nusheen come?"

"No, and Alistair was disappointed, but then he spent the whole time talkin' to Christine with Tony, which she seemed to be enjoyin'. She's lookin' good, isn't she? I like her shorter, curlier hair."

"Yes, it suits her. She's an attractive girl. What about this man you met?"

"Steve's a cousin of Nigel's. I must say we had an immediate rapport. We discussed the datin' agencies we'd tried. Tinder was too aggressive, Bumble gives one control, but one can only go through hundreds of different profiles if one is young, there are very few older ones. Silver Singles, Elite, eHarmony and Match – the people on those seemed too old. We really got on well, despite the fact that I've almost forgotten how to flirt, and vaccinated, masked and socially distanced have become the new tall, dark and handsome."

"Has he been married?"

"Yes, but three years ago his wife died. Horrible. She had a headache, which he didn't worry about, as she often had migraines. He gave her the usual medication and a hot drink and sent her to bed early. He watched somethin' on TV and then when he went up, she seemed to be asleep and her breathin' was light. He drifted off to sleep, and when he woke in the mornin', she was cold next to him. Can you imagine the shock! And one would blame oneself. He said they had drifted apart, but he could never have imagined an end like that. He's so nice. Such a warm, good listener, positive and helpful, and his smile lights up his face. He hums a lot and sometimes breaks into song. His singin' voice is deeper than his speakin' voice. He's a baritone in his local choir. He lives in Wiltshire, in a village – his own house. We've done some video calls and he's comin' up to take me out, tonight actually."

"Mmm, so pleased for you."

*

When Ruth got home, Gerry wasn't in his study, she called his name and a faint response from the conservatory led her there.

"The light's not good now. I'll finish soon," he said, mixing colours together on his palate, squeezing and stirring, then studying his canvas carefully, leaning forward and back, as if examining a picture inside his head which he hoped to transfer.

She spotted an Artemisia Gentileschi artwork print they had bought when they went to the National Gallery exhibition propped on her easel nearby. He had sketched her reaching forward to pick a rose, as in her self-portrait. Their garden was the background.

"That's promising," she said. "You haven't lost your touch."

He waved his paintbrush vaguely. "Just been too busy. You haven't painted either."

"No, I'm thinking of weaving. I've sent for a weaving kit, am renting a loom and have enrolled on an online course. If I don't get on with it, I'll make another wool rug."

As he returned to his painting, she could see that his paintbrush was trembling slightly and his shoulders were more kyphotic than she had noticed before.

*

She had dressed with care, changing four times. The red lace might be too young, the black too sophisticatedly formal for a first dinner date. The blue suit was smart but made her into just another older woman ruling the roost at work. The zip-through, pale green, knitted knee-length, with the long silver earrings? Yes.

The doorbell rang. Already? She ran down the stairs and flung the door open. "Come in," she said. "Go into the lounge, nearly ready." Then she dashed back up to the bathroom, checked for lipstick on her teeth and chin hairs. Dusted her eyes with green shadow, another pat of powder and a look at the back of her hair, into her bedroom for her jacket and she was downstairs apologising for keeping him waiting.

"Oh, it's OK, I've been snooping around and needed a bit of a rest. It's a long drive."

In the car, she nervously chatted, drowning her fears in a great river of words.

The restaurant she had chosen was Italian. Delicious smells of garlic and grilled meat reached them as they parked across the road. She had chosen it because the tables were in the garden. Sitting near the gently pattering fountain, a vase of rosebuds and lavender and a glass of white wine in front of her, and the pale evening sun slowly sinking behind the buildings, she started to feel calmer. *This is ridiculous*, she thought. *How many scores of men have taken me out?*

Flattered by the soft light under the awning, which shaded out the marks of ageing in their faces and gave them a healthy glow, they looked a golden couple.

She borrowed his glasses to read the menu, and discussed his friendship with his cousin Nigel, how lucky it was that he had been visiting him the day of the party, and how Nigel had a problem with being on time. "I find it arrogant that unpunctual people think that their time is more precious than other people's," she said.

"Exactly. But he's a dear, kind man otherwise," he agreed.

They talked about their favourite writers, films, holiday destinations, looking for common ground on which to build a relationship. He was amused by her audacious frankness; her wide-eyed, intense, articulate delivery. She was as striking as a tropical bird in these darkening surroundings.

Then with the coffee, Steve reached across the table for her hand. "I hope you're going to visit me in Wiltshire. Do you like being in the countryside? And nature, feeling the dirt under your fingers?" He looked at her expectantly.

Debs nodded and smiled across at him, but her thoughts were rampaging, her heart banging in her chest, agreeing she did, while all the time her mind was engaged in a different dialogue, about cold and mud and loneliness. "I love to walk," she said. But wellington boots, wet dogs and no tennis or opportunity to wear her beautiful clothes and go to parties, opening nights, concerts and theatre were foremost in her head. She could feel her sparkle and enthusiasm draining, leaving her quiet, subdued and stale.

Finishing her coffee, while he chatted about the delights of living in his village, she could see that he too was less animated.

"I've promised Nigel I won't be late, he wanted to go to bed early," he said. And drove her home.

*

Vicky lay in bed, a card from Malcolm, which he had sent during the first lockdown to thank her for calling and asking her to come again as soon as was possible, next to her pillow. She felt the tears seeping out of the corners of her eyes, wetting the pillow, and she reached for a tissue to blow her nose. The card was of Vincent van Gogh's *Chair*. It depicted loneliness. That yellow chair in a kitchen corner, on battered brown tiles, next to a closed blue door. Emotion choked her.

4 October 2020

> The R number has gone up from 1.3 to 1.6. President Trump is being administered an experimental drug for his COVID-19 and apparently his 'vital signs' are impaired. Paris is imposing more restrictions, closing bars for two weeks, and Italy is worried they are getting a second wave. Public Health England says that 15,841 positive cases have been left out of the UK daily totals by an IT error; the Excel spreadsheet was full and so new names couldn't be added! Which means that efforts to trace the contacts have been delayed. So today there have been 22,961 total cases and thirty-nine deaths.

"Can you believe this, yesterday was the wettest day since records began in 1891! There was enough rain to fill Loch Ness."

Gerry and Ruth were sitting in their heated conservatory, heavy rain battering on the perspex roof. The TV was showing the French Open tennis, which Ruth, curled up in an armchair, was watching. "Incredible!" He shook his head.

"What else are you reading about?" she asked with a smile.

"Trump had a party in the rose garden and inside the White House, where people were crammed together, maskless, and even embracing one another! Now at least eight of them have the virus. A petri dish of contagion and arrogant denial. Not to mention that yesterday he sat in a car with others for a drive-by, waving to his supporters. Everyone with him should quarantine now."

"After he mocked Biden for excessive mask-wearing and joked about and rolled his eyes at scientific advice and said he now understood all about COVID and it's nothing to be scared of! So disrespectful to those whose loved ones, over 2,000 of them, have died."

"And I've just read the article that Andrew Marr talked about this morning."

"What, about the lack of infectious potential of COVID on contaminated surfaces?"

"Billions have been spent on deep cleaning, yet Italian researchers say that they couldn't grow the virus from samples taken from surfaces. People catch it from other people, from their noses and mouths."

"All those weeks when I washed or wiped every item that came into the house, particularly food packaging. I was feeling guilty because my standards of doing that have slipped. What a relief. However, there is so much misinformation in the press. It's really well researched that the virus lives for seventy-two hours on stainless steel. So probably of no concern in the home, but an enormous problem in public areas. Someone coughs or sneezes into their hand and then holds onto a rail, they are surely passing it on. I'm off for a swim now."

"Isn't the ladies' pond closed?"

"Mmm, some sort of problem with the water quality. I'm meeting Vic at the sports centre. We've booked to swim there."

"More sensible than that freezing pond." He shuddered at the thought.

"I ignore the chalkboard with the temperature on and think about how great I'll feel after. It's so exhilarating! We'll go back to it next week. I'm trying to help Vic through this agonising period of Malcolm nearing death."

"Madness. You could wear a hair shirt and walk barefoot, they'd be good for you too."

"I often recommended patients to take up cold water swimming. It recalibrates stress and anxiety and wards off colds and flu. Kick-starts the recovery process…"

"I'm with Herodotus. Cold water is dangerous for our health."

"Isn't he the Ancient Greek who also said that when a woman removes an item of clothing, she also removes her respect? Not the kind of guy I'd have been inviting for dinner! See you later."

*

The last couple of months had altered Malcolm a great deal. Not that she had known him well. But when his deep-set, bright eyes had been open, his effort of will had kept up the illusion that he was still a vigorous, lively, handsome man in his seventies, with a temporary problem, rather than the wasted, crumbling, deeply shrunken, sealed, bluish face she saw now.

Deep down in the smallest, steel-enforced compartment of Vicky's mind, where her main dreams were stored, she had kept the hope of Sophie returning and Malcolm recovering.

Although she knew it was unlikely, and she had been waking in the night, full of nightmarish dread and never felt rested, it was still a terrible shock when he died.

Talking to Ruth about him as they sipped hot drinks in the

gazebo after their swim, she said, "He looked death squarely in the eye and kept on looking outwards to the people he loved, showing all the qualities that we know really matter – courage, compassion and love." She could feel the tears brimming, dripping down her face, plopping as they fell onto the metal garden table. Ruth's tender face made her cry harder – unstoppably.

It had been raining ceaselessly – great sheets pelting from the leaden sky. They could hardly see the garden and had got soaked between the pool and car, then the car and Ruth and Gerry's house.

Ruth wanted to give her a hug. "Imagine I'm hugging you. It takes courage to give love when all of the things of this world are impermanent and fleeting. It's safer to protect oneself by building walls, hiding – protecting one's heart. You would have regretted not caring about him enough, even though it's so painful now. The intensity is what makes us human. The love and tenderness you gave is what counted for him in the end. You know the poem:

> 'Better by far you should forget and smile
> Than you should remember and be sad'?"

"Yes, yes, it's one of my favourites. Christina Rossetti."

*

She chose not to ask to see his body. She remembered Rob; the light had fallen from his eyes, they were glass, his long, brown eyelashes on the made-up skin – strangely smooth and soft before decay. She had wondered if his spirit was still present, whether he would be able to hear her. No, she didn't want to see Malcolm in the hospital morgue.

It, of course, wasn't her job to register the death and arrange dates with the funeral directors and church. She knew there would be a short church service, as Alison had rung to give her the details…

*

"How are you?"

There it was on her little screen, and underneath, "Ted x". Jo's heart started racing.

Garry came back with the tickets for *La Haine*. "Shall I get you a drink?"

She felt flustered; she needed to take in this message from Ted. "Um, yes please, a white wine?"

He wandered off, mask in place, and she stared again at her phone. "How are you?" It had been six months since he chose Moria over her, weeks since she had heard from him, and here he was texting her… How to reply? Whether to reply? What could she say? How could she express her range of complex, ambiguous feelings?

She typed, "How are YOU?"

Garry came back, having ordered, and slid down the bench to be more than two metres away from her. She sent it quickly, turned her phone off and took her wine from the waiter who appeared with two full glasses. "Thanks for this," she said, and took a sip. She wasn't attracted to Garry. He was short, thin, with spectacles. He looked as if she could break his bones with a hug. They were like giant clothes hangers, holding up the sagging flesh, and the artificial light gave his lips and cheeks a clayish colour. Her brain was racing, and she wished she could go home to think about Ted.

They were sitting on the end of a long counter, making bland comments about the weather cooling down. She wondered if it would have been any better if they had been allowed to touch. But no, he wasn't attractive and seemed to have nothing to say; she had already asked what his favourite food and best film were. She took a gulp of the wine, wishing he would go away again so she could see if Ted had replied. However, she was being rude. She took a deep breath and turned to him with a smile. "Yes, the summer seems to have gone for good."

He grimaced. "And with this lockdown, the whole of my life now seems to consist of wasting time. I never feel really well, always some part of me is aching or painful. I was energetic and fit, now arthritis and angina have slowed me up." His voice cracked into a squeak.

*

Vicky was in bed, crying and crying. She really must stop this, but still the tears came.

Stop, stop, think how lucky you are. Lucky to be healthy, to have a lovely house and garden, to have known Rob and Malcolm, to have good friends. Lucky, lucky, lucky, but tears poured down.

She could just hear the clock on the distant church striking three, but the night seemed to stand still, as whichever way she lay, sleep evaded her.

After another hour or so, when her face ached and her nose was sore from being blown, she thought, surely all this sadness could inspire some deeply felt poetry? She reached for her notebook and pen.

*

What am I doing here? Jo asked herself as she eased out from under a sleeping Garry. She felt cheated. No orgasm, just a sticky trickle between her legs and all over in minutes. Back too soon into her own possession. She gazed around his platform bedroom, above a big lounge with massive windows looking out at the Thames, through trees, moving in the breeze. It was sparsely furnished; their clothes were scattered across the floor and there were books everywhere.

He was shorter than her, not attractive, and the few strands left of his greying hair had fallen across his face. His big brown eyes were his best feature; they were closed, his lids flickering with dream life.

Moving carefully, so as not to wake him, she slid towards the edge of the bed, wondering if this had been planned, as the sheet and duvet smelt fresh and clean. Carefully, she got her feet onto the floor and, heaving herself up, gathered her clothes and headed for the bathroom.

When she came out again, he was still asleep, lying on his front, breathing heavily.

There was no need to leave a note, she didn't want to see him again. She opened the outside door quietly and slipped out, hoping that she would have a further message from Ted before she reached home.

8 October 2020

There have been 14,542 new cases in the UK and seventy-six deaths announced today. Manchester, Liverpool, Newcastle and Leeds have most cases, and there are fifty-three cases in two Edinburgh care homes. The area across the central belt of Scotland is to have all pubs and restaurants closed after 6pm indoors, for sixteen days.

The first ray of sun for days peered through the kitchen window, where Vicky was washing up last night's supper things. How dirty the windows looked after so much rain. They were a positive insult to the kitchen which she had just cleaned. The lawn was sodden and there were pools in the streets. At night the moon had had a yellowish ring, which meant more rain. She hadn't slept, too much buzzing through her head. On nights like this, she couldn't keep still and was on the move all the time. She'd lie on her back, then after a few minutes roll over onto her front. This was bad for her neck, so onto her side, hands under her pillow, knees in an embryo position. A few more minutes, then onto the other side, legs straight, to legs bent and back onto the back. If she was lucky she would doze at dawn.

The phone rang. "It's going up and up, 17,540 positive infections today, 2,000 more than yesterday. Who are these people?" Jo asked.

"Well, it's great that we don't know any of them. I heard that over 3,000 are in hospital. No wonder so many of us are waiting for routine operations. I mean, I can walk on my knee, but it's getting worse by the day. Have you heard again from Ted?"

"This morning. I had a long email. Maybe he'll come home. He'd well and truly had enough after the fire. Twenty-six thousand people having to sleep on the side of a road, with the police at either end to stop them going off somewhere else. The camp had violence, disease and mental illness, and the locals hated the noise and sewage stench. It felt like hell, and they aided its incineration. He stayed to help, especially as COVID was around too. Will you be OK? Shall I come to Windsor with you and look around while you go to the funeral? We could have something to eat or a walk after?"

"That's very sweet of you, but don't worry, I won't stay for the wake. I'll be OK."

*

Vicky was early to the church. First, in fact. Feeling drained after little sleep and too much weeping. It was a sunny day, in the middle of the week of heavy rain.

There's Bec. Perhaps that's her son, Will, supporting her.

Perhaps that's Sylvia's sister with her family, and maybe Sylvia's brother? Though he looks rather like Malcolm, so perhaps his brother? Does he have one?

By the time that they were ushered into the chapel, there must have been thirty mourners and she had given up trying to identify them. Alison hurried in at the last minute, managing a little wave to her as she passed.

Her mind went back to the last day of Malcolm's life. He had been unable to speak, and she wasn't sure if he could hear her, though she tried to talk to him as if he could. Alison had come, and when she came back from a walk around the back streets with their tall Georgian houses, there was a couple she hadn't seen before, leaving. He had still been alive when she had left for bed.

She sat and wept silently with convulsive sobs which shook her body and made her intercostal muscles ache in the effort to not make any noise.

A gleaming hearse arrived, and the coffin was wheeled past her, hiding at the back, her tears wet on her face. Funerals make one realise how unimportant, ephemeral we are… The short service started and Vicky's red eyes were open, but her sight and mind were switched off. Members of the family said nice things about him, so many things she hadn't known. Then horrors, the coffin was to be wheeled out to the graveside, to be buried with Sylvia. As it reached the side door, it slammed shut before the coffin could exit. Was he saying he didn't want to go? *Oh, Malcolm, are you here?*

The mask-wearing mourners, with social distance between them, slowly left the church. She didn't join the group around the grave. Alison had given her Bec's address for refreshments. *But most of the family don't know I exist. I need a walk.*

She left her car and walked out of the village and up a road of expensive-looking houses. At first, she walked slowly as if in a daze, feeling a little dizzy and having to tell each foot to take the next step as she wiped away tears which refused to stop. She had never felt so lonely. The houses petered out, and in front of her was a grassy hill. She made herself stride, and as the sun warmed her face and head, she promised herself a new life.

At the top of the slope, heart racing, the breeze stroking her skin, lifting her hair and drying her tears, she stood taking deep breaths of the clear air. Then with each stride downhill she became surer of what she wanted for her future. More than anything she wished for her daughter and grandchildren to come back and live in the house and garden she loved so much. But young people want to make new lives, build their own nest, while the parents they have left drift without focus, all the paraphernalia of family life now redundant.

She had to forget her dreams of Sophie coming back and downsize, however deeply painful. While she still had lots of energy…

*

Jo had exchanged emails with Ted again. He was OK, was still around the camp, even though it had been largely burnt down. There were so many young, keen, unskilled volunteers in the dirty, dangerous conditions, he felt duty bound to stay and try to help them keep safe. He told her a little about the situation he lived in, without even the basic amenities and the poor quality, inadequate food provided by local caterers and paid for by a national NGO. Despite the privations, there had been no suggestion of him returning in the near future. She wished she had bothered to go to the second Silver Foxes meeting Vicky and Debs had organised, but she hadn't, so video dating, here I come, she thought.

*

Michelle had chosen twelve paintings to exhibit. Stella was very reluctant. "This is embarrassing, my daubs aren't worthy," but she gave in, and let Michelle choose four. The day came for the opening. Michelle pinned up her hair, which had grown quite long in lockdown, and chose a long, green dress with a wide waistband. The heavy material clung or swung appropriately. Stella wore smart trousers and a long-sleeved sequinned blouse. To their surprise the cafe was crowded with well-dressed people, all wearing masks, except when sipping wine on the terrace.

Teaching had been good for Michelle; there were so many

of her students there, everyone chatting, caught up in the spell of the evening. Very soon, green stickers appeared underneath quite a few paintings.

14 October 2020

There have been 19,724 positive cases and 137 deaths. Boris refuses to do a nationwide 'circuit breaker' lockdown as demanded by Labour – "The cure is worse than the disease!" But probably London will be in Tier 2 in a few days if Sadiq Khan gets his way. There is a curfew from 9pm in Paris and nine major French cities. Spain, with 1 million cases, has imposed a nationwide curfew and a six-month state of emergency. Italy has closed cinemas, theatres, gyms and swimming pools, and bars and restaurants must stop in-house dining from 6pm.

"There are mutinous mutterings among backbenchers against lockdown, and local government leaders in the North are fighting not to be put into Tier 3. Yet our mayor has come out of his slumber and is demanding to lock down London. Nine million Londoners in severe restrictions – again! Has he seen how empty the West End and City are? Is this becoming a police state?" Gerry shook his head in disbelief.

Ruth nodded and took a sip of her orange juice. "Yes, SAGE suggested it three weeks ago, but there are so many conflicting opinions amongst the 'experts'. Many of them say it probably won't work and will hugely damage the economy. The contact tracing is still costing massive amounts and managing to contact at best only forty per cent of those they should. We're living in a hokey-cokey world. In/out, in/out. Public Health England needs sacking. Tier 3 will bankrupt so many businesses and put too many people out of work. What can we do if we're put into Tier 2 in a couple of days?"

"It's pretty similar. No unnecessary travel, no meeting with people outside our area or meeting anyone outside our household, in *any* setting. That's no more friends coming for your socially distanced teas in the garden, or supper inside, and probably no meeting in restaurants! I'm off to the golf club, I'll have lunch there, while it's still allowed." Gerald pulled himself up and moving round the table, gave Ruth a peck on the back of her neck.

"OK, I suppose the curfew means for all but the most determined social partying people, more sleep, boredom, isolation, frustration, weight gain and reduced mental capacity as we head towards the gloom of a socially distanced winter! Hey ho," she said.

*

Vicky, while walking around during lockdown, had often gone past a little row of what had obviously been workmen's cottages, with tiny gardens in front and from what she could see from the first one, a bigger one behind. The middle one was for sale. She rang the estate agent, who said, "My colleague is going to show someone round at four, shall I tell him to stay for 4.30, for you? No time like the present."

Dove Cottage was in an immaculate condition. Everything seemed to have been updated, and luckily, although the atmosphere felt dense with the lives of past owners, it was all to her taste. Only two bedrooms, but they both had ensuite bathrooms, and the kitchen cupboards were oak and the floor limestone tiles. It had been partially knocked into the big lounge which opened out into the perfect-sized garden, with so much potential. The lowering sun was turning the sky orange, above yellow and gold trees. *Just for me, this miracle of colours, like the tresses of party girls?* Could she move from a big five-bedroom house to this? *I'm nearly eighty, I'm forgetting words, dates, pin numbers, stiffening up, and the computer is starting to have a life of its own, typing gobbledegook. How much longer will I be able to cope with my wonderful home on my own? I need to stay in my neighbourhood, though, I can't start making friends again...*

Getting rid of all the things I don't need will be a good exercise and when I die be less to clear out, for whoever gets that job.

*

"Are you sure?" Ruth asked. "Don't rush into anything. Remember that Paul Theroux said something like, 'If you haven't found a person and a place you love, a house that suits you, and a bit of garden, I feel sorry for you.' You did, and you've been so happy here, or does it remind you of Rob too much?"

"Well, yes, it's full of memories, but are those stopping me moving forward? I just think it's probably better that I make a complete change now. I expected to live the rest of my life in my house, but what happens when I can't get up the stairs or do the garden? There's a kind of low-level depression inside me, underpinning everything, because I need things that keep me active and engaged with life. Meeting up with you is the highlight of my day today. I'm just so gloomy and down. Life is going to get increasingly hard for me, coping with my big house and garden. It's surely better to have less to worry about, especially as a second lockdown and isolation is looming and a vast amount of pent-up rage, anxiety, anger and grief is building up in everyone over it. If I do this incredibly painful thing now, I'll eventually have more time to devote to more challenging, enjoyable things. I'll have more control of my life."

Ruth smiled. "I'm sure that COVID has caused millions of people to reappraise their lives. Being at home more with our own company has given us the time to think, as well as all the sourdough baking and sorting out our clothes and books."

*

Debs and Vicky were chatting, sitting on a bench near the courts after their game.

"Sartorially, lockdown has not been good for the fashion industry and our self-images. If we get lockdown again like Wales, we'll have to meet outside in our fleeces, cagoules and thick trousers and huddle in a socially distanced way around one of those outdoor patio heaters – if there are any left to buy."

"I haven't worn a dress since March. If I keep on eating as much, I won't be able to get into any of them anyway. Have you been seeing Steve?"

"Not since that dinner date two or three weeks ago. He didn't even phone for a week and I thought it must be over."

"Were you upset, then?"

"Yes, definitely! At my failure to communicate and be attractive enough for him to want to see me. And I admit that, I had hoped that this time…"

"Mmm, so what's happening now?"

"I'm drivin' down there a week Saturday. It'll be crunch time, I think."

*

"The government has announced that couples living apart are no longer able to have sex indoors, under Tier 2 restrictions!" Barry scratched his head.

"What? The Heath will be even more packed in the evenings. But seriously, it's getting too cold to do it outdoors in my garden."

"If I can get it up, it'll probably be quick."

"I'd better wear a long skirt and no knickers, then. But if we're minimising the chance of catching COVID… we wouldn't be doing it for fun!"

"Can't do face to face, then. How about doggy, wheelbarrow, downward donkey? Don't know what they are, but they don't sound facing."

"Masturbating seems simpler."
"Or I move in with you?"

*

"How are we going to cope with lockdown yet again?" Nusheen asked Vicky as they sat in her garden for tea, for the last time for a while.

"Shall we suggest things for people to do in our local newsletter?"

"Good idea. Like exercising, learning something new, sewing, making things?"

"Yes, and I've got a friend who says she does colouring, mindful colouring, whatever that is, and she keeps a thoughts diary and does visualisation. Imagining herself in a beautiful, calm, relaxed place."

"Writing a few good things that one has done that day, before going to bed?"

"Sounds good. Well, we can try. It might be helpful to some people..."

*

Michelle had a call from Hannah, who said that thirty-five per cent had sold in the view and another thirty per cent in single sales since. A brilliant result for this time, when they were only open for takeaways.

What a wonderful compensation for growing old. How lucky am I, she thought.

23–24 October 2020

Complete lockdown started in Wales yesterday (Friday) until 7 November, even though cases are concentrated in specific places, for instance Cardiff has 207 per 100,000 compared to twenty-five in Ceredigion. Businesses will have to close

again. There were 241 deaths and 21,242 new cases in the UK – the highest figure since June. More of the north of England has been put into the highest level – Tier 3. So now South Yorkshire, Greater Manchester, Liverpool, Lancashire and Warrington are in Tier 3. Northern Ireland and Scotland have five tiers. Our national debt now exceeds our GDP at 103 per cent. We borrowed £36.1 billion in September, £28.4 billion more than in September 2019!

It was done. A family had made an offer on her house. They seemed nice, liked the house as it was, and apparently didn't want to pull it to pieces, which Vicky would have found hard to have witnessed, living so near. Her offer for the cottage had been accepted and things were moving towards completion.

Was she doing the right thing? She loved her house. The stained glass, the tessellated tiled hall floor – the colours had seeped into her soul. She couldn't sleep for worrying and wandered around her garden, her sanctuary, from very early morning, wondering if she could go through with it. Today the early morning sky was overcast and getting darker. She raised her face to the sunless heavens and breathed in the cold air. Swathes of mist lay under the apple trees, and her feet made a dark green trail over the dewy grass. As she reached the bottom of the garden, there was a sudden downpour as the black clouds sent spiteful, stingingly cold sheets of water hurtling down. Her cardigan was drenched in a minute and plastered to her skin as she ran for the house.

Later, she was half-heartedly looking through the kitchen cupboards wondering which dishes and glasses she should take to a charity shop. *Take? I like the British Heart Foundation and if I get enough stuff and fill in the online form, they'll come and fetch it. Or I could do what I read that Joan Bakewell did when she was moving from her four-storey Victorian home. Give things I have loved to friends, asking them to throw them away without telling me.* Tears coursed down her face as she imagined her empty house, her home. A house that she had filled with furniture from parents and friends, with parties and people. The smell of polish from the oak floorboards, from flowers in vases, from whatever was cooking. The kitchen was a warm, welcoming place, with the wood-burning stove and the enormous oak table which could seat ten. She would have to sell it, together with so much furniture and the gym equipment. Though it felt as if she would be abandoning part of herself.

It's easy to forget that generations of other people have called this their home and generations more will do the same. I'm glad my dear house won't be on my route to catch a tube or bus, I couldn't bear to walk past and see the changes, they're bound to do some. She thought of the house on the corner, where close friends had lived but had downsized. It had been ripped apart and the lovingly tended garden looked like a bombsite, covered with skips for the last five years. Too hurtful to a home one had loved. *Life moves on. I must be grateful to still be part of it.* A sob escaped her, and she determinedly pulled dishes out of the cupboard and packed them into a box.

There was a ring at the doorbell. Quickly taking out her rollers, which she wore indoors in her now too-long hair, she went to answer it. Opening the main door, she saw a young, slender giantess standing on the step, looking in through the glass of the porch door. Her hair was long and honey-coloured, pulled back in a ponytail, her grey-blue eyes wide and shining. *What is she trying to sell me? Religion? To volunteer for something? Is she a neighbour?* The girl smiled. "Hello, Nana," she mouthed.

In shock, Vicky reached forward and opened the outside door. The girl standing there with big case and rucksack did look familiar. "Hello?"

"Hi, Nana, I'm Daisy. I haven't seen you since I was six or seven, was it?"

"Come in, come in. This is wonderful, what are you doing here?"

"Didn't you get Mum's letter?"

"Not yet, no."

"I don't know why she didn't email. I should have texted you. I was going to ring when the plane landed, then got caught up coming through passport control. I thought you'd know I was coming. So glad you're in!"

They were standing in the hall. Daisy, with the rucksack on her back and a large case next to her, was a few inches taller than her five-foot nine-inches grandmother.

"Have you had breakfast?"

"On the plane, some hours ago, yes, but I've come straight here. I'd love a herb tea."

"Leave your bags and come into the kitchen. You probably don't remember the house?"

"I dream about it and the lovely garden, but think I've altered it a bit over time. What are these boxes? You're not moving, are you?"

Vicky explained about having to downsize. "What are you doing here?" she asked.

"As you know, I've done my med school training and thought I'd like to do the two-year foundation training in London. I applied, and here I am. I'm hoping to live with you, that's why Mum wrote you a long letter, so you'd be able to think about it. Actually, we did wonder why you hadn't replied."

In shock, Vicky went to the kettle, filled it and put it on. "Toast or cake?" she asked.

"Ooh, cake please. But, Nana, Ben wants to come over when he leaves school and Mum is talking about coming back at the same time. He'll finish next summer, and Mum will have given in her notice and have applied to teach back here."

Vicky handed her granddaughter the cake tin and a mug of lemon and ginger tea. "Honey in your tea? This is all too much.

I don't want to lose the cottage and have to cope with this big house on my own when you all change your minds."

"Let's take this step by step, Nana. I'll speak to Mum. Not now, she'll be asleep, then running off to teach. Later? When she comes home? Perhaps we could keep both? We've all got to live somewhere, and London is where we want to be. We came from here, from you, and we're coming back."

In a daze, Vicky listened to Daisy's explanation of the hospital she had been accepted at and her five-year medical training, straining to find a resemblance in this self-possessed young woman with the fresh, sweet-faced, clear-eyed, smiling child in the last photograph she had been sent of her. Perhaps the shape of her nose, and certainly the colour of her eyes and of course the hair.

"There are only two med schools in New Zealand and thousands of people apply. I was lucky to get in. I'm so pleased to be here, Nana, I've missed you all these years!"

Vicky's brain was working overtime wondering what to do. Of course she'd love Sophie, Daisy and Ben to have the house and garden she had loved for so long, but what if everything fell through and she lost the little house? Could she buy it anyway? Remortgage this house and when they were all back, Sophie could perhaps pay it off, or some of it...? The evening passed in a blur of talking and planning...

*

Debs had driven down the motorway, past trees with their leaves in shades of gold, brown and green and the grass which had been bleached silver, to Steve's village in Wiltshire. She followed his instructions and parked in front of a grey stone cottage in a small lane, opening off the village green. She stretched as she got out of the car, having stiffened up after an hour and a half on the M3, and got the roses, wine and chocolates out of the boot.

His front garden was a profusion of cottage garden flowers and some vegetables. When he opened the door to her, a smile of pleasure spread across his face and into his eyes. "Come in, come in. How was your journey?"

They went through the house into a well-equipped kitchen, where he made her some tea while they chatted about her journey and what they had been doing. Then into a big, plant-filled conservatory to drink it. He had a way of cocking his head towards her, as if he didn't want to miss a word. *Perhaps his hearing isn't what it was?* However, she liked the sprung tension in his body, his mobile face, his nice firm mouth and wondered how it would feel on hers.

They strolled around the ancient village with its timber-framed, stone houses, the church and old workhouse. She could see why it had been used so often by film and TV producers. Then toured his garden and the orchard at the back, where he had been pruning trees. A tiny brook ran in and out of the orchard. They stared down at the water together. He concentrated on peeling a twig as he asked what she thought of the village.

"Quaintly beautiful," she said. "The sort of place that busloads of elderly ladies in their fleeces and comfortable shoes visit. Or where the super-rich and perennially absent have a third or fourth home. I'm not sure villages are for me, though. But perhaps I'm just not used to them, I've always lived in cities." *Mustn't be bitchy*, she thought, *I'm an elderly lady…*

He had bought smoked salmon, cheeses and wholewheat bread for a picnic lunch. The day was sullen and humid, with thunder in the air, so they sat in the conservatory, examining one another appreciatively. He had kicked off his sandals; his feet and legs in shorts were strong and brown. She was wearing a blue, low-necked, cap-sleeved midi dress, cinched in with a wide belt, and a long, blue, cashmere cardigan. Her model's legs were bare. She had coiled her blonde hair up in a loose bun. He thought she looked voluptuous, ripe.

"Would you like a glass of prosecco?" he asked.

She nodded. "Please."

They started talking about dietary supplements. He said that his current interest was in acetylcholine, a chemical neurotransmitter helping in memory and thinking. "I am almost a vegetarian," he said looking at her closely to see how she would take the news. "I mostly eat phytochemicals. I will eat some meat, but not beef liver, which is the food one finds most in."

She shuddered. "No, I can't eat offal, or anything rare. What other foods have it?"

"Eggs, cod, chicken, quinoa, yoghurt, broccoli and sprouts, but there is far less in these. So sorry, Debs, my wife was a nutritionist, a lecturer, I had to get interested. Ask me anything about nutrition and cancer. Actually, don't, if you want to keep enjoying sugar and alcohol."

"When did you move here?"

"About fifteen years ago. I could project manage in the computer industry from here. I wanted to retire, so they agreed I could work from home. Let's go for a lovely walk by the river."

Going for a walk was the Rich Tea biscuit of invitations for Debs. No fun. In fact, a punishment. "OK, but I need to use the bathroom…"

They went upstairs. He showed her around, then something about their closeness as he helped her open the bathroom door – "the handle sometimes sticks" – triggered passion, and ten minutes later she was arching beneath him, all the doubts and fears of a new relationship swept away. Later, she lay damply inside his arm as he stroked her hair, the scar from her caesarean and her soft, fine pubic hairs. Occasional street sounds drifting in through the partly open window.

28 October 2020

It is thought that 100,000 people are catching COVID every day in England and one in a hundred people has been infected already. Yesterday there were 367 deaths – the most

> since May. France had 500 deaths, and they and Germany are going into partial lockdown. Europe's total daily deaths have risen by forty per cent this week, with the highest number in Spain, the UK, the Netherlands, Belgium, Russia and Austria. China, Taiwan, Singapore and South Korea are doing better, because people focus more on doing the right thing and their test and trace system works better. October has been the wettest month since 1797 and the dullest since 1894…

"Mmm, that's interesting," Ruth mused, and went back to eating her half a grapefruit.

Gerry looked up from his newspaper. "What are you reading about?'

"You know that Imperial College has been researching into population immunity? They screened 365,000 people."

"Well?"

"The initial findings suggest that the spread of the virus hasn't improved our collective resistance, we can be reinfected!"

"The government's initial hope that we could develop 'herd immunity' while shielding the old and vulnerable was way off the mark, then. Hundreds of thousands would have died. What good will vaccines be?"

"I would guess that immunisation won't be the saviour as hoped and booster jabs will be necessary, perhaps as often as twice a year! Think we're way away from developing a full inoculation. It's going to take a lot longer than we thought…" She scraped the last of the juice out of the skin and looked longingly at the toast…

*

Debs woke early. The light was just beginning to creep into her bedroom; her pictures were still pits of darkness against her peach-coloured walls. She felt happy, joyful, still in her dream, before she came to complete consciousness. Mostly her dreams were a jumbled nightmare of petty anxieties, sexual desires and repressed longings, but this had been delicious. Pictures and aftershocks of Steve and their lovemaking swept back into her thoughts. She reached for her vibrator.

*

"People don't generally celebrate Halloween in New Zealand, but we did. Mum used to tell us stories of the parties you had." Daisy and Vicky were eating a vegetable curry for supper.

"Yes, she used to go out trick-or-treating with her friends, and we had teams of our friends apple bobbing, biting apples on strings, seeing who could peel the longest piece of apple skin, then throwing it over their shoulder to see what letter it made. Meant to indicate the name of one's future partner. We did quizzes. Oh, lots of things, as well as eating Halloween food. There's a box of spiders, rats, webs, witches' hats, all things scary under the stairs, but no chance of even having two friends here now, I'm afraid."

The phone rang. "Hello, Vicky," said Alison. "How are you?"

They chit-chatted, then Vicky explained about her granddaughter and her predicament about the little house she was buying.

"Well, I've got some good news for you. Malcolm wanted you to have half a million from his estate. He was so fond of you and was so grateful for your company and support during the last months. Of course, his estate and investments are not yet valued, he had taken out trusts a long time ago, for Bec and myself. Tax will be taken and probate proceed, but I think there will be plenty left for his wishes. Trouble is, you won't get it for a while, you know how probate drags on…"

"I'm totally shocked! Do you and Bec mind?"

"No, not at all. We're pleased that his last few months were spent happily with you. Don't let's lose touch. We will be able to visit one another when this lockdown is over. Malcolm would have been so pleased if he'd known about you using this money towards buying a little house. We look forward to meeting your family sometime."

*

"Will you be able to keep both houses now, Nana? If you get a mortgage on the little house, Mum will be able to pay it when she gets a job next September, and when you get the money from Malcolm's estate it will pay off most of it."

"Yes, I've got over half the value of it, which I can put down, so I can probably get a bridging loan for the rest."

She sighed with relief. It was all going to work out well. She would be able to live in either house and her dream of seeing her daughter and grandchildren had come true. Daisy had proved to be a wonderful housemate. She was thoughtful, tidy, eager to clean and garden and wanted to learn how to make her grandmother's favourite dishes and cakes. *How lucky am I?* she thought.

Daisy didn't remember much about the UK, so in her free time they planned to visit various places. Vicky explained that this time of year was the peak of beautiful autumn colour. They could see it in their own garden, so they planned trips to Osterley House and Petworth, and talked about others. Wading through the ankle-deep London plane, cherry and sycamore tree leaves in stunning colours in their road, they puzzled about which word described the noise their feet made.

"It sounds a bit like paddling through water if one shuffles. Shushing? Swooshing?" suggested Vicky.

"But the dry ones crackle, crunch and rustle. None of them are quite right, we need a new word."

They found a walk in Winchmore Hill in a newspaper, and one sunny day, drove to Buckinghamshire to do it. Daisy fell in love with the quaint hamlet, ancient woodlands and the gentle countryside, crisscrossed with permissive paths.

The sun was warm on their heads and the slight wind brought the trees to life.

*

"Alex has died." Diana had telephoned Vicky.

"What? Dead? How?"

"Yes, I should have told you when he had a stroke last week, but he was in hospital and everything was drama. He had another massive one a few days ago and it killed him."

"I'm SO sorry, Di. You must be devastated."

"It was a shock. No one knew he had been having TIAs."

"I didn't get to meet him. Was he overweight, did he drink or eat too much, smoke?"

"All of those, and he had high cholesterol and high blood pressure. After the first stroke he could barely speak or swallow, and his left side was paralysed."

"You poor girl! How terrible for you, just when you were selling up and changing your life. How tragic!"

"Will you come to the funeral? His three daughters are organising it. I'll let you know where and when. He was noisy and talked a lot, as if he knew everything, though I think he was bluffing half the time, but I miss him and feel a pain, a terrible pain, but was it love? Did I love him? It was too early to tell. Can we have a run around the tennis court this week. I'll probably be rubbish, but I need some exercise."

"Of course, tomorrow? Twelve o'clock? I booked a court and Sue can't play now."

"Great, see you then."

*

Christine had braved the first public transport she had taken since the pandemic began, to go to Alistair's little gallery in Notting Hill. There didn't seem to be less on the roads. It was, as ever, unending, dirty traffic, spraying water up from the wet road. Shoppers, their waterproofs slick with wet, crammed onto the bus. There was the smell of wet fleeces, hair and trainers from the passengers, huddled over their shopping and mobile phones. She was strap-hanging. *Where have all those liver spots suddenly appeared from? They've jumped up like mushrooms on my arthritic old claws – ugh!* A woman, a few seats away, had stood up and was pointing to her seat.

"It's OK, I can stand," said Christine.

"I wouldn't let my mother stand, why should I let you?" she replied and pulled her down onto it.

At the Silver Foxes meeting, she and Alistair had talked about her watercolour and oil botanical art, her hobby for many years. She was carrying her portfolio to show him and arrived at 6pm as he closed up.

"Ah, Christine, how lovely to see you. It seems we may have to close again on 5 November. It's a tragedy, and puts all the museums and galleries back into precarious financial positions. I'm hoping that the furlough scheme will be extended. Come in, let's have a glass of wine to cheer me up anyway. Shall I take your coat?" His voice was gentle as if he intuited that she was nervous.

She had been hiding inside her big duster coat for months now, feeling plain, worn out. It was her fortress against the world. When she took it off at night, she would heave a sigh of relief that she had got through another day. But it was warm in the gallery.

He locked the door and, carrying her coat, pulled down the blind and shambled his rather overweight, soft, shapeless body ahead of her to a high table containing wine and glasses.

They sipped their wine as he pored over her paintings, chatting about the Silver Foxes meetings as he did so. He talked about the people he knew from the tennis club. She was surprised when he described Debs as 'frightening'. She was feeling very anxious; no one had ever looked at her work before, but frightening? "Why?"

"She doesn't see me. I don't exist for her. I'm a shadow she doesn't deign to speak to, and certainly not play with."

"Really? I've always found her very warm and friendly."

He focused his pale blue eyes on her, as if wondering whether he was digging a hole for himself. "Hmm, well, she's rather a goddess. She's afforded popularity and celebrity simply from her looks. Her dazzling radiance and presence diminish everyone else."

Getting out his spectacles from his blue shirt pocket, he examined more of her paintings.

"Now, these are strong. The underpainting is particularly special. It's the rhythm and the bass, so the detail on the leaves shines out. So different from the crop of young artists coming from art school. I think we could have a small exhibition together with a young artist challenging the status quo. Can you leave a few with me?"

She was amazed, overcome. "Well, yes of course. I don't need them, keep them as long as you like."

"My car is parked around the corner, I'll give you a lift home. We don't live too far away from one another."

As they drove, her brain was whirling around. Should she invite him in, offer him something to eat? What? She hadn't been bothering to cook much since John died. Would he be interested in an omelette? With courgettes, mushrooms and cheese and that half a loaf of seeded wholewheat Vicky had made in her machine and given her this morning…?

4–5 November 2020

There have been 25,177 positive cases and 492 deaths in the UK. Lockdown in England is from the 5th. Schools and colleges are to stay open and food shops, but theatres, cinemas, concert and bingo halls, salons, zoos, botanical gardens, shops selling non-essential items, indoor and

outdoor facilities, pubs, bars, restaurants are all to close. The furlough scheme has been extended until next March. Countries across Europe are tightening their restrictions and introducing curfews. Various research has shown that even if there are rising numbers of infections in the country, there are few outbreaks in schools, particularly with six- to ten-year-olds. Adult staff are more likely to be infected. In the US election, Biden is nearing 270 electoral votes and Trump says he has easily won with legal votes. He has filed a series of lawsuits in the key battleground states.

"Theresa May made some excellent points in the Commons today, accusing the government of picking data to suit their coronavirus policies. She said the second national lockdown in England was based on the prediction that the country could see 1,000 deaths by the end of October. She challenged the validity of the data and asked if the house could see it, because what she had worked out from the available figures was nothing like that, and she quoted her analyses. I forget the figures. I've got a lot of time for her."

Gerald put his *Telegraph* down on the table and looked for the dish of fruit.

Ruth handed him the blackberries and raspberries. "Didn't Boris Johnson get up and walk out? So rude! And I had thought the same when I watched Sir Patrick Vallance and Chris Whitty presenting the case. That some of their points weren't borne out with the graphs and figures they showed us. How many graphs with incorrect, overstated figures have been used to justify this damaging lockdown?"

"Indeed, amateurish. The latest statistics for London do not justify this economic devastation. We're a lucky generation, not having fought in a war. This battle against COVID is being compared to one. Not knowing how long we'll be fighting this invisible enemy – where it is, how many people will die and how huge the collateral economic damage will be." He popped a spoonful of fruit into his mouth.

Ruth opened a pot of Greek yoghurt, took some and passed it across the table. "History tells us that nothing lasts forever and quite soon we'll be celebrating the discovery of a vaccine, as they did in 1942 when penicillin was first rolled out."

Gerald smiled. "But there will be no Marshall Plan, with which the US provided massive financial support for Western Europe."

"Didn't they give five per cent of their national income for four or five years?"

He nodded. "Their financial position is now far worse than after the Second World War with the medical costs of COVID and their ageing population. We're so lucky to be retired, not having to be furloughed or losing our jobs and looking around for support schemes. We're definitely 'the haves', not worrying about our incomes and how we're going to survive."

"Mmm, agreed. Poor Vicky won't be playing tennis for a while. Ridiculous closing tennis clubs when I can walk with her but not stand on the opposite side of the net and hit a ball! I'll ring her for a walk, it's a bit cold for swimming."

"Thought you said it was refreshing, and you were going to swim all the year."

Ruth looked sheepish. "It has got very cold, but yes, I'll ask her if she'd like to."

"Are you sure it's open?"

Ruth picked up her phone to look. "Well, it's outdoors, surely it should be? Oh no, it's closed too. How ridiculous. Come back Theresa May!"

*

Vicky dragged herself out of bed and pulled on her track trousers, T-shirt, old jumper, socks and trainers. It was a grey day and life seemed grey too. *Shall I get back into bed?* She paced around the room. *I know I should get on with the day, go out, rather than stay here in this half-world, where I lose my sense of time. Unless Daisy is here, I sit every evening looking for something to watch on TV and either making the coverlet or knitting mittens out of that jumper wool I never finished. I need to see and be with people – see them doing things in the real world. This is a half-life. When will normality return?*

She parted the curtains to let in the morning light. The cold mist was breaking up, to reveal the familiar shape of her shrubs and trees. The young silver birch, with its skirt of yellowing leaves and long whips of twigs, danced in the breeze, as if it were straining to leave its comfy bed in the soil.

*

Gerald picked up the phone; Amelia's name was showing on the handset screen. "Hi, Pops, no golf again?"

"Ridiculous decision. Who makes these ignorant, illogical decrees? England Golf has the highest possible standards to keep participants safe. Surely in a round of golf one is less likely to catch or pass on COVID than running, cycling or walking in urban areas."

"You'll have to go walking with Ruth now. You must keep fit. I've been glued to the news, with horror and total fascination. I'm addicted to Trump v Biden. The plot becomes more and more absorbing and shocking. People's right to vote has been sacred in the US for 200 years and Trump is denying the validity of postal votes! And 70 million people voted for him, despite his racism and misogyny."

"Agreed, and the longer it goes on, the more polarised and fractured the US becomes. At least the Republican solicitors are not prepared to help him, other than Giuliani of course."

"The girls are asking when we're going to have another lockdown quiz."

"Ruth organises our social life. She'll be back later. I'll ask her to ring you."

"Did you realise that the UK has one of the highest rates of obesity in the world and the second highest in its 50,000 deaths? There's a correlation between obesity and dying from COVID. In Japan, I read that the law requires people between forty and seventy-four to have their waist measured every year and if they are over a certain size they have to go to weight loss classes!" said Ruth as she and Vicky walked on the Heath.

"Can you imagine the outcry if that was law here?" Vicky sighed. "A whole month in which our resolve, patience and mental health will be challenged with no tennis or golf in England. I've signed petitions, written to my MP, even though she's a waste of space. I've even written to Number 10 asking them to reconsider."

"Yes, the first lockdown was a novelty in gorgeous weather, and so many Brits pulled together against the virus. Didn't a million sign up to be NHS volunteers and there were all the local support groups to help the most vulnerable, via Nextdoor and WhatsApp? People were helped with food parcels, and restaurants supplied hospitals with meals. Despite food shortages, we made bread, cakes and life felt energising, hopeful. We thought society was changing for the better. I don't think people are taking this second one seriously. They're annoyed at being told what or what not to do."

"Agreed. Just look at all the groups of people here! Wandering along, close to one another and not wearing masks! We banged pots for the NHS and felt emotional when we heard others doing it in nearby places. There was more commitment to doing what we were asked the last time."

"It was after the Dominic Cummings incident. People started bending the rules and using their 'common sense'. And then in July, when the hospitality industry opened up and we were allowed to go abroad, life was becoming normal again. But now, what hope is there that Christmas is going to be as we'd like it?"

"Yes, our 'world beating' test and trace system has been an abject failure. Before the summer it was given a target of 500,000 a day, but it's only now with the army being deployed that this looks as if it could be achieved."

"Mmm. All the endless, different 'experts' on our TVs contradicting one another. It makes people rebellious – has *anyone* got a clue what will happen next? Blanket lockdowns punish the careful, inflame the resentful and are destroying what's left of the economy!"

Vicky sighed. "Everything has been closed and we don't want to walk around the streets or be in brown, wet gardens in this cold greyness – even the birds have flown off to somewhere warmer. People who live alone are so lonely. Being permitted 'recreation outdoors with one other person' but no tennis and golf is irrational. The good feelings of the first lockdown have evaporated and it's obvious that people are fed up and not feeling at all compliant!"

"At least Trump v Biden was a welcome distraction from the C word. How is Daisy getting on?"

"She seems to be loving it. I'm just going to be seeing her on her days off from now. It's got too much, coming back from the hospital, stripping in the hall and disinfecting her shoes, bag and anything which wasn't going into the washing machine, and leaving them in the lobby. She would have a shower, and I wouldn't use that bathroom and then she'd eat the meal I'd left for her, in her bedroom. So we weren't communicating much. She was paranoid about bringing COVID back to someone of my age, even though I don't have any underlying health issues. Anyway, now Dove Cottage is mine, she's going to be there on her hospital days. We've taken some furniture and kitchen things over."

"That's a great idea. Will you be able to manage financially without letting it?"

"I hope so. For a few months anyway."

"It could be until the spring and the various vaccines being approved."

*

Vicky was starting to feel more human again, she had been locked inside herself in misery, just going through the motions of life. It was suddenly November and she hadn't made her Christmas puddings. Every year she made four, with a much-loved and honed recipe. She had spent every Christmas Day with friends since Rob died, and always took the pudding. She sent one to New Zealand and others to a local charity who cooked Christmas lunch for those unable to.

She got up at 7.30. The kitchen was warming up as the heating came on at seven. The fruit had been weighed, and together with the suet, breadcrumbs, sugar, spices and grated zest was soaking overnight in alcohol. She put the big aluminium pan on to boil and put the rest of the ingredients into a big bowl. The mixing was always the hardest part, but when done, the mixture went into the greased basins, then was covered with foil tied on with string, which she also ran over the tops to act as handles with which to lift them out of the boiling water.

Daisy slept longer on her days off, and by the time she had come down they were cooking. "Lovely smell. Who are all these puddings for, Nana?"

"One for us, one for Ruth and two for a charity which cooks Christmas lunch for the homeless and people who can't do it for themselves."

"That's good, it will make them very happy to have a nice Christmas lunch."

"Yes, and the majority are rather lonely older people. Some are poor, not healthy and have no family. Being old can be such a difficult stage of life, because it's the end, there's no future other than death."

"I hadn't thought much about being old, but a lady came into the emergency department yesterday with an upsetting story. She said: 'As I get to my front door and get my key out, I think, perhaps I need to pee soon, and then suddenly it's gushing out of me. Nothing I can do to stop it, however hard I try to control my muscles. I can't go to the cinema or theatre anymore. I can't wait in a queue. My sphincter doesn't work, even though I practise it and my pelvic floor, tightening and lifting 'n' times a day. I can't walk briskly, or I'm spraying wee every time my feet hit the ground. I've had various treatments – some tape put under my urethra, which only lasted a few years. Then radio-frequency sessions and a platelet-rich plasma injection, which is supposed to last a year or so. But I'm back to having no control. I can't go on like this, I'm at my wits' end, suicidal!' She was a smartly dressed lady, I felt so sorry for her."

"What on earth did you do?"

"Well, it isn't my specialism. I made her an emergency appointment with a consultant. I do know that there are various treatments. Colposuspension, an artificial urinary sphincter, Botox injections into the side of the bladder and a sling round the base of the bladder, though it sounded as if she'd had that procedure. It's probably vaginal laxity, and I've read about radio-frequency sessions to regenerate the vaginal walls. The appointment is next week, so I think she was glad she came."

"You'll have to give me some advice, very soon, I seem to be losing control. Have to get up in the night and if I think about going, it starts. My mum used to wear a sanitary towel. It's a seldom-discussed older woman's nightmare."

9–13 November 2020

9th: 24,957 cases and 413 deaths in the UK. The Evening Standard and senior business leaders are now continually

making the case for London, the powerhouse of the UK economy, to come out of lockdown ASAP. London's infection rate is 145 per 100,000 of population, whereas Manchester is 463, Bristol 408 and Leicester 434. 10th: 20,412 cases and 532 deaths, the highest since May. Pfizer/BioNTech have a promising vaccine, but testing is not completed. 11th: 33,470 cases, 560 deaths. People with learning disabilities were up to six times more likely to die in the first wave of the virus. 13th: 27,301 cases, 376 deaths. There have been 51,304 deaths from coronavirus since the beginning of the outbreak.

"How on earth are all these emergency funds that Rishi Sunak is paying out going to be recouped?" Gerald grimaced in pain as he got up from his chair after breakfast.

"Mindboggling amounts, goodness knows," Ruth sighed. "Eight months of everyone suffering and the only good news has been Biden's win, until this possible vaccine."

"Shares in IAG which owns British Airways flew up by forty per cent. The travel industry might yet be saved," he groaned.

"A glimmer of hope. Why are you walking like an old man?"

"My back is painful, knees stiff, I *am* an old man. I need some young blood, or a miracle." He stopped his laboured progress at the door. "I hope you don't feel that I'm not still very attracted to you. I've just not been in fine fettle recently."

Ruth smiled. "That's a relief. But there's no evidence that young people's blood is the elixir of life, though it appears to be, in experiments with rats. You really need to exercise more. Your inactivity is the root cause of your problems. Remember I told you about that research on drivers and conductors on double-decker buses? The conductors were half as likely to die of a heart attack, and there is no illness, even Alzheimer's, which isn't improved or prevented through exercise. You can't play golf for a month, but even that once or twice a week isn't enough. What are you going to do about your inactivity? I'll be having to push you around in a wheelchair soon if you carry on sitting down all day."

He transferred his weight painfully from one foot to another. "You're right. I'll ring up Neville and get him to come for a walk with me. It's no good going with you, I'd be lagging behind."

"Shall I ask Vicky if we can use her gym? She has offered so many times. We might even get some cake afterwards if we go in the afternoon?"

Gerald sighed. "The cake is tempting."

*

Diana dressed with care for the funeral, dreading that Alex's three daughters and Daniel would detect her relief at his death and deduce that she hadn't cared deeply. She didn't often wear makeup, but felt the need for it today, before she felt she could show her face. The cliché 'it's for the best' had been used quite often, as after two strokes in quick succession, so many people said he "wouldn't have wanted to live, if he was unable to move or communicate". She didn't say, but it had, perhaps, been a relief for her. She didn't want the task of looking after him for the rest of his life, especially as she wasn't at all sure that she had really been in love with him. Flattered, yes, but had she loved him? She would never know now.

Why were men so selfish? She thought back to her ex-husband. He was generally cheerful – liked his job, a drink, other women and his sport – but not exciting. *I wasn't the centre of his life. He enjoyed playing away, dipping his wick too much to value me. All he wanted was for me to be a good housekeeper and mother, an occasional companion, a willing lover and not to need anything from him. Then, when he was having the affair with his secretary, he was too cowardly to burn his boats with me, his wife, until that thin creature with her earnest, big brown eyes got pregnant.*

So, she had dressed in black and had even bought a black hat with a veil to hide her face. Adam had supported her in and out of the church. She was shocked at how easily she had got over Alex's death and how almost relieved she had felt not to have to look after him.

They all drove back to his house, and Mrs Gilbert, the housekeeper, who had laid out the finger buffet, was standing at the door with glasses of wine. There was a flood of chatter in the room from people Diana had never seen before. They looked theatrical, spoke loudly and seemed to know one another. She refilled glasses, moving around, with a sad little smile on her carefully made-up face.

Some people asked if there was going to be tea, so she went into the kitchen to make some, but when she emerged with the teapot and milk, her heart almost stopped. Who was that talking to Adam? It had been at least thirty years, but it could be Robin; this man looked rather like him. She suddenly went ice cold and her hands shook. The teapot rattled in her grasp; some of the milk escaped from the jug. She hastily put them down on the table and turned her back on the throng behind her, trying to calm herself, gain composure. A hand held her elbow and a voice said: "Mum, Dad is here."

She turned, trying not to tremble, trying to make her face light and bright, and there he was, standing in front of her. It felt as if there were a lead weight attached to her vocal cords. "What are you doing here? You didn't know Alex. Were you confused? Did you hope it was my funeral?" She tried to smile, but her face was stiff.

"I wondered what sort of man would want to take you on."

He had aged well. Looked slim, fit, relaxed, not too lined. The old irritation was spreading like a rash inside her. Anger boiling up from her stomach into her throat, making her want to scream at him. She spat out, "One who wouldn't have walked out on his son and wife."

"Walked out? Driven would be more applicable. And Adam has just traced me, and we wanted to meet."

Their voices had risen, were fighting for supremacy, getting overwrought. "Stop it, you two," said Adam firmly. "It's all a long time ago. It doesn't matter anymore."

They both looked at him and Diana blew her nose loudly, sneezed and turned to pick up a sandwich, though she knew it would taste like chalk in her dry mouth.

"All these years I thought you were dead," Adam said to his father.

"Why, did she tell you that?"

"I was protecting you, thought it would be less hurtful than saying he had been an alcoholic and unfaithful," Diana blurted out, her anger fizzling away, like air out of a balloon. She put the unbitten sandwich down on the table.

"I did drink, and did end up with my secretary, but only because you were destroying me with your endless prattle, your demands and lack of warmth. I'm sorry to have not been around for you, son, but I've never hidden, hoping you'd want to find me one day."

Mrs Gilbert came up, closely followed by Kate and Ellen, Alex's daughters. "Would you like a drink, or tea?" she asked Robin. "Is everything OK, Diana?" asked Kate.

Adam introduced them to his father, while Diana tried to recover her composure. People were leaving, and Mrs Gilbert and the daughters had to get coats and say goodbye.

"You left us, finally, thirty years ago. We've had no word and no help from you in all that time. How dare you turn up now, at this sad occasion," Diana exclaimed.

"Adam found me, luckily. He was looking for my grave, records about the car accident, and he turned up me and my wife and two children." Turning to his son: "I'm sorry I kept away, I was ashamed, thought it was for the best."

"You lied to me," Adam said to his mother.

"I protected you," she said again. "Don't look at me like that, you'd do the same for Ellie and Mark."

"You've got children?" asked Robin. "I've got grandchildren?" He looked excited.

"Are grandchildren more important than your own child?" she squeaked.

"For thirty years I believed my father was dead. It never occurred to me that he might have been alive. I'm so angry about your lies! How can I forgive that?" Adam was wringing his hands in his distress.

"Tell him about all the other women. How you were out all the time, drinking and womanising," she said desperately. "I was left in, hiding it all from you. You were too young to know what he was up to."

They were the only people left, still standing by the food table, glasses in their hands. "I've got to help clear up, please go," she said and started picking up plates and glasses. She felt tired, so tired, as if she could crumble into a heap. Her heart bled to see them walking out together, both tall, nice looking, father and son.

*

Vicky didn't get to speak to Diana at the funeral and didn't go to the wake, so rang her next morning.

"How are you feeling, Diana? You must be in shock."

"Shock, yes, but he wouldn't have wanted to live as a disabled person. I miss the person he thought I was. I've realised that when someone dies, the person you were in their eyes dies with them and leaves you with the old you. The one you were when you met them. Maybe I was quite enjoying the different me. Though to tell you the truth, don't tell anyone else, but I was thinking I'd made a mistake, giving up my independence to live with someone used to getting their own way. Thank goodness my sale hadn't gone through, so we hadn't yet bought the house on the south coast." She sounded lugubrious, unsettled, and rushed on. "But even more shocking, Robin, Adam's father, turned up. Adam had traced him and they wanted to meet straight away, so Robin came to the wake. Adam is angry with me, having told him his father was dead all these years."

"No, really? I didn't know him, but wow, could anything be a bigger shock?"

"Alex has left me the house on Bute, as long as I allow his daughters and grandchildren to holiday there when they want to. He's controlling me from the grave, getting me to organise who goes there when."

"Is it a big house?"

"Four bedrooms. Kate wondered if we should keep it. Glasgow is a long way away and the family have preferred holidays in hotter places for the past few years. I've decided to go and look. I've booked a train ticket for tomorrow. Need to get away."

*

She took a train from London to Glasgow, a smaller train to Wemyss Bay and then the ferryboat to Rothesay. The sea was rough, so the boat chugged very slowly and noisily through the powerful waves. Spray rained down over her, the only passenger. She started to feel sick. The boatman was grimly staring ahead, gripping the wheel. It seemed to go on for far more than the advertised thirty-five minutes. She closed her eyes… Then suddenly she felt the boat slow down, the harsh throbbing changing to a steady rhythm, and they were at the mouth of a harbour, sheltered from the harsh winds.

It was still raining heavily, and the dark clouds made any buildings on the island invisible. The boat's engine cut out as it moved towards the jetty, and a man got out of a truck parked where they were to pull in, so he could secure it to a capstan. The wind howled and rocked the boat, so he put out his hand to steady her. "Macpherson," he said as an introduction. "Dae ye ken whaur ye're gaun?"

She nodded. "I've got the address."

When she was safe on dry land and he had put her bag on the truck, the two men started to unload the cargo, mostly food and DIY orders for people on the island.

The house was detached, but in a road of other houses a mile or so from the harbour. She was cold and tired and was dreading arriving to a damp, freezing house, but Kate had rung the neighbour and the heating was going and the house seemed very comfortable and well equipped. She took out the sandwiches she had bought in Euston, looked for some tea and found plenty of varieties and tins of soup. She heated up minestrone and put on the TV.

*

Marion came walking up the road as Vicky was walking down. The dry autumn leaves rustled under their feet and skittered along the pavements in the breeze, like a plague of brightly coloured cockroaches. They smiled at one another; though their masks hid their mouths, they could tell from one another's eyes that they were pleased at the chance encounter.

"How are you getting on?" Vicky asked.

"My world has shrunk and me with it." At this thought, she straightened up and pushed back her kyphotic shoulders. "But I don't mind my own company. I seem to go inside myself to a portion of my past and examine and reinterpret it. My parents came here from Germany between the wars, you know. They set up a suit-making company and worked so hard that they became wealthy, though they never took the time off to enjoy it. Having time to think has been interesting, though being trapped inside in a cold, wet winter isn't a good prospect."

"TV is so undemanding and boring. So much about cooking, animals, quizzes, doing up one's house or buying one. I find the only programmes I watch are the news and political programmes."

"True, and I'm older than everyone in the books I read and the TV I watch. If ever there are older characters, they are stereotypes, smiley old dears or rancorous, cantankerous curmudgeons."

"Not computer literate, eccentric, radical women, full of energy and quirky oddballness."

"I'm waiting for my cat to die, then I'm off to Switzerland. Most of my friends are dead or confined to care homes or their homes."

They both grinned and carried on their way.

19–24 November 2020

19th: 22,915 cases and 501 deaths. The Oxford-AstraZeneca vaccine shows a strong immune response in sixty- and seventy-year-olds and doesn't have to be stored at minus seventy degrees like the Pfizer-BioNTech vaccine. The Moderna vaccine is £28 a dose, the Pfizer £15 and the Oxford-AstraZeneca less than £3. 24th: 18,213 cases, but 696 deaths, the highest since mid-May.

Gerald and Ruth were walking on the Heath, with what seemed like half the population of London and their dogs. A biting east wind rattled the bare branches of trees together and cut through their clothes. Grey clouds raced overhead. Ruth shivered. "This lockdown feels very different from the first, where we had a sense of togetherness. The roads are full of cars, no one cares if they are doing non-essential journeys. Walking anywhere is hazardous. Everyone seems to be out with their dogs, a coffee and a few friends, and social distancing is rare. They march along three or four abreast, shouting at one another, oblivious to us practically in hedges, or in the road, trying to avoid them. Do they WANT to catch COVID? The polls may say that the majority of the country approves of lockdown, but actual observations of the restrictions are certainly not communitarian." She sighed as they made a muddy detour to avoid a group of six, filling the path in front of them.

"The government, like many across the world, seems to have nationalised personal responsibility. Why don't they leave us to our own devices? People have got 'lockdown fatigue' and are bored and would prefer to decide for themselves how we cope with it."

"Trump is still trying to stay in power. Did you see that he fired the director who vouched for the reliability of the result, is demanding recounts and filing suits in various states to block the certification of results?"

"Yes, he is trying to get Republican-friendly legislators to ignore the popular vote and appoint their own electors, which they can do if fraud is suspected."

"So shocking. Malignant, orange, stupid man. Did you see the Midwest, whose governors laugh at social distancing and masks, has the world's highest fatality rates! Trump's still saying that there has been massive fraud and they're checking graveyards to see how many dead people voted! And Christmas is up to three households who can meet indoors for up to five days."

"That's going to be a problem. I'll have to have Catherine and leave out Amelia and family, and of course Charles."

"Shall we see who wants to come?"

"With your wonderful cooking? Just hope no one gets upset…"

*

When Daisy had time off, she and Vicky were doing walks around famous parts of London, which were currently quiet, with people working from home and no tourists. This morning they were walking Royal Westminster and aristocratic St James's. They took an empty tube to Westminster and Daisy was introduced to Big Ben, which was shrouded in scaffolding. Then the Houses of Parliament, Downing Street, the Treasury,

Ministry of Defence, Foreign and Commonwealth Office, Horse Guards Parade, Buckingham Palace, the gentlemen's clubs, Westminster Abbey, St James's Palace, Green Park and many more famous streets and buildings. They read the guide/walk book to one another and marvelled at the amazing architecture, the elegance and history.

*

Janet and Barry decided to get married, without asking for the blessings of their expectant heirs.

They telephoned Vicky to be their best woman.

Blasts of wind had been tearing through her garden, rattling the windows. The lawn was strewn with leaves and twigs, and she was trying to brush them up in the biting gusts, but stopped, and went to see them, scuffing through the leaves from the London planes which had drifted into heaps and were skittishly whirling in the flurries of polluted city wind. The sky was grey and heavy. She hardly noticed, as she was deep in thought about why they were bothering with this ceremony aged seventy-eight, rather than just carrying on living as they were. Perhaps they were hoping marriage would make their relationship better? Or did they miss the state of being married? Or was it because they felt they should have married one another years ago?

"My daughters go to church. They seem to think our sexual congress is immoral. We both had small registry office weddings, so this time, we're going to do it in style, but not until the summer, when hopefully we will be free again."

Vicky looked at their glowingly happy faces and surprisingly felt a pang of envy.

26 November 2020

There are now 17,555 cases and 498 deaths today. It's Thanksgiving in the US, the world COVID capital, with four per

> cent of the world's population and more than twenty per cent of its deaths. London is back in Tier 2 next week. Only one per cent of England has been put into Tier 1. £394 billion has been borrowed this year – approximately £4,000 per UK citizen.

"So that's still no socialisin' indoors, apart from Christmas!" Debs sighed gloomily.

"All the parties we can't give or go to, it's tragic, but at least we'll be able to play tennis again," said Vicky.

They were sitting on a bench overlooking Highgate pond, watching the swans, herons and ducks. A rare excursion for Debs; she wasn't a walker.

"Germany has been hit hard by COVID cases recently and Merkel can't get the regional leaders to have a unified response and lock down together. The Germans are very keen on their civil liberties. Thousands of people demonstrated for their freedom in Berlin. She has an uphill battle to do a national lockdown."

"Yes, and the Swedish libertarian approach is changin'. I guess nowhere is immune. We all have to keep away from one another and change our way of life until we get vaccinated. I may go mad, though, if I can't cuddle my grandchildren soon. Danni is sayin' we shouldn't meet at Christmas and risk the dance macabre in January but Zoom – the fast food of contactin' our loved ones – instead."

"If only getting a test was easy! So all those of us who live alone, who are old and desperate for a hug, could feel safer with our families. Have you seen the ridiculous Christmas rules?"

"What, the takin' your own plate, glass and cutlery, don't pass dishes around, don't sing and keep the windows open."

"Or cancel Christmas until the summer?"

"How do we know some other mutation won't appear when we've been vaccinated against this one?"

"And do you think that spending all this time at home

will make the thought of restarting our normal social lives seem just too exhausting? Why go to a restaurant and then cinema, when one could curl up on the sofa with a takeaway and Netflix?"

"Yeah, a year's subscription to Netflix costs less than a night out at the cinema for four people. I know the big screen is infinitely more captivatin' than watchin' a small one, but will we want to bother? Perhaps it's the end of cinemas."

"Shouldn't we be planning the next Silver Foxes meeting? Doesn't sound very exciting on Zoom, unless we have a focus. How about a quiz?"

"Hate quizzes, I'm hopeless at them… But I'll work out the joinin' info, send out the Zoom link, put everyone into their breakout groups and make a PowerPoint of the questions – if you work them out and get a quiz master?"

"Mmm, Jo would probably be good at that. I'll do the publicity. Do you think we should widen our pool and advertise through the community centre, or keep it to current people and their friends?"

"Keep it small and the people we know already, I think, so it feels as if we're a group, and let's have it before Christmas."

"Sounds good, let's go for it."

They sat either end of the bench, hunched against the cold, planning the event in their heads while staring at the birds leading their normal lives, wishing more than anything that they could too. The trees on the hill above them were black skeletons against the unbroken dome of grey sky, darkening as the afternoon moved towards evening.

3–7 December 2020

There are 14,979 cases and 414 deaths today, bringing the total to 60,113. Lockdown has finished and London was put into Tier 2 yesterday, which means that pubs and bars could

open if they provide meals; hairdressers, shops, pools, gyms, tennis and golf clubs are allowed to open, and the Rule of Six applies outside with only support bubbles inside. In the US, the daily total of deaths is a record high of 2,800 and 100,267 hospitalisations. The first batch of the Pfizer-BioNTech coronavirus vaccine came through the Channel Tunnel from Belgium. It will be distributed to hospital vaccination centres around the UK, which is the first Western country to vaccinate the public.

Vicky and Diana were having a drink outside, after their game of tennis.

"I don't think I want this Pfizer vaccine. I'd like to wait for the Oxford-AstraZeneca."

"Why?"

"Possibly the fact that it will be cheaper and easier to distribute, not sure, it's just a feeling. This Pfizer one was supposed to go to the care homes and care staff after the hospitals, but because it has to be stored at minus seventy degrees, it's now thought that it won't be possible. Anyway, one has to have two full doses, and if that happens, say, next week and just after Christmas, one doesn't have immunity until January."

"This always happens. The government announces something and it's as if they haven't been given accurate facts by the scientists, because then the PHE, BMA, GPC and all these other bodies, including the NHS, say it's not possible when it comes to it. Why don't they work it all out before? It's depressing. It makes the government look so stupid."

"Agreed. Anyway, tell me about the house on Bute."

"It's lovely, everything one could need is there. Nice, helpful, friendly, local neighbours with lovely gardens. A stunning view, plenty of shops, some great walks and I saw deer, a hare, loads of birds. There's a Gothic mansion – not open at the moment – a castle, sandy bays *and* a golf course! I went there. Didn't play, but people were very friendly and offered to lend me clubs. In fact, my neighbour plays. Who wants to go to the south coast!"

"How brilliant! So, it's perfect for holidays, then?"

"Holidays? I'm going to see if I can live there! My flat here can be for holidays."

"Oh NO! I'll miss you. Won't you miss your tennis?"

"Apart from three golf courses, there are six tennis courts and four bowls clubs, what more could I want? It will be a new start, getting to know the place and people. My bones are weakening, nails crumbling, hair thinning, waist disappeared. I've turned into a toad and am not going to find anyone now to kiss me and turn me into a princess. You'll have to come and stay."

"I certainly will. When are you going back?"

"Probably next week, and Adam is coming for Christmas with Ruby, Ellie and Mark. He seems to have forgiven me. Ellen might come too, if we're allowed. How about that?"

"Perfect!"

*

Vicky stood at her kitchen window looking out at the sodden garden. A blustery wind was tugging at tiles, blowing twigs to tap on doors and windows, but there were still plenty of flowers everywhere. Almost all the roses seemed to be having their last fling, and the mountain ash was covered in pink berries, the cotoneaster in orange ones, and the white-flowered viburnum tinus looked beautiful against the red-leaved Virginia creeper. Her gaze went down to the window box, the other side of the glass. Beautiful, with pansies, cyclamen, innumerable bulbs just peeping through, a golden cypress and grey-green eucalyptus either end and variegated ivy trailing over the edges.

Daisy had two days off, beginning tonight – they could do a walk. Unless of course she had organised something else. *I mustn't assume that all her time will be spent with me.* She sighed. *The last nine months have turned lives upside down,* mentally, physically and emotionally. Social calendars have been empty, and day after monotonous day has passed with no quick fix of being able to go out with friends, or invite them round.

I've hugged my very closest friends tight. Zooming, phoning, emailing and meeting up in the garden or at tennis, but there are dozens in my outer circle who have disappeared from my world, and I miss them.

Though some, who were in my outer circle, have moved to the inner one, just by the fact that they live near and are up for socially distanced walks. And some close friends have moved to be less close because of their attitude towards risk.

In the summer there was a brief period of normality, but I've felt myself drifting away from friends who don't walk and those who take no care to mask up and socially distance. Oh, for this to be over.

*

The local theatre had opened at last and very socially distanced tickets had been on sale.

Vicky bought tickets for herself and Daisy, with almost insane excitement. There's something uniquely wonderful about live shows. She hadn't watched any plays from theatres during lockdown; she had already seen many of them and hadn't wanted to see others. She loved finding out which friends wanted to go, booking the seats, meeting for something to eat, because plays don't usually start until eight. Then the expectant hush when the lights dim and the absorbing magic when the curtain rises.

She hadn't liked this play when she had seen it years before and it hadn't improved with time, but Daisy found it intriguing and they bumped into three women Vicky knew. So, it was a sociable and successful evening.

And she wore proper shoes and a skirt, instead of her lockdown uniform: her K Swiss trainers and black jogging pants…

8 December 2020

> The mass vaccination programme with the Pfizer-BioNTech vaccine started today at University Hospital, Coventry, with Margaret Keenan who will be ninety-one next week. She was the first person in the world to receive it, and the Christmas T-shirt she was wearing sold out. Thousands more vaccinations followed across the UK. Neath Port Talbot has the highest COVID case rate in the UK, with 693.6 per 100,000.

Gerald had finished his breakfast and looked over at Ruth. "I'm reading an article asking why there is such a song and dance about the COVID deaths, because the fatalities are mostly among the elderly and/or people with 'underlying conditions'. The *Telegraph* is saying that more under-sixties died on roads last year than those with no underlying conditions from coronavirus. Fuel for the view that the old and sick are those dying, so can't the rest of us get on with our lives? It's saying that this is why Harold Shipman got away with murdering so many people – there was a view that they would have died soon anyway. Similarly, when over 450 patients at Gosport War Memorial Hospital were injected with diamorphine, even though they hadn't been dying, the doctor wasn't prosecuted or even struck off. Yet, the three most popular people in this country are old, so we as a nation can't despise the elderly."

"Let me guess who they are: Captain Tom? The Queen? David Attenborough?"

*

Liz had designed a Christmas card to look like a fun mask. "Can't you write a poem to stick inside?" she asked Paul. He had a distinctive way with words, was working on an anthology, though he was modest about his efforts.

"My poems are a work-in-progress, perhaps like my life."

He read for a long time every night; she wondered how many hours' sleep he got.

"How about doggerel? That's easy, and people don't want to read anything heavy."

An hour or so later, he came in with one, which they arranged four on a page, photocopied, cut them up and stuck one on each card:

> We thought it would be over, before the summer came.
> They said it was a type of flu, though not quite the same.
> It started in a market, Chinese pangolin from bat
> Skied in Europe, then to here, and really that was that.
> What if it's just nature, teaching us to care?
> What if it's just nature asking us to share?
> Some of us have lots of friends to talk to and to phone
> But many now can't work or play and live quite alone.
> Our Christmas happiness depends on seeing all our lovely friends,
> No parties for us all this year, so where will be the Christmas cheer?
> Please keep in touch, don't eat too much and exercise, the task.
> Until we get the vaccine, Santasize, space and wear your Christmask!

Then he went back to painting the hall, a very pale mint colour. It looked sophisticated, cool and of course, clean.

*

Gerald had a phone call from the Royal Free, inviting him to telephone for a vaccination this week.

"Impressive, don't think any of my golf friends have been summoned, and one or two are also over eighty. Life seems to rush from one birthday to the next. All too soon I'll be old and powerless, though I hope not helpless for my young wife to have to look after me!" He put his arms around Ruth. "I hope you don't regret marrying such an old man?"

She giggled. "Silly person. You're only a few years older than me, perhaps you'll be pushing me about one day?"

15 December 2020

>There are now 20,263 cases and 232 deaths today; London, Essex and parts of Hertfordshire have been put into Tier 3. A new variant may be associated with the faster spread, as cases are doubling every seven days. Theatres, cinemas, pubs, restaurants will close. More than 34 million people will be in Tier 3. Schoolchildren, particularly, are spreading the virus. Wales has the most cases. The number of jobs lost in the UK during the pandemic is 800,000. The Netherlands has 8,496 new cases, so is locking down till 19 January. All non-essential shops are closed in Germany and there is a curfew, also in France. Italy has the highest number of cases and deaths since March.

"At last! The electoral college formally elected Biden as the next president of the US, though he won't assume the role till 20 January. At last the destructive tenure of Trump, who has disdained truth, the norms of democracy and has shown no respect for the dignity of his office, will be over," sighed Gerald in relief.

"Hopefully there will be some progress in gender equality before the next election. There are now twenty countries with a woman head of state, yet America produces two old men to vote for… By the way, did you see that two of the health journals, the *BMJ* and the *HSJ*, are urging the government not to allow household mixing at Christmas?" Ruth asked as she and Gerry chatted over the breakfast table.

"I don't think they will rethink now. People have made arrangements and are looking forward to it. And anyway, Parliament voted for three households to be able to mix and would have to vote for the change."

"There seems to be a growing frustration and anger at our being told what to do and how to behave. You can see the rules being broken daily. I don't think a lot of people would take any notice if Christmas mixing was banned."

"You may well be right. The teens and twenty-somethings seem to be rebelling the most, and it's having such disastrous consequences for our economy and so many people's mental health."

"Shall we go for a walk this morning?"

"Not keen, but I know you're right, we need to." He tried to push himself up from his chair, but like a man drowning who painfully manages to rise to the surface, but not quite, the chair reclaimed him. He flushed, embarrassed, pulled his chair nearer the table and with its aid, pulled himself up. "Yes, I know, I should practise 'sit down, stand up' every day. I will."

Hmm, Ruth thought. *How many times have I reminded him? I wonder sometimes if what I say penetrates. He's entertained by my opinions and knowledge, but does he take notice of them, adapt because of them? He likes to talk with men and is amused by women, but are we a lesser species? It's how he was brought up. Like an aristocrat from another era, where the little woman manages homelife. He will never have done housework or cooking. But I do love him, am very happy with him and will not be able to change him now.*

*

Nusheen and Vicky were walking in the local park, and Nusheen was talking quite angrily. "It's irritating that each decade after one's thirties is increasingly sad, petering out from our golden heyday. So is the rest of life going to be miserable and anticlimactic? We are expected to always give the impression that we are younger and more flexible than we are, both physically and mentally, so we're not thought to be a decrepit crone. The only way to be visible is to look young. If you look your age, you're not listened to." Her luminous skin crinkled slightly into a frown. "Yesterday after our walk, I went up to the bathroom, and when I was washing, I peered closely in the mirror and eased the skin at the side of my temples back, then the side of my cheeks, like *this*… Look, wouldn't I look better like this?" And she pushed the skin at the side of her face backwards. "I'm getting pouchy bags and a saggy, crepey neck. My face was red and pinched with cold, but *also drooping*! I must have a facelift! Wonder who knows a top-class cosmetic surgeon?"

"*Drooping?* Where?"

"Here, under my jaw and there are *pouches, crepey pouches*, under my eyes! I'm going to have cosmetic surgery. Farzad won't want an old woman for a wife!"

"How do you know that they won't mess up your lovely face?" Vicky asked. "You could end up looking like those weird American women, freaky death heads with Donald Duck lips! I wish that there were more celebrity women who dared to age."

"Oh, I'm not going to have much, just a pull-up here and a pull-back there. It'll be fine. So many women have it now."

"I read about a woman dying after she'd had liposuction in Turkey. Please be very careful!"

"I'll find one with great references."

Vicky laughed. "Really?"

"And don't say I'm doing it for others, it's for me – so I feel better about myself. You've had knee and shoulder surgery. You could have put up with them and given up tennis, but you improved yourself."

"Changing the subject, did you see that hundreds of puppies, bought enthusiastically in the pandemic, some for

£3,000, are now being offered for sale on websites or handed in to charities?"

"People didn't realise how much time and attention they need."

"True, I read that the Dogs Trust charity is getting thousands of calls from people wanting to get rid of their puppies, and they're worried that many will be abandoned."

"Puppies are being stolen and offered for sale, they're so expensive now. I don't understand why people didn't think it through, having to get up at 6am to give them a walk before work. That they need training, so they know how the owner wants them to behave."

"And they live for ten to fifteen years, which is a big commitment for an owner."

17 December 2020

There were 612 deaths yesterday and Wales is restricting Christmas socialising to two households. Bristol was put down to Tier 2, but two-thirds of the country – 38 million people – are in Tier 3, and it sounds as if most of the UK will be in lockdown after Christmas.

"I've had my vaccine jab," Marion called proudly as she and Vicky saw one another across the street.

"Oh great, where did you go?" Vicky called back as she put a picnic basket in the back of her car.

Daisy and Vicky had decided to go to the sea on Daisy's day off. To breathe in clear, cold air. She would be working on Christmas Day and Boxing Day. Whitstable and London were both in Tier 3. They set off for the Kent coast.

"Why is it assumed that retired people live in the past, Nana? You and your friends and neighbours seem to be very involved in your present and future, use computers and are actively engaged in life."

"Yes, irritating, isn't it. There's a huge difference between people who are looking after themselves and those in care homes. They tend not to look forwards, but backwards at the life they had. But when you're paying bills, shopping, organising repairs to your house, your social life and so on, you're very much in the present."

The day was cool and cloudy with a forecast of showers, but all they encountered was a few stray drops on the windscreen. Vicky parked on Marine Parade, and they walked into the charming, old-fashioned town, avoiding people coming the other way. They then retraced their steps, past the harbour, and decided to walk towards Herne Bay on the coastal path.

"Not the whole way. I think it's about five miles, so ten will take too long."

"OK. What an amazing number of beach huts, there are hundreds."

They walked and walked next to the shingle beach, with groynes installed to protect the beach from being washed away. A fisherman was reeling in his catch from the calm, silver water.

At last they left the beach huts behind and were on a grassy path overlooking the bleak, grey sea, now breaking gently onto broken rocks.

"Nana, I've got something to tell you, which is as upsetting to me as it will be to you." Daisy pulled her grandmother down onto a seat that they were passing. The nippy wind blew her fringe back, exposing her thin face and worried expression.

Vicky leant against the back and tried not to think that it could be about Sophie. She could feel sweat gathering under her arms, her forehead and face, though she was as cold as ice. Her heart was a stone. The sea blurred into the sky, grey and more grey, with no demarcation. The grey was reflected in her; she felt dead, dull, grey.

"I was so angry with Mum," Daisy said rather bitterly, biting her bottom lip and gazing out to sea.

Vicky looked at her quizzically and tried to breathe deeply to stop her heart beating faster, to relax. *Is she going to say that Sophie isn't coming back?*

"She never did send that letter telling you I was coming! She said she'd hoped I'd change my mind…" she blurted out.

"Is she still coming herself at the end of the school year?"

Daisy turned with a surprised face, her recently cut fine fair hair like a halo in the breeze. "Well, yes, I think so, she hasn't said she's not, and she won't want to stay there without Ben or me."

"She must have lots of friends. Hasn't she got a boyfriend? Your father and grandfather have been dead a long time now."

"Fifteen years. Boyfriend? Well, she had someone, Richard, about five years ago, but no one since. Perhaps she'll meet someone over here."

The sun came out weakly and the air was warming up. They walked on the beach and Daisy made sketches of the cliffs, the shape of some pebbles, rubbed smooth by the sea and showing different colours as she moved them in her hands. "I wanted to be an artist when I was younger."

Vicky went for a walk, then sat on a rock and wrote a poem:

Shades of grey, a bleak, stark day.
Clear, cold sea and heavy sky.
Prostrate, shiny granite, towering cliffs,
I yearn for no more than this.

Alone I stride, scramble and sit.
Comforting, soft sea sounds, bird calls
Suffuse the air. I leap and soar
And never feel solitary here.

Water caresses, fondles, licks
The gleaming rocks, searching, prying

Bubbling, rushing, enveloping
All but me, its companion.

You too would love this December day
So subtly lovely in shades of grey.
I do not miss you, or feel incomplete.
I am content that we were friends

20 December 2020

There have been 67,000 deaths – 534 yesterday – and 27,052 cases. The new COVID variant is seventy per cent easier to catch. Put into Tier 4 are: thirty-two boroughs, City of London and parts of Kent, Buckinghamshire, Berkshire, Surrey, Gosport, Havant, Portsmouth, Rother and Hastings, which together with the current Tier 4 is 16 million people. Wales is already locked down. Plans for Christmas have to be scrapped – no travel out of London. There were crowds at London stations as people tried to leave before Tier 4 came into effect. No mixing with anyone at Christmas unless people are living alone, and only with their bubble. Scotland goes into Tier 4 on Boxing Day. Italy, Germany and the Netherlands are in full lockdown, with 68,441 deaths in Italy. Germany is storing bodies in shipping containers as the pandemic spirals. Newspapers are reporting that forty-three nations are slamming doors on Britain.

"You're early. You can't be going swimming, can you?" Gerald came downstairs to see Ruth with her coat on, doing up her outdoor shoes.

"No, all the pools and ponds are closed. As Christmas is cancelled, it's a relief I hadn't bought the turkey yet, now we don't need a big one. I'm off to get one. It was a ridiculous idea that we could have different households mingling in hot, poorly ventilated houses, in the middle of a pandemic, but now there's this superspreading variant it would have been crazy."

"We can still have Catherine, though? We're allowed to have someone who is living alone to be in our support bubble?"

"Yes, apparently. It's all so disappointing, and Catherine isn't going to enjoy being here with two old fogies."

"The rules aren't ours. She'll enjoy seeing your decorations and tree."

"Well, we won't let the Tier 4 rules spoil our day and it'll give me a chance to get to know her better. I've hoped that one day I'll find the key to unlocking her rare and special psyche, which seemed to bury itself when Annabelle was ill and stopped communicating with her. She was much more outgoing when I met your family first."

*

Debs and Vicky had booked a court and were chatting across the net. They weren't allowed to sit and talk in the clubhouse, only walk through the building, wearing masks.

"It went really well, don't you think?"

"Yes, surprisingly it was fun. Though I don't think you should have let Ruth enter a team, they won every round!"

"She does family quizzes every week and memorises stuff easily. You, Steve, Sam, her husband and Danni were second, though. It was nice to see so many people and their relatives. I thought Jo was good and she'd put together interesting questions. Are you still going to Danni's for Christmas?"

"Christmas is all about children. Thank goodness as someone livin' alone I'm allowed to go to hers for the day. Can't wait to hug Andy and Suzie, though I probably shouldn't. What are you doin'?"

"Eating late, when Daisy gets back from the hospital. It's a freak Christmas. The tree and decorations are up. We'll just have to make the best of it on Sunday and Monday when she's off. I'll go for a walk and do the cooking, that'll take up most of the day. When are you seeing Steve?"

"He's gone to Sam's to see his grandson, Dylan. I'm lookin' forward to meetin' them properly when this is over."

*

"A real tree? We haven't had one of those for years. I got too cross with still finding needles in the lounge in the summer!" Nusheen was standing on a chair chatting to Vicky over the fence, who had been emptying her compost bin onto her big heap at the bottom of the garden.

"Did you try a Nordmann or a Douglas fir? Their smell is delicious."

"Don't remember what they were, but Farzad won't have another. Anyway, we only celebrate a little, as the Qur'an venerates Jesus and the Virgin Mary, but not on the scale of Eid and Ramadan. Thanks for your Christmas card, though."

"I don't expect one back, but don't like leaving you out. It's going to be a very subdued celebration anyway, being in lockdown."

"Like Eid was. Why are Europe's coronavirus cases and deaths so much higher than in East Asia, do you think?"

"Well, they had a practice run with SARS, and some politicians have said that they are automata who do what they're told, while the G7 Western nations are individualists. There could be a lot of truth in that."

"But Taiwan's death toll is seven and ours is over 70,000! And their economy has *grown* by 2.5 per cent. If a European country had that success, we would all be copying by improving Test, Track and Trace, isolating and better border control. By ignoring successful eastern countries' success, we've had a gulf in outcomes. It's shocking that, and I suspect it's for cultural reasons. Don't you think?"

"Mmm. Yes, you're right, but at least the West has produced

vaccines, though Russia and China are supposed to have the Sputnik and two by Sinopharm. We haven't heard much about them though…"

Christmas Eve 2020

> The number of people inoculated is 600,000. There were 39,237 who tested positive and 574 died. The UK now has 19,000 people in hospital. Cases have risen by fifty-seven per cent in the past week. On Boxing Day, 6 million more people will move into Tier 4, including Norfolk, Suffolk, Sussex, Cambridgeshire and parts of Hampshire. Other areas will be moved up to 3 from 2. Italy has had more than 70,000 deaths, the UK 69,000 and France 62,000, though Italy has the smallest population. There are more than 5,000 lorries at Dover, which have been waiting for three or four nights to cross to France which has stopped crossings because of the new variant of coronavirus in the UK. Forty countries have closed their borders to the UK because of it.

"I'm sure this new variant is present all over Europe, they just haven't tested for it," said Ruth, reaching for the hot water jug.

"You could well be right," said Gerald. "And this other strain they have found in two people who have come from South Africa would support that. At least they have quarantined them."

"I wonder when we'll find out what we have given way on to get a Brexit deal?"

"Sovereignty issues are said to be agreed, but they're still negotiating over fishing rights…"

*

The lawn was white with frost and the sun shone pale and wintry, reflecting into the kitchen where Vicky and Daisy were preparing the vegetables for the next day.

"My mother made me cut crosses on the bottom of sprouts, as if they wouldn't cook through without it. Then she boiled them to death anyway. All one has to do is to cut a sliver off the bottom and take off the outside leaves. We can cook the roasted root vegetables tonight and the red cabbage, then they can be warmed up and there will only be bread sauce, potatoes, beans, broccoli and peas to cook tomorrow. Do we need kale? I could pick some."

"Think it might be one vegetable too many, Nana. I've never had the chance to eat as many vegetables in one sitting. Will we fit them all on the plate?"

*

"Have you seen that we have passed 70,000 deaths, like Italy? Who has the biggest population?" Janet called.

Barry carefully put down the spoon with which he was stirring cranberries to make a sauce, turned the heat down and put the lid back on the saucepan, leaving a gap for the steam to escape. He turned and went into the lounge where Janet was laying the table. "France has the biggest population and we're next with 66 million. I think Italy has about 60, and of course France is a larger country. The UK is smaller than both."

"I love Christmas, all except Boxing Day. It's such a sad, deflated, angry day."

"Why angry?"

"Because one has eaten too much the day before, feels fat, hungover, dreary and anticlimactic, and so didn't sleep well. And this year there are no Boxing Day sales. One spends it nibbling at all the food left and picking up paper, tangerine peel and half-eaten chocolates."

"Well, as we're not cooking here, that won't be our problem."

"And sitting too much makes one stiff and achy, old. One minute one is young and confident, strong and positive, and going to change this mess of a world. Then suddenly, we're old and tired and somehow had minimum impact."

"You're a real misery today, what's wrong with you?"

Janet screwed up her face. "Not sure. Perhaps I'm disappointed not to be spending our first Christmas since we've met up again, together. And you're even cooking lunch for Fiona's family! Perhaps I'm jealous of them having you."

He smiled and gave her a hug. "Let's enjoy our Christmas Eve supper together anyway. Perhaps next year we'll be able to have both our families, and we'll be married."

29 December 2020

There has been the highest number of new cases reported today – 53,135 – and 414 deaths. It's so worrying the hospitals are full, with some patients having to wait in ambulances. The ambulance service reports the busiest ever time – in history.

"This is an interesting article!" Ruth waved a newspaper page at Gerry.

He looked up over the top of his spectacles, from the 'Business and Money' section of the *Sunday Times*. "Yes?"

"It's listing the bestselling products in John Lewis, month by month, and some of them are surprising. Like loaf tins in April, loungewear in May, picnic rugs in July, Christmas trees in September and jigsaws in October!"

*

Vicky was alone for the next few days, as Daisy had gone back to work and the little house. She had spent a few hours cleaning with the radio blasting pop music, had made soup with leftover vegetables, bread in her machine, played a game of tennis and was now eating lunch. The phone rang. It was Janet. They chit-chatted, then Janet said she was worried about herself.

"I was accustomed to making my own life decisions with no

thought of anyone else, so as you know, living with Barry has been a big adjustment. Not least because I used to dance about my lounge, whooping and hollering to my favourite feminist anthems. I've had to quieten down, but also cohabiting has made me co-dependent."

"You?" Vicky was surprised. "What do you mean?"

"On Christmas Day I went to David's and he went to Fiona's and the grandkids. I only went for the day, so had a few days on my own when I came back. I thought I was looking forward to the alone time but had a bit of a panic attack at going out to do my food shop. Barry has always done the shopping. I wore my mask and kept checking I had my keys the whole time. When I got back, I thought I'd order a takeaway. But the thought of someone cooking it who might have the virus, or the one delivering it could be positive, made me freak, so I was forced to cook something. Then I realised I hadn't cooked completely alone since Barry moved in. During this last period of living together we've done everything together – meal plans, walks, workouts, cleaning, TV watching – he's become my world because we're not supposed to see anyone else. I had a meltdown, just thinking of having to cook on my own!"

"You are funny, Janet. I hope you got over it and danced drunkenly to your favourite pop songs before he came back?"

"You're right, that's what I should have done. No, I just sank back into my helpless version of coupledom, when he appeared. It's ridiculous, I'm seventy-eight! Barry says lockdown is fine for him. He's perfectly happy with an empty diary and says whatever time of day or night he wants to exercise he can turn on his laptop for a video session, or go out for a run or walk. Yet I'm embarrassed at dancing about to loud pop music. I *will* be more independent. I *must* be more confident and self-sufficient."

"You'll work it out, Janet."

31 December 2020

There have been 55,892 new cases and 964 deaths, and this doesn't include Wales and Northern Ireland. Hospitals are overwhelmed, but the Nightingale hospitals can't be used because there are not enough staff. Three-quarters of the population of England is now in Tier 4, plus all of Wales and mainland Scotland. Police broke up hundreds of New Year's Eve parties and gatherings all over the UK, arrested people and handed out fines, with £10,000 fines to the organisers. Germany is getting 1,000 deaths a day and is extending lockdown until mid-January. The UK left the EU at 11pm.

Ruth breathed out impatiently. "This lockdown life has led to such a lot of preachy-type articles. Every day some journalist tells us how we should be living our lives."

"Yes, one can't avoid them. But they have had an effect. So many completely unathletic people are jogging and most are walking. They, and you, have even convinced me. What is this one saying?"

"Absolutely nothing new, it's all becoming a mantra." She read in a singsong voice: "'The key to healthy old age is sense of purpose, be active, exercise a lot. Aerobic exercise strengthens the brain, which stretching and toning don't do. Have strong social networks, don't sit down for long, eat healthily and not too much. Work for longer and learn new things.'"

Gerald smiled. "It never says that if you live this perfect existence you can still die young of a myriad of things over which one has no control."

*

It was New Year's Eve and Vicky was on her own. It was a dark, quiet day. The sun had disappeared, the wind had dropped, and a few flakes of snow drifted past the window. She went out into the winter garden and looked up into the snowy sky. *Shall I have a dry January?* she asked herself. *Alcohol can't be good for my body, and self-denial will feel like an achievement, especially if coupled with vegan January. That poll said that 6.5 million people are going to participate, compared with 3.9 million last year. Hmm, could these sacrifices be to do with control, at a time when one is feeling anxious during this increased COVID period?*

Ruth will be Zooming a quiz, I'll ring Diana in Bute.

"Hi, Vicky, what are you doing tonight?"

"Absolutely nothing, Daisy's working. I've not got a diary full of social engagements and parties, like we used to have. I'm bored and lonely! I need to top up my stores of seeing actual people and talking to them. If only travelling was allowed and meeting in each other's houses, but we've got Tier 4 rules! How are you getting on? How was Christmas?"

"Perhaps surprisingly, great. I've settled into this house quickly and everyone loved this island. It's cold but seems to have more sun than the mainland. We did wonderful walks, and everyone is friendly. I'm going to a neighbour's this evening, wearing a mask of course, but I think I'm doing the right thing being here, there's not been anyone with COVID."

"Oh, so glad it's turning out well for you."

"I've played tennis with another neighbour, but then tennis and golf were banned, so I'm just walking now. Of course, loads of houses are second homes. I don't meet many people out walking like you do on Hampstead Heath."

"Yes, it's a scrum, particularly at weekends, and the mud is ankle deep."

"As soon as you are allowed to travel, why don't you come for a visit? The restaurants and pubs should be open then too, and Mount Stuart, Rothesay Castle and various gardens."

"Love to. I'm so missing the theatre, galleries and tennis. The first lockdown we were constantly delighted by the glorious weather and our stunning gardens we spent so much time in, wearing shorts and flipflops. We were relaxed, though a bit scared in case the virus was lurking on our shopping, or on that person who got too close. But the sunshine made everything better, even the way we looked. And friends could come for tea or barbecues in the garden. Now it's freezing cold, horribly muddy everywhere, raining perpetually, and no one is allowed into our house or garden. The weather matches the national mood. I'm patrolling the neighbourhood streets, like an animal pacing its cage, passing overweight joggers and people scuttling along to their homes to tick off another day on their cell wall."

"I remember it well. I have been thinking about you and feeling sorry for you. I've done a lot of Zooming, though not with you, as I knew you weren't keen. Whoever would have guessed that most of 2020 would be spent at home, talking to a screen of disembodied heads in front of bookcases? Yes, there's one here too, for me, full of plays and classics."

3–6 January 2021

There are now 58,784 cases, with 407 deaths today and more patients in hospital than in the first wave of infections – 2,600 in England. Hospital pressure and the last six days with infection rates over 50,000 has forced the Prime Minister's hand to decide on a new lockdown from 4 January to last until mid-February, when hopefully the first four priority groups will have all been vaccinated. Schools and universities and outside sports venues are now closed. 5th: It gets worse: there were 60,916 cases and 830 deaths, and more than 30,000 people are in hospital. One in fifty of the population has symptoms and one in thirty in London. 1.3 million people have been vaccinated. 6th: 62,322 cases – the highest daily figure and 1,041 deaths… Moderna's vaccine is the third to be approved in the UK.

Debs and Vicky had finished their game and were chatting as they walked down from the courts.

"Lockdown again! This is the Monday-est of Mondays, how are we going to cope with no tennis, no going out, no nothing?!"

"I'm goin' to go and stay with Steve. I can't stand yet another lockdown on my own."

"But you've never wanted to live in the country."

"No, but I've convinced myself that I've been prejudiced against it. How often do I go to London's theatres, shops, galleries? Twice a month? In fact, I've felt guilty how I always intended to grab more of the culture offered. Livin' in one of the world's great cities, how often do I partake of its cultural delights? And most of the time, the loneliness freezes me, alienates me from life, so even gettin' out of bed is an effort. I've realised that one has to have another livin' body near to validate one's existence. Well, I do, anyway. Perhaps we only exist in others' eyes, and alone – do we exist?

"I'll come up to see Danni and the twins. I'll babysit for a couple of days a week so she can start workin' again, but Steve is too good to let go of, and I've been so unhappy on my own in lockdown. And to tell you the truth, drivin' back last time, when the concrete began to rise up either side of the motorway, the congestion around me felt alien, not where I've been most comfortable all my life."

"At least you've not been suffering from FOMO."

"What's that?"

"The fear of missing out, the curse of the connected person."

"No, that hasn't been me for quite a few years. A lot of the influencers I knew have dropped off the perch. And how am I goin' to impress the next generation? I'm no longer sexy. Bein' admired was good, bein' respected was essential, but bein' loved is what I crave."

"Well, go for it. You can't expect Danni to give you all the companionship you need! The Mental Health Foundation found that nearly half of the UK population had felt anxious and half of those had been lonely since everything we might have done to make life bearable has been taken away, banned. Meeting friends indoors is banned, outdoors is forbidden, so we're stuck alone indoors. If you're here for part of the week, you won't have burnt your boats. Hope you'll fit in a regular game with me?"

"Yes of course. But the human cost since this virus has appeared is incomprehensible."

"We're supposed to do one thing every day that makes us happy. And start the day by deciding what will spark happiness."

"Like what?"

"Perhaps play songs you love and make you want to dance and feel wonderful. Take up arts and crafts. In all these lockdowns, I've made a quilt, two sets of mittens, a small rug, and I might knit a jumper next. I don't want to be trapped indoors every evening staring at the TV, without doing something creative. And dancing about is the quickest way to boost my mood, uncoil all the knots, open the chest and make my body feel lighter, more fluid and improve my emotional wellbeing. It's supposed to release toxins and produce dopamine, oxytocin, serotonin and endorphins and give one greater neuroplasticity. I think that means that the brain is more adaptable and resilient!"

"Well, bein' with Steve makes me happy. Though I have to admit that I'm a jealous cow… I'm jealous of the person he was, those he loved and the life he had before we met. I'm probably mournin' my own past as well as his. I've just got to get on with life as it is, how we are. Let's keep in touch. I know we're all weary and wary of Zoom, but if we're lonely and we ration it…? Or if not, let's phone chat."

*

"What terrible scenes last night at Capitol Hill, with Trump the right-wing rabble rouser, coercing and encouraging his fans to 'take back control'. Is he right in the head? They actually broke into the House of Representatives gallery, where Congress members were meeting to confirm Biden's victory. His legacy will be of hate, division, confusion! Where was the excessive law enforcement that the 'Black Lives Matter' peaceful protesters endured? For them, there were thousands of national guard troops, police and other federal agencies, *and* they were tear-gassed and hit with batons from horses, so Trump could stage a photo opportunity! Hope they invoke the Twenty-fifth Amendment against him and impeach him multiple times. He's a complete fascist!" Ruth put her head in her hands. "After 350 years of US democracy what on earth is the rest of the world thinking of us?"

Gerald leant across the breakfast table to pat an arm which she had stretched out to bang on the table in her agony. "Well, it's been evident almost from the start that he's an oligarch, kleptocratic, xenophobic, authoritarian, violent, racist, but no, I don't think he's a fascist. He's too individualist, fascism is a collectivist philosophy."

Ruth looked up and half grinned. "Have you seen that joke doing the rounds? 'After the events on Capitol Hill, Mexico will pay for the wall and Canada wants one too!'"

*

Marion had her second vaccination, though there was a decision a few weeks ago that second ones weren't happening for twelve weeks so the vaccine could go further. "I'm so relieved," she said. "COVID would probably finish me off. I would be so weak that they wouldn't let me go home, I'd be sent to a nursing home for continuing care."

"I'd visit you. I'm sure lots of people would," said Vicky, from standing in the road. She had knocked to check that Marion was OK.

"Hmm. When one is old, and in a care home, and getting perfunctory duty visits from relatives and friends, one has no status and have done nothing interesting, so the relief in visitors' faces when they can escape is palpable. I've been a visitor myself. And what can one do to avoid putting such expressions on loved one's faces? I don't sing or dance and haven't got lots of money to hand out. No, I want to keep well away from care homes!"

"We all, consciously or unconsciously, think quite a bit about death, but we try to distract ourselves from the fear of it. I've read that if you can reconcile yourself to your own death and try to live as if you only had, say, six months left, life becomes happier, you live better."

*

Vicky telephoned Michelle, not having heard from her. "Hi, Michelle, how are things? Haven't seen you for a couple of months, since you and Stella exhibited in Hannah's cafe. Did you sell a lot?"

"Oh, Vic, so sorry, I've had the worst week or so of my life. Stella is in hospital on a mechanical ventilator and ECMO machine, she's dying!"

"Oh no, no, how absolutely terrible! How did she get COVID?"

"She insisted on seeing Dominic, her son, and his kids at Christmas and less than a week later she had a high temperature, was coughing and couldn't smell or taste. All the classic symptoms. I'm not allowed to see her. She's fighting a battle for her life, alone. It's hell!"

"How tragic, Michelle, I'm so very sorry. You haven't had symptoms, have you?"

"No, not yet, perhaps I'll be lucky. Dominic is suicidal, he's probably killed his mother and hasn't any symptoms himself. It's so strange. Oh, and yes, we did well, we both sold most we hung at the cafe."

*

Michelle parked her bike and stood on the embankment, watching the broad, brown Thames slipping past, en route to the sea. Oily mud banks, glinting in the half light. Stella was dying! Stella was dying! *Why* was this happening? She looked up at the faint moon and prayed, something she hadn't done since she was a child. As she finished her prayer, a single flash of light came from the sun as it disappeared back behind heavy cloud and the houses on the opposite side.

Staining her cigarette with her red lipstick, she flicked on her lighter and drew the smoke into her lungs.

13 January 2021

> There are 47,525 cases today, so they're going down, but the deaths have reached an all-time high – 1,564! There have been more deaths than in World War II – 84,767. The UK has soared past Italy, France, Spain and Germany in deaths but doing well in having vaccinated 4.3 people out of every 100. In the US it is 3, Italy 1.3, Germany 0.8 and France 0.3. The House of Representatives voted for Trump's impeachment after he incited the mob to storm Congress last week, where five people lost their lives. The Senate now has to endorse it, which is unlikely, as a two-thirds majority is needed.

"I watched that programme I had recorded on Tuesday, yesterday evening, when you were clearing up and showering."

"Oh, which one was that? Could you pass the fruit, please?" Gerald stirred yoghurt into his muesli and reached forward to take the mix of fruit which Ruth passed across the table.

"*Are Women the Fitter Sex?* It was on Channel 4 on Tuesday. I'm going to have to look after you. Apparently our two X chromosomes means that we have more antibodies than men with their XY. So, men are forty to fifty per cent more likely to die if infected. This was evident in the SARS pandemic, but also in the cancer, diabetes and COVID statistics. For many years it had been thought that this was because they smoked and drank alcohol more, but apparently it's their Y chromosome."

"Mmm, so I can eat and sleep well, exercise and look after myself, but I'm doomed because of my chromosomes. Doesn't seem fair!"

*

Vicky went to hospital for an echocardiogram and ECG monitoring, after months of having them cancelled. She had seen her GP when she started having the little bouts of feeling she might faint. Ruth rang up when she got home. "How was it?"

"The echocardiogram was rather traumatic. The operator took nearly two hours! I was lying there on my side with him tucked into my back, his arm over me and a probe thing under my left breast. He wouldn't tell me anything about it but panicked a few times and had to get other people in to look at the computer evidence of what he was doing. The second time, three little operators and nurses came rushing in to do the 'bubble test'. Their English wasn't great, but they took a load of blood. Hate giving blood, it makes me faint. Shook it up with saline and four times sprayed it back into my arm. I had to bear down – like pooing – and the bubbles were forced into my heart, as they thought I had a hole between the two sides. I know that this is nothing compared to what other people have had, I'm just a baby. Anyway, apparently, I didn't, but they wouldn't tell me what was wrong. I have to wait for a consultant to contact me… Am now wearing a Holter monitor for twenty-four hours.

"I was traumatised after nearly three hours of people doing things to me, then there was signal failure so sat on the tube for ages then walked most of the way home. Paddington is now a truly enormous building site, just more massive buildings going up. The hospital crouches behind it. If that's what going out is like, plus too many maskless people in the streets to catch things from, I'll stop moaning about lockdown and be happy to stay in for a while."

18–20 January 2021

All of Britain's quarantine-free travel corridors are suspended due to new coronavirus variants. Everyone entering Britain must produce a negative test taken within the last seventy-two hours and go into immediate isolation for ten days. The worldwide death toll has passed 2 million. A third of the people in Bradford have had COVID! Four million people in the UK have been vaccinated. On the 20th there were 1,820 deaths, the highest so far, 38,905 cases and 93,290 total UK deaths.

"Journalists keep saying that we've seen the best of humanity in these lockdowns. Do you think that's true?" Gerald mused.

"There have been a lot of frontline workers and people volunteering for clinical trials who have put their own health at risk for the public good. There are rule breakers, but the critical mass of people are willing to do the right thing. So yes, I think we have seen enough small actions to be optimistic. If nothing else, it's reminded us that the actions of each and all of us count."

"Particularly that Michigan Republican whose job it was to certify the result of the vote and was aware that his career in the party may depend on his loyalty to it. He upheld the rule of law, despite the pressure. So yes, in this case, but I worry about my own lack of community spirit. What have I done to help anyone in this crisis?"

"You've been donating to various charities. And age is definitely a barrier. I wasn't wanted as a volunteer to help in a hospital setting. And I would have volunteered to give vaccine injections, but the ridiculous, endless forms were too off-putting. Perhaps we're meant to keep quietly out of the way and not catch the virus. And the mantra, 'we are all in this together' is one we should have been living by before. So much of our stress comes from having competitive and jealous feelings. A sense of community and kindness may be the result of this horrific period. Look at our children. Half the time they can't make time for a call, as they are playing bridge, going for a walk, got a Zoom. What are they doing that they can't put off? How can they be so busy? Do you think they all find us boring? They're looking at other screens when we're on a call to them and they're always wanting to recipe-share – agh!"

"I have wondered. Charles has irresponsibly bought a dog, though he's always mocked people with them. He talks about 'their bubble', but it's the people they fancy seeing, and not the same ones every time."

"And Naomi and Josie competing, sending pictures of things they've made, cooked, or rooms they've painted, which makes us feel guilty. Not to mention them boasting about losing weight, because they're going running every day. They say they're quite enjoying lockdowns!"

"Oh well, at least we're lucky having a garden and not having to go to work."

*

Vicky hadn't seen Debs for a while, now she was living in the country, with no tennis allowed. But they had spoken on the phone and currently she was in London. So, after having her COVID jab, she walked in her direction. Rain was falling in earnest, slapping on the pavement in front of her. It was miserably cold. Debs came to the door with a big smile, dressed in an old paint-splattered shirt and leggings.

"Hi, how are you? What on earth are you doing?"

"As you can see from the mess I've got into, I'm paintin'! Compensatin' for not bein' able to do anythin' more to prevent my agein' looks, I've spent some time makin' the space I live in look younger and fresher. And I suppose to show Steve that I'm not a total slut."

"You are funny. Isn't love an acceptance of all that has been, is and always will be?"

"Yes, yes, but we're still in the courtin' stage, tryin' to look our best to impress. Well, I am anyway. Old people can't charm anyone with a meltin' smile or hide wrinkles, bulges and sags. Not to mention their hearin' aids, lack of sphincter control and balance. I am realistic. But I want to expend some effort, not accept and sink into it. I can at least redecorate, try to improve my nest."

"You're right. When the world seems scary and unpredictable, we need to feel soothed and happy in homes we're not allowed to leave. This third lockdown is *so* draining. We don't know when it's going to end, so we can't plan for anything, even having a haircut!" Vicky was standing in the porch with her hood off. She lifted her rather lank, longer hair, and made a face. "Let alone plan a holiday, a trip, or have a game of tennis. It would be energising to give ourselves some purpose... instead of which, long, cold, grey, empty days, one after another, with no changes, no end. Men are so lucky with their very short hair. Look at mine, it desperately needs a trim. Wearing a bobble hat in this freezing weather flattens it into rats' tails. And staying in, eating, means I've put on half a stone. Thought my metabolism was fast, but sitting so much seems to have slowed it down. I've got a half a stone more on my bottom. And I never dress up or put makeup on – why bother?

"This lockdown is far harder. TV tells us about bereavements, job losses and massive national debt – so walking seems an indulgence, and in these dull, grey, cold, damp days I have to bully myself out. Trudging through this endless winter, head down, teeth gritted, a few snowdrops, violets, primroses in people's gardens really lift my heart and spirit."

"Well, you *are* depressed! Perhaps you should take a

vitamin D tablet? They help with tiredness, or you might be low on iron… Hang on a minute and I'll come for a walk with you and try to cheer you up. You've cheered me so often!"

A few minutes later, she appeared wearing a big turquoise parka with a fur-lined hood and walking boots.

"Thanks for coming. It's not so good on one's own. I read that walking is a way of escaping oneself – getting lost in perceptions and sensations of a body in motion, atoms moving through space. I find it hard to get lost in motion, though, unless there is someone to chat to."

"I need to practise anyway. Steve gets me out every day. It's not so crowded there, though. Other walkers give way, beckonin' us on, or they do a circuit around cars, not to pass too close. We nod or wave our gratitude. It so rarely happens in London. It's always us gettin' out of people's way."

*

Janet had a letter inviting her to make an appointment for her vaccine. All the chemists they had listed were miles away, in places she had never been to. She was a few months older than Barry; presumably he would hear soon. She rang her GP practice to ask if it would be offered at somewhere nearer. The receptionist said she would be ringing patients of her age in the next few days, but why didn't she go to a nearby mosque that afternoon at 3pm? Barry came with her for the walk, and they found that there wasn't a list of names; groups were herded in every half an hour and dealt with together. So he had his Pfizer too.

She hated needles, but the doctor distracted her adeptly and it didn't hurt. After twenty minutes of rest, they set off back home with big smiles on their faces, thankful that they would have a bulletproof vest under their clothes in three weeks' time. "As the WHO has said, no one's safe until everyone's safe. Your shoulders seem to have relaxed down from your ears now," Barry said.

"Such a relief. But wish we'd had the Oxford one, the testing of that seems to have been more rigorous. But at least life might start getting back to normal soon."

*

"Hello, Michelle, haven't heard from you, so how is Stella? I've been scared to ask." Vicky had telephoned.

"We thought she was going to die, but she is recovering slowly. She was supposed to be going to the Nightingale but hasn't gone yet. She's totally exhausted, can't sleep, got throat, chewing and swallowing problems and is not interested in eating. She's weak, lost muscle mass, loses her balance and her whole body aches, but hopefully she'll be able to come home soon and I'll look after her."

"Oh, wonderful! I'm SO pleased, Michelle. Thrilled! Good for her, fighting off COVID!"

27 January 2021

There were 1,725 deaths yesterday and 25,308 new cases, so they are going down, but the UK is the first European country to have more than 100,000 deaths in total. Over 38,000 people are in hospital. It is to be mandatory for people arriving into the UK to have to go to hotels, paid for by them. France is saying that it must have another lockdown, as its cases and deaths are rising again. 6.5 million people have been vaccinated and the EU is complaining about AstraZeneca's production delays. The company is having problems producing so much, but the UK deal was signed three months before the EU, so there are fewer delay problems.

"Interesting," said Ruth. Gerald looked up from his *Times* and wholewheat toast.

"The *Camden New Journal* has an article here which says that the Crick Institute, which has looked at the Israeli analysis of the 200,000 people who had the first dose of Pfizer, found there was thirty-three per cent efficacy. So Public Health England might be putting us at risk with their twelve-week ruling until the second dose. Surely it will be reconsidered now? Pfizer itself says the second dose should be in three to five weeks. The *BMJ* asked them last week to revisit this decision, based on emerging scientific evidence."

"Well, I was lucky to have had both before the change was made, but it affects you and so many thousands of others. We're not going on the Heath today, I hope? It was ankle-deep mud and very unpleasant the last few times, and it has rained most days since."

"The Regent's Canal path, round the streets or the City, then?"

"Let's do it tomorrow. I haven't seen Catherine since Christmas Day and she's not good at answering her phone. She always seems to be out, and goodness knows what happened to the two mobiles we gave her. I'll go to her flat, to see if I can catch her in. She works at the community centre with the elderly groups, playing board games and helping to cook lunch. If I go early, I'll probably catch her before she goes."

"Why don't you take the cake I made yesterday? I'll make another one for us today."

*

Catherine lived in a one-bed flat that they had bought her, in an undistinguished late-Victorian terrace, just two stops away on the tube. Coming out of the station, he saw her on the other side of the road, outside Tesco, packing her shopping into her rucksack. He called and she looked up and smiled. "Are you coming to see me?"

"Yes, of course. We haven't heard from you since Christmas." He walked across the road, feeling puzzled at her appearance. She seemed to have swelled in the front, though her wrists, ankles and collar bones were thin and protruding. Ruth had said at Christmas that she had put on weight, but this was a serious bulge in her otherwise slim frame. He took her rucksack, deciding to wait before he mentioned anything. They chit-chatted as they walked. Catherine wasn't beautiful, but her movements were slow and sinuous; he could see that she had sex appeal, but he felt like pulling her along. She said the centre was helping a lot of immigrants from Afghanistan. Finding them places to stay, work and teaching them English.

They were soon at her flat. She opened the door into the small, dimly lit living room; a stale smell of bodies and cooking assailed him. Stepping in after her, he saw a black-haired, swarthy man jumping up from the couch in front of their TV, which they had passed on to her when they had bought a new one.

"This is my dad, Ashtak. Dad this is Ashtak." They touched elbows and he indicated for Gerald to sit in the one armchair. "Tea, Dad?" she asked as she went over to the windows, where a few slim rays of sun strained in through the slats of the blinds. She pulled at the dangling cords, hand over hand, dust flying off them as they grumpily, reluctantly rose, but finally the sunlight flooded into the untidy room. Before sitting down, Gerald followed her into the kitchen with the cake. The sink was full of dirty dishes, the bin overflowing with takeaway packaging.

Handing over the cake, he asked, "What's going on, Catherine? Is he living here with you?" He still couldn't bring himself to ask if she was pregnant. She was forty and they hadn't been aware of her having boyfriends since she was in her teens.

She had filled the electric kettle and put it on, and was slowly washing three mugs. "He's my partner, we may get married," she said lightly.

"What have you got yourself into? Are you OK?" he asked. She pulled her cardigan round on to her front and stroked her bulge, blinking behind her glasses. "Yes, we're very happy, we want this baby."

"It's fine if it's what you want, Catherine. Do you know him well enough? How old is he? What work did he do before?" He couldn't see her face; her shoulders were hunched and her long, brown hair had fallen forwards.

She had poured water onto teabags and was unwrapping the cake. "I knew you wouldn't understand," she said defiantly, blinking behind her glasses. "Let's have tea and you can talk to him."

They sat talking, with the tea and Ruth's delicious apple cake, while all the time the TV spewed endless news of the pandemic. Which only seemed to bother Gerald.

Ashtak's English was rudimentary, but he seemed fond of Catherine and said he would be looking for work, painting, when he had finished the language course. He would make money to look after his baby and Catherine, so she could stay home and make the house nice.

Gerald didn't comment but wondered if this was possible. The flat was a grubby mess and he remembered her bedroom when she had lived at home.

*

Ruth was thrilled. "You'll have another grandchild. It'll be good for Catherine, being responsible for a baby, and if it doesn't work out with Ashtak we can help."

"We're not to tell Charles or Amelia yet. She begged me not to."

*

It had rained for days. The parks and Heath were ankle-deep mud and Vicky's lawn was too soggy to walk on. She gazed out of the window, hearing water sluicing down the slate roof and hammering onto the terrace below, before causing the pond to overflow and drowning the new growth on the lawn. *The hopper must be blocked again*, she thought. *I must get someone with a very long ladder to clear it out.*

3 February 2021

There have been 1,322 deaths and 19,202 new cases today and over 10 million people have now received their first vaccine dose. France now has a travel ban on all but essential travel from non-EU countries. Their schools are open, but there is a 6pm curfew for everyone. Portugal's health service is overwhelmed, as it has had the most cases and highest death rate in the world. Germany has sent them intensive care specialists and ventilators. Captain Sir Tom Moore died. He had raised £39 million after the addition of Gift Aid.

"Amazing that because of COVID, the development of other drugs will probably now speed up," said Ruth.

"What do you mean? Why?"

"Well, all the elements of creating a vaccine have been done simultaneously. The work of discovery, scaling up the manufacture, speeding up clinical trials, planning the distribution and engaging with the health systems has pioneered rapid pathways… Not to mention Zoom consultations, transforming healthcare and indeed producing multi-purpose vaccines, where one shot could target several deadly diseases at the same time."

Gerald looked enquiringly at her. "We should be better placed to face the next pandemic, then?"

"Precisely."

*

Ruth and Vicky had met up for a walk around the streets. The Heath and parks were too muddy and could be so crowded.

"We're not even midway through this third lockdown and it's difficult to be cheerful with dark, freezing weather and continual variants being discovered," Ruth said.

"I've always been a 'glass half full' person, but even for me, the tedious routine of sleeping, eating, doing housework, eating, having a walk, eating, watching TV, eating is dragging me down. Though the alternative of being in hospital, fighting COVID, is even less attractive… I've read that video dating is still very popular, as are Zoom and the sales of vibrators. Will anyone want to see real-life people when we go back to normal?"

Ruth nodded. "I'm starting to think that we've all gone mad. We've all cracked. There's a collective mental stress. People on TV and radio sound desperate and depressed about the dullest, tiniest minutiae, or manic and hysterical if something is even slightly funny. Like the Texas lawyer who was in a court hearing on Zoom and a cat's face was in the filter, not his."

"We're all stuck at home, going around the same wheel, with nothing to report, nowhere to go and watching the entire world grind to a halt. Apparently, because we're not able to go off and do our own thing and are stuck indoors twenty-four hours a day, divorces have increased. OK, the pace of life and its demands were sometimes miserable and alienating, but our high streets have been decimated, the arts devastated, the hospitality industry will take years to recover. In our heart of hearts, we were hoping for a short break at Easter and a longer one in the summer, then we're told not to book anything yet, and so we're back to feeling mad and despairing again."

"Oh, to be back in our former lives, our normality – buzzy streets, offices, packed theatres, restaurants, nightlife, seeing more people."

"There have been a few good things. I've got closer to you and a few other friends as we've spent more time together, and I do think we'll feel more grateful for what we had and perhaps rebuild a better normal?"

*

After Gerald had seen Catherine, his routines, which he had enjoyed, didn't seem as satisfying. He felt restless and worried about her; he couldn't sit at his computer and absorb himself in anything. Was it his fault he hadn't given Catherine enough attention? He had rarely had enough emotional energy left over for his family. Would this have happened if Annabelle had still been alive?

Did she imagine that her aimless life had been taken out of her own hands? That she would be looked after by this small, younger, broad-chested man as she had been sheltered by her mother? Should he go and see her again? Check that she was OK? She hadn't done well since Annabelle had died.

There was no time like the present. He took an empty tube to her stop and walked briskly to her flat.

He rang her bell, waited and rang it again. It was eleven, perhaps she had left for the community centre. Then her voice came over the intercom. "Who's that?"

"Catherine, it's Dad, come to see you again."

"Shit, Dad, it's not a good time. Can you come another day?"

"But I'm here now, please let me in."

There was quiet and then she appeared at the door, wearing the same cardigan over pyjamas and slippers. She looked pale and her hair was a greasy mess.

There was no Ashtak, though the TV was blasting forth and there was a prevailing smell of what could have been marijuana. He hoped that she hadn't got back into taking mind-altering substances, which had left her barely able to think, so she had had to give up her medical degree. He asked if she had been seen by a doctor as he followed her into the still-messy kitchen. She washed out two mugs and put the kettle on. She was vague. Said she had seen someone and thought she was now twenty or so weeks.

"There's a smell of dope in this flat, hope it's not you smoking it. Your mother would have been horrified for the foetus." She grunted, and they sat down with their tea.

He studied her and wondered what she did every day. "Are you still helping with the lunch at the community centre?"

"Not since I got pregnant, I was being sick, and the lunch smell made it worse."

"Are you doing anything at all there now, then?"

She narrowed her eyes. "Yes! I play board games or read to some of the older local people in the afternoon, or help with the Afghans learning English."

He imagined what her mornings were like, probably sleeping late, tidying half-heartedly, sitting about. "You won't be able to get up so late when you have the baby."

"I know. You don't think I'll be able to do anything!" She got up, took a comb from the mantlepiece and tried to drag it through her tangled hair.

All the way home he was wondering how he could persuade his daughter, who had always been protected and had never really had a proper job, to come home and let her family look after her.

*

Daisy had a couple of days off and Vicky had cooked her favourite meal of salmon roll, green vegetables and parsley sauce. They were sitting in the kitchen at the big polished pine table, eating and sipping prosecco.

"How does your mum like teaching? She always said she wouldn't teach and worked in a library when she was here."

"She's very active and pumped in term time. Seems to get on with the children, taking netball teams in the evenings and Saturdays and doing a lot of preparation and marking. She's always relieved when the holidays come around."

"Do you think she'll teach when she comes here?"

"She seemed to think she would. The holidays are better. That's why she didn't go for librarian jobs back home. What happened to Rob? I can hardly remember him, but my impression was that he was strong and healthy."

"Mmm, we thought he was. He'd been cutting back trees and shrubs, chopping the wood smaller for the green bin. He came in for tea, gave me a kiss and walked over to the table, picked up his cup, then dropped to the floor with a crash. I was more worried about the smashed mug and hot tea everywhere, thought he might have tripped over the doormat, though he hadn't been near enough to it. He didn't shout, didn't say anything, just breathed out and dropped. A horrible shock!"

"Then Dad and Pops in the accident and all the men had gone. Mum should have brought us home here after that, but she seemed shellshocked, went into herself." She reached out her hand across the table and squeezed Vicky's. "I missed you, Nana, and you must have missed us. You've coped with a lot on your own. And don't worry, leaking heart valves aren't serious. Most older people have leakage, but you do such a lot of exercise, you're pretty fit and healthy. And now I'm here, always ask me if you're worried about anything." She pulled Vicky's hand to her mouth and kissed it. "Love you, Nana."

10 February 2021

Deaths in London have halved in the past two weeks and new cases have gone down by a fifth from New Year's Day. There have been 13,013 new cases and 1,001 deaths. One quarter of all adults in the UK – 13 million – have had their first vaccine dose . Britons flying home from any of thirty-three countries on the UK 'red list' will have to pay £1,750 for hotel quarantine and compulsory tests and imprisonment and fines for failing to follow this procedure. The Pfizer vaccine scientists are saying that the second dose

should be given three to five weeks after the first, as one dose may offer only limited protection. The UK variant has been found in Australia. They will probably have to lock down again. Poland has reopened cinemas, theatres and operas to fifty per cent capacity, with mask-wearing and no eating. Portugal still has the highest number of deaths by size of population.

"Look at all the crowd, packed in together with no masks!" Gerry was watching the England cricket team playing India in Chennai.

"Yet the cases and deaths in India have recently soared ten times over. There were fears it would overtake the US in deaths, and their vaccinations wouldn't make a difference, as they've only just started."

"Was it herd immunity at first?"

"Or that they have antibodies from other infections."

Gerald was trying to push himself up from his chair. "I'm feeling very old and stiff today."

"It happens to us all sooner or later and you have been sitting for over an hour," Ruth smiled.

"Makes one wonder what was the point of it all. Will I have left anything, anyone, better? And is there an afterlife with old friends and flowers? Perhaps this is all there is?"

*

Janet had a second letter from the NHS and Barry had two texts, inviting them to 'receive the free NHS coronavirus vaccine, as experts recommend that people in your age group should be among the first to have it'.

"I thought that our world-beating healthcare system was the only one in the world to have records of everyone in the country. Why don't they know we had it three weeks ago?" She looked at her diary. "It was 20 January, and we completed forms, a record should be on the system." She was wearing her hair pulled up into a ponytail, exposing the greying parts and making her face look bare and older.

"Not good, is it. Peter has had five invitations from hospitals, NHS and his GP, though he had the first one six weeks ago, and the second one a couple of weeks later. Don't think their database is very accurate!"

"And Pfizer is questioning delaying the second dose as the data they're using is based on the AstraZeneca trials, which did compare different spacing."

"Israeli data shows three weeks is the optimum between doses for the Pfizer. Hopefully the government will change its mind and it'll be given earlier. Where are we going for a walk today?"

"I was wondering about Kensington Gardens, but it's below freezing, might snow, and there's a chill wind."

"Thought I'd freeze to death yesterday and it was supposed to be minus seven last night, but we can't stay in all day!"

They took the tube to Lancaster Gate. It seemed much safer than a few weeks ago, because almost everyone now wore a mask and tried to sit or stand away from others. The sun was shining as they crossed the road into the nineteenth-century Italian garden and passed the Peter Pan and the Physical Energy statues, to the Round Pond, where there were hundreds, if not thousands, of birds. The swans were feeding in the water, turning themselves upside down to reach the bottom, but geese, coots, ducks, seagulls and pigeons fought for the bread thrown to them. They passed a man whose arm and shoulders were covered with parakeets.

"They're actually rather beautiful," Janet said.

"Yes, but they're like vermin, taking over London and the South East. Should be culled. But we haven't seen them so close up before. Such shiny, smooth plumage and bright red rings." As more arrived to sit on the fence close to the man, Barry said,

"I read about this, that they like to spend time with people they bond with."

By the time they had reached the Queen Victoria statue and the Albert Memorial, the sun had gone and they couldn't feel their extremities. "Shall we go back?" she asked. "It's too cold to do the whole walk today."

He took his small flask out from his greatcoat, unscrewed the top and handed it to her. "For emergencies," he said, and they both had a swig of brandy.

She could feel the heat returning to her body. "Let's go, enough is enough. I don't want to stagger around drunk. I wouldn't be taking it in anyway."

*

Gerald's phone rang in the early hours of the morning. He got out of bed; it was in his trouser pocket on the chair. Ruth had woken and sat up, naked against the pillows, watching him. "Who on earth is that?"

It stopped before he got there. He took it out of his pocket and turned to see Ruth, drinking in her reality, her beauty, her sexuality. "Probably a nuisance call from another country, no one rings at 3am!"

"Have a look."

It was a mobile number. He rang it back. It was Catherine. "Dad, I'm walking home now. Can you come and meet me, it's too far to walk all the way."

"Shall I go?" Ruth asked.

"No, she's my responsibility." And if truth be told he was rather thrilled to be rescuing his daughter when she needed him. "I wonder what has happened with Ashtak?"

He dressed quickly and got in the car before he rang her. "Where are you?" She was in a service station that he knew, so was there in minutes. She was standing outside, wearing her green, fur-lined parka, her rucksack at her feet.

"So glad you came, people are staring at me." Her face was pale and her hair pulled back in a low ponytail. There was a crease between her eyebrows; she looked strained.

"I expect they're wondering what a pregnant woman is doing here at 3.30 in the morning."

They touched elbows and he took her full rucksack as she got into the car.

"What has happened? Why have you left in the middle of the night?"

She leant back against the upholstery. "Nothing, don't worry about it." She turned to look out of the window on her side as he reversed out and set off for home.

"Where is Ashtak? Have you had an argument? I'm worried about you, Catherine."

"Well, don't be. I'm OK with everything. I just made a mistake, but I want this baby."

"What sort of mistake?"

She had her head turned to the window again and was shifting round in the seat, trying to hold the belt away from her bump. "I'm not talking about it now, I'm tired."

They were home. He drove into the small drive, got out and opened her door. "Do you want a hot drink?"

Her voice was small and desolate; he wondered if she was crying. "No thanks, I want to sleep. We can talk tomorrow."

18 February 2021

New infections are two-thirds down since the beginning of lockdown, to 12,027, and there were 454 deaths. 31.2 per cent of people aged nineteen and over in the UK have had their first dose of vaccine.

What had taken place with Catherine in the past week?

She had stayed in bed for three days and hadn't wanted to

talk. Ruth took her meals and on the fourth day persuaded her into the bath and then downstairs for lunch. She was wearing a dressing gown of Ruth's, her wet hair was tousled and curling, and her face was pale and puffy, probably from crying.

They exchanged a few remarks about the cold weather and then she blurted out, "He was married. Ashtak is married with two children."

"How did you find out?" Ruth asked softly.

"One of the other guys, Bibi, told me."

"Where is his wife?" Gerald asked.

"Bibi said she'd come when he had a home."

"So presumably you asked Ashtak if this was true?"

"Yes, of course. He said no at first, then he was sorry, he'd been lonely and I was kind to him. I don't want to see him again, but I want the baby. Can I stay here for a while? Will you tell Ashtak he has to leave my flat?" And spotting a huge card with a heart on the dresser: "Is that soppy Valentine's card from you, Dad?"

Despite himself, Gerald was feeling rather sorry for Ashtak. It wasn't surprising that after a dangerous and hazardous journey to the UK, he would have accepted a place to stay and sex with an unattached woman. Perhaps he thought she was taking precautions or was too old to conceive.

"To me, from Ruth. I forgot, as usual. Why don't you stay here, and we'll tell Ashtak that as soon as he has an offer of a flat or job, he must leave your flat? And meanwhile he must look after it?"

*

They were chatting at teatime, and a crumb of the rhubarb cake Vicky had given them had stuck to Liz's cheek. Paul's eyes kept being drawn to it, dancing about as she talked. She was animated, lively and attractive, despite her thin, fine hair starting to go white, as she couldn't get the blonde topped up with all the hairdressers closed. Age had made her face lose its distinct lines, but Paul could see how she had looked when young. Then, because she was eating too fast, she dipped her chin into her wrinkling neck to prevent a burp and he saw the old woman she was becoming.

Salutary, he thought. *But then I've got high blood pressure and have had a stroke. I'm no young buck. I pant going up hills and I've got an age-spotted, bald pate and am going deaf. And before we met, I was wondering what to do with the time that is left to me. Get more seedy, wrinkled and graceless? After the safety and pleasure of my working life, I was awake half the night and having to listen to the* World Service *or* Farming News. *The world is full of old people lying awake in the dark and then dropping off in the afternoons. I felt in a tribe of the forsaken and forgotten. How lucky am I now? I feel more love and tenderness towards her than anyone else who has been in my life.* Certainly more than Emily, who'd been sympathetic at first when his company had folded. She had no patience with failure and soon got sick of seeing him sitting about the house recovering his equilibrium, confidence and self-respect, while reading and writing poetry. She had taken a job with a law firm where she spent most of the time in other countries. They had divorced soon after.

We're all going to die, let's enjoy the last chapter. What's that Robert Browning quote about growing old with me, the best is yet to come? Maybe, hope so.

"Have you heard?" she asked.

"Heard what?"

"Janet and Barry are going to get married."

"I've only met them once. Weren't they childhood sweethearts?"

"Yes. If people ask me about us, I say, I don't have to, I'm not pregnant!"

He smiled. "Do you know, I'd have liked to have had a child with you. But seriously, we seem to be getting what we need from the way it is, so why do we need a compulsory contract? Though if you want to, of course…"

She came over and sat on his lap. He knocked the annoying crumb from her cheek and they kissed. Her eyelashes, thick with mascara, fluttered against his cheek. "I'm perfectly happy, I've never felt so loving and loved. This is everything I need."

*

Ruth, Gerry and Catherine were having dinner together.

"All the different vaccine technologies will be able to be compared because of this pandemic. It's the dream study!" Ruth said as she put dishes of chicken and leek casserole, rice and green vegetables on the table, and indicated for them to help themselves.

"What do you mean?" Catherine asked.

"Well, you know that vaccines can be made from inactivated virus, messenger RNA, protein subunits or adenovirus vectors, which can never be compared in humans, it would just be too expensive. This time there are a dozen vaccines using several technologies which hopefully will report their results."

"The Oxford-AstraZeneca one isn't having a good reception in Europe, is it? People are refusing it and want the Pfizer-BioNTech instead. Even though there is no evidence against it, and WHO has approved it." Catherine had been reading every article about COVID-19. Two red spots appeared on her pale cheeks as she spoke with passion. Gerry smiled at her proudly.

"The mRNA vaccines do seem to be the most effective, with the least side effects. A year ago their technology had never been used for a vaccine. Their disadvantage is the need for extreme cold storage, but Pfizer is now saying it has been overcautious and after taking the vaccine from the deep freeze, it will last for up to a month in a normal fridge. Anyway, we may need all these different vaccines, as our bodies might learn to fight them. And different people may need different types of vaccine. It's fascinating."

"Yes, it is, isn't it. Perhaps I could get some part-time, lowly research job when this baby starts school."

"You've got your BSc. No reason why not. Delicious, as usual, Ruth. Is there a pudding?"

"Great idea, Catherine. I can help you with the baby. It's your favourite, tiramisu!"

22 February 2021

> There were 178 deaths and 10,641 new cases today. The roadmap out of lockdown was announced today by the Prime Minister. He said that because of the unparalleled vaccine effort, we can begin to start our lives again, safely, with a four-step plan: 8 March – schools return and care-home residents will be allowed a visitor. 29 March – two households or up to six people can meet outside, including in gardens. Amateur sport returns outdoors, so tennis and golf will start. 12 April – pub gardens, shops, hairdressers, nail salons, holiday lets, indoor pools for individual or family use and campsites can open. 17 May – pubs, restaurants, hotels, cinemas, indoor gyms can open and international travel will be allowed. The weeks in between are so that the data can be reviewed before moving forwards.

"That's interesting," Gerald mused.

"What is?" Ruth queried before she popped a piece of grapefruit into her mouth.

"Well, according to the Office for National Statistics' analyses of the pandemic, the average age of people who have died with COVID is above eighty with more than nine in ten of the deaths among the over-sixty-fives. The total number of deaths involving COVID in England and Wales is approaching 130,000 up to 19 February 2021."

"And your point is?"

"A hundred thousand people with a pension of £9,000 per year equals £900,000,000, nearly £1 billion that the government doesn't have to pay out in pensions, and there are other amounts to save, like attendance allowance, winter fuel and personal independent allowances – all helping with our balance of payments."

*

"Why not tennis singles on 8 March?" Vicky asked as she and Ruth did a walk around the financial centre of the City from Moorgate station. "It's far safer than walking in the streets or parks… where one spends the whole time dodging out of the way of people. Doubles could be the 29th. Boris is a tennis player, he must know that. Think I'll email him."

"Can you?"

"Nothing ventured. It's just so ignorant to lump singles and doubles together. The days pass, bland, indistinguishable and unexciting. Our ordinary lives being so savagely disrupted. I know we're lucky to have avoided COVID, but this confinement stretches on and on, and there's another five weeks of it – until there is something to look forward to."

"Yes, I don't understand how non-essential retail, commercial art galleries, libraries and community centres can open on 12 April, but museums and galleries not until 17 May. What is the difference in COVID exposure in the British Library and the British Museum? It doesn't make sense. Presumably one will be able to go in the Tate Modern shop, but not their Turbine Hall? But isn't the end in sight? Easter socialising? Dinner parties, theatre and cinema, weekends away – life as we know it? We are a sociable species and like the company of others. I was wondering if this deprivation has made us more insular and selfish?"

"Maybe. And socialising keeps one on one's toes in terms of how one looks. I haven't kept up my figure or appearance. Wearing old baggy clothes and comfort eating and drinking. When I emerge from my cocoon, it will be track pants be gone and hopefully dressing like the best version of myself. Wearing proper shoes, losing weight, having a haircut, and launching myself back into the world! The desire to think about what I put on will intensify. I hope I will be going out almost every night, as I used to. No nights in, in boring clothes. Bliss! But should I start the 5:2 diet now?"

"You look the same as ever to me. This period, communicating electronically, has been good for the environment, if not for one's mental state. And it has ravaged some people's lives, with deaths, breakups and job losses. Hopefully we'll all be joyfully celebrating our freedom by Easter! The high street won't be the same though. Debenhams' 130 stores will be closed. Arcadia had already collapsed and only Topshop and Miss Selfridge brands have been bought – not the seventy stores. Shopping online is convenient, but it doesn't give the adrenaline rush of trawling fashion rails for inspiration… and those two Oxford Street stores are Meccas for the latest trends and social hubs, where models are spotted. Oasis and Warehouse have gone, with Boohoo only buying their online businesses – not the shops. Did you know that the fashion and textiles industries contribute more to our GDP than the fishing, music, film and motor industries combined? £35 billion! The government has offered the fishing industry a £23 million support package, but nothing for fashion. They need our help, our custom."

"Changing the subject, what has happened about Catherine and her flat?"

"Gerald went there one evening last week, hoping to find Ashtak. He was in, was very concerned about Catherine and agreed to move as soon as he could. I went a few days later, thinking I'd give it a good clean, but found it spotless and the key in an envelope just inside the door, with the pile of post. He'd gone but had left it much better than he found it."

"He sounds like a nice guy."

"Indeed. Shame he's married. One of those poor people who try to get here, lured by empty promises of a land flowing in milk and honey, homes, education, healthcare and jobs for all."

"We seem to have passed half a dozen churches in the last ten minutes."

"I looked up how many after our last walk, and before the Great Fire in 1666 there were a hundred in the Square Mile. Now there are forty-five, plus extra towers and remains."

"Incredible. It just shows how many houses were crammed in. Would love to be able to go back in time and see how it was."

*

Catherine was getting up later every day. It was nearly lunchtime when she came down, to find Ruth in her floral pinafore, stuffing a joint of pork for dinner. She stood, hopping from foot to foot, in her green coat, buttons straining across her bulge. Hair, thin and lank, desperately needing a cut. "Will you come for a walk with me?"

"I'm a bit busy and I did a walk with Vicky this morning. Get your father, he hasn't been out today."

Catherine frowned. She kept trying to forge a link with Ruth, who always made her feel pale, colourless, ordinary and ignorant – very ignorant – next to her. In the same way, Ruth would like to be closer to Catherine, but she, Naomi and Josie were bright, confident go-getters and she could feel Catherine diminishing in their presence.

Catherine turned and waddled off, shoulders hunched, in the direction of Gerald's study.

Gerald duly went for a quick walk around the nearby park before lunch. He came back puzzled. "Why does she want this baby? I thought she seemed happy to be single – doing whatever she wanted in life. She's seemed too wrapped up in herself."

"Well, women's bodies are ticking time bombs, we have expiry dates. By the time a woman is forty, the chance of getting pregnant is depressingly small."

"But she's never seemed interested in even having a boyfriend, let alone having a baby!"

"Perhaps she has been stuck, helplessly thinking it was all too difficult, then suddenly Ashtak showed interest in her and she woke up to the fact that there was a chance."

"Well, we'll have to hope that it's healthy and she commits herself to looking after it."

*

"I can play tennis, Nana," Daisy had said just after she arrived. She had won some junior tournaments but hadn't played while at university. She was keen to start again, so Vicky had paid for her to be a member at her club and they were going to book for the 30th in the morning when she was free.

*

Barry put his arms around Janet's waist as she stood at the sink washing the breakfast dishes. "Shall we book our wedding for 21 June when mass gatherings are allowed?"

"You mean if everything goes to plan? If there are variants or stupid people mixing before we're allowed, it may well not happen and we'll have restrictions imposed again!"

"But if we want a big wedding, we can't have one before. Let's book a hotel and pay for our families and invite our closest friends? They probably won't mind paying for themselves."

"Yes, great. Let's look for suitable places, particularly ones where we won't lose everything if it has to be cancelled?" She turned to face him and they hugged and kissed…

*

Vicky rang Maggie, wondering how she was, after months

presumably on her own. "Are you still luxuriating in solitude, watching four episodes of something wearing your pyjamas?"

"Well, it's definitely palled. A year alone has taken its toll. I thought I was a cheerfully solitary person, but I'm also an extrovert and do need people, so I've felt depressed and lonely to some extent. I've realised how important small talk is. Regular shared confidences over a meal are endlessly fascinating and sources of energy for me. They lift my mood and make me feel I'm part of the world. And Zoom just doesn't cut it. I just want to hug the shit out of all my friends – be *with* them. I just want my life back! How about you?"

"Agreed. Haven't you been going out walking with different friends?"

"How many bubbles can one have? I thought it wasn't allowed to meet different people?"

"You can talk at a social distance with anyone. And cutting down on the people one sees means that friendships get stronger. I think you've met Ruth? We've walked most days, chatting, peering into other people's properties, laughing, putting the world to rights. It's been a lifeline for both of us and definitely stopped me from losing the plot!"

"I've had enough now. I want to *go* somewhere and *do* something, *see* people and shows and films. I keep playing that song 'All By Myself' at full volume, singing my head off. I'll stick it out because hopefully we're near the end of it, but BLOODY HELL, I want my life back!"

8 March 2021

It's International Women's Day. Children went back to school, the first step in easing lockdown. Secondary pupils are being tested three times at school and then regularly at home, and wear masks when they cannot socially distance. The R rate is between 0.7 and 0.9. If it goes above 1, lockdown

may be applied again. After the weekend the numbers are lower: sixty-five deaths and 124,566 in total, with 4,712 cases. Lombardy was the epicentre of the first wave of infections; it is now considering going into lockdown again.

"Deaths from COVID across the year haven't been much more than double the winter flu deaths, but we've closed society down for COVID. Is the plan to create a country where people still die of many things but never of COVID?" Gerald mused.

"Mmm, did you see that Denmark and eight other countries are probably going to suspend the use of the Oxford-AstraZeneca vaccine after reports of blood clots. The trouble is, how do you distinguish a causal effect from a coincidence? And COVID itself is strongly associated with blood clotting and has caused thousands of deaths from it. The EMA and the UK's regulatory body said that there is no indication that it's linked to thromboembolic events."

"Initially the problem was shortfall, then doubts about giving it to people over sixty-five and now it's safety concerns. Would this have happened without Brexit?"

*

"Are you going to go back to the community centre to help out?"

Ruth and Catherine were sitting in the conservatory having tea.

"Maybe, I don't know. I'd be embarrassed to see Ashtak or any of the other guys. They all know this baby is his."

"Does it matter?"

"Mmm... I shouldn't have got involved, should I?"

"Did you enjoy being involved?"

Catherine screwed up her face in thought. "It made me feel special to feel he wanted me. But I don't know if he found me sexy, or I was just someone for sex, or if I did the right things."

"Did you enjoy the sex?"

There was a long pause while she considered the question. "I hadn't had sex before, so didn't have anything to compare it with. I didn't know how it could be better. It wasn't that enjoyable, and it hurt at first."

The door opened and Gerald, wearing his painting overall, came in. "Any tea left?"

"You'll have to put more hot water in the pot," said Ruth, handing it to him. "Hopefully you'll meet someone else one day, after you've had the baby," she said to Catherine as Gerald disappeared.

*

Vicky was sitting in her conservatory engrossed in a novel, turning the pages with a hand impatient for her eyes to catch up. She was only half concentrating, and eager to know how the story ended. *Is this it, the beginning of the crumpling and crumbling, as I move forwards through the one-way valve to disintegration? Those little few-second blank-outs I get, are they the first stage of dementia? I can't remember names of plants, and sometimes where I am and how to get places. Oh God, is anything worse than dementia?*

It doesn't help that I'm constantly worried that Sophie might renege on coming back. But then, as Daisy says that Ben is definitely coming and applying for universities in London, surely she will. And when all this is over, I'll probably be able to rent out the little house...

She gave up trying to read and went inside to play feminist anthems – 'It's Raining Men', 'Sisters Are Doin' It For Themselves' and 'Make Your Own Kind of Music' – and dancing about, singing loudly, thinking about her life. She had written a feminist thesis as part of an MA, set up organisations and classes to support women, brought up her daughter virtually on her own, rebuilt her life a few times, and had many close women friends, but men? *The two most important ones have died, but then again how many people find one wonderful soulmate in their lives, and I've had two.* "'Cause it hangs them up to see someone like you'," she sang along at the top of her voice. "'But you gotta make your own kind...'" The door had opened and Daisy was singing with her: "'Sing your own special song'." They danced around, waving their arms, staying a metre away from one another and laughing their heads off...

"Here's to strong women!"

*

Christine was eating breakfast, her usual coffee and cheese on toast, when her doorbell rang. She went down the stairs and saw Alistair through the glass of the front door.

"Don't worry, I know you keep to rules. I won't ask to come in. The good thing about living alone is that one can act on impulse. We've had quite a coup this morning." He stepped back a few feet and with a huge smile, said, "Ben Hooper was meant to exhibit at the Dulwich Picture Gallery from January to mid-May, but of course it was cancelled."

Christine looked puzzled.

"Commercial galleries can open on 12 April, so he's going to exhibit with you! He does big abstracts, the opposite of your meticulous detail and subtle touch. Such a contrast – perfect!"

Christine didn't know what to say. Wouldn't her little botanical watercolours or still life oil paintings be lost on the tranquil, pale walls next to big, bold works? "I can't imagine it."

"Don't worry, all is in hand. You just need to price them for the catalogue. Come in a few weeks and see how they're hung. I have to go, but we'll get together very soon." He saluted and went back down the path to his car.

Christine was in shock. *I don't belong in the art world, I'm too naive and shy. I just copy, I've no imagination. And I don't* know any of these arty types. The tentacles of his connections stretch everywhere. Why is he bothering with someone like me? She went back upstairs, the smell of turps and linseed greeting her, the pots of brushes and pencils and a lily in a vase on the table with her breakfast and her latest botanical painting on her easel. *I suppose I couldn't have been doing this if John was still here*, she thought. The solitude and silence had become sensuous pleasures, which she would lose next week – when she started giving vaccinations at the church hall.

*

"Three weeks till we can play tennis." Vicky and Debs were chatting on the phone.

"Then another six weeks or so till life goes back to normal. Whatever normal was. Having lived for so long comfort eating and drinking and in a state of stress, how are we going to be able to rise like phoenixes from the sofa and go back to how we were? I can't imagine jumping into a full-throttle social whirl straight away, can you?"

"No, much too tiring," said Vicky. "The first lockdown wasn't too bad. It was different, the weather was beautiful, the air clear, with so little traffic. We could hear the birds and see the plants growing in warm silence. I almost enjoyed it."

"Yes, it was a holiday for some, while for others it was like being in jail. Especially for children without a garden. By the way, when I come back to London next week, I'm going to book a non-surgical mini facelift."

"What? You don't need it, Debs, why?"

"It's Zoom and FaceTime, having to look at one's face! Apparently, thousands more people have asked for virtual consultations with plastic surgeons. There are now techy treatments that don't require needles or knives, but radiofrequency or ultrasound waves to increase the collagen and tone and tighten the skin."

"I bet it's expensive."

"Of course, £2,000 or so. But my mum left me some money which she said to use when I was feeling old, to give myself a lift. This might be the time to go for it."

"It feels like five years has passed since we've been in lockdown. The newspapers are constantly telling us the stresses of COVID. Too much alcohol and inactivity have pushed us into physical-ageing overdrive. Our telomeres have shortened considerably – which hastens the ageing process."

"What on earth is a telomere?"

"Segments of DNA at the ends of each chromosome that become shorter every time a cell divides. When they become too short, the cell can't do its job and ages."

"Is that it, then? Or can retinal cream, good sleep, good food and exercise improve their length? Doesn't too much activity increase wear and tear? And make one scraggy? A lot of fanatical men who exercise a lot look scraggy."

"Well, I have read that the more one sticks to a Mediterranean diet, the longer one's telomeres are. Plus, different types of exercise – not doing one too extremely – and of course, learning new things and socialising. Hey ho, if we lead the perfect healthy lives, our telomeres might be longer, but won't the boredom have some other dastardly effect? Anyway, who is booking the court for the first day?"

"I will. And shall we have a Silver Foxes meeting? Book a couple of tables in a pub garden on the 12th? It's going to take a while to get used to our old ways of life. It could be a start for us all. But we'd better book soon."

"OK, good idea. Remember last July when we were allowed to see friends again? It was awkward, we didn't know whether to hug, or poke elbows. What is the post-lockdown etiquette? Should we sanitise our hands before passing a glass to a friend? Should we all wear masks?"

"I know something we mustn't do and that's have Zoom

drinks if it's raining on our pub night. Let's insist on meeting in our raincoats and umbrellas. I can't take any more Zooms. A lot of people are uneasy about returning to the rush hour, the office, their social life. The pandemic has ravaged so many people's lives, with deaths, job losses or breakups!"

"We'll need to start little by little, like training for something, so we don't get social jetlag. This social evening in a pub can be our launching pad, a distraction, a comfortable connection to reality?"

"OK, I'll book it. I'm on it now."

16 March 2021

There have been 110 deaths, which makes 125,690 in total, 5,294 new cases, and nearly 25 million people have had their first vaccination. France, Germany and Italy have joined the other fourteen European countries suspending the use of the Oxford-AstraZeneca vaccine. Despite the WHO and the EMA, the European regulator is saying that there is no indication of a link between the vaccine and reports of blood clots, and that the vaccine is safe. Ursula von der Leyen threatened to seize EU-made vaccine exports, as there is not enough vaccine to stop the third wave, though there are 7 million doses not being used, and as the Pfizer vaccine has also been linked to blood clots, this has also caused vaccine hesitancies. Many regions have been forced into lockdown in Italy, Germany and France. There will be a stamp duty holiday until the end of June as properties outside cities are snapped up. Londoners bought 74,000 homes outside London last year – people want to spend lockdown time in villages, in the country.

"Apparently Belgium – where the Pfizer vaccine is manufactured – is opposed to export bans."

"I read that Germany, France and Italy are threatening holding our supplies hostage?"

Gerry reached over for a piece of toast. "Delicious bread, is this Vicky's again? Yes, an export ban would damage the pharmaceutical industry. And aren't some of the components made by Croda, based in Yorkshire?"

"Yes, Vicky's. We're just getting blamed for the EU's slow rollout of jabs. Surely, they won't take control of factories or seize vaccines? We paid towards the development of the Oxford vaccine and ordered it well before the EU. Brexit has caused far too much aggro."

"And the experts are worried about a new wave. Our Italian holiday looks unlikely."

"Unless most of the world accepts that we should all have a vaccine passport with which to travel, go to the theatre, even apply for jobs, but the ethical and moral issues need discussion."

*

Vicky walked round to see Jo. It was 10.30, but when Jo eventually came to the door, she was wearing her dressing gown and slippers. She looked exhausted. "Sorry, I'm just not getting to sleep. I must have 'COVID-somnia.'"

"Does that exist?"

"Apparently so. This period has had dire consequences for a large number of people's ability to have a good night's sleep. And I keep reading how people are having vivid and bizarre dreams, which I've started having too."

"It's the months of uncertainty, loneliness, anxiety, loss of our routines, boredom, disruption of our body clocks and possibly, for some, lack of exercise. You don't take your computer to bed, or look at it too much before bedtime, do you?"

"No, but I do watch TV, and that's got a blue light, hasn't it? One shouldn't look at either for two hours before going to bed.

That's a hard thing to stick to. I watch the news. Don't you have sleep problems?"

"No, not at all. I've been sleeping well recently. I lie down and go to sleep, even though I watch the late news too, and I don't dream – which I used to do."

Jo rubbed her eyes and yawned. "I have the weirdest dreams, so vivid. I'm shattered when it's time to get up. I used to be asleep in seconds, now nothing happens. I wriggle about and when I finally pass out, along come the nightmares. I've got a constant headache, tinnitus and can't remember anything. I've tried melatonin, Nytol, Night Nurse, lavender sprays, guided meditation and even read Gwyneth Paltrow's sleep guru's book. None of it works."

"Maybe when lockdown is over and we can do normal social things, your sleep patterns will go back to normal."

"Mmm, when that happens, there's something I must do."

"What's that?"

Jo didn't answer for a few minutes, she seemed to be going pink all over. "Come in for a minute." She led the way down the hall and into the sitting room, where she picked up an urn off the sideboard. "I need to part with this."

Vicky was puzzled.

"It's Al, crouched in there, like a little mole in a tunnel. We talk to one another. I've needed him."

What could Vicky say...?

*

Catherine and Ruth were walking in single file around the Brent Reservoir.

"Will I be a bad mother? I've made a mess of my life so far. Should I be having a child when I've got no source of income or partner?"

Ruth strained to hear from behind, and hoped she'd picked up the gist.

"Perhaps taking responsibility for a baby will change your life. Perhaps it will be the spur you've needed, and you'll soar from now."

"Ashtak was my first boyfriend, you know. He got lucky. I was ripe for it at my time of life. I was clever at school and I wanted a proper career, then I got in with some friends and we smoked pot. We smoked our brains silly when Mum was ill."

She was now walking backwards in her eagerness to help Ruth understand her life so far. The wind on her back whipped her hair across her face and glasses, and she stumbled over roots and twigs. The track ran along the side of parkland; they could hear the roar of traffic from the North Circular muffled by the hornbeam, holly, beech and lime trees. Wembley Stadium could be seen in the distance. They stopped to see the huge sheet of water sparkling in front of them. A band of sunlight crossed the reservoir towards them, lighting up the dozens of ducks, geese, grebe and gulls, busily competing for food.

23 March 2021

There are 5,379 new cases, with 112 deaths, making a total of 126,284. Over 28 million people have had their first vaccination in the UK. Germany is to extend its current lockdown by three weeks, as there are 2,667,225 cases and less than ten per cent of people have been vaccinated. Poland has its highest number of cases, ever, and the Czech Republic and Hungary have more than in their previous peak in December. Leaving the UK without a reasonable excuse will be illegal and attract a £5,000 fine under new coronavirus laws. Boris has braced the nation for the third wave, which will undoubtedly "wash up on our shores from Europe". He said that SAGE's biggest "mistake" was not knowing that one in three people who has COVID has no symptoms. This is to be the National Day of Reflection, to remember the victims of the COVID pandemic. At midday there will be a minute's silence, and at 8pm people are encouraged to stand on their doorsteps with a light – a candle or torch – to remember the people who have died this past year. London landmarks will be lit up, like Wembley Stadium, the London Eye, Leicester Square. A trial involving 32,000 people in the US has shown that the Oxford-AstraZeneca jab cut coronavirus deaths to zero in every age group, with no serious side effects. Twenty per cent of people were over sixty-five. After European leaders have repeatedly criticised this life-saving vaccine, these results are consistent with Oxford-led trials. Hopefully this will boost confidence across the EU, where 13 million doses are lying unused.

"Interesting. The *BMJ* has at last concurred with all the research showing that transmission after touching surfaces is minimal. *The Lancet* published research to that effect nine months ago," Ruth said.

Gerald breathed out in annoyance. "So the hygiene dictatorship in all the homes and public places was in vain?"

"Yes, the virus is overwhelmingly airborne, transmitted through speaking, sneezing and even breathing."

"Not sure if that's a relief or worry. I'm meeting Nigel for a stroll today, should we be wearing masks as he's not my usual companion?"

"I suppose you could. He's not in your bubble. But you've both had your two vaccinations. You should be safe."

*

It was a year ago today that all the theatres were closed, everything stopped, and as seventy per cent of people working in the theatre are freelance, they have had no government support. Vicky thought as she went through her new emails from the theatres she had been going to for many years. Suddenly her heart lifted, and she was right back in the old normal life. *Can't wait to start going again!* She had credits at two theatres, so excitedly booked tickets for the end of May and June. One could only book with one's support bubble, so she couldn't get a group of friends together as usual, but hopefully soon.

And thinking about that, groups of six can meet in a garden. Why don't I ask some friends over for a six o'clock picnic in the garden on the 29th? I can cook chicken and sausages in the oven and make various dishes, like caponata, potato salad and a mixed salad, with lentils, beetroot, spinach and goat's cheese. Who shall I ask?

The year of staying home is nearly over. We've coped and there are better times to come! Wonder if Debs booked some pub tables for the next release on the 12th? I'll phone her.

*

"No, it seems that every single restaurant table and pub garden in London is fully booked! There's been a frenzy of booking in the optimism about freedom and the future. Some pubs said they were overwhelmed and fully booked till the end of May. We'd better think of alternatives, or we'll have no social life at all."

Vicky's elation dimmed. This nirvana of social life which seemed to be returning had already stalled.

A few phone calls later, Ruth and Gerry and Janet and Barry couldn't come to her garden picnic, they were seeing family. Nusheen was out of London, looking at estates to buy. Jo could come, as could Liz and Paul, Christine, and Debs and Steve. That made seven, with her, but who was counting?

Debs rang back later with the news that their favourite pub had had a cancellation and offered them two tables for the 12th.

"Brilliant. Though you know, I think I'm terrified of launching myself into my old social life after so many months of restrictions!" said Vicky. "Lockdown is rather like an elimination diet, perhaps we'll find that we won't want to go back to some things, or spend time with some people?"

"Well, it'll be good to get dressed again. You'll hopefully be taking off the joggin' pants and old jumper and put on a dress in a bright colour and proper shoes. A handbag instead of a rucksack or carrier bag and even big, bold bling! You're probably nervous of the change, havin' to leave the house and re-enter society!"

"You're right. And I should fit into my clothes. For the past three weeks I've been trying to stick to the 5:2 and not drink alcohol every night, and I've lost five pounds. I'm slowly returning to my old shape like a tired piece of elastic!"

29 March 2021

> There have been twenty-three deaths, bringing the total to 126,615, with 4,654 new cases. More than 30 million people have had their first vaccination in the UK, though only fifteen per cent of the EU population. Europe is struggling to contain the virus, with many countries tightening their borders and locking down. Tennis, golf and outdoor sports are allowed, and six people from different households can meet up outside or in a private garden from today. Adults are going to be asked to take twice-weekly COVID tests, and nationwide sewage monitoring may also be used to spot outbreaks.

"Shame we can't go to Vicky's tonight. No social engagements for months and then two on the same evening!"

"You see Vicky most days and it's been months since we saw Charles, and Catherine can come with us." Gerald reached for the toast.

"This is interesting. Economic forecasters say that in the pandemic, the world moved forward ten years in its predicted shift to remote working, learning, medical consultation, phasing out of cash, commuter travel and video conferencing. We keep saying that HS2 is twenty years too late, now there's even more reason to scrap it."

Gerald smiled. "I don't expect we will have the satisfaction of it being stopped now though."

*

The garden was full of birdsong, from robins, blackbirds, chaffinches, thrushes. And as the day became lighter and warmer, the tits, sparrows and finches added their voices.

The defining emotions of lockdown will soon be behind us, thought Vicky. *Boredom, eating for the sake of it, anxiety, confusion, sleeplessness and sleepiness, and the dread that our lives will never be the same again.*

It was at last permitted for Marion to come over for tea in the garden. They sat companionably, admiring the wallflowers, the last of the daffodils, tulips, forsythia, different-coloured primroses and hyacinths, the armandii, hypericum and euphorbia.

"Maureen had her dog stolen a few days ago," said Marion.

"Oh no. There's apparently been an unprecedented demand in owning dogs, and stealing them to sell on is obviously lucrative."

"She's devastated. Annie's been her companion for nine years. Two men just came up, grabbed her, pushed Maureen out of the way, jumped into a car and were gone."

"Terrible. So cruel. Hope the police find her. The thieves sometimes let the dogs go if they don't manage to sell them. By the way, I'm so impressed how well you've coped in this long, lonely lockdown," Vicky said.

"I've found it an interesting time. I've lived on my own for so many years, I'm used to just getting on with things, and I've found the help from so many neighbours quite cheering. It's made me realise how amazing humans can be, you just have to give them the opportunity to be so." She smiled her asymmetric grin, which squeezed her wrinkles together.

"The question is, will it go back to how it was? Will we want it to? What have we learnt which might change our futures? I know I'm much more tired. Sort of fuzzy-headed, dazed, self-conscious, probably because I've been more anxious and Zoom has convinced me I'm grotesquely ugly, with my liver spots and wrinkles and words disappearing before I can say them. I no longer think of my death in a remote philosophical way. It's no longer an abstract, but when and how. My world has shrunk and me with it. I've lost my mojo. It must be post-pandemic stress disorder!"

Marion smiled sympathetically. "We don't really know if we're post-pandemic. We're supposed to be happy about reopening and supposed to get back out there to resume lifestyles we've almost forgotten we led, but part of us is tensed for the next wave. It's a tiring way to exist. However, I must say social media, WhatsApp and Nextdoor have kept me going. Reading about missing cats, how to discourage visits from foxes and all the strange things that people want or want to get rid of. My new path of five paving slabs came from a Nextdoor post."

They grinned at one another and tucked into their cake.

*

Vicky and Daisy managed to erect the big garden table, which together with two smaller tables meant that the seven could sit socially distanced.

As the guests arrived, dressed up for their evening out, a drink was poured for them and vaccination information was exchanged. Who had had their first and second, who had had which vaccine and did anyone have after-effects from it. Debs hugged everyone; she was so pleased to see them. Vicky couldn't help recoiling inside and submitted unhappily. *Yes, hugging is a normalised way of greeting, but now?*

When the dishes had been brought out and everyone was settled with their food and drink, Vicky said: "Shall we have a discussion about the strangest year in our lives? A year when we've been forced into elderly behaviours and doing everything on a screen?"

"Won't the trauma of it change our value systems, because we have been unable to mourn, to process our grief adequately if we needed to?" asked Steve.

"Yes, social isolation, bereavement, depression and stress have affected so many people's mental health. And being trapped at home, seeing no one – social isolation – accentuates the problems. It's the people in our lives who make us who we are. Who are we now?" said Liz.

"I'll never forget how many people have died lonely deaths in the ICU. That terrible cycle of coming into hospital and leaving in a body bag!" Jo added.

"Depends on our experiences of COVID and death, I guess. We have to keep our heads up, feel grateful that we're still here and have hope that we'll be able to socialise and live as we used to. There was a before, so there will be an after," said Paul.

"But the time we've lost! Before lockdown, time seemed to be impenetrable, misty, our futures, old age were far in the distance. Perhaps I was in denial," said Jo. "Getting COVID and then being unable to lead my normal life has put time, not ahead anymore, but behind me. No more anticipation of a future, but only a memory of a past. Time has run out!"

"Have there been any good things that the year of eating, sleeping, being at home have brought? There's been no variety, nothing to separate each day, have we been productive in any new way?" asked Vicky.

Everyone agreed that they had saved money, as they hadn't bought clothes, gone to restaurants, had holidays, or gone to cinemas, theatres and pubs.

"I shop locally more," said Liz.

"I feel fitter from all the walkin'. My daughter says she has enjoyed workin' from home and not havin' to commute," said Debs. The feathers on her cape fluttered in the little breeze and her eyelashes, thick with mascara, quivered with her smile.

Feathers which had insulated birds from the cold, thought Jo, *poor birds*. "Despite my good intentions, the novelty of at-home workouts soon faded, walks round the block were frankly boring, and I've added a few inches to my waistline by sitting about too much and doing emails in the kitchen, too near food. And look at my flabby, prawn-pink arms!" She waved them in the air, causing smiles from her friends.

Steve raised his glass. "You won't want to hear this, but most of us need to cut down on alcohol, it's empty calories, enlarges the liver, and when it's in our system one doesn't burn stored body fat." He slid his arm around Debs' blue silk waist. She couldn't help hoping that there would be no stain from the salted nuts he had been dipping in to.

"And doesn't it increase cortisol, the stress hormone, which apparently increases fat round the abdomen?" asked Liz.

Steve nodded. "'Fraid so. Just when the pubs and restaurants are opening. I must say, though, that my neighbours either side have kept me sane. I had barely talked to them before, but they've often been the only people I've talked to all day. I chat over the fence with my fellow prisoners. Not being able to travel to see family and friends, I've relied on neighbours as the world shrunk to the size of our neighbourhood."

"How about changes in what we've been doing?" asked Debs. "Apparently more than one third of adults have taken up a hobby in lockdown."

"I've been learning French," agreed Christine.

"Italian for me," said Paul. "Written some poems and I've done lots of useful jobs."

"Learning dance moves from TikTok, and more painting," Christine added. "And last week I joined a Goddess Circle."

And seeing all the puzzled faces, she continued: "It's for spiritual maintenance, post-pandemic resurgence. We sit cross-legged on the floor around a cloth. It's not conversational, but people can offload – we listen but don't give advice. There's no hierarchy, no competing or comparing – we learn to listen, to have empathy and compassion. Sharing stories is cathartic and everything is so still that the answers you're looking for seem to be reflected back to you, like a mirror. I hope I can learn to find what I am looking for in life, within myself rather than in someone else."

"Do you have crystals, candles, burn sage to get rid of negative energy?" asked Steve.

"All of them, and we have a drink. It's about just being. Perfect for me."

"Sounds brilliant! I've read that the most popular activities are walking, reading, exercise and gardening. The question is, will people keep doing them?" Vicky summed up. "Is national hibernation at an end? The long-awaited beginning of the return of our lives as we knew it. It's like VE Day must have been! Will we resume our familiar routines? Be confident to join crowds, in theatres, concerts, hotels, restaurants, classes, churches, sports events? Do we want to? We've forced ourselves to live in lockdown ways, can we resume our old freedoms?"

Debs squeezed Steve's hand. "It's made me more introspective. I missed people. I'm a social creature so I'm valuin' my friendships more... but we might need another year off to reintroduce our old lives, slowly, and do the things we promised ourselves we'd do, and didn't. But at least I'm less confused with the two realities of social media and the real world, and so less obsessed with doom scrollin'."

"We've endured and adapted, though, and things will get better. Let's drink to the return of normal life," said Vicky as they clinked glasses and sipped their prosecco.

"We will all be so thankful when COVID is vanquished, though we must know in our heart of hearts that viruses don't disappear, they mutate and reappear in a different form.

"But in the end, I guess every country and person will have to learn to live with this disease and any other viruses that come along, and balance medical against other human needs, by developing coping strategies, but meanwhile let's be grateful for the precious gift of life. We're old and getting older, but we live and breathe, how wonderful is that…!"

For writing and publishing news, or recommendations of new titles to read, sign up to the Book Guild newsletter: